Praise for *Women of Good Fortune* by Sophie Wan

"Sophie Wan's glittering debut is a delightful romp inside an elite Shanghai wedding and the complicated women who are determined to stage a heist there."
—Carley Fortune, #1 *New York Times* bestselling author of *Meet Me at the Lake*

"A love letter to Shanghai and complicated female friendships, *Women of Good Fortune* is a joyous, indulgent, immensely clever debut. I loved every second."
—Grace D. Li, *New York Times* bestselling author of *Portrait of a Thief*

"*Crazy Rich Asians*, but add a heist? YES PLEASE. I loved every second of this fun, fast-paced book with hilarious hijinks that begs the question: can women really ever have it all?"
—Colleen Oakley, *USA TODAY* bestselling author of *The Mostly True Story of Tanner & Louise*

"With an incredibly entertaining cast, sharp insights into class and gender, and glamorous settings, this is a most delectable read."
—Kyla Zhao, author of *The Fraud Squad*

"Sharp, biting, brilliant." —*Booklist* (starred review)

"This was one of the most unique books I've read and a must-read." —*New York Post*, Best Books of March

"[A] crackling debut. . . . The novel moves along briskly while dutifully adhering to the tropes of the heist genre, but this stands out for its unexpected depth. . . . Wan pulls this off without a hitch." —*Publishers Weekly*

"This fun novel has it all." —*Woman's World*

"*Women of Good Fortune* recalls the extravagant wedding fanfare of *Crazy Rich Asians* and the minute-by-minute scheming of *Ocean's Eleven*. . . . The story's urgency will keep readers captivated. But it is what these women learn along the way—about themselves and about one another—that gives the novel its heart."
—*Shelf Awareness* (starred review)

Also by Sophie Wan

Women of Good Fortune

the social circle

A NOVEL

Sophie Wan

*Dear Reader,
I hope you enjoy this book!*

PARK
ROW
BOOKS™

Recycling programs
for this product may
not exist in your area.

ISBN-13: 978-1-525-80006-1

The Social Circle

Copyright © 2026 by Sophie Wan

All rights reserved. No part of this book may be used or reproduced in any manner whatsoever without written permission.

Without limiting the exclusive rights of any author, contributor or the publisher of this publication, any unauthorized use of this publication to train generative artificial intelligence (AI) technologies is expressly prohibited. Harlequin also exercises their rights under Article 4(3) of the Digital Single Market Directive 2019/790 and expressly reserve this publication from the text and data mining exception.

This is a work of fiction. Names, characters, places, and incidents are either the product of the author's imagination or are used fictitiously. Any resemblance to actual persons, living or dead, businesses, companies, events or locales is entirely coincidental.

TM is a trademark of Harlequin Enterprises ULC.

Park Row Books
22 Adelaide St. West, 41st Floor
Toronto, Ontario M5H 4E3, Canada
ParkRowBooks.com

HarperCollins Publishers
Macken House, 39/40 Mayor Street Upper,
Dublin 1, D01 C9W8, Ireland
www.HarperCollins.com

Printed in U.S.A.

For Daniel

the
social
circle

Chapter One

WEDNESDAY

Circle is ten years old today.

Maggie is reminded of this everywhere she goes. All her usual news outlets are covering it. She overheard her employees talking about it in the microkitchen.

Ranch 99 is the only safe place for her. With its speakers blaring Chinese music from the '70s and old ladies shuffling between sauce aisles and patting cabbages, it's not hard to pretend that the screens and algorithms that normally consume her life are far away. She shifts on the vinyl chair beneath her, the sort guaranteed to make the sound of a wet fart when it's time to peel yourself off and leave. It was either this or the Philz across the road, where stressed-out Apple ants like to congregate, their badges flapping from their waists as they clutch their mint mojitos and discuss product delays like the very fabric of the planet is ripping apart.

Today, Maggie has brought her COO, Lisa, into this hallowed space. Lisa insisted that their one-on-one couldn't wait, so here they are, except now Lisa has just announced that she's quitting, and Maggie realizes that bad things still happen in sacred places.

"Don't you want to know why?" Lisa asks.

"I won't stop you if that's what you want," Maggie tells her as she looks over her shoulder at an old lady who's slowly placing items from her grocery cart onto the conveyor belt, one by one. When the young man behind her tries to help, she warns him off and resumes her slow pace. The man throws up his hands and swerves his cart to another lane.

Of the three COOs she's had, Maggie thought Lisa would be the one to stay. For one, she hasn't made a face over the fact that they're meeting in a supermarket that smells like roast duck, nor does she care that Maggie prefers extended silence to small talk. Lisa's jacked résumé of scaling far larger companies has helped with OurSpot's credibility immensely, especially when most VCs still see Maggie as a kid with a bad rap. Since Lisa joined, they've even established retirement funds for their employees and installed a coffeemaker in the microkitchen that's capable of brewing more than hot shit.

She needs Lisa, she realizes. She really needs Lisa. Maggie has to try to make her stay, even if it means putting aside her pride.

But just as Maggie is about to open her mouth, Lisa folds her arms and says, "I'm considering an offer from Circle."

Maggie's stomach plunges.

Lisa is watching her closely, waiting for her reaction, but Maggie keeps complete control over her body and expression.

Lisa decides to press harder, as if she wants to elicit a reaction. "Did you know Adam Fink personally interviewed me?"

It feels wrong for that name to have entered the sanctity of this Ranch 99, and yet here it is, invading her life again. Maggie has no doubt that Adam promised Lisa the world to get her to leave.

"He only did it to pass you a message." From her bag, Lisa pulls out an envelope. Slides it across the greasy table. "I can see why you guys were friends. Neither of you really cares about anyone. All of us—we're bugs to you. Worker bees meant to carry out a task."

A small sliver of remorse opens up inside Maggie. After she left Circle, licked her wounds and decided to start another company, all she had known was that she didn't want to make the same mistakes. This time, she would hold on tightly to the thing that she created. Everyone else would come close enough to see it, maybe even touch it, but nobody would own it the way she did. The cost of sharing ownership was clear. She needs people to listen to her, not see her as a friend.

Still, she misses it sometimes. The crackling energy of collaboration, the heat of an argument where each side is willing to go down fighting for what they believe in. Nobody except Lisa dares to argue with her now. She wonders if Lisa will take the Circle offer anyway, despite her disdain for Adam. If there's anything he taught Maggie, it's that everyone has a price, and Maggie has heard all about Circle's sprawling Palo Alto campus, the smoothie bars and Michelin-chef-made lunches, along with the on-site gym and laundry service. And Lisa will be there, making her stellar PowerPoint presentations for Adam instead of for Maggie. Going to company town halls where she can ask Hari questions. Listening to Charles talk about new product launches.

She slams a wall up against those thoughts. "Make sure to document everything you've worked on. I'll take this as your two weeks' notice."

Lisa stands, throwing her bag over her shoulder. She doesn't look angry, only resigned. "Can I say one thing, not as a COO but just as someone who's worked with you and gotten to know you a tiny bit better than anyone else?"

Maggie gives a short nod. This will probably not be something she wants to hear, but it will allow Lisa a sense of satisfaction. Maybe it'll take some of the heat out of whatever gossip she'll whisper about OurSpot to her future colleagues.

"You've got the chops to succeed. Not only are you capable, you've got that all-consuming obsessiveness that I think all good entrepreneurs need. But OurSpot is not going to make it if you don't open yourself up. There's a reason these venture capitalists don't want to invest. They can't connect to who you are now, so they believe you're still the person you used to be. If you don't change how you run things, you'll never beat Circle. And I know, deep down, that's what you want." Lisa looks at her for a long moment, but when Maggie doesn't answer, she sighs. "I'll see you back at the office."

Once she's gone, Maggie rubs her forehead, already anticipating the headache of writing up another job description and sorting through thousands of tech-bro résumés for someone who will accept low pay and uncommon work hours for the promise of making it big. Ideally another woman, but she knows how unlikely that is. Lisa was a unicorn, someone who'd actually wanted to help grow an early-stage company she didn't cofound. Morale is going to dip again once Maggie announces Lisa's departure. And she'll have to take on all of Lisa's work until she finds a replacement, including the miserable search for funding. They have about three months of runway left before she has to start pawning office supplies to make payroll.

She groans, dropping her head against her seat. This is not something she wants to deal with right now.

When she sits up again, her eyes go to the envelope, unassuming yet threatening. She stares at it for a long moment, trying to set it on fire with her eyes. OurSpot has only been around for a year and a half, and Adam is already in her business.

She grabs the envelope, intending to throw it away. But then, as if acting separately from her brain, her finger slides under the flap. She'll just take a peek at what's inside, then forget about it. Better to do that than to wonder.

Inside is a card that says *Happy Anniversary*. Someone has handwritten *10th* in between the words. There's a slash through the zero that tells her immediately this is Adam's handwriting.

A plane ticket slips out of the card. The destination: Oslo, Norway.

The date: Tomorrow.

A slightly hysterical laugh leaps out of her throat. The lady at the deli counter gives her a squinty look before shrugging and returning to watching dramas on her phone.

Norway, of all places. And so last minute. Adam has a sick sense of humor.

She opens the card, about to stuff the ticket back in and throw it in the trash, when her eyes catch on more handwriting at the bottom.

Come. Please.

She fingers the invitation. Ten years. Unbelievable, that the little website she coded with Charles in their grungy apartment is now turning the age she was when her dad first brought dial-up internet into their home.

It's been too long. She is not part of Circle anymore, and the people she built it with are no longer part of her life. Accepting this invitation would mean that she still wants to remember what she's spent almost a decade trying to forget.

Her phone pings, and she sets down the invitation to scroll through the pile-up of messages. She needs to get back to her employees, not wallow in the past.

There is a trash can by the exit. She hovers in front of it, the envelope loosely held between her fingers. Instead, she shoves it into her jacket pocket and goes through the sliding doors.

Chapter Two

AUGUST 2005

Maggie stood on Durant Street, eyeing the peeling apartment building while her dad searched for parking. After two years of attending community college while commuting from home, she'd been eager to move out and start her life as an independent adult. But now, apprehension swept through her. She'd chosen the cheapest off-campus housing she could find, thinking *how bad could it be?*

The answer was *bad*. The building before her looked like it might crumble at the first loud noise, and the limited windows on its exterior were grimy and dark.

Best to get this over with. She heaved her first suitcase up the handful of steps, then returned for the second. Once she had them both beside her on the narrow doorstep, she went to unlock the door, but her key didn't work no matter how she twisted it.

The sun shone unrelentingly down on her, and her backpack, stuffed full with her hardware and notebooks, strained her shoulders. Sweat beaded on her forehead as she withdrew the key, staring at the road helplessly, wondering when her dad would show.

Two guys came up the steps behind her, one balancing three pizza boxes while the other had a liter of Coke under one arm and a handle of Smirnoff under the other. Awkwardly, she tried to make space on the doorstep so they could pass, squishing to the side with her two giant suitcases. Smirnoff boy jogged to the door, jimmied his key, and held it open so his friend could enter. She caught it just before it closed behind them.

Her Nokia rang then, and when she scrambled to pick up, she lost her hold on the door. It shut with a final-sounding click, and she cursed inwardly as her dad said through the speakers, "Parking is impossible. I'm just going to head home. You can get in on your own, right?"

On their way there, they'd driven past the dorms, entire families on the curb, parents pushing wagons piled high with belongings and grandparents embracing their grandkids. She hadn't expected that from her father, but she also hadn't expected to be dumped here so unceremoniously. She'd thought he'd say goodbye at least, offer a perfunctory *good luck*.

"Yeah, but I—" she began, but her dad had already hung up.

With renewed effort, she jammed her key into the lock and managed to barge inside, though she wasn't confident she'd be able to repeat her success next time. The inside of the building was no better than the outside. The carpet was dark with stains. It smelled, oddly, like melted crayons and burnt food.

There was an elevator, which was good, though it seemed more appropriate for a horror movie set than transporting people. The light in the ceiling didn't work, and the only thing that separated her from plunging down the shaft was a rusty gate that she had to manually pull shut. Only one of her suitcases fit inside. When she pressed the button for the third floor, the metal cage made a horrible shrieking noise as it sealed her in. The elevator rattled and groaned its way up to the third floor, and she stood stock-still, afraid that any movement would send her back down through the chute and into the underworld.

The elevator opened to pandemonium. Doors were open along the hall, the strains of a pop punk song she always heard on

Star 101.3 coming through one of them. People were congregated at the far end, loudly talking. The burning smell was even more intense here.

She dragged her suitcase along, ending up on the border of the crowd. A *whoa* went through it and people backed up a few steps, enough for Maggie to see *fire* licking up through what looked like the metal door to a trash chute.

"If the landlady from hell finds out about this, there's no way she's giving our deposits back!"

"Your deposit was gone the moment you left a human-shaped hole in the drywall."

"I'm not the one who got drunk and thought he could suddenly walk through matter—"

"I got it, I got it!" A boy with curly blond hair and a bright orange Hawaiian shirt came barreling down the hallway, holding a stockpot with water sloshing over the sides. He took off the lid with a flourish, frisbeeing it over the heads of the crowd. The lid carved its way straight toward Maggie, who reflexively put her arms up in defense. It smacked into her elbow, sending vibrations through her funny bone.

The crowd parted for the boy to approach the chute and dump the water down. The flames disappeared, replaced by a belch of smoke and the smell of wet trash. A cheer went up.

He slammed the trash chute door shut with finality, looking incredibly pleased with himself. Maggie got a good look at his face, and shock burned through her. She let go of her suitcase, and it flopped inelegantly over onto its frame.

"Adam?" It was him, she was sure of it. The curly hair and high nose were hints, but it was all but confirmed by the fact that he was, as always, the center of attention.

He looked in Maggie's direction at the sound of his name, but his eyes ran right over her. "Where'd I put the lid?"

She bent down to pick it up, but someone else reached for it at the same time. A tall boy in a Cal T-shirt and wire-framed glasses. He was frowning.

"I'll take that," he said. "It was my pot he was using."

He held the lid with two fingers, like he was well aware of how dirty it was. He looked at Maggie again. "You know him?"

He'd heard her? She wished she'd actually thought before opening her mouth.

Adam suddenly appeared from the crowd again, the pot cradled in his arms like a baby. "Sorry I took your pot, but duty called." His eyes went to Maggie, and his expression lightened. "A new friend? Charlie-boy, I didn't know you knew how to talk to strangers without me!"

Maggie was about to redo introductions, but Charles said, "Dude, she already knows you."

"You do?" Adam tilted his head. "How?"

Maggie flushed, embarrassed by how little of an impression she'd made on him. "Summer camp in '02. Santa Cruz." Summer before senior year of high school. The camp was supposed to turn the youth of today into the leaders of tomorrow. Maggie had applied because she was desperate to get out of the house, and one of the camp electives was "computer lab." It was free too, which was what convinced her dad to let her go. Otherwise, summer would have been aimless walks in their boring cul-de-sac, math problem sets that her dad downloaded from Chinese prep sites, and trudging three miles to the closest GameStop to play demos and browse through games she'd never be able to buy.

"Oh, I remember now!" Adam made finger guns at her. "Rebecca!"

Maggie's face burned hotter. Rebecca Wang had been one of those cool Asian girls who'd figured out how to fit in. She'd owned a bedazzled Walkman, listened to Paramore, and worn layered camis from Hollister. They might've looked alike, but they couldn't have been more different.

Charles smacked Adam in the head. "Racist. That's obviously not her name."

She wanted to disappear into the ground.

But Adam didn't look perturbed. "Shit, I *am* racist. Sorry. What's your name?"

"Maggie."

"Maggie!" Adam opened his arms wide, like he was about to give her a hug, and then he actually did. She was so surprised that all she could do was stand there, stiff as a board. He smelled like burnt bacon and Old Spice. When he pulled back, he was grinning, his eyes an electrifying blue. "I'm Adam, but you already know that. That's Grumpy." He pointed at the guy who was scowling at him. "Just kidding, his name is Charles, and we live together. We're having a pizza party today. You should come."

She hesitated. If Adam had actually remembered her, he wouldn't have invited her to his party. At camp bonfires, guys called him "bro" and girls sidled up to him and pretended to be cold so he'd lend them his hoodie. Even the counselors, who were in college and infinitely cooler, never gave him hell for skipping mandatory events. Meanwhile, Maggie would sit shivering on the fringes, waiting for a free moment when she could slink off to the computer lab, where she was teaching herself Java and PHP. By the end of the summer, she'd coded a computer game and felt very proud of herself until she realized she'd re-created Minesweeper.

He'd find out the truth soon, that she was no Rebecca Wang.

Charles piped up then. "Yeah, come. Domino's had a buy-five-get-five deal, and half our group is starting to develop lactose intolerance."

They stood there looking at her earnestly, like they actually wanted her to come, and her confidence expanded a teeny bit.

Here, in this smoky, sketchy apartment, she could be someone new. A person who might fit in with someone like Adam Fink.

"I'll see if I can stop by," she said, proud of herself for the answer. Not too desperate.

"Is that all you brought?" Charles asked, his attention going to her single suitcase. "Not much for a girl."

"Oh, shoot. My second suitcase is downstairs—" She hadn't even finished her sentence before Charles and Adam were tromping down the stairs.

Moments later, they reappeared with her suitcase. "Don't take the elevator," Adam told her with a wink. "A kid got stuck in it for five hours the other day."

MAGGIE ONLY HAD one mission for her first week of college: make a friend. It couldn't be that hard, on a campus with thirty thousand people.

Attempt one: she tried to become friendly with the roommate who'd come with their Craigslist apartment. She was a stylish art history major who spent an hour in the bathroom every morning talking to her New York boyfriend while she curled her hair. Then Maggie had overheard her mention "my weirdo roommate" during one of these calls and it was clear she did not mean it affectionately.

Attempt two: she struck up a conversation with the girl sitting next to her in her Compiler Optimization class. She'd asked about her iBook G4 and whether she'd noticed the benefits of the upgraded processor, only for her seatmate to stare at her like she had two heads. She certainly showed no interest in Maggie's secondhand Thinkpad, which was less futuristic-looking but that she'd customized with upgraded RAM and a larger battery.

Attempt three: she succeeded in making conversation with a kind girl handing out flyers on Sproul Plaza, until the girl asked

Maggie if she was interested in the Cal Christian Club and Maggie noticed the flyer she was holding had Jesus on it. For a moment, she had debated pretending to be religious, then decided that would probably not win her any divine favors.

Mission: failed. By the end of the week, she had stopped paying attention to the people around her, going straight from class to home. Cal was no different from community college. Everyone had already found their place. She was the only loser.

She was trudging down the third-floor hallway the following Monday, contemplating what kind of pity lunch to cook up, when a door opened and Charles backed out into her with a box overflowing with bottles and cartons.

"Sorry!" Charles said, dropping the box. Bottles went tumbling over the sides onto the carpet. He turned around. Wet black hair curled over his forehead, and he smelled faintly like chlorine. "Adam always shoves so much shit in the recycling, and then I end up being the one to carry it out."

Adam poked his head out the door. There was a blanket around his shoulders, and he was wearing plaid pajama pants like he'd just woken up, even though it was two in the afternoon. "Talking shit again? Oh, hey, Maggie."

"Hi," she said. She grabbed onto this moment, not wanting to step into the oppressive isolation of her apartment. "I can help you with these." She started picking up the dropped bottles.

"Thanks. We haven't seen you around. You must've had a busy first week," Charles said.

If only they knew that it was because she'd spent it inside her room, wallowing.

Another bottle fell out of Charles's box, but Maggie caught it before it dropped to the ground. Charles glared at Adam. "Asshole, give us a hand."

Adam gave them a little wave. "Looks like you guys got it handled. Once you're done, come watch cartoons with us." This, he directed at Maggie.

She wasn't sure if it was a serious invitation, so after she accompanied Charles to the recycling bin, she headed in the direction of her room.

"Where are you going?" Charles asked. "Our room is that way."

"Oh." She followed him into their apartment, feeling like she was entering uncharted territory. Two desks were joined up against the back wall, with a Lego Millennium Falcon serving as a divider between the two workspaces. One was well-organized, while the other was a mess of Skittles wrappers, torn-out notebook pages, and open textbooks. In the middle of the living room was a ratty couch on which Adam was sprawled.

"You guys have your own bedrooms?" Maggie observed. She and her roommate lived in a studio that was all but empty save for their two beds, shoved up against their respective walls.

"Yeah, Adam needs privacy to jerk off."

Adam flipped Charles off. "Have you had lunch yet?" Adam asked Maggie. Before she could answer, he jumped up and went to the kitchen, emerging with Charles's pot. He opened the lid and waved his hand over whatever was inside, like a chef presenting the soup du jour. "We made curry. I can heat it up for you. Want a sunny-side egg on top?"

Charles folded his arms. "You have no idea how to make an egg sunny-side up."

"I can set up the movie," Maggie volunteered, eager to be helpful and stay out of their squabble. "And, um, you don't need to fry me an egg."

Charles gave her a look, like the egg was a done deal and there was no use arguing. He snatched the pot from Adam's grip. "Unless we want another trash chute fiasco, I'll do it."

"Thank you," she said as she leaned behind the TV and plugged

Charles's laptop in, making sure the audio was coming from the right source, before settling on the couch next to him. "Your TV is huge." She marveled at the plasma-screen centerpiece. Some *Transformers* action figures stood on top, alongside a hula girl bobblehead and a creepy Oski plush.

"Gift from my dad," Adam said. "He wanted to buy me a car, but what would I do with that?"

"Drive to the grocery store so we don't have to ride the bus carrying four gallons of milk," Charles said.

"It's for our gains, Charlie-boy."

"What's the show?" Maggie asked.

"*Fullmetal Alchemist*," Charles called from the kitchen.

"*Fullmetal Alchemist*!" Maggie exclaimed. When Adam had said *cartoons*, she thought he'd meant Cartoon Network or Nickelodeon. "What episode is this? Have they explained the alchemy yet?"

Charles stuck his head out of the kitchen. "See?" he said to Adam. "I told you normal people watch this stuff."

"Who says she's normal?" Adam asked.

Maggie's smile slipped as she remembered her failed attempts to make friends, all because she probably projected something decidedly *abnormal*. Had she exposed herself already?

She realized Adam was holding out his fist for her to bump, his expression utterly serious. "Weirdos unite."

Charles came out of the kitchen and held a plate out to Maggie. On it was a mound of rice, topped with what she immediately knew by scent to be Golden Curry, as well as a single fried egg. He'd even added chopped scallions on top. It was basically fine dining.

Charles sat between her and Adam, unfolding a pink blanket with patterns of birds and flowers. It looked a lot like the blanket Maggie's dad brought out in the winter, the one he'd shipped from China. "It gets cold in here," Charles said, before he draped the blanket over her legs.

It didn't take long before they were totally absorbed by the show. Sometimes, the guys would ask Maggie to clarify some part of the plot. When she got up to put the empty dishes away, Charles paused it.

"I've already seen it. You can keep watching."

"No," he said gravely. "You have to be here for all of it."

After five episodes, Charles rose from the couch.

"Wait, don't you want to know what happens to Alphonse?" Maggie exclaimed. She'd definitely overstayed her welcome, but she wanted this afternoon to go on forever. She thought Charles would say no, it was too late, she should go back to her room.

Instead, he gave her an amused smile. "Chill, I just need to piss."

At six, Adam announced he was starving and asked Maggie how she felt about Bagel Bites. Even though she knew the sodium and fake cheese would trigger her eczema, there was no way she would interrupt the flow of this evening.

She watched Charles and Adam shovel down Bagel Bites like they were in a competition. "Hey, you free tomorrow?" asked Adam through a mouthful of soggy crust. "Charles and I are getting omelets at Café 3."

"I have an eight a.m.," Maggie said ruefully.

"Forget that," Adam said. "Charles and I will get you at eight thirty."

The next day, they knocked on her door at the promised time. Adam summoned a freshman to swipe them into the Unit 3 Café, and they sat in one of the booths. Breakfast stretched into two hours, and then Adam offered to give her the "campus tour: Fink edition." Instead of going to her classes that day, Maggie learned which bars didn't card, where to go for dollar scoops of ice cream, and the least hilly route from one end of campus to the other.

"This is the real education," Adam told her. "Stick around, and you'll learn what life's all about."

It sounded like a promise.

Chapter Three

WEDNESDAY

After staring at her computer long enough for her eyeballs to go bone dry, Maggie drives ten minutes from work to the garage she calls home. An enterprising couple decided they might as well make a buck from the skyrocketing housing prices in Silicon Valley and renovated their garage into a living space. The Wongs have been nothing but kind to her, inviting her grocery shopping or to Chinese New Year celebrations, but Maggie has always turned the invitations down. If she befriends her landlords, she'll be incapable of negotiating rent or will feel too guilty to trouble them to fix the old hand-me-down appliances.

By the time Maggie parks in the driveway, it's 9:00 p.m. Mrs. Wong, who is taking out the trash, immediately hurries over, and Maggie steels herself to refuse whatever she's about to offer, whether it's mooncakes, an extra blanket, or her son's hand in marriage. "Your dad's here!" she says instead, gesturing toward the Wongs' house.

Maggie follows her inside, wondering whether something terrible has happened. She sees her dad on holidays, but they mainly communicate through text. After a number of inflammatory phone calls from her college days, she sticks to iMessage, where she can send him unserious Asian-dad memes. Today's meme said,

Blood Type A-? Why Not A+? He dutifully replies to all of them with *LOL!* She taught him that.

Her dad sits in the Wongs' dining room, drinking tea and chatting in Mandarin with Mr. Wong, who's once again speaking grandly about his son who works at Google. Based on his bragging, Maggie has deduced that his son is a mere grunt whose main job is shuffling protobufs around, but she has decided not to pierce their delusion that their precious boy is solely responsible for Google's growing stock price.

"Margaret, join us!" Mr. Wong cries. "I already grabbed your mug!" The Wongs have assigned her, of all things, a Circle mug that their son got from a career fair. She tries to back away from it, but he shoves it into her hands.

"What are you doing here?" she asks her dad. He's in the Berkeley Dad shirt she bought him last Father's Day. She hadn't expected him to wear it, but every time she's seen him since, he's had it on.

"I was just in town playing badminton," he says, but there's something shifty in his gaze.

Her dad used to be a loner like her. But the '08 financial crisis forced him out of his comfort zone. While Maggie sank deeper into herself during her unemployment, her dad took the opposite course, throwing himself into networking until he could find a new job. Now he's *popular*. She's lucky that he LOLs at her once a day.

"Did you just come back from work? It's late." He's searching her face, like there are secrets folded into the crevices by her eyes or in the permanent pinch between her brows. She's unused to his scrutiny. During college, they went long periods without speaking, and now here he is, showing up unprompted to check in on her.

Mrs. Wong, who has taken a seat next to her dad, shakes her head as she peels a tangerine. "Aiya, this is early! Usually she comes back at midnight."

She really should move to an apartment where her comings and goings aren't monitored by nosy empty nesters.

"You should have more fun. You're only just thirty." Her dad frowns, probably remembering how quietly her thirtieth passed. They'd gone on a walk in his neighborhood, her dad had made her favorite dish—Golden Curry with a fried egg—and he'd insisted on singing her "Happy Birthday" while she waited to blow out the candle on the slice of cake he'd bought. Then she'd driven home and kept working until it wasn't her birthday anymore.

"When you were thirty, you were trying to make a living in the US with fifty dollars in your pocket, as you like to remind me." That was also the year her mom left.

"I did that so you wouldn't have to." He looks, briefly, unsure. Like there's more he wants to say, but he doesn't know how.

Mr. Wong says something to her dad in Mandarin that she doesn't understand, but she hears her name. She wishes she'd made a better attempt at learning Mandarin when she was little. It's her dad's preferred language, what he speaks with all his friends. With her, though, he speaks English, and it feels like seeing him through frosted glass.

Mrs. Wong smacks her husband in the shoulder. "Aiya, speak English when Maggie's here! She'll think you're insulting her."

She feels bad that everyone has to accommodate her monolingualism. Mr. Wong grins sheepishly. "I was just saying that he must be so proud of you, a two-time entrepreneur! I saw on Circle that it's ten years old today!"

Maggie wishes she could throw the Circle mug at the wall. The invitation to the anniversary reunion hasn't been far from her mind. Why would Adam issue such a personal invitation? Why are reminders of this damn company all around her, and why can't she just ignore the curiosity gnawing at her?

Her dad is staring at her, and she knows that this is the real reason he came. He wanted to see if she was okay. After all, at the five-year mark, he'd found her in the darkness of her bedroom, staring at the site while tears streamed down her face.

"How amazing!" Mrs. Wong says, clapping her hands. "You know, when I told George—who works at Google—that one of the founders of Circle was living in our garage, he didn't believe me."

"Yeah," Mr. Wong says, nodding. "He kept saying Circle was founded by three guys, then when I said, no, there was a girl, he finally remembered! He just forgot because you weren't there for very long. He still doesn't believe me, though. Doesn't think someone who founded Circle would be living in a garage." At this, Mr. Wong peers at her curiously. She knows the Wongs wonder why she's not living in a mansion in Atherton. Her personal finances are a mystery they're determined to solve.

Her dad clears his throat loudly. "What are your plans this weekend? Doing something with your friends?" It's a poor attempt to change the subject. Despite herself, Maggie is bothered by George's ignorance. Is this what most people think? That she was an insignificant part of Circle? Has the company she founded and devoted herself to for two years erased her from its history so easily?

"I'm too busy to have friends." OurSpot has gained some traction in the saturated social media landscape because it's her entire world. At all hours of the day, users log onto their Spots desiring connection, and she and her lean team must be on-call to serve it to them. She can't get distracted by group dinners and weekend outings.

Mrs. Wong gasps. "George is visiting this weekend! Maybe we should all go hike Mission Peak together."

Nothing in this sentence appeals to Maggie. "I'm sorry, but I'll be busy." She'll just hide out at the office. Then she remembers it will be closed because they're fixing a water leak there this weekend.

She envisions running into scrawny George Wong, with his Google-issued Timbuk2 and love for name-dropping Larry Page.

Mrs. Wong has not given up on matchmaking the two of them, even though Maggie is certain that George must think he's superior to her. After all, he has dental insurance and she lives in his parents' garage.

She sticks her hand in her pocket, her finger poking against the corner of Adam's invitation. "I'll be busy because I'm going to Norway. I got invited to a Circle reunion." This second part she says for the Wongs' benefit. Maybe they'll tell their smug son.

The Wongs and her dad gape at her.

"You didn't mention this," her dad finally says.

She shrugs. "Last-minute decision." She should probably spend more time thinking this through, but deciding to go feels right. She *should* be there, on the tenth anniversary of the company she helped create. If she doesn't respond to Adam's invitation, it will only contribute to her ever-fading part in its history. "I think it's time I took a vacation."

"Are those other boys going?" her dad asks.

Boys. This is how her dad has always referred to them. In his mind, Adam, Charles, and Hari are forever the college hooligans who prevented her from focusing on her studies.

"Probably."

Mrs. Wong is excited for her. "Norway! That sounds so fun! Do you need help packing?"

Her dad's forehead is all scrunched up. "It's been so long. Are you sure about this?"

"Positive," she says, donning a smile that feels like it doesn't fit properly on her face. Nothing these men could say or do could possibly hurt worse than what happened in 2007, and she has since climbed out of that hole. Now she runs a company with product market fit and manages to get out of bed every morning to do it. She'll go to this thing, make sure everyone remembers the role she played in Circle's success, and return to OurSpot to resume her search for a new COO. And she'll get out of meeting George Wong, the pride and glory of Google.

Her dad still looks worried, but there's nothing he can say, not when the Wongs are eagerly hanging on to every word. "You seem to know what you're doing."

She nods, using all her hard-learned executive presence to convey that yes, she *totally* knows what she's doing.

Chapter Four

DAY 1: THURSDAY

When Maggie disembarks in Oslo, she's groggy and disoriented. She spent the entire flight working, pausing briefly to scarf down the three-course meal that came with actual silverware, barely registering that this would be one of the few times she'd get to fly business. In Arrivals, a tall blond man who looks like Armie Hammer holds a placard with her name, and waiting with him is the last person she expected to see.

"Margaret Tang?" Sylvia Kim asks. Beside the Scandinavian giant, Sylvia looks like a doll, and her wardrobe—bright blue blazer and red pumps, topped with a knee-length white puffer—only amplifies the effect. There's no reason for Sylvia to dress like this; she's a reporter in Silicon Valley, where the typical dress code is joggers, hoodies, and a patina of entitlement.

Still, Sylvia's appearance is jarring. Maggie has never spoken to the journalist, who hosts an annual tech conference that costs five hundred dollars to attend and has interviewed the top twenty of the Bloomberg Billionaire Index. Her popularity sprouted from her posts on Circle—short, punchy quips that cover the tech industry and its titans. Nobody has been spared from her remarks. Maggie recalls a pull quote where Sylvia called Adam a "subhuman jock captaining the Death Star." And, of course, she had bet on Maggie getting kicked out of Circle long before anyone else had.

They couldn't possibly be going to the same place, could they? "Are you here for the—"

"The reunion! Wow, up until I saw you, I was *not* expecting you to show up. You have no idea how much I've wanted to meet you." Sylvia loops an arm through Maggie's with a bright smile, like they've known each other for years, and drags her along as they follow their escort. She puffs on a vape that is as thin as a pencil, her dyed-black hair swinging loosely around her face. "This is going to be a fun piece to write."

"Wait, what piece?" The very fact that there's a journalist here is a red flag. Maggie dislikes journalists on principle, though she does kind of admire Sylvia. She cuts people down yet has been able to maintain her insider status. Pretty impressive.

Sylvia peers at her with an expression of disbelief. "You haven't heard?"

It seems like there's some important context that Adam left out of his little invitation. "What piece?" she repeats.

Sylvia exhales cherry-scented smoke, considering her with curious eyes. "Adam wants to grow Circle into a full-fledged media company. There's so much homegrown talent on the site, especially within news. So he's handpicked a group of journalists to write newsworthy stories that will be the first to go live on the new platform, Circle Net, when it launches later this year. And I was the lucky one tapped to write about your reunion."

A news product. Maggie pushes down her distaste. Adam's sphere of control, it seems, is expanding. "Is that really news?" She finds it hard to believe that the general public cares that much about their friendship.

Sylvia clicks her tongue. "The four of you, being interviewed together? That's front-page material. Nobody knows the real story behind Circle's inner circle."

Like George Wong. He thinks that she played an insignificant role at the company, there and gone in a blink. Soon, her name will just be a footnote in Circle's sprawling history. Maggie processes this new information. Figures that Adam had an ulterior motive for bringing her here, but why does he want to revisit her departure? Is he trying to punish her?

Their escort leads them toward a black helicopter, and that's when it occurs to Maggie that Oslo isn't the final destination. She should turn around before she gets taken to a remote location from which she can't escape.

Adam isn't the sort to give people access without asking something in return, especially not a journalist who's had bad things to say about him in the past. "I'm assuming he's going to read it before you publish it?"

Sylvia narrows her eyes at that. "Journalistic integrity is a thing, Margaret. Adam has made it clear that I will be the sole author of this article."

She's offended her, but Sylvia is the fool if she thinks that Adam would invite her into his inner life and let her write whatever she wants.

When they arrive at the helicopter, Sylvia's first question is whether she can vape inside. Maggie sits, clamps the headphones over her head, and stares out the window, strategizing. Sylvia's presence is a double-edged sword. Everything she says, everything she does, must be filtered carefully. But maybe she can convince Sylvia that she's outgrown the immaturity that characterized the early years of her career and get coverage for OurSpot. A sly smile spreads over her face. That would be a sweet victory, to get her company mentioned on the front page of Circle.

The helicopter lifts off, and Maggie spends the journey watching the wide channels of water, bordered by idyllic red-and-white houses. In the distance are mountains, proud and tall, still covered in snow. From this height, everything looks distinctly fantastical, like a well-designed adventure RPG. Is she actually in Norway right now, when just yesterday, she was being dumped by her COO in a Ranch 99? Even Sylvia is silenced by the unreal views.

After thirty minutes, they land on a helipad on the beach, just inches from the churning waves. The moment Maggie steps off, an icy wind darts at her face, shocking her back into the reality of her situation. She is going to see the guys again after almost eight years of not speaking.

Ahead, a paved path leaves the beach and winds through a bright green field dotted with wildflowers. She sees a lone figure standing at the end.

"That must be Adam," Sylvia says. She's taken off her pumps and holds them by the heels as she walks, barefoot, toward the path. Already, she's got her phone out. "Do you have any service?"

Maggie follows behind Sylvia, her resolve already wavering. This distance is too short to figure out what the appropriate words are for a stranger who used to be a friend.

Adam wears a black trucker jacket and joggers that expose tanned ankles. When he spots them, he lifts a hand. He greets Sylvia with a cheek kiss, then turns to Maggie. Her throat constricts, and any words she could've said immediately vanish from her brain.

For the last eight years, she has tried to forget Adam Fink exists. But the internet and media would never let her, and he's constantly loomed larger than life. A dynamic innovator who rubs shoulders with actors and politicians, with a net worth that exceeds the GDPs of some countries. This image has replaced the real person from her memories, the boy who could drink implausible amounts of Fireball and thought cats dressed up as dogs were hilarious.

Up close, she notices how much older he looks. There's some gray at his temples, like he's been seasoned by life and the countless experiences it has gifted him. There are creases along his brow, and he's thinner.

Then he smiles wide, and at least that has stayed the same.

Sylvia preempts their greeting. "Adam, look! Margaret came. You made it sound like she wasn't going to show."

So, he hadn't been certain. That gives her a measure of comfort. The handwritten note was a last-ditch attempt, not proof of how well he still knows her.

Adam steps toward her. Sylvia, who doesn't seem to think this is a private moment, watches as he goes in for a hug, just like he did the day they first met. And just like back then, Maggie is stiff in his arms. "It's so good to see you, Maggie." His voice hasn't changed either. It's suffused with warmth, like stepping into a steaming bath.

She pulls away quickly. "It's Margaret now," she says, businesslike. *Maggie* is for friends and loved ones. And Adam hasn't been a friend in a long time.

"Right, I forgot." A beat passes, then he says, "Let me help with your bag," picking up the duffel she'd dropped before she can stop him. "This is heavy. What's in here?"

"Rocks," she replies. "I can carry it." She'd brought her work laptop, along with various devices to supplement her internet and security needs, just in case the accommodations didn't meet her standards.

Adam shakes his head. "No, allow me." He puts the bag on Sylvia's suitcase and pulls it along while the two of them follow.

"I'm not getting any service here," Sylvia says.

"That's on purpose," Adam says. "There's Wi-Fi in the rooms, but I think it's nice to disconnect."

"That's ironic," Sylvia says. "Considering you're the reason everyone's obsessed with their phones."

"Come on, Sylvia," Adam says playfully. He catches Maggie's eye, as if they're sharing a joke. "You just got here, and you're already throwing down?"

"I'm getting the festivities started."

"Let's party, then. This is your cabin." Adam sounds amused

as he leads them down the path, not annoyed, like this is an exchange that they've had often. They're on a rocky outcropping now, and in front of them is a cabin of glass and wood. Maggie can see through the wraparound windows into the living room, where a long, curving white couch is lined with knitted throws and fuzzy pillows. She's only seen places like this in Costco timeshare magazines.

Adam lifts Maggie's duffel off Sylvia's suitcase, and Sylvia grabs the handle, jabbing a finger at him. "You won't escape me for long."

"Don't I know it." Adam salutes her, then it's just him and Maggie.

"I'll take that," she says, grabbing for her duffel, but he pretends he doesn't hear her and continues ahead. She walks faster to keep up, then catches herself and slows. Adam's strides were always unfairly long.

Adam notices after a few minutes and stops to wait for her.

When she reaches him, she says, "You had time to write me a note, but not mention the journalist you invited along?" She pauses and reminds herself to take a breath. Be levelheaded, not accusatory.

"I'll explain when everyone gets here," Adam says.

"You stole my COO," she says. So much for not being accusatory.

"I wasn't the one who filled out the job application."

"Asshole."

This doesn't even make Adam flinch. Instead, he laughs loudly. "Nobody's called me that to my face in a long time. But Mag—Margaret, this could be great for you, too. You're raising, right? Sylvia will definitely post about you and your company. It'll be good exposure with the VCs."

He's landed on the same conclusion that she did on the helicopter ride. Early-stage founders would be begging for a journalist with as much cachet as Sylvia to mention them. A positive word from her is rumored to improve stock prices.

"She says you're not going to proofread her article," Maggie says. "That doesn't sound like you."

This makes Adam's shoulders rise, before he drops them with a chuckle. "I chose her because Sylvia's known in the Valley for being fair. But there are other, less obvious ways of influencing a story."

He's still so *Adam*. Calculating every action, thinking about the best way to position himself. He's probably even better at it now. She walks ahead, aware that by coming, she's agreed to participate in his games. The air here is crisp and clean, but also a kind of cold that seems unfazed by her fleece. She hears Adam behind her, the sound of their shoes against the rocky dirt.

"We're here," Adam calls up to her. They're at the top of a path that leads down to the water. The sea is lined with black rocks, and on top of those rocks is another fancy cabin that looks slightly bigger than Sylvia's.

When Adam reaches her, he says, "I didn't want you to have a reason not to come, so I didn't tell you. Even if Sylvia wasn't writing this article, I'd have wanted you to be here." He says the last part softly, like he's confiding a secret.

It's disarming to hear him tell her so directly that her presence is wanted. She looks up at him, keeping the emotion out of her voice. "Well, it worked. I'm here now."

He puts his hand on her shoulder, the weight warm and familiar. "Don't worry. This weekend will be fun. It'll be just like old times."

Chapter Five

SEPTEMBER 2005

"You can choose from three: skydiving, poker, or belly dancing." Adam fanned out pamphlets from the three clubs, waving them in front of Maggie tantalizingly. "Come on, the skydiving club calls themselves the Air Bears! Isn't that adorable?"

"Adam, you realize the average terminal velocity for humans is a hundred and twenty miles per hour? Can you conceptualize how fast that is?" Maggie smacked his hand away. She'd accepted his invitation to Calapalooza with the intention of checking out a *normal* club. Like Dungeons & Dragons or Robotics. But Adam had dragged her to the most crowded part of Memorial Glade, the grassy field teeming with wide-eyed freshmen looking for a place to belong. Maggie felt like that, too. It was all so overwhelming—the signs, the free swag people were handing out, the beaming upperclassmen in customized T-shirts shoving flyers in her face.

Adam shrugged. "You're small, maybe yours is lower." He turned to the intense-looking guy staffing the skydiving table before Maggie could school him in physics. Even though there were three other people in front of him, Adam was so tall that he immediately caught the guy's attention. "How do I sign up?" he asked.

She'd come to Calapalooza determined to find her community on campus. She was getting too dependent on Adam and Charles, basically living in their apartment, and when both of them were busy with extracurriculars or other friends, she felt invisible. She had to make more of an effort.

"If you're not signing up, you need to move," someone at the Air Bears table ordered her.

There were so many people crowded around the tables that digging an underground tunnel would've taken less time than waiting to get to the front. "I'll be over there," she told Adam, as she tried to move out of the crowd. Adam nodded in acknowledgment but didn't follow.

The sun, combined with the heat of all the bodies, was suffocating. As she waded out of the sea of bodies, she spotted the far less crowded Engineering Honor Society table, staffed by two pale guys in hoodies. She'd forgotten, but she had emailed them before even arriving on campus.

"Are you interested in going Greek?" Somehow, she had ended up near the Panhellenics, surrounded by pretty girls who all looked and dressed unnervingly alike. One of them was currently addressing her.

"No, I'm trying to go over there," Maggie said, pointing.

The girl followed her gaze. Her bright smile flickered, replaced by confusion. But Maggie was already moving past her.

The two guys were having a conversation about open source, something she knew a lot about. She'd been a regular contributor to projects since high school.

She approached them eagerly. "Hi!"

They stopped their conversation and stared at her. "Are you lost?" the Asian one finally asked.

"What? No, I want to join." She smiled wide. "I'm a computer science major. Actually, I sent an email—"

"We don't usually take underclassmen."

"I'm a junior."

"This isn't really a beginners' club," his white friend said. "We're not going to teach you basic stuff, like Javascript or whatever."

"Trust me, I know the basics already. Including Basic." She thought they'd at least appreciate her pun, but neither cracked a smile.

They glanced at each other. Then the Asian guy shrugged and said, "I guess we could use a girl."

It took all her effort to keep smiling as she gave them her email address again. Only once she turned around did she let the disillusionment crash through her. What was the point of transferring to a world-class university if this was going to be just like high school, where the guys assumed she didn't know shit, and the girls thought she was weird for being interested in computers?

Maggie ended up at the edge of the Glade, feeling worse off than when she'd started. She had no idea where Adam was and was debating heading back alone when he found her.

"There you are!" He smelled like grass and candy, and he was holding at least ten flyers, a newly won T-shirt around his neck. "Just came from the Furries table where they had Haribo gummy bears," he said, waving a bag in front of her. "Find anything interesting?"

"Yeah," she said with a sad shrug.

Adam tilted his head at her. "That is the saddest *yeah* I've ever heard."

"I found clubs I wanted to join, but they don't want *me*." She felt like a loser admitting this to Adam, who had probably never been rejected by anything or anyone in his life.

"Then they're idiots," Adam concluded immediately. Even if he was only trying to make her feel better, Maggie felt comforted by the speed of this denial. For some reason, she had won Adam's favor, and that was a far greater achievement. "What club was this?"

"The Engineering Honor Society."

Adam snorted. "That place isn't worth your time. They don't even look at applications. They just choose people that the president personally knows."

As they walked in the direction of the apartment, she filled him in on her interaction. Adam reacted with the appropriate indignation, and Maggie felt her disappointment replaced by anger. Why *did* they get to make assumptions about her before they even knew her? Why were any of these club officers gatekeepers, when they were all students on the same campus? It struck her as deeply unfair.

"We need a better way for students to join clubs," Maggie said as they headed through Sproul Plaza. "And to share information about them. People deserve to know if they're wasting their time by filling out an application." She could already imagine how disheartened she would be if she'd spent hours on an application to the Honor Society only to be immediately rejected based on someone else's whims.

"Like a forum?" Adam asked, chewing on a gummy bear. He offered her one.

"Sort of. Less anonymous. More organized."

"That would be cool," he said. "You know who'd love that? Charles. Actually, funny story—freshman year, Charles joined this design club because he wanted to learn more about prototyping and design, fancy woo-woo Charles stuff, you know? But everyone else in the club just wanted to learn how to Photoshop their heads onto animals' bodies. Charles was *pissed*." He chuckled. "Anyway, this sounds like something he'd use."

The idea began to take shape in Maggie's head. It wouldn't be that hard to build. The current directory of clubs was a static webpage that looked like it'd been built at the dawn of the World Wide Web. If they could export that data, she could make it easier to search clubs and leave testimonials. Then it wouldn't be necessary for everyone to sweat on Memorial Glade, wasting time on clubs that didn't want them anyway.

"What if . . ." she started, but then she stopped. Yes, she could build something, but she lacked the insider knowledge Adam had. Even if she could scrape everything from the official directory, something like this would only have value if other students contributed to it.

"Finish your thought," Adam said, his head turned toward her. He seemed invested, and Maggie had never had someone actually want to hear her weird little ideas. Usually people didn't have that kind of patience for her. Certainly not her dad, who was always working or doing chores, like life would bury him if he stopped.

So for the rest of their walk, she explained her thinking, pausing to catch her breath as they climbed the three flights to their floor. When she described her uncertainty around getting information, Adam flapped a hand dismissively. "I could help you with that, if you wanted."

She nodded so quickly that she got a crick in her neck.

They were in front of his and Charles's apartment, and Maggie was ready to part ways, but Adam said, "Maybe Charles has some thoughts. Let's go talk to him."

In their living room, Charles was on his knees in front of the coffee table, studying a stainless steel teakettle. He cupped his hand around its silver belly, as if he were caressing a lover's face.

"What are you doing?" Adam asked.

Charles wasn't bothered by the interruption. "I'm admiring the design of this teakettle."

"You fished that out of the dumpster."

"Whoever tossed it is a moron. The handle is the perfect distance from the cap so you get a balanced lift. The spout opens automatically. No water or steam burns. And the pitch from the spout is a perfect D sharp." He seemed to sense the friendly judgment coming from Adam's direction. "I've been challenging myself to find the beauty in common things. The paradox of good design is that you don't notice it. But I won't be tricked into taking it for granted."

Adam gave Maggie an exasperated, *this is what happens when I leave him unattended* look. "Maggie had a big epiphany while we were out."

Charles looked at her. "Was it that clubs are just another way of creating hierarchy in an already overachieving student body?"

Adam headed into the kitchen for a snack. "Maggie, tell him."

"Kind of," she said as she sat on the floor by Charles. He sank down beside her as she introduced her idea. "What we need is an easy way of consolidating and delivering the combined knowledge of the student body."

Charles brought the kettle into his lap and clicked the spout open and shut as he thought. "We'd have to surface the most useful and relevant information for it to be of any value."

"We create a ranking system and let users vote on what's most helpful to them." She had literally come up with this idea twenty minutes ago, and now they were pulling it apart like it was as legitimate as free trade or cybersecurity. She'd started plenty of random projects from her wandering thoughts: chatbots, mini games, an interest calculator for her dad. But this was the first time there were other people involved, building on the original premise.

"Charlie-boy, this sounds right up your alley," Adam said, coming out of the kitchen with a stack of Kraft cheese slices and sleeve of Oreos. He took a seat at their desk, rolling his chair toward them. Maggie had never actually seen him do any work there. "You spent, like, an hour the other day listing all the reasons you think MySpace is an overpopulated, buggy piece of crap with an identity crisis. Can you really do better than Tom?"

Charles stood and returned the teakettle to the kitchen stove. Then, he came back to their desk, which was really two dining tables pushed together. The other day, he and Adam had spent an hour explaining to Maggie why a mega-desk was superior to two separate desks.

Maggie watched Charles boot up his laptop. He glanced over his shoulder at her, cocking an eyebrow. "Aren't we going to get started? I've got to prove this bastard wrong."

Adam smirked as he tore a slice of Kraft cheese in half. "What are you waiting for, Maggie?"

She jumped to her feet, then ran down the hallway for her laptop. They were really doing this.

Circle's Inner Circle: Part One

By Sylvia Kim

When I head to Janteloven, a peculiar little island in Norway that doesn't show up on Google Maps, I think I know what to expect for the weekend. It is ten years from when Circle, the tech company and social network that has become a daily part of all our lives—like it or not—was founded. I'm here because Adam Fink, Circle's CEO, well-known for his Captain America looks and equally golden charisma, has invited me to the executive team's reunion so that I can gather color for an anniversary retrospective, which will launch at the same time as Circle Net, Circle's news engine. It promises to replace traditional media, delivering readers well-curated selections of the topics they're interested in.

I've only been able to observe Circle's top executives in large, public formats previously. In those settings, they are like most tech founders in Silicon Valley: obsessed with their work, driven by an almost mad desire to expand their influence across the world, possibly half-robot. I'm hoping that this weekend will give me a deeper look into their origin stories and the friendship that preceded their partnership. Really, I'm hoping for evidence that we haven't handed off the future of our society to a group of unwieldy man-children.

Founders Adam Fink, Margaret Tang, Charles Xu, and Hari Acharya met while students at the University of California, Berkeley. In its earliest iteration, Circle was known as Clubb and gave college students the ability to easily find, rate, and review clubs. It was a new way to tap into the campus grapevine at a time when broadband had only been introduced commercially five years before. At its one-year mark, Circle was present in campuses across the country. By the time it turned two, Tang had been voted out. She left in a flurry of rage that led to that famous GIF of her violently stabbing a chair. We heard nothing of her for six years until 2013, when she released an app called OurSpot, a competitor to Circle's core product.

Fink insists that the four of them are still friends. He even tells me that for the tenth anniversary, he's invited Tang to join us. I love the intrigue, but I'm skeptical she'll show. And yet, when I step off the plane, Tang is there, on the tarmac. She's dressed in all black, her hair cut short at a perilous slant, looking equally surprised to see me. As if Fink didn't give her the full story, either.

It should be an interesting weekend.

Chapter Six

DAY 1: THURSDAY

The cabin is nice. *Too* nice. The interior is all light wood, and the entire side facing the ocean is glass. The sun, high in the sky despite the lateness of the day, spills over minimalist Scandinavian furniture. There's a small kitchen to the side of the entryway with a fully stocked minifridge and pour-over setup, a marble bathroom with a scented rain shower and Aesop soaps. On the walls are still lifes of randomly modern objects done in vibrant colors: a pencil sharpener, a Big Mac, a tangled set of earbuds.

The luxury of it all disquiets her. She wants to be back in her cramped garage, with her small workspace and the muffled sound of car doors slamming whenever the Wongs go anywhere. Yet again, she wonders what she's doing here.

Work will settle her and take her mind off the weekend ahead. Maggie pulls her laptop out of her backpack. It's seven in the evening in Norway, which means she still has time to dial into her daily stand-up with her engineers.

She joins the call just as she hears one of the program managers saying, "It's going to be in February."

"Margaret's here. Hey, Margaret," one of the engineers says quickly, alerting everyone to her presence.

"What's in February?"

A pause, and then the program manager says nervously, "My wedding," like she's admitting to a crime.

After the meeting ends and Maggie sends off some emails and drafts a company-wide announcement about Lisa's departure, she feels wiped. She should really catch up on the sleep she missed on the plane, but she needs to wind down a bit. She grabs her old iPhone and swipes through her mobile games, patiently dealing with the lag, before deciding she should take some pictures of this island to send to her dad. She'd texted him when she landed, but he's probably still fretting over her spontaneous decision to fuck off to Norway.

After a shower, she throws on a sweater and the bird-embroidered scarf Mrs. Wong insisted she borrow, and ventures out. She follows the path along the beach that brought her here, quickening her pace as she passes Sylvia's cabin. It takes her into a forest where another cabin is nestled in the trees. When she exits the forest, she's on the beach again. She sees a wooden building that looks like it's floating in the sea, connected to the shore by a series of stepping stones, and ahead, a large lodge that must be some kind of community center. She keeps going, until she reaches wooden steps that go up a cliff, to another cabin, smaller than the others. That's where the path ends.

She climbs the steps. There's no railing, so she's careful, core tightened. The waves crash beneath her. When she arrives in front of the cabin, she realizes what is so unsettling. She hasn't seen another soul on this island. Either she's wandered into the setup of a murder mystery, or . . .

Just then, the door opens, startling her. Adam comes out, holding a picnic basket stuffed with items she can't easily identify, wrapped in plastic and topped with a giant red bow.

His eyes go wide. "I was just about to come looking for you. Guess you found me first."

"Why isn't there anyone else here?" she asks.

"Hari and Charles get in later today."

Maggie ignores the jolt she gets from hearing their names. "I mean, why are there no tourists?" She can't imagine that people would pass up the chance to visit a place as beautiful and untarnished as this. "Did you book this place out or something? Can you rent a whole island?"

Adam chuckles. "I guess you could say that."

The weird art that's probably really expensive, the fact that there are only five buildings on the island, the way Adam had answered Sylvia's question about the lack of service like he'd personally decided where it would be available . . .

"You own this entire island!" Maggie exclaims, loudly enough for the seagulls circling above them to hear. Adam rubs the back of his neck. It's enough of a confirmation. She wants to ask him how much it costs to *buy an island.* Now she understands the Wongs' obsession with her financials. Adam already came from wealth; his father is an architect who designed a number of famous buildings in New York and San Francisco. He'd only lived in that shitty apartment in Berkeley because it was all Charles could afford, and Maggie suspected he was curious about how normal people live.

But this is a whole other level.

"I was actually going to come looking for you," Adam says, lifting the basket, unperturbed by the massive piece of land he owns. "This is for you. A welcome gift."

"Oh, that's okay," Maggie says. In her head, she knew that Circle had made them rich, but it's different to see what that money has actually allowed him to do. *A whole island.*

"Take it." He shoves the basket at her, and she accepts it reluctantly. "Come in, it's too cold outside," he says, and then he's standing to the side and she is walking inside his cabin, which smells just like hers. It's smaller, but it has an incredible view. The sea stretches in front of her and below her, its dark blue waves hypnotic. It feels like she's suspended above the world, within reach of the sky.

She sets the basket on his round dining table, untying the ribbon and taking off the plastic. It's full of products that look like they belong in a department store or Whole Foods. Artisanal cheeses, aged balsamic, a blanket embroidered with Gucci logos, a bottle of something called "body butter" that Maggie can't determine is for eating or skincare.

"You forgot the diamond necklace," she says to Adam as he brings her a mug of hot water.

Adam laughs, sitting at the table. "Dig deeper."

"Really?" she asks, not sure whether to take him seriously, but he just waits. She starts pulling things out and laying them to the side. That's when she sees what's hidden underneath.

Stuffed-crust pizza. Kraft cheese slices. Double Stuf Oreos. Bags of Skittles. Endless ramen. Her amusement grows with each item of junk food she uncovers, all of them mementos of their caffeine-fueled, sodium-laden college days. She keeps waiting for Golden Curry to make an appearance, though it does not.

Finally, the basket is empty and, shaking her head, she begins putting everything back. "Thanks. Though this basket makes me think you don't have a ton of faith in Norway's cuisine."

There's a brief pause, and she looks over at Adam, notes that he's staring at her, not listening to what she's saying.

He seems to realize that he's let the silence go too long. He gives a small smile. "Sorry, I was checking you out."

Once, a comment like that would've made her blush, maybe even come up with something clever to say. That was the power of Adam—his confidence could make you confident, too.

This time, though, she lets his comment hang in the air, until even Adam looks a little discomfited and adds, "You never post anything online. It's kind of weird, how little I know about you now."

She can't believe he just admitted to internet-stalking her. That he cared enough to even type her name into Google, when he probably has a million things he has to do every day. "Yeah, you've basically invited a stranger to your island."

"You're never going to be a stranger."

She studies the man in front of her, with his weathered features and a new remoteness he didn't have before. Those are only the changes she can see. There must be so much more that isn't visible to her. "Not even after eight years?"

He folds his arms on the table and gazes at her, the same way he used to when she was offering a new idea. There's an openness to his face, like he's game for whatever leaves her mouth. "Then catch me up. Tell me everything that's happened."

Does she start from the two years of unemployment, when her bad reputation haunted her everywhere she went? Or the three years after that, when she languished at an IT job inspecting people's laptops because of a problem that almost always could be fixed by a restart? The trail of failed apps she left behind her, until she finally came up with the idea for OurSpot? Telling him any of this would reveal that she hasn't made it far from the floundering community college transfer who hadn't found her place in the world, and she's not about to admit that when Adam owns an entire island and commands legions of employees across several continents.

She picks at the wood grain on his table, a sense of futility hitting her. "I wouldn't know where to begin."

Chapter Seven

OCTOBER 2005

Maggie had never been very good at time management, and this turned out to bite her in the butt when it came to balancing friends and schoolwork. Case in point: she was rushing to finish her *Hamlet* paper due that night while Adam dramatically told a story about finding a bug in his Café 3 omelet.

"Maggie, Maggie, Maggie," Adam said, getting up from the couch and coming to stand behind her. He tugged on her ponytail. "Are you listening?"

"Yes, you found a bug and then you ate it."

He tutted at her. "No, I didn't eat it, though that's a very good guess. I put it in Charles's bowl and waited for *him* to eat it."

"Which I didn't." Charles was seated at his desk next to her, working on Clubb, the name they'd assigned to their project to identify and classify all Berkeley clubs. She'd built the web scraper to import all the available data on the clubs and their officers, and Charles was designing the interface so that it would be easy to search for clubs and leave reviews. All Maggie wanted to do right now was work on it, but she had to focus on a stupid play about a crazy dude.

"Liar, you thought it was a bean!"

"That I immediately spat out because it was crunchy."

"Gross," Maggie said, even as she continued staring at her laptop screen, wishing Shakespeare had never existed.

Adam leaned over her shoulder, blocking her view of her screen. He smelled good. It was Old Spice; she'd confirmed when peeking at the bottles in their bathroom one time. "What are you working on so diligently? '*Hamlet* makes no sense. He talks to skulls and says he's pretending to be crazy but I don't think he's pretending.'"

"It's a work in progress," Maggie said, shoving him back.

Adam didn't budge. "By the way, I've finished cleaning up the club database. All eight hundred and fifty-five of them."

She stopped attempting to move him and instead stared at Adam in shock. "Already?" It was a Herculean task when there were so many clubs without websites indicating whether they were still active or who their officers were.

Charles sounded suspicious, too. "Who did you bribe?"

Adam grinned down at her. The lamplight made his curls glow. "I have a friend who's a senator at the ASUC. He got me the emails of all the current presidents. I reached out to them and said we were collecting data for a research project, and participants would be rewarded."

Maggie's face fell. "Adam, we can't actually pay them." Her dad gave her just enough money to cover rent and basic living expenses each month. After spending far too much on textbooks she'd never opened, she was barely scraping by.

Adam waved her off. "Think of it as my investment in us. I sent you guys the spreadsheet." Adam spent money without a second thought. He never hesitated to pick up the bill when they got takeout from Asian Ghetto and often forgot to ask them to pay him back, even though Charles and Maggie now privately maintained a shared ledger of what they owed him, which they cleared at the end of each month.

Charles opened the file on his laptop. "We could launch this thing now."

She abandoned her essay.

As she fiddled with the code, Charles went into the kitchen for a snack. He reappeared with his mom's five spice peanuts. At first, Maggie had been jealous of Charles, whose mom delivered food every month and idled on the curb in front of the apartment without caring who honked at her. Her own mom was a mystery. She knew nothing about her, except that she had not cared enough about either her or her dad to stay.

But if Charles didn't have his mom, she wouldn't be sitting here, being fed delicious peanuts.

Without looking away from the laptop, Maggie opened her mouth, and Charles dropped in a peanut before he slotted another chair next to hers at the mega-desk. The two of them fell into a charged silence, the tapping on their keyboards the only noise.

Working with Charles felt natural. They flowed around each other, their brain waves moving in synchrony. Neither got offended when the other had feedback. Maggie knew Charles was a damn good programmer, and he believed the same about her.

"Nut me," Adam called from the couch. He'd sacrificed his chair to Charles and was back on the sofa, earbuds in his ears as he did his homework. At first, he'd tried to involve himself in their process, straining to wrap his head around how clients and servers functioned. But after Maggie attempted to explain how websites operated over packet-switched networks, he stopped. Now he let Maggie and Charles work, while he took on the stuff they didn't want to do, like talking to people.

Maggie pinched a single peanut out of the container with Charles's chopsticks and flicked it. Charles paused his work to turn and watch as it soared through the air. Adam emerged from behind the couch like a breaching whale, mouth wide-open. She held her breath as the peanut landed on his tongue, and Adam shut his mouth, a victorious grin on his face. Charles and Maggie clapped. "Thank you, thank you. I'm here every night." Then everyone went back to what they were doing without another comment.

This was the kind of thing that made her smile at night when she was falling asleep. *Friendship* was such a big word, but it was engineered by all these tiny, shared moments. It made everything less scary, knowing she had these two people, and this apartment, to return to at the end of the day.

By midnight, they had a functioning, if bare-bones, website. Anyone could easily search a club, explore its leadership, and leave a rating or testimonial. It had the Charles Xu touch: streamlined but cohesive.

"I also wanted to try something," Charles said to Maggie gravely, like whatever was going to come next was incredibly important to him. Unlike Adam, who was constantly distracted by shiny new things, Charles honed in with laser precision.

"What is it?" she asked. On the couch, Adam tugged his earbuds out of his ears and stretched.

"We've been discussing how we want people to engage with content in a way that feels intuitive." Charles indicated a purple circle hovering next to the comment box. As he held his mouse over the button, a circle appeared, expanding and contracting over the comment it accompanied. "So I designed this circle. You can 'circle' a comment, a club, or a post to indicate support. The size is a measure of *how much*. Then, the site aggregates all the feedback and uses it to rank the content."

Maggie clicked on the circle. It was satisfying to watch the purple circle grow bigger, then smaller. "I like the kinesis of it. And the color."

"I spent the last two days trying to get it to do that. At first, it was expanding too slowly. Then I thought the shade was off, and I got lost in Pantone swatches. I can't believe you noticed." Charles sounded happy.

"Is that why you haven't left the house?" Adam asked. "Dude. It's just a button."

"No!" Charles said, his expression turning thunderous. "It is not *just* a button. Every single thing we put on this site is important. Whether it's the shape of the scroll bar or the color of the header, we should be obsessing over every detail, even if it goes unappreciated. Because *we* are going to live with the reality of what we've created, and *we* should believe that we created the absolute best version we could."

Sometimes, Charles went along with things so willingly Maggie felt like she was just forcing him into it, and he was saying yes because he was nice. But his desire to perfect these features showed her that wasn't the case. The results mattered to him. His design philosophy was both beautiful and impractical, and she wanted him to believe in it for as long as he could. "Follow your heart, Charles," she said, playing with his circles. They really were satisfying to use. "Delight the fuck out of our users with your Pantone palette and circular circles."

Charles looked pleased by this. "Do you want to see the color wheel I made for the webpage?"

"Maybe later. There's something else I wanted to discuss. I don't think visitors should be anonymous," Maggie said. As they'd been working on Clubb, she'd thought constantly about what differentiated it from the forums, chat rooms, and other social sites that already existed. In high school, she'd been so eager to make friends that she hadn't hesitated to accept any MSN messenger request she got. She'd wanted so badly to fit into her mostly white high school, which meant boycotting speaking Chinese and laughing when other kids poked their fingers into the corners of their eyes and pretended they couldn't see. All it ultimately resulted in were messages from people like <<xtrEMEgurl333>> going "y r u so weird" or toNyHawkluvr<3 telling her she was a loser.

"Seriously?" Adam asked. "You want people to just give their names to the internet? That's literally what our parents always tell us not to do."

Maggie gave a firm nod. This was supposed to be a way for students on this campus to find community, and how were they supposed to get that in a sea of faceless numbers and letters? "We'll keep it limited to people with Berkeley emails for now."

Charles started typing on his laptop again. "I'll make that a requirement on the sign-up page. Done."

"Like, done done?" Adam asked eagerly, walking over to peer over their shoulders.

"Yeah," Charles said. "It's a living thing and will need updates, but as of now, it's done."

"Let's launch it then. Right now."

"Whoa, whoa, wait," Maggie said, feeling like she was in a car that had just accelerated to warp speed. "Not yet."

"Why not?" Adam asked impatiently. "Most people will be in clubs by now. We've probably already missed the train."

"There might still be bugs we haven't caught. We haven't looked for all the edge cases yet. And I don't know . . ." She trailed off.

"What?" Adam asked.

In a smaller voice, she asked, "What if people hate it?" It had been easy when it was a fun side project, but now that she knew real people were going to access it, she felt shaky. What if it totally flopped, nobody used it, and Adam and Charles saw how much time they'd wasted, chasing a silly idea with her?

"Maggie." Adam pulled out her chair and got her out of her seat. He put his hands on her shoulders. They were warm and strong. "You've been spending all your time on this thing for the past few weeks. I've never seen you pay so much attention to something in all the time I've known you."

"You've known me for two months."

His eyes were blue and full of faith. Faith in her. "Regardless, it's time to let this thing loose."

After a moment, Maggie extricated herself from Adam's grasp. She could still feel the warm pressure of his fingers on her shoulders. "We'll launch it after I finish my essay."

"That may never happen at the rate you've been going." Adam's voice was cajoling. "If we don't do it tonight, Maggie, we never will."

"Besides," Charles said reasonably, "one of the ways you make your user experience better is to first get users."

She couldn't put up a fight against this mix of goading and logic. "Fine! We'll do it now."

"You do it," Charles said. "Launch it."

She sat back down, and the two of them gathered behind her. She was pressing a button on a laptop, and yet it felt like readying herself for a mission to outer space. Maggie drew in a breath. It almost felt like an accident, the light tap of her finger against a key, sending this secret shared with Adam and Charles into the vast world.

Adam squeezed her shoulder excitedly. Even Charles was smiling.

Their secret was out. Now their peers would decide what came next.

Chapter Eight

DAY 2: FRIDAY

Maggie wakes far earlier than she intended, but the cabin is already illuminated with light. Adam had told her last night about the blackout curtains, but she'd forgotten to turn on the feature from the iPad on the nightstand. Their conversation had quickly run out of steam. She didn't want to talk about how miserable life had been for the past eight years, and she also didn't want to hear about Circle, so all they could talk about was college, or how nice the clouds looked outside. Eventually, Maggie faked tiredness, refusing Adam's offer to walk her back. What did she have to be afraid of on Adam's big private island, anyway?

As she rubs cream into the dry patches at her elbows and behind her ears, she wonders if Hari and Charles have arrived. The island feels too big with just her, Adam, and Sylvia on it, but she's not sure if additional company in the form of those two will alleviate the isolation she feels.

Before she leaves for breakfast, she plays one more game to calm herself. Her 2007 iPhone is unforgivably laggy and no longer updates, but it still works, so she refuses to replace it. The value is not in the hardware, but in all the mobile games it contains. When Apple launched the App Store eight years ago, some random guy who probably confused her email with his kid's started sending her games through Apple's gifting feature. Despite the risk of viruses, she accepted, and the games kept coming. The purchases stopped sometime in 2013, but now she's got a collection of two hundred games, including ones no longer available to purchase.

After about ten minutes of getting knocked out by the same pipe in *Flappy Bird*, she is feeling more anxious. There's no use procrastinating any longer.

The smile she tries on in the mirror looks demented. No smiling, then.

By the time she leaves the cabin, fog has swept in from the ocean and blankets the landscape. She heads toward the lodge she saw yesterday, walking on the dirt path that parallels the shore.

The poor visibility is the reason she doesn't realize there are other people ahead of her.

"—appreciated a heads-up."

She stops. The voice is unmistakably Charles's. It's even, but there's a forcefulness behind it that says he's angry.

"I wasn't even sure you'd show." Adam, sounding exasperated, as if they've been arguing for a while. "Honestly, dude. You get pissed at me for withholding information, but you can't even bother to respond to a text. Look, it's only three days. Besides, it's about time that you did an interview."

"But why this place again?" It's a new voice this time, but still familiar. Hari. "I told you I wasn't hanging out with you on this godforsaken island until you got better cell service. It took me ten minutes to post a photo last night."

"Your followers will understand," Charles replies dryly.

A pause, then Hari asks, "So . . . what's she like now? Did we mess her up permanently?"

Adam coughs. Maggie can almost see him rubbing his neck. "She's more . . . reserved. It's harder to tell what she's thinking."

If she were braver, she would make her way through the mist and tell them to look for themselves. But her heart is pounding, and the fog has seeped into her, chilling her bones.

"Are we talking about the same person?" Hari asks, incredulous. "I bet Charles can still read her mind."

"People change, Hari," Charles says.

"Not that much."

"We should get to breakfast," Adam says. "Charles, you can drop your stuff off at my cabin for now; it's closer."

Hari starts talking about meetings next week and people whose names she doesn't recognize, his voice growing farther away. Maggie hangs back until she can't hear them anymore. She's not sure if she can face them just yet, at least not without any coffee in her.

She waits a few more minutes before heading toward the lodge, a two-story rectangle that looms out of the fog. Inside, a big wood-burning fireplace releases an oaky scent. There are a few small nooks with squat lounge chairs, and the decor is in shades of blond and ash, radiating coziness, especially with the toastiness of the fire. Even the smell seems to be customized for the space, a blend of wool, smoke, and something sweet.

At the end of the wood-paneled hallway is a glass enclosure that seems to be elevated right above the sea, though the fog has turned everything gray. Sylvia is inside, her back to the entrance as she peruses the breakfast spread.

Maggie stops just outside of the doors, gathering the courage that brought her here in the first place, ready to stake her claim on Circle's history. But Hari's and Charles's voices are a punch to the heart, proof that they've continued on without her, strengthening their bond while their memory of her grows more distant.

The whole weekend stretches in front of her like a marathon she hasn't trained for. Sylvia will inevitably ask what happened that day Maggie walked out of Circle's doors forever. And for the sake of her company and her dignity, she will have to pretend it didn't break her heart, didn't lead to years of unemployment and sitting alone at home, marinating in her failure, not knowing who she was anymore.

She rubs her wrist, an old habit in response to the itchy eczema patches that habitually sprout up on her arms and neck. The movement usually gives her something else to focus on.

But right now it can't conceal what a terrible idea it was to come here.

Chapter Nine
OCTOBER 2005

Maggie went straight to the guys' apartment after class. They kept the door unlocked if one of them was home. Clubb had been live since last night and life was going on as usual. It was disappointingly anticlimactic. She hoped Adam would alleviate some of her anxiety, the emptiness she felt now that they weren't actively working to launch it.

Instead, Charles was standing in the living room, shirtless.

"Whoa!" she exclaimed, flinging her hands over her face.

"Oh, hey. Do you want to go to the pool with me?" She heard him rustling around. "Adam hid my towel again . . . all because I refused to let him wash his boxers with mine . . ."

"Where is he?" she asked, keeping her hands up.

"On a date," Charles answered.

Huh, a date. Briefly, she wondered what kind of girl Adam might be interested in. Probably someone really pretty. Charles came out of Adam's room, holding a towel that he sniffed cautiously. He gagged, then looked at her. "You don't have a towel I could borrow, do you?"

While Charles swam, Maggie tried the Stairmaster, decided that was too ambitious after two minutes, and switched over to a stationary bike. She played a game of Snake on her Nokia, stared enviously at the girl next to her who had the newest iPod Nano, and periodically glanced at the TVs overhead that were playing some muted CW show with hot thirty-year-olds masquerading as teens. Once she was sufficiently bored, she went to the pool. Every lane was occupied, but she recognized Charles immediately by his purple swim cap. She took off her shoes and socks, letting the wet concrete cool her feet as she walked to his lane, sliding her feet in.

Maggie kicked the water, watching the small waves bounce against the sides of the pool. It had been so fun working on Clubb, and she was disappointed it hadn't amounted to much. Clearly, Adam had already moved on, likely with a blonde sorority girl who knew how to use a hair iron.

Something yanked at her foot, and she let out a squeal just as Charles's head burst from the water. He leaned against the edge and lifted his goggles, which left faint indents around his eyes.

"What if that wasn't me, and you just pissed off some stranger?" Maggie demanded.

"I recognized your tiny feet."

"They are *not* tiny. They're normal sized."

"You said you shop in the kids' shoes section."

"Because it's cheaper!" She kicked water at him.

He chuckled and wiped it from his eyes, then reached out again and tugged at her ankle. "Whatever, Tiny. What were you thinking about?"

"Nothing."

His grip tightened on her leg, and he yanked her closer to the ledge. "Liar. You're always thinking about *something*."

"Okay, okay!" She scrabbled against the tiles. "I was thinking about what we could work on next. After Clubb."

He raised his eyebrows, releasing her foot. "Already? It hasn't even been live for twenty-four hours."

She shrugged. "It's probably not going anywhere. And I had a lot of fun building it. Did you and Adam have fun?" She realized she was starting to sound desperate and willed herself to chill out. It was hard, though. She wanted to give Adam and Charles a reason to keep hanging out with her, and just offering herself didn't seem like enough.

Charles braced his hands against the ledge and pulled himself out of the pool. Water gushed down his broad shoulders. Adam was the one who'd pointed them out to Maggie as Charles's best feature while claiming his lacrosse-trained quads were his. "Let's give it some time. Me and Adam aren't going anywhere. I'll change and meet you out front?"

She nodded, even though Charles was channeling a patience she didn't possess. She didn't want to lose the shimmer of collaboration she'd felt, the three of them driving toward the same goal.

In the guys' apartment, she and Charles put together a fulfilling and healthful meal of microwaved dino nuggets, Kraft cheese, and rice. Maggie had moved her rice cooker to their kitchen because it made better rice and she basically ate all her meals there anyway. After, they played Flash games on Charles's laptop while arguing about which was superior: the GameCube or the Xbox. She lingered, waiting for Adam to come back, but there was no sign of him. Finally, Charles lay down on the couch, yawning, and Maggie knew it was time for her to go.

When she returned to her apartment, she tried to do her homework, but her roommate was fighting with her long-distance boyfriend on the phone, not caring at all that Maggie could hear every insult. Unable to focus, Maggie opened up the diagnostics for the Clubb site, and five minutes later, she was pounding down the hallway with her laptop under her arm, banging open Adam and Charles's door.

"Charles! Charles!" He was lying on the couch playing a video game, and Maggie nearly tackled him. "Tell me you see what I see."

He yawned loudly and dragged a hand through his hair. He

looked like he hadn't moved since the dino nuggets had sent him into a food coma. "Play for me." He tossed her his Game Boy, and she took over *Pokémon Crystal* while he scrolled through their analytics, his head propped against the side of her thigh.

At one point, he tipped his head up. "Your shampoo smells good."

"It's Head & Shoulders," Maggie said. She almost mentioned that it was the only shampoo that didn't give her dandruff but caught herself in time. That wasn't something Charles would care to know.

Maggie finished three battles before Charles said, "This looks right."

"That's bonkers!" she said, returning his Game Boy to him. "You're saying we have ten thousand active users? In one day? That's, like, a third of the school."

People were actually posting, then using Charles's purple circle to upvote clubs and posts they liked. Already, Women in Business and The Daily Cal were rising to the top of the ranking board on the home page. Their ranking system, determined by the size and quantity of circles given, seemed to be working. She opened the page for the Engineering Honor Society. It was blank; nobody had written anything or circled it. There was an empty text box that invited her to *be the first!*

She wrote, *Avoid at all costs unless you want death by testosterone. Full of bigots who operate under the assumption that there exists no woman who understands Java and PHP.* Then left the smallest possible circle she could.

With satisfaction, she submitted her post. Then, someone circled it. And another person. Someone named Maria F commented, *One of their members copy pasted my CS project and accused me of plagiarism. DISHONOR!!!*

The door opened and Adam came through, a satisfied smirk on his face. "Your boy scored today," he said. Then he saw Maggie sitting on the couch next to Charles, and his smirk turned sheepish. "Maggie! What are you doing here so late?"

"Ten thousand!" she exclaimed, too elated to dwell on the first half of his statement. She ran toward him and leaped on his back when he dropped his backpack.

Adam's hands came under her thighs, and he squatted slightly so that he could lift her higher. "Dollars? Puppies? Chocolate truffles? What units are we talking?"

"People," she said, thumping his shoulder. "People on our website. On Clubb."

He craned his neck around to look back at her, and for a second, they just stared at each other, until Adam determined that she wasn't messing with him. Then, the biggest, brightest grin broke out over his face and he began to spin her in circles until she got dizzy and begged to be let off.

As she lay down on the floor to wait for the room to stop whirling, she heard Adam exclaim, "This is huge! Charlie-boy, why the fuck are you still playing games? There's work to be done!"

"I just turned in my CS project, dude. I'm resting."

"Ten thousand is a lot, but there are thirty thousand people on this campus. That means there are twenty thousand more people who haven't heard about us."

She'd felt so validated by the number of sign-ups, but Adam was already pushing them to go for more, and she didn't want to him to lose interest, to go back to his dates and the parts of his life that didn't involve her. She got to her feet. "So let's make them hear about us."

Adam thought for a moment. "There's a party happening at Acacia tonight. Let's go and sign people up on the spot."

"How are we supposed to do that?" Charles asked. "Everyone's going to be drunk."

"We'll meet people and make accounts for them. Get your lazy ass off the couch. Let's move."

Charles resisted. "Do you know how many people have puked on that lawn?"

"So don't step in the grass."

Maggie looked at the laptop screen, where the numbers were continuing to tick up. Adam was right. It felt like she was on a rocket, and if she didn't reach out and hold on, she'd be left on the earth with the rest of the civilians while other, braver people got to colonize the moon. She'd never been to a frat party, and she was kind of afraid, but nothing would happen to her if Charles and Adam were both there. "Charles, I know you secretly want to come," she said.

Charles groaned. But he got off the couch.

Chapter Ten

OCTOBER 2005

"What kind of alien thinks this is fun?" Maggie asked an hour later as she and Charles stood in a less crowded corner in the basement of a frat house. She scanned the room around her. It was dark, packed with bodies, the floor sticking to her soles. If she'd thought Calapalooza was bad, this was ten times worse and smellier.

"The drunk kind." Charles stuck his hands into his pockets, making a very heroic effort to not look at the people nearby who were basically having sex with all their clothes on.

At the bar, Adam was flirting with a girl. He threw an arm around her and pointed the lens of his disposable camera toward them. They'd bought three disposables from Walgreens on the way over, along with some mini legal pads, with plans to develop the film tomorrow, scan it, and upload it to Circle's home page alongside people's names so they could claim their profiles. Maggie wasn't sure of the permissibility of creating accounts for people who hadn't explicitly agreed, but Adam didn't seem worried, so she wouldn't be, either.

Maggie watched him snap the photo, then continue chatting with the girl. She felt a tug of impatience. Wasn't it time for him to move on?

"We should complete our mission so that we can leave," Charles said. Maggie tore her gaze away from Adam and his target. The two of them nodded grimly at each other, then plunged into the crowd. Maggie avoided the girls, who all seemed to have come out of the womb knowing how to achieve an intimidatingly good cat-eye and wore tiny shirts that exposed belly button piercings. She was a blob in her sweatpants and *Princess Bride* T-shirt, but when she'd asked Adam and Charles if her outfit was okay before they left, they'd said yes.

A body brushed up against her, leaving behind a slick of sweat along her upper arm. She wanted to blast everyone with hand sanitizer.

Then someone grabbed her by the waist. A tall guy with a backwards baseball cap, wearing sunglasses. He started grinding into her, and Maggie leaped forward like her butt was on fire. The guy held up his hands, like *what's the deal?*

"What's your name?" Maggie shouted at him.

"Rupert," he replied. "Do you want to dance or not?"

"No," she said. She pulled out her disposable camera. "But I do want to take a photo of you!"

The flash illuminated the bodies around them for a brief second. The guy blinked while she scrawled *Rupert* on her legal pad. Bass thumped around them. "Last name?" she asked.

Rupert stared at her, then shrugged and answered, "Jones."

The drunkenness made people a lot more amenable to sharing their surnames with a random girl. When Maggie returned to the corner, she was out of film, sweating, and sure she didn't want to go to another frat party again. Charles was waiting for her, looking like he'd never left, but there was a guy standing next to him. He was Indian, with the beginnings of a beard and eyebrows that looked like they were mere centimeters away from becoming conjoined twins.

Charles leaned in slightly. "He helped me get photos but now he won't leave."

The guy yelled something that sounded like *Harry*, holding his Solo cup out. "Want some? It's good!"

Maggie politely refused.

The guy bopped his head like he could actually hear the music over all the other noise. "I want to see your website!" he shouted, his accent heavy. "It sounds cool!"

"Thanks!" Maggie yelled back, warming to him.

A warm hand briefly cupped her elbow. She looked up to find Charles, who tilted his head toward the exit.

Just as they were mapping out their escape route, Adam surged out of the crowd.

"I was looking for you guys!" He wiped his sweaty hair off his forehead, and Maggie prepared for him to invite them to beer pong or something.

Instead, he said, "This was horrible. Let's go home."

They exited the frat house single file, like kindergarteners going back to class after recess.

It wasn't until they were almost home that they realized there was a hanger-on. The guy from earlier—Harry—was following a few steps behind, a dopey grin on his face.

"Um, do you live around here?" Maggie asked.

"No," he said, smiling serenely.

She glanced over at the guys, unsure what to do. He was clearly intoxicated, and Maggie didn't want to wake up tomorrow morning and see him on a missing-persons notice.

Charles shook his head slightly. Adam yawned.

"Where do you live?" she asked.

"Near University and MLK."

That was way too far. She was too tired to escort him and too poor to call a taxi. Charles and Adam didn't seem to think he was their responsibility, but Maggie couldn't just leave him like this.

She sighed, then started walking in the direction of their apartment. "Just come with us. You can crash on their couch."

"Thanks for that," Charles muttered.

Adam chortled. "Or you can snuggle up with Charles. He doesn't bite. That hard." He ducked behind Maggie when Charles lunged at him. "You wouldn't hit a girl!"

Maggie snorted, removing herself from between them. She was annoyed at Adam for a reason she couldn't pinpoint. "Go get him."

They were distracted by the sound of violent vomiting. Their new friend was bent over behind a bush, but then he popped up, wiping his mouth. "I feel *amazing*. Let's go home."

"Our home, not yours," Charles corrected him.

Back in Adam and Charles's apartment, the three of them sat on the couch and started cataloging names. Tomorrow, Charles and Maggie would replace the home page with a carousel of all the unclaimed profiles. They thought this was a sure way of getting the rest of their classmates' attention.

"I feel like it should be more than just a photo and a name," Adam said as he scrolled through the test landing page. "Like, they should be able to do more than just check out clubs. They should be able to check each other out, too."

He had a point. All the testimonials on the clubs were about the people in them, not the club itself. That, Maggie was beginning to realize, was why people were coming to the site. Like Adam had said from the beginning, people loved gossip. "We should let people interact with one another. Write up bios and connect with each other." She gasped. "We could use Charles's circling thing and let them circle people they know!"

"It should be mutual, though," Charles said, his laptop on his thighs, already making the changes live. "What if we let them add three interests instead of a full bio? To keep it succinct. And if two people circle each other, they become friends."

"Can I make a profile?" Harry said suddenly from the ground. Maggie had thought he was dozing.

"Yeah, of course." Maggie opened up the registration page, passing her laptop down to him.

Harry pecked at the keys. "What do you think my top three interests are?"

"Following strangers home," Charles said. He went to the kitchen, returning with a glass of water and handing it to Harry. "You better hydrate if you don't want to feel like you came out of an armadillo's asshole tomorrow."

"Making new friends," Maggie corrected, before Harry got himself labeled as the new campus creep.

"Pizza," Adam added.

"That's so boring," Maggie said.

"No, it's universal," Adam argued. "Only fascists hate pizza."

"I love Hawaiian," Harry chimed in.

Adam pressed a hand to his chest. "Definitely don't put that on your profile."

Maggie stopped Harry before he uploaded his profile. "I think you spelled your name wrong." Was he still that drunk?

"No, it's H-A-R-I. You actually pronounce it Hah-ri. But you can keep calling me Harry. Everyone calls me that anyway."

Adam laughed, not understanding. "Why would you let people call you by a name that isn't yours?"

Discomfort landed on Hari's face. In a blink, it was gone, replaced with his sunny smile. "Easier that way. What should my third interest be?"

Maggie studied him, sitting cross-legged on the ground with no complaints. She'd gone through the same thing as Hari back when her legal name was still her Chinese name, dreading when teachers would struggle to pronounce it during roll call, or even worse, insist that she say it aloud in front of the whole class so they could get it right. They never did. Maggie battled her dad to change her legal name to Margaret in high school.

She and Hari were kindred spirits, she thought, and she was glad he had tagged along after the frat party.

"Going with the flow," she said.

"I like that," he said, typing it. "There, submitted! Oh, cool," he said, clicking into his profile page. Three neat rectangles displayed his interests. A separate box would show his activity on club pages. "Will you guys circle me back, if I circle you?" This he asked shyly.

"Of course. Charles, we should add another box for people you know," Maggie said.

Charles nodded, already working on the changes.

"Welcome to Clubb," Adam said, fist-bumping Hari.

Maggie made a face. The name sounded like they were offering entrance to something exclusive, rather than a portal for everyone. They would need to change it.

Charles got off the couch to shower, leaving her and Adam. Hari stretched himself out on the floor, and moments later, she heard him snoring.

"We haven't made profiles yet," Adam said, scooting closer to her.

She felt her body tense at his nearness. She thought of him pressed up against that girl at the party and inched away, not knowing why she was suddenly so sensitive to his proximity. Her voice was a bit too loud when she said, "Do *not* make one of your interests *pizza*."

"What, pizza's not deep?" At the expression on her face, Adam relented, pressing backspace with unnecessary drama. "Okay."

Before he published his profile, he bumped her with his shoulder. It was like he'd sensed her mood, and he was trying to get back in her good graces. "I need approval from my overlord before I make this official."

It was hard to ignore Adam when he acted like he cared what she thought. Maggie turned to look at his laptop. She was about to chide him for his first two interests—sleep and being funny—when she saw the third one.

Being around people who make me want to live forever.

Something in her became gooey, like the inside of a freshly baked chocolate chip cookie, her frustration melting away. She thought of how Adam had left the frat party to finish out the night at home, with them. He'd actively chosen them. "Are you talking about us?"

He offered a smile that felt like it was meant just for her.

Chapter Eleven

DAY 2: FRIDAY

"Hey, I'm glad I caught you before you went in."

Maggie jumps at Adam's presence beside her. She's not sure how long she's been standing outside the breakfast area, but she must have zoned out. He looks troubled, and she wonders if it's because of his earlier conversation with Charles and Hari.

"Charles and Hari are here. Let's chat after breakfast, just the four of us." His voice is low, serious.

Nerves blossom in her belly. She hasn't even officially seen Hari and Charles yet. Whatever Adam wants to discuss later, she'll be outnumbered. Sylvia spots them and comes to the door, popping it open. "Can one of you tell me what brown cheese is?" she asks.

The seriousness melts right off Adam's face, and he turns his charming smile on Sylvia. "It's a Norwegian delicacy. Really good with waffles."

Sylvia looks at Maggie. "You look a little worse for wear, Margaret. Jet lag?"

"Had to work," Maggie says, following her into the dining room. *Snap out of it.* She needs to appear competent and put-together. "No vacations when you're running your own company."

"You, too?" Adam asks sympathetically.

"I love it, though," she says. She doesn't need anybody's pity when she chose this life. Nobody will accuse her of not working hard enough.

"Me, too. Work has been the most constant thing in my life," Adam says with ease. Maggie grits her teeth. Somehow, it feels like they're competing again. Like they both want to show Sylvia just how passionate they are about their jobs.

Sylvia isn't impressed. "Well, both of you still have to eat."

The breakfast spread is all cold cuts. Sylvia's plate is piled high with smoked salmon. "I saw the helicopter out on the pad again this morning. Have the others arrived?" she asks.

"Yup," Adam says, shooting Maggie a look. She recognizes it. *Let me talk*, he's saying.

But Sylvia directs her next question at Maggie. "The guys see each other every day at the office, but how often do all of you get together like this?"

Maggie grabs a plate, ready to inform Sylvia that, actually, it's been eight years. "Never—"

"—too long goes by," Adam quickly jumps in. "Our offices aren't that far from each other, and we make the time."

An olive rolls off Sylvia's plate. As she goes to fetch it, Maggie glares at Adam. Did he just lie? Why does he want to pretend that they still hang out?

A loud voice turns their attention toward the doors. Through the glass, she sees Charles and Hari clearly now. Hari is complaining about the president of Brazil, saying how she doesn't follow him on Circle, until Charles elbows him and he sees her and Sylvia watching. He jumps, but then a smile crinkles his face and he purposefully strides toward the doors, shoving them open. "What's up, everyone?"

Her eyes drink them in even as her body tenses. The last time she saw Charles and Hari, the cloud of rage and betrayal had been so thick that she'd barely remembered how they'd looked. It's been easier to avoid mentions of them when the media spotlight is usually on Adam. But here they are. Hari's black hair is styled and swept upward, his beard gleams, and his eyebrows are impeccably groomed. He's stocky and packed with energy, a heavy watch on his wrist. He sees her and basically zooms over, exclaiming, "Maggie, you made it! Whoa, you look different. Don't tell me—did you get a haircut?" His old accent has eroded, replaced by sharp, crisp enunciation.

"Margaret," she mutters, but her voice is snuffed out as he grabs her and squeezes her.

Hari booms a laugh, putting her down. "*Margaret?* What are you, an old lady who owns three Persian cats and crochets doilies on the weekends? You're Maggie." He releases her and her eyes catch on Charles's. He hangs back, caution clinging to the lines of his body. But he seems to accept that he needs to match the vigor of Hari's greeting, because he moves forward and then wraps her into a hug, too. "Hey, Tiny."

The nickname ricochets through her insides, but Charles is already stepping back and heading toward the breakfast buffet. His hair is longer, curling around his ears and at the nape of his neck. His glasses are more stylish than the wire-rimmed ones he wore in college, the frames tortoiseshell.

Hari chortles. "So, none of us are calling her Margaret? That's settled, then?"

The old Maggie would punch Hari in the arm, but she wouldn't want Sylvia to think she's violent, so she pastes a pleasant smile on her face and shuffles toward the table with her oatmeal.

The table is farmhouse style with benches long enough to seat five on each side. Charles approaches it, puts his plate of toast down, then smooths a hand over the surface. "When did you get this?"

Adam beams as Charles sits on the edge of the bench. "It arrived last week. Remember those trips I was making to Minnesota?

I was working with a carpenter and furniture maker there. Chose the tree myself. It's white pine. Sauna's made of the same wood. I've added a lot of things since the last time you were here. You'll see."

Last time. The passing of days and weeks, not years. Her nerves give way to a deeper ache.

"As long as the sauna works and we don't spend an hour sitting in a wooden box convincing each other that it's getting hotter," Hari grumbles.

As Adam joins Sylvia at the breakfast buffet, Maggie tries to decide where to sit. She's about to put her plate down next to Hari, when he says, "I need to save two spots."

She waits for him to smile and say he's joking, but he keeps looking at her, like he expects her to move.

"Oh," she says, then collects her things again, feeling like someone who just got rejected in the middle of the high school cafeteria. It stings a little. There's no reason to save seats. He just doesn't want to sit next to her.

"Sit across from Charles," Hari suggests.

She obeys, swings her leg over the bench opposite from where Charles is buttering his toast, not acknowledging her.

Adam drops his plate next to hers. He's managed to make himself a breakfast salad out of all the ingredients on offer, along with a bowl of Special K cereal, the kind with freeze-dried strawberries. They used to go through five boxes a week.

Sylvia sits down on Adam's other side, but Adam is focused on picking through the Special K like he's excavating dinosaur bones, plucking freeze-dried strawberries out of the sugary mountains of cornflakes and putting them on a saucer.

A waiter comes by for drink orders, and Hari requests a latte, a hot chocolate, and an Americano. It's an excessive number of beverages for one person, but nobody comments. Maggie orders hot water, planning to pour some of it into her oatmeal to loosen its sludgy texture. Maybe Adam was right to give her that snacks basket; she's going to need it.

"So, everyone's all together," Sylvia says, layering smoked salmon onto her bagel. "How do you guys typically orchestrate these reunions?"

Maggie blinks at her in confusion. Sylvia seems to be lumping her in with the rest of the group, like she's been present for all of this.

"A hike first," Adam says, completing his task and sliding the saucer of strawberries toward Maggie. She doesn't want to accept, but also, the oatmeal is inedible. She takes a strawberry. "There's a spot with an incredible view, and it'll only take three hours round trip. Sylvia, that'll be a good time for you to talk to everyone, get the lay of the land. We've got a fun lunch planned, then free time afterward. Tomorrow, we'll go on a drive around the island and take photos. And the last day is a surprise." He crunches on his cornflakes. "It'll be fun. These trips always are." He sounds genuinely excited.

"Now that Margaret's got her own company, are you guys going to have to be careful what you say around each other? Actually, when did they find out about OurSpot?" Sylvia asks Maggie. "Were you working on it secretly, since you knew it was a competitor?"

Hari's knife clangs loudly against his plate. Charles coughs slightly. Maggie clears her throat, but Adam speaks for her again.

"Of course she told us," Adam says without hesitation. "She's one of us."

"I *was*," she corrects him, her ire rising. She's done with Adam putting words in her mouth, and it's becoming more evident that he wants Sylvia to believe they've kept in touch all this time, though she has no idea why.

Sylvia swivels her head between her and Adam. "Seems like there's a disconnect here."

Before Maggie can confirm that *yes, there is*, Hari blurts, "You *have* been really busy with OurSpot lately, Maggie. Have you had time for other stuff? Hobbies?"

She tries to swallow her oatmeal, but it sticks in her throat. A hand pushes a glass of water into her field of vision. She looks up at Charles, but his eyes are on her wrist, where the sleeve of her sweater has fallen down. The red marks she rubbed into it last night are still there. Quickly, she adjusts the fabric and swigs from the water. For some reason, everyone is interested in her answer. Maggie reaches through the suddenly empty cavern of her mind for a hobby but can't come up with anything. Her days are a blur of working, sleeping, and eating enough to sustain herself, but if she admits that, she knows how it makes her sound. Like someone with no life.

She finds herself grasping for proof that there are still people in her life who care about her. "Um, I hang out with my dad."

"That's sweet," Sylvia remarks. Maggie takes that as a win.

"Your dad?" Adam is looking at her strangely, and she realizes how this must sound to him. He's only known the dysfunctional father-daughter duo who fought often over her choice to pursue Circle.

If there's one thing outside of OurSpot she's proud of, it's how she and her dad managed to rescue their relationship. She's not afraid to brag about that. "Yeah, we've been bonded by memes. How's your dad doing?" She used to wish her dad could be more open and honest like Mr. Fink, even if he and Adam had a tricky dynamic.

She knows immediately that she's said something wrong by the way Adam's eyes pinch and the sound of Hari's fork dropping to the ground. Charles winces infinitesimally, which is basically a megaphone saying she's fucked up somehow. She prays that the floor gives way and she falls deep down into the earth's core. Better that than navigating this conversational minefield.

Adam clears his throat. "Wherever he is, I'm sure he's doing well." He addresses Charles. "How was the flight in, Charles? I thought you weren't going to make it after your flight got canceled."

Maggie sinks into her seat, exhausted all of a sudden. At least the limelight is off her now.

"Tashie got me rebooked," Charles says.

"Perks of an influencer girlfriend," Hari says, wiggling his eyebrows.

Girlfriend? She sits up straight again, glancing at Charles. She'd forgotten that, with the time that's passed, the guys might have found partners. Does Adam have a girlfriend, too?

And Hari. Is he still with—

Just as the thought crosses her mind, the door opens again, and something small comes darting through them, jumping onto Charles's back. "Uncle Chars!" a voice cries, and she sees a girl of around five clinging to Charles's neck. Her black hair is in two braids, and she's wearing a magenta puffer.

Someone else speaks from behind her. "Jaya, that's not a proper way to greet people."

Maggie turns and sees the woman standing there with her hands on her hips. She's tall and lithe, wearing a vest with a fur-lined hood and fuzzy boots, but none of that takes away from the ferocity in her face. Priya Kumar always looked vaguely irked, and it seems like the expression has dug its way into her features and made its home there. She still has the same voice, too. The bossy one that could command a thousand ships.

"She's not bothering me," Charles says, doing some kind of acrobatics so the girl is in his lap instead of on his back.

Priya makes her way over to the table and takes a seat next to Hari.

"Your latte," Hari says, pushing her drink toward her. Maggie gapes at the two of them, then at the little girl currently climbing all over Charles, the pieces fitting together.

"You're married," she blurts. She sees the matching gold rings on their hands. She should've expected this, but still—it's a shock to see them formally joined.

Hari slants his eyes at Sylvia, then laughs. "You don't need to keep reminding us, Maggie. We know."

Priya skims Maggie's face, and Maggie instantly inventories the flaws she will see. The wrinkles that have formed on the bridge of her nose, the gray strands in her hair, the dark patches beneath her jaw from the eczema scars that never fully faded.

"You made it," Priya says finally, and her words are accompanied by a warm smile that surprises Maggie.

"Daddy, who's that?" the little girl asks, pointing at Maggie. Charles has cut his waffle into smaller pieces for the girl.

Hari looks momentarily panicked. "Jaya, you know. This is your Aunt Maggie."

Maggie blinks. She's never been called *aunt* before.

"Yes, say hello to Auntie Maggie," Priya says.

Jaya looks at Maggie, suddenly growing shy. "Hello," she says in a whisper.

"Look at me, Jaya." Adam peekaboos at her, and Jaya releases a bubbly laugh.

Seeing the ease that they have, how comfortable Jaya is with everyone else, makes something hot and thick rise in Maggie's throat. She's barely sat down for breakfast, and she already acutely feels the loss of the past eight years.

"I'm going to get ready," she mumbles, standing up. "Excuse me." She squeezes past Charles then basically runs out of there, only taking a breath when the doors shut behind her. Except the entire building is made of glass, so she slows her pace and keeps her back straight as she walks away, in case anyone is watching. The fog has barely lifted, but she can hear the waves thrashing against the shore.

Hari and Priya, married, with a kid. Charles has a girlfriend. Adam probably also has an entire other life she doesn't know about.

Her heart clenches, and she gasps a little. It's one thing to be vaguely aware that there's a not-so-distant world where these three have continued their lives together. It is a whole other thing to come face-to-face with that reality.

In the cabin, the blackout curtains are pulled shut, making the entire room dark. She sinks to the ground by the bed and hugs her arms around her legs. Then, she lets the burning work its way up her throat until it comes out in a low cry. Two fat tears gather at the corners of her eyes before crawling their way down her cheeks.

Seeing them has wrenched her loneliness to the surface. She can feel its weight, taste its bitterness. All this time, they have had each other. Adam, Charles, and Hari turned Circle into a success while she struggled to survive. Their lives have flourished, while hers has stayed fixed in place. She pulls her phone toward her, intent on texting her dad, telling him that she made a mistake and will be coming back on the next flight out of Oslo—

The door opens, and Maggie leaps up, swiping a quick hand across her cheeks just as she hears someone coming down the hall.

Charles stands there, a duffel strapped across his chest. He sees her, his stoicism briefly giving way to surprise. "How did you— never mind. Are you okay?" His voice is gruff, but not unkind. "You didn't finish your food."

"It's nothing." She needs him to leave. She can't think of anything more humiliating than for the guys to know she was crying. "I just need a moment."

A pause. "Okay, I'm just going to drop my things off and change for the hike."

That makes her look up, confused. "Don't you have your own cabin?"

Charles blinks. "This *is* my cabin."

"Well, it's mine, too." Snappiness creeps into her tone, her sadness momentarily forgotten.

The two of them stare at each other in confusion, and then Charles growls, "*Adam.*" There's the thud of his duffel bag against the ground, and then he's jogging out the door. Hurriedly wiping her face of residual tears, Maggie runs after him.

Chapter Twelve

NOVEMBER 2005

They were onto something. Maggie realized it when she went to the library and saw a bunch of students scrolling the Clubb site instead of studying. The website wasn't about campus clubs anymore. It was about the people. The students whose photos they'd taken without their permission weren't even mad about the profiles that got created on their behalf. Instead, it became a bragging right. Others started following the trend, changing their profile photos to the dramatic close-ups that they'd produced with their disposables. Adam's guerrilla tactics had worked. The students of Berkeley wanted to be seen. Clubb had given them a way to create an online footprint, and nobody wanted to miss out.

Nobody was more obsessed with it than Maggie, though. She thought about it when she was walking to class, when she was *in* class, when she was supposed to be doing homework. And she knew Adam felt similarly. They now had basically the whole school on there, but he still insisted on trawling through the user logs so he could become their campus ambassador and make sure anyone he crossed paths with had an account. Charles was more reserved with his enthusiasm, but she could tell he cared more than he let on. It was in the tiny tweaks he made all over the website: a more pleasing font, the positioning of boxes, the icons on the sidebar that allowed people to navigate to different pages. Hari, who had quickly become a fixture of their group and came over multiple times a week, helped with user support and outreach to other universities that had expressed interest in Clubb.

It was rewarding in a way that Maggie hadn't expected. Coding a website wasn't new to her, but having people doing it along with her, eager for what was next? That was a revelation. Transferring to Berkeley had been her second chance. She'd remade herself. People knew her, but not as some friendless dork. She was the girl coder who'd started Clubb. Those jerks from the Engineering Society could *suck it*.

There was still the matter of the name, though. Clubb didn't represent what the website offered anymore. They brainstormed and discarded hundreds of names, all of them bad. Until one night, when she was hanging out with Adam and Charles, hopped up on energy drinks. Charles was doodling potential logos for the company on McDonald's napkins when a knock came at the door and Hari's butt came through first. The three of them stood, watching as he dragged in a wide green chair with scratched-up wooden legs. Once both he and the chair were fully inside the apartment, he faced them and waved his fingers. "Ta-da! I finally found something for me to sit on!" He dragged it right next to the couch.

"Did you steal that from a homeless man?" Charles asked. "I'm pretty sure I've seen a chair just like that in People's Park."

"Nooo," Hari said unconvincingly. He patted the green cushion. "I've decided that serious stuff will happen in this chair."

"Staph is pretty serious," Adam said, eyeing the chair with skepticism.

Hari waved a hand. "I sanitized it. Anyway, new rule: if you're sitting in the chair, you can ask anything you want, and nobody will judge you. I'll go first." He sat on the chair. The leather squeaked beneath him. "How do I tell if a girl likes me back?"

Charles shot up. "I'm getting bleach so we can clean that thing properly."

Adam sat back down on the couch and kicked his feet up on the coffee table. "Hari, my man. You've come to the right place. Let me tell you everything I know about the elusive female sex . . ."

Hari rolled his eyes, then turned to Maggie, who had taken Adam's desk chair. "I want to hear from an actual girl. Maggie, what do you do if you like someone?"

She wasn't sure she knew the answer to Hari's question. Maybe she'd crushed on boys before, but it was always at a respectful distance because she didn't have a chance. "I don't know. I guess . . . I pay more attention to what they say and what they like. I try to find reasons to hang out with them." As she explained, she glanced at Adam. He wasn't paying attention, instead texting on his phone.

"She's blushing!" Hari exclaimed. "Maggie, do you like someone?"

"No!" she said, valiantly keeping her eyes from flickering in Adam's direction again. The beginnings of a realization were creeping in, but she would not deal with it right now.

Charles came out of the kitchen with a box of Clorox wipes. "Are you asking this because you're into someone? Who is it?"

Hari grew shy. He grabbed their ugly Oski plush and hugged it to his chest. "She was the TA for my Corporate Finance class last year. I circled her on Clubb, and then she circled me back, and, well . . . now we're talking."

Adam hooted. "An *older woman*?"

"Just two years!"

"Quit wasting time and ask her out," Charles said. "Before another hairy brown dude snatches her up."

Hari got up from the chair, seized by urgency. "I need a phone!"

Adam tossed him his BlackBerry. "Go nuts."

Hari darted into Charles's bedroom, slamming the door shut. Adam and Maggie exchanged an amused smile while Charles started wiping down the chair.

"He circled her, then she circled him . . ." Maggie repeated to herself softly. The right name had been in front of them all along. "Circle," she said loudly. "We should name our company Circle." It had all begun because users had circled clubs and posts. Now being friends meant being part of each other's "circle." The average user had fifty people in their circles, a number that was steadily growing. Geometrically, every point around a circle was equidistant from the center. Every point, every *person*, having equal significance.

Adam smacked his forehead. "I can't believe I thought of FriendZone before I thought of that."

"We should plan a relaunch with the new name and logo." Charles grabbed his napkin sketches, holding them close to his face. Then he said, "I'm going to do some shower thinking." He went into his room.

They heard Hari let out an offended squawk. "Can't a guy get some privacy around here?"

Charles emerged moments later with his clothes and towel before disappearing into the bathroom.

Then, it was just her and Adam. His praise of her had turned her insides frothy and light, like a slushy. "I can't believe we didn't arrive at this conclusion sooner." She couldn't imagine Circle being called anything else now. "Although I have a feeling the domain is going to cost us."

"Whatever it costs, we'll pay it. Circle," Adam said, as if he was tasting the name on his tongue. He nodded approvingly. "That's a name people are going to remember."

Maggie threw a pillow at him. "Is that all you care about? Being remembered?"

Adam looked at her then, an inquisitiveness to his eyes. "What should I care about instead? Being loved?"

"Why can't it be both?"

"What if you can only choose one?"

"I'd rather be loved." Better to be loved by a few than remembered by all. Sometimes she thought she was just a dotted line moving through the world. With her mom gone, no real friends during her childhood, and her dad busy working, she'd felt like she was fading. If nobody loved her, did she exist at all?

Every time Hari came to her for advice, Charles bought her the taro boba she liked, or Adam saw her across Sproul and ran toward her to give her a hug, she became more solid. Their friendship connected those lines and made her real. "What about you?"

"Being remembered."

"You're only saying that because you take love for granted."

"If you're remembered, that means you fulfilled some kind of purpose. It means you did something with your life." Adam sat up, reaching toward the stack of Kraft cheese on the coffee table. He peeled one out of its plastic wrapper, ripped it in half, and offered part of it to her.

Maggie ate the cheese and considered the chair Hari had brought. Shrugging, she got up and sat in it. It smelled like Clorox, and the leather was firm, with a little bit of give. The walnut arms were smooth beneath her arms. She could tell Adam was in one of his contemplative moods.

Adam tipped his head back on the couch, lost in his thoughts.

"Here, sit in the Feels Chair." Maggie vacated her seat.

"Is that what we're calling it now?"

"If you sit here, you can say what's on your mind, no judgment. I don't make the rules." She moved to the couch, and after a moment, Adam traded it for the Feels Chair.

He spread his hands over its armrests and leaned back again, his eyes closed. "I've been thinking a lot about what comes next."

She scooted closer on the couch, until her knees nearly bumped his. "Like, what you have to do tomorrow?"

"No, silly," he said affectionately, opening his eyes and smiling at her. "Like, after college. Did you know my dad worked on a project with Frank Gehry when he was twenty? It was some rich dude's house. He never shuts up about it."

"So you want to find your Frank Gehry?" Maggie asked.

"No, I want to *be* Frank Gehry," Adam said. "Isn't it sad that people will only remember my dad as that guy who worked with Frank Gehry?"

Maggie had admired famous figures, sure, but she didn't want to *be* them. This hunger Adam had was foreign to her. It was a hunger for greatness, for legacy. Things she'd never thought to take for herself. "That's not how you'll remember him. Or how the people who love him will remember him." And yet, even as she said it, she felt an undercurrent of doubt. Was she small-minded for not wanting bigger things? If she had made a greater effort to be remembered, people in her life might have paid more attention to her. Perhaps greatness led to love.

"My dad always asks me what my Empire State Building will be. And I never had a good answer. But now I do." Adam was excited now. Their knees bumped, and he was leaning toward her, his eyes alight. "It'll be Circle."

He wasn't looking for assurance, but she could tell that his dad's words exerted pressure on him. The same way her dad's axioms about getting a good education and a good job weighed on her. "Adam, you don't need to impress everyone. Just because the world doesn't know who you are doesn't make your life a waste. And people are already impressed by you."

"Are you?" he asked. There was gentle teasing in his question, but he was gazing at her like he really wanted to know the answer.

"Of course." Adam was bright on his own, but his glow extended to the people around him, including her. He was the reason Circle had grown so quickly. He'd pushed her to believe she could reach beyond the constraints of her tiny life and make a dent in the universe. Did he not see the impact he had on people?

Adam's lips curved. She realized how close they were to each other, this moment between them as fragile as butterfly wings. His ambition, his confidence, his *vision*—it mesmerized her.

"You impress me, too," Adam said, his eyes not leaving hers. He stated it like it was a fact, like everyone felt the same way about her. "I'm glad I'm your friend."

Friend. She should've been ecstatic to hear him call her that, but instead, something inside her deflated. She *liked* Adam, as more than a friend. It was why she seemed to always know exactly where he was in the room. Why things that she should've found weird, like his insistence on smelling everything before tasting it, were now endlessly charming.

Adam held his pinky finger out to her. "Let's promise that no matter what, we'll always be impressed by each other."

He had no idea how easy that was for her to promise. She linked her finger with his.

Chapter Thirteen

DAY 2: FRIDAY

Sylvia is nowhere in sight when Charles and Maggie reach the lodge to meet up for the hike, but Adam, Hari, and Priya are standing outside, Jaya running between the adults' legs.

"Maggie!" Adam calls, spotting them. There's a look of relief on his face. "You left so abruptly, I didn't get the chance to brief you all."

Charles plants himself right in front of Adam. "Why don't you start by telling me why Maggie and I are roommates?" He sounds incensed, and Maggie feels her own hackles raise.

"It's not like I want to be your roommate either," she snaps. The irritability is a nice distraction from the sadness that racked her earlier. After everything, he should be begging *her* for forgiveness. He is *not* the one who's entitled to a hissy fit here.

Charles turns toward her, and his fury seems to gutter a little. "That's not what I'm saying."

"Then you *want* to be roommates?" Hari asks with a touch of glee.

"That's definitely not what I'm saying either," Charles growls.

Adam puts his hands up. "There are only four residential buildings. Obviously, I was going to give Sylvia her own. Hari and Priya got the biggest one since they brought Jaya. That leaves yours and Maggie's cabin, which is also the only one with extra beds."

"Why not give Maggie your cabin?" Charles demands. "You and I can share."

Adam makes a face of displeasure. "You know I'm very particular about my sleeping environment, and I've built my cabin to accommodate that."

"Right, I forgot you're the princess from *The Princess and the Pea*."

"*Or*," Adam says, and Maggie doesn't like the turn in his voice, like he's decided to play the game another way, "Maggie could come sleep with me."

"Maggie can take my spot, and *I'll* sleep with you," Hari volunteers.

"Not happening," Priya says.

Hari pouts. "But I want to try out his intelligent mattress. It's a prototype!"

A muscle ticks in Charles's jaw. He turns to Maggie. "What do *you* want to do?"

What does Maggie want to do? She wants to move on from this extremely uncomfortable discussion. She'll deal with the consequences later. "Let's just keep things as is. It's not like we didn't live together before."

"Easy enough," Adam says, clapping his hands once. "On to business. You all know Sylvia's writing about us. Maggie, I briefed Charles and Hari earlier, but I don't want this to be another critique of Circle's influence or philosophical garbage about how we're ruining humanity. I want it to be about our friendship, and how it's helped the company grow."

So that's why he kept interjecting during breakfast today. Maggie thinks of how confident Sylvia had been when she told her Adam wouldn't be allowed to see the article. Little does she know that it's because he basically wants to write it for her.

Once again, Adam's gall amazes her. Only he would believe that they're capable of lying to a reporter across this entire weekend. "You don't need me for that," she says, gesturing toward Charles and Hari. "You have them."

"She's right," Charles says. "You didn't have to involve her."

He's agreeing, but it stings anyway.

Adam's shaking his head. "You were there at the beginning, so you should be here for this." He fans his hands out, like he's framing his vision for them all to see. "We're about to launch a product that tells people that they should trust us to curate the best content for them. To earn that trust, we need to humanize ourselves. The recent discourse around Circle hasn't been conducive to that. We need Sylvia to focus her article on *us*, not the company."

"You think that pretending we're still friends is going to *build trust*?" Maggie demands. The guys have to pretend they've kept in touch with only her, but she will need to give the impression that she's stayed close with *all three* of them. Three people whose lives she's shut out for the last eight years.

Adam looks worried now, like her reaction is more extreme than what he'd budgeted for. "I'm only asking you to give the impression that we've kept in touch. Today's and tomorrow's activities will give us time to catch up before the official group interview on Sunday. It won't be hard, I promise."

Maggie scoffs. Adam's promises don't hold water anymore.

"Sylvia's coming," Priya says, her eyes on the path. "Better wrap this up."

"Maggie, please," Adam says, and she thinks again of the note he wrote her. *Come. Please.* He normally doesn't need to beg. People were always eager to fulfill Adam's requests. "This is going to help your image, too. You're passionate and smart and innovative. Don't you want people to know that side of you? I think they should."

She knows this is just his way of building up an argument, but when Adam Fink is doling out compliments, it's hard to remember how to say *no*.

"Fine," she says, aware that she's surrendering. But maybe she can turn this to her advantage. "I make you look good, and you do the same for me."

Adam nods. "Of course. Venture capitalists will be demanding to be on your term sheet after that article's out."

"What about us?" Hari asks, gesturing to him and Charles. "I want you to call me smart and passionate too, Adam."

Charles runs a hand down his face. "If I knew how to act, I wouldn't have been an engineer."

Sylvia cuts off the conversation with a bright "What are we talking about?"

Adam gives them all a nod, like they are now in agreement, though Maggie's not completely sure how they're going to pull off lying to a reporter. "Logistics," he says. "Shall we go?"

Chapter Fourteen

DAY 2: FRIDAY

Maggie decides not to change and heads to the trailhead with the group. She's already in leggings and Nikes, which she figures will be sufficient for this hike, and she can't think of anything more awkward than walking back to the cabin with Charles, the two of them changing in different rooms. He doesn't want to be around her, and she can't say she feels any differently.

Even fast walking to catch the crosswalk signal winds her, but maybe the adrenaline will spur her to the top of this mountain. She feels newly motivated. All the facts are in front of her. Adam wants to manipulate Sylvia's article, which is so typical of him that she wants to laugh. If he wants her to play along, he'll have to make her look good, too. This is her chance to rehabilitate her image, especially when people find out she's lost yet another COO.

The wind blows her loose hair into her mouth. She checks her wrist, but it's bare.

"I got you." Hari holds his arm toward her, and she sees three black hair ties crammed on his wrist. "Priya always forgets, too."

Once Charles joins them, they start hiking. The trail begins to climb almost immediately, and Maggie disposes of her delusions of keeping up with the group, instead focusing on staying alive.

Even Jaya is faster than her, bounding up like she's half gazelle. Priya shouts at her to slow down.

Just like in the animal kingdom, Maggie's pace turns her into the first victim. As she hears Jaya's chattering fade and the blue dot of Charles's backpack grows farther away, Sylvia closes in. "I was curious about how all four of you came to the decision to work together. You were from such different backgrounds." Sylvia hits her vape, unleashing a cloud of kiwi-scented smoke in Maggie's direction. How is she managing to breathe and vape right now?

"We weren't that different," Maggie replies between huffs. The greenery is dense here, and her arm brushes against leaves, coming away damp with morning dew. It takes everything she has to concentrate on this conversation and maintain her footing. "We all wanted the same thing—for Circle to succeed. OurSpot exists because that drive never left me."

"How come you don't have a cofounder now?"

"I wanted to challenge myself." She hears the rushing of water, catches the sparkle of a river through the greenery. Circle's runaway success was like winning the lottery. Nowadays, there's far more competition, and her own self-doubt, but she asserts herself. "When it's just you, there's no ducking responsibility. I take full ownership of everything I do." *I'm a control freak*, she thinks.

"It must be lonely, being the outcast." Sylvia holds her hands up. "I don't mean that as an insult, by the way. I think you've made a remarkable recovery. Would you have built Circle by yourself, knowing what you do now?"

She's parched. She should've brought a water bottle. They've lost sight of everyone else. "No," she says, even though she'd thought that exact thing after she got ousted. That she never should've left her fate in the hands of others. Now she digs for a reason their partnership had been worthwhile, despite how it ended. "The idea never would've even left my brain if Adam wasn't there to listen. When the three of us were working on it together, I couldn't imagine doing anything else. It was pure fun."

That's the difference, isn't it? All she does now is work. She can't remember the last time she had fun, when she was doing something for the pure joy of *doing*, rather than moving toward an objective.

They turn a corner, and Maggie sees Charles contemplating a rock. He lifts his head and waves at them. Maggie approaches with caution.

"I wanted to make sure you didn't get lost," Charles says, even though Maggie only sees one obvious path. He must have no faith in her sense of direction. "Water?" He hands her a bottle from his backpack, and Maggie gratefully takes it.

The three of them end up clustered together, Charles ahead, followed by Sylvia and Maggie. The trail flattens. Small bluebells spring up in the grass. Her calves finally stop screaming at her.

"Do you want to ask me any questions?" Charles asks Sylvia, and Maggie eyes him suspiciously. She's still annoyed after he threw such a stink about their room arrangements, but if he's going to take some of Sylvia's heat, she won't object.

"What was your favorite part of working with everyone?" Sylvia asks, and Maggie finds herself waiting for his answer.

"The unwavering faith," Charles says.

"You'll have to explain that to me," Sylvia says.

"I wasn't sure I wanted to go into designing software. I thought that I'd design objects, things I could touch. I didn't take Circle that seriously at first. It was Adam and Maggie's project. But they had so much faith that Circle would become part of people's lives, and I think that conviction is the magic that made it real."

She hears the wonder in his voice, and something inside her thaws. Charles was the most rational of them, but here he is, admitting there was something magical in those early years. "I wasn't like that in the beginning. You believed, too," she says. "Remember when I was ready to give it up after one day of the site being live? But you told me to be patient."

"That's because you were acting like you'd failed. Which you hadn't."

"So, if Circle didn't exist, would you be doing something totally different now?" Sylvia asks.

"I'm not sure," Charles says, but his voice is guarded. "I haven't really imagined my life without Circle."

They round a bend and catch up to the rest of the group, standing beside a wall of fallen trees. Hari calls, "This is the trail, right?"

The pile of trunks looks like a giant was playing pickup sticks and didn't bother cleaning up. It's taller than Adam, the logs wet, their roots exposed and tangled like uncombed hair.

Charles says, "This wasn't here last time."

"We can't let a bunch of dead plants stop us," Adam insists, even though there's a sheen of sweat on his forehead and a dark patch on the back of his shirt. Maggie is surprised he's so visibly spent. Adam was always naturally athletic. "This hike is a tradition."

"We've only done this, like, once," Hari says. He looks from Adam to Charles. "Unless you two have come here without me."

Maggie catches the way Charles and Adam exchange a glance. "It was while you were on pat leave," Adam says. "We assumed you were busy."

"He was," Priya interjects, shooting Hari a look that makes him shut his mouth. But disgruntlement lingers in the furrow of his brow.

"We can climb it," Charles says.

"It's unsafe for Jaya," Priya says. "We'll head down first and wait for you."

Maggie considers asking if she can go with them. But she can already hear Hari calling her a wimp.

"Catch you later," Hari says. He doesn't seem to notice the way Priya frowns.

Even as they head back down the trail, Maggie hears Jaya asking why Daddy isn't coming with them.

Hari is rubbing his hands, assessing the obstacle in front of him. "This reminds me of that survival camp we did in Atacama." He grins at Maggie. "Just so you know, if the zombies ever come for us, you should stick with Charles. He's very good at finding water."

Charles doesn't hide his disapproval. "That place should've gone out of business. You can't just make people sign a waiver and think that absolves you of all liability." He decides he'll go first so he can guide everyone else. He expertly finds the right handholds, and Maggie watches anxiously as he makes his way up. At one point, his foot slides on a slippery branch, and she expels an audible *ah* before he regains his footing.

"I can't watch," she finally says, turning toward Adam. Hari and Sylvia are chatting a few steps away.

"There's nothing to be scared of," Adam says soothingly. Like it's still his job to allay her fears.

"I'm not scared," she says stubbornly, before turning back to watch Charles reach the top. She can't be afraid in front of Adam, even if fear is her state of being.

She's scared all the time. Scared she doesn't really know how to run a company. That she will let down the people in her employ, the users who have given OurSpot a chance. Scared that she's a one-hit wonder, and the world has already moved on without her. She pushes the thought away and focuses on the present. "I haven't congratulated you," she tells Adam while Sylvia starts climbing, Charles directing her on where to put her feet. Sylvia casually stops halfway up the root wall for a vape break.

"On what?"

"You told me once that you wouldn't be satisfied until you left a mark on the world. Now you've got a Wikipedia page, a building with your name on it at Berkeley, and a product that might replace legacy news media. Safe to say, you'll be remembered." More accurately, he'll be able to *make* people remember him.

Adam laughs. "Looks like we've both kept our promises."

"What promise?"

"To be impressed by each other, always."

There's no hiding the surprise on her face. His comment sends her back to that living room, their pinkies linked. It had been a moment steeped with importance, yet it's somehow faded from her memory. "It's okay, you don't need to uphold your half of the bargain."

"It's not hard," Adam replies. "Look at you, CEO of a second company, while I've only got the one. I was glad when I heard you'd started something new, Maggie." She imagines what it would've been like, to have Adam gassing her up when she started OurSpot. She probably would've launched it much sooner, instead of second-guessing herself for weeks.

Still, she notices how easily he has made her the topic of conversation, instead of acknowledging everything he's accomplished. It makes her think he *isn't* satisfied. That none of it has been enough. She wonders if he holds any regret at all about the other parts of life that he must have missed in his endless quest to exceed expectations. "You're not married too, are you?"

Sylvia's reached the top, and now it's Hari's turn. He climbs daintily, like he doesn't want to get his hands too dirty.

Adam shrugs. "I don't really think that kind of stuff is meant for me. What about you, Maggie? Do you have someone?"

She snorts. "Yeah. Workaholism."

The wrinkles smooth out of Adam's forehead. "You had me going for a second there. Let's get you over this wall."

Their conversation had been so normal, so pleasant, that she didn't even notice Hari disappear over the top of the wall. Maggie grabs one of the slick pieces of wood. It's slippery, especially under the well-worn treads of her sneakers.

Charles's instructions are precise, like he can see exactly what she sees. When the soles of her shoes slip against a root, and she pauses there, her heart thumping away in her chest, Charles says, "You're almost there. It's more trouble to go back down at this point." His tone is practical, but encouraging, and she grits her teeth and keeps pulling herself up.

"You did that way faster than Hari," Charles says once she's close to the top.

"I heard that!" Hari yells from somewhere behind him.

Charles reaches toward her. "You might need some stability to get your leg over."

She shies away from his hand, but the sharpness of her movement makes her wobble. She doesn't want to accept Charles's help. Charles, with his influencer girlfriend and his zombie-fighting skills, who's only being nice because Sylvia's watching.

"Maggie, you good?" Adam yells from below.

"I'm good!" she calls as she climbs the rest of the way up.

"Good job!" Hari exclaims, holding his hand up for a high five. Delirious with the adrenaline of the climb, Maggie returns it, grinning at him. "Hey, wait, let's take a selfie." He holds his phone out, already pulling Maggie toward him. "Sylvia, get in. Charles, look over here! Damn, I should've brought my selfie stick."

"I'm making sure Adam doesn't fall on his ass," Charles says.

"Don't worry about me!" Adam shouts from farther down. "Take the photo!"

Hari, Maggie, and Sylvia crowd together, and Hari lifts the phone high enough to capture the back of Charles's head. Maggie smells the kiwi on Sylvia's breath and hears Hari's breaths rustling through his nose. At the last second, Charles turns his head and smiles, and that moment becomes frozen on the screen of Hari's iPhone.

"Aw," Hari says, showing Maggie the photo. With their smiles and casual clothing, they look like they've been friends for ages.

"What's the right caption? Should I go for short and punny or turn this logjam into a metaphor for the countless seemingly insurmountable obstacles of life?"

Adam makes it to the top and squeezes Charles's shoulder as he climbs past him. He admires the selfie that Hari took. "Okay, Maggie?" he asks when he reaches her.

"Okay," she replies. "Are you okay?" He looks actually winded.

"I will be." Before she can verify his statement, he's turned away, toward Sylvia.

Hari nudges Maggie. "You should give me your number so I can send this photo to you later."

She nods, even though she plans to forget he even asked. There's no need for a photo reminding her of that one time she saw her college friends before she never spoke to them again.

Chapter Fifteen

DECEMBER 2005

"Are those girls looking at us?" Hari asked as he dipped his quesadilla into an absurd amount of sour cream.

Adam had gotten one of his freshman acolytes to swipe them into Late Night at the Crossroads Cafeteria, and they'd taken over one of the tables with tater tots, wings, quesadillas, and waffle fries, spreading their textbooks and notes out. It was Dead Week, the week before finals when there was no class so students could study.

For someone who claimed his visa situation depended on him not flunking out of school, Hari was doing remarkably little studying. Instead, he was feverishly exchanging emails with his not-girlfriend through his nonschool email. He hadn't wanted to add her on AIM on account of his username being sexiiidesi, or post on her Circle profile, where everything was public. Hari had solicited their opinions on every message he'd sent and received. She wondered if this girl had any idea that she, Adam, and Charles had read every word of her communications and pontificated on what it meant when she wrote out "you" instead of "U." It also made her realize how inefficient email was. She wanted to build private messaging into Circle and remove the need for users to migrate onto GChat, AIM, or email to have conversations.

"They're looking at Adam," Charles said, bored.

Maggie followed Hari's gaze to where a table of what looked like freshmen were staring at them. One of them made eye contact with her and started waving frantically.

"Looks like you have fans," Adam said. He wasn't even trying to study and was instead building a tower of tater tots. "Better look away before they come over for an autograph."

She stuck her tongue out at him. "You're just jealous because you're not the center of attention."

Adam stood up and stretched, letting his shirt ride up over his abs. The freshmen dissolved into giggles. He sat back down and shot Maggie a victorious look. She had no comeback, not when the sight had rendered her speechless.

Charles sighed loudly. "There's no more ketchup."

"Maggie and I will get more." Adam pulled his legs out from under the table and waited for Maggie to join him.

She had no good reason to refuse, and the two of them walked toward the condiments table, Maggie wondering why Adam had summoned her when he was very capable of carrying ketchup on his own. As they wound around the lines of students waiting for buffalo wings and steak and rice, Adam stopped every few feet to knock fists with someone.

"You've been acting weird," Adam said after his fifth such greeting. "Ever since we developed the new logo."

Maggie froze in the middle of the cafeteria, her brain short-circuiting. That was the night of the pinky promise. Charles had come out of his shower and seen them, shouted, "Wait! Stay there!" Then, with his hair still dripping and a towel around his waist, he'd grabbed a napkin and sketched their hands, before taking the lines of their wrists and connecting them to form a full circle. In the center, he wrote *Circle* in cursive. "I knew there was a reason my teacher taught me cursive," he'd said with satisfaction.

After pulling up the site for the hundredth time to stare at the logo, Maggie had to admit that she had it bad. There was something so romantic about her and Adam's hands, memorialized forever. She tried to remind herself of how he'd so assuredly called her a *friend*. Whatever she felt for him, she needed to bury it, and the only way she could think of doing it was by avoiding being alone with him.

"Weird? Me?" She inched farther away from him. She'd rather die than tell him she had a crush on him.

"You're not keeping something from me, are you?" Adam reached out and cupped her elbows, and that was when she saw that she was crossing her arms. She quit fidgeting, the heat of his palms traveling through her skin.

"It sounds like there's something you want to tell *me*."

The tension left his face, as if he'd been waiting for her to say those words. He tugged her toward the salad bar, the least populated part of the cafeteria. "So, my dad was not very happy about me skipping Thanksgiving to stay here. He told me Circle was a waste of my time, and to quit." The corner of his mouth tugged down, and Maggie forgot about maintaining her distance. She grabbed a handful of his sleeve, suddenly afraid.

"He doesn't get it. My dad doesn't, either. Nobody who didn't grow up with the internet understands."

Her fierce response made Adam smile slightly. "I know. My dad responds to legitimacy and contracts, which is why he's not buying that Circle is a real company. So, I've been looking into incorporating. That should be the next step, right?"

Maggie nodded, her panic subsiding slightly. It seemed that Adam was searching for a way to stay.

"If we do that, we have to decide how to split up equity in the company."

"Oh," Maggie said softly. It was too soon. They'd just developed their logo, bought the domain. She could still pretend that Circle was a well-functioning group project. Having a conversation about how much of it they each could get felt like chopping up a baby. Once they did that, they would never have Circle as it was now, whole and perfect.

"I wanted to talk to you about it before we go back to Hari and Charles," Adam said. "We'll probably want to model it out, choose a lawyer—"

"No." She shook her head. She didn't want to get caught in a morass of legalities and negotiations, and besides, if Adam wanted it, it meant it was important to him. "Let's just do it tonight."

Adam squeezed her arm, but his eyes were concerned. "Are you sure?"

"Yeah." She turned, about to return to their table, but Adam tugged her back.

"Thanks, Maggie." She had never seen him look so serious. His thumb brushed against the inside of her wrist, and she knew she'd done something right.

A moment passed, and then Adam let her go. She led the way back to their table, trying to calm her heartbeat. When he touched her like that, she wanted to believe that he felt at least a smidge of what she felt for him. Maybe she should tell him? But it seemed like too great a risk for their friendship.

"Where's the ketchup?" Hari asked when the two of them got back. Maggie and Adam took the bench opposite him and Charles. "You guys were gone so long, I thought you started your own tomato farm."

"It doesn't matter. We ate all the fries anyway," Charles said. He watched as Adam pulled a Five Star notebook out of his backpack and set it on the table. "It's a little late to start taking notes, dude."

Adam uncapped his pen. "We need to split up equity."

Hari closed his laptop. Charles's eyes narrowed. "You can't cut up the *Mona Lisa* and expect it to retain its full value."

The softness in Adam's expression was gone, replaced by a steely determination. "Circle is about to become a business, Charlie-boy. This is a necessary evil."

A business. The word was a foreign substance entering her bloodstream. She realized Charles was looking at her. "You agree with this?" he asked.

She could feel Adam's expectant gaze. This was why he'd pulled her aside earlier. So that they could present a united front. "Yeah."

Charles didn't look pleased, but he didn't mount another protest. "How do we do this?"

"Should we go around and say how much we each think we should get?" Adam suggested, sounding a bit uncertain now.

"And then what?" Charles asked. "We negotiate with each other for less or more?"

"That's going to take forever. Maybe Maggie takes the largest chunk, and the three of us split the rest," Hari said.

Adam scratched his head. "Why does Maggie take the largest chunk?"

"Didn't she come up with the idea?" Hari asked.

"Ideas aren't worth that much," Maggie said. The thought of getting the largest share didn't sit well with her. She didn't want to single herself out, like she was better than everyone else.

The air grew thick. They couldn't even agree on an approach. How would they find a split that worked for all of them?

"Let's split it equally," Maggie decided. She didn't want to drag this out, for them to start pointing out one another's flaws in the hopes of increasing their stakes in the company. This way, nobody would be resented for getting more.

The guys all looked at her. "Are you sure?" Adam said.

"Any one of us would put the company first. If we ever disagree over something, we'll always choose the path that benefits Circle most. Do you guys agree on that?"

Hari and Adam nodded. Charles, after a split-second pause, followed suit.

Maggie ripped a piece of paper out of the notebook. Adam handed her the pen, and she wrote each of their names. Then, beside each name, she wrote *25%*. Finally, she scrawled her signature at the bottom. She thrust the paper back into the center of the table.

A few minutes passed and nobody reached for it. Then Adam slid the paper toward himself and signed his name beneath hers. He dropped the pen on the table like it was a hot potato. Then Hari took it and did the same.

Charles was the only one left.

"Charles, come on," Maggie said, impatient for this to be over, so they could move onto less stressful things, like studying for finals.

"You know that because we're splitting the company equally, three of us could gang up on the fourth?"

She laughed at that. Of all the reservations Charles could've shared, this one she was not worried about at all. They were friends first. Circle would never get in the way of that. "If that happened, it must be because the person deserved it."

Charles still hesitated. There was something indecipherable about the way he was looking at her. Like he saw something she didn't yet. He was always so much more careful than any of them. She chalked it up to his paranoia.

Finally, Charles picked up the pen and signed.

Hari sat back. He dramatically wiped his brow. "Wow, why was that so nerve-racking?"

Adam seized the paper and tucked it away into a manila folder, which had materialized from his backpack. "I'll give this to our family lawyer. He'll probably ask if I'm serious, but whatever. All he said was to get it in writing."

Beneath the table, his knee rested against hers. Maggie settled back, happy because he was happy. They were in this together, and that was what mattered.

Chapter Sixteen

DAY 2: FRIDAY

They are granted a flat, smooth path after the root wall. Maggie takes the opportunity to speed up, hoping she can leave Sylvia in the dust. But when she takes a break to catch her breath, it turns out she hasn't gotten much of a lead. Sylvia trots over, Adam beside her. Hari and Charles are trailing after them.

Sylvia sends her a cheeky smile, as if she can read her thoughts. "Doing alright?"

"Of course." She adjusts her grimace into something more welcoming. "Any more questions I can answer for you?"

"This is more for my own curiosity, but why choose to start a company when you've got the money to do whatever you want?"

She meets Adam's eye over Sylvia's head, mind going blank. He knows as well as her that this is not a question she can answer truthfully. She sold her full stake in Circle long before the IPO, which means she made no money when the company went public. But explaining that to Sylvia would mean telling her who she'd sold it to, and why. "Because starting a company should never be about making money." It was about proving herself. About impacting other people's lives, at scale. And beating her enemies. "I put the Circle money toward paying my debts and helping out my dad. The rest can wait."

It's a half-truth, at least.

"I find it hard to believe you didn't do anything irresponsible. No chartering a private jet? Building an estate on Kauai? We all know that Adam here tried to buy part of Patagonia."

Adam coughs. "That's a rumor."

Maggie gives her a weak smile before turning back around. "I'm not into that stuff." Sylvia thinks that she occupies the same income bracket as the guys, but that couldn't be further from the truth. It's a discomfiting feeling, to realize the people she once regarded as her peers have far exceeded her. At one point, Adam let slip that everything he eats at home is produced by a farm he started with some Nobu chefs. Hari mentioned he outbid a bunch of other parents for his nanny, and that he has to bribe her with saffron and a week off every Diwali so she doesn't leave them for another family. And the thing is, they don't realize they're doing it. They've gotten used to talking about large sums of money, accustomed to deploying it whenever necessary to make their lives easier. Her meager salary, paid for by OurSpot's seed funding and barely enough for her rent and essentials each month, is pennies in comparison.

The smooth road ends, and the five of them gather at the base of the ropes portion. She tips her neck back to look. It's so steep that it's impossible to walk up without holding on to a rope, anchored into the rock beside them with metal stakes. No way is she going up that thing.

"It's not that bad," Charles says from beside her, reading her mind.

She scratches her wrist. Between the logjam, this, and keeping track of the falsehoods she's been feeding Sylvia, she feels both physically and mentally spent. "I might be good."

"It's a really great view," Adam promises. "Really, it'll be worth it."

"What if I fall and roll all the way to the bottom of this mountain?"

"Come on," Adam wheedles. "It'll be just like hiking the Big C."
She stiffens at that.

"That's the hill that all the Cal students like to climb, right?" Sylvia asks.

"Yeah, we used to hike it every time we accomplished something. It's a special place."

"Anyone want a Gatorade?" Charles asks. She looks up in time to see a bottle of Gatorade go shooting past Adam.

Adam picks the dirt-encrusted bottle off the ground. "I didn't ask for one," he says.

"Sorry, thought you raised your hand," Charles says. He addresses Maggie now. "If you bail, we're all going to have to turn around."

"Yeah," Hari chimes in. "And you can't deprive us of the view when we're so close."

"You don't want to miss it," Adam says. "Seriously."

She'd forgotten how impossible it is to refuse when the three of them are peer pressuring her at once. They could go without her, but for some reason, they are all invested in getting her up this mountain. It reminds her of how they would always do everything as a unit. If even one of them was missing, the group would feel incomplete.

"Okay," she says finally.

"Yes!" The guys cheer, as if they've closed a hundred-million-dollar deal.

They arrange themselves in a line, Charles in the front, then Maggie, Adam, and Hari. Sylvia tells them to go ahead because she wants to jot down some notes, and she'll catch up.

Charles grabs the rope, pulling it taut as he starts working his way up. Maggie follows closely behind, but then realizes that each step pushes her phone farther out of her pocket. She glances behind her. Adam is a couple feet down, moving slower than expected. "Charles," she calls.

He immediately stops and looks over his shoulder.

"Can I put my phone in your bag?" she asks.

He nods, swinging his backpack off his back so that he can unzip the outside compartment. She grabs her phone from her pocket, then hands it up to him.

He stares at the old iPhone. "Is this . . ." He trails off, as if unsure he wants to even ask the question. Zips the phone into his backpack. Pats the compartment once, as if checking it's safe. Then he turns back around, and they resume walking.

If the logjam worked out her shoulders and arms, this is a workout for her quads. She wishes she'd exercised before arriving on this blasted island. Finally, they reach a clearing, and Charles drops the rope, grabbing onto a boulder and pulling himself up.

She releases the rope. For a terrifying moment, she is untethered, and that's when she looks down. The narrow trail snakes between the trees, and on either side is a steep drop. Adam and Hari are close behind her, and she can see the strain in Adam's expression. He takes a break to massage his shoulder.

A sudden burst of wind whistles past her ears, and a chill ripples through her body. One wrong move . . .

A nervous laugh emits from her chest. Adam hears. She sees his head snap toward hers, the rapid fall of his chest. When their eyes meet, he gives her a thumbs-up.

"This last part is the worst," he calls. "But it'll be worth it. I promise."

When she turns back to the ledge, Charles is there, his hand held out toward her. She grabs it, and he pulls her up, his grip strong and sure. She half-flails her way over, but then it's done, and she's lying on blessedly flat ground. Slowly, she stands and then faces the way they came.

The colors. They punch her in the gut with their vividness. The ocean washing up against the white shore of the beach, bright turquoise transitioning into mysterious, deep blue, dotted with tiny green islands. A halo of clouds floats around the peaks of one of the nearby mountains, an ethereal necklace on the throat of a great goddess. She can see now how this place inspired wild myths of one-eyed gods and lightning hammers.

"It's awesome up here!" she shouts down to Adam, feeling a begrudging respect for his good choice in islands.

She hears his answering laughter, then his head appears over the rock. "I told you!"

Charles starts to walk toward him, but Adam waves off his outstretched arm. "Let me do this myself." He pulls himself over, lies there a second, breathing hard, before rising. Then, he walks away from them and sits on a rock overlooking the view. Maggie watches him, concerned.

"What's going on with him?" she asks. Adam rises from his rock and starts stretching his quads, looking oddly frail off by himself.

"Just old age and joint pain. You should take this back." Charles opens his backpack, holding her phone out to her.

"Hold on to it for me. We still have to get down, don't we?" she says.

"Charles, you bastard, give me a hand!" Hari calls from below.

But Charles is too busy examining the iPhone in his hand. He turns it over. The breath catches in her throat. She knows what he's looking for, but luckily the phone is covered with a case.

Hari hoists himself up, grumbling. "Yeah, give Maggie the special treatment while your bosom bro gets nada."

Sylvia, astonishingly, doesn't get there that much longer after them, nor does she need help reaching the top.

"Wow, this is great!" she exclaims, walking to the very edge of the viewpoint to snap photos. Charles puts Maggie's phone away and starts unwrapping a protein bar.

"Give me some," Hari says, already opening his mouth wide.

Charles holds it out to him, and Hari takes a big bite, leaving only a nub behind. Charles examines the remnants of the bar, unamused, then snatches the strings of Hari's hoodie, pulling them hard. Hari's hood tightens around his head, covering his eyes.

"You—" Hari chases Charles off somewhere. Maggie snorts. Incredible that these two are grown men now.

Adam comes up alongside Maggie. He seems to have finished stretching. "I have something to show you," Adam says, lowering his voice. "Open my backpack."

Cautiously, she goes behind him and unzips his backpack. Inside is a sweating six-pack of Miller High Lifes. "Are you serious?" she says, exasperated.

"Do you think shotgunning these in front of Sylvia is a good idea?" Adam asks.

"Absolutely not."

"I thought you'd say that," Adam says, but he doesn't sound defeated. "That's okay. The weekend's still young."

She zips up his backpack with finality. "I might've agreed to go along with this scheme, but let's not go around resurrecting old rituals."

"Why not? It couldn't be that you're afraid?" There's a taunting edge to his question as he turns to face her again.

"Afraid of *what*?" She intends it to come out challenging, but the words sound inquisitive instead.

"Maybe you're afraid that you're going to like hanging out with us too much, and when this weekend ends, you won't know how to say goodbye."

"I'm the only one who'll *have* to say goodbye," she shoots back. One weekend isn't enough to erase the past. She needs to remember that. She tries to relax her posture, look like she doesn't care all that much.

"Why do you have to?" Adam searches her face, but she's not sure what he's looking for. "When you hit me up, a year later . . . I thought you wanted to be friends again."

Maggie turns from him, surveying the landscape. Her throat is tight. "I don't want to talk about that."

Adam is quiet for a minute. "You asked me to keep it secret, and I have. I won't tell anyone about how you sold your shares to me."

She sucks in a breath through her teeth. She'd asked Adam for his help when she and her dad were stranded in the depths of the recession, and even though it was a necessary move, it doesn't mean she's not ashamed of it. She'd been a shit negotiator and thought that what Adam was paying her for them was plenty. Even though she'd been on the losing end of that deal, she's made her peace with it. If she'd become rich so young, while she'd felt aimless and wronged, she doesn't know what she would've become. "Thanks," she mumbles. Hearing him promise this soothes her worries. She's glad that he hasn't told anyone.

"It doesn't feel right, though," Adam says. "You sold them to me without knowing how much they'd be worth. If you wanted, I could—"

"No," she cuts him off. She meets his eyes and hopes that he can see her gratitude, and her desire to leave this decision behind them, for good and bad. "You did enough, Adam. Thank you."

"What are we talking about?" Sylvia asks, appearing like a pop-up ad.

Adam's expression, which had been so intent a second ago, clears. He smiles amiably at Sylvia. "Privilege."

"Oh?" Sylvia asks with a curious lift of her brows. "Whose privilege? Yours?"

"Of course. How many people get to know and learn from someone like Margaret Tang?"

Her instinct is to pass this off as a compliment given for Sylvia's sake. But Adam has stuffed his hands into his pockets, and there's a wryness in his expression that tells Maggie he's being genuine. She thinks of the beers he lugged all the way up here, how he remembers a pinky promise they made a decade ago.

Maggie shrugs. "Circle was a training ground for all of us. Everything I've learned, I'm applying to how I run OurSpot now, so I don't make the same mistakes."

"It's definitely tough out there for women," Sylvia agrees. "Do you get impostor syndrome?"

"Less than before," Maggie says, even though impostor syndrome has become her lifelong partner. She's just learned how to cope with it. Every time she thinks that she's not good enough, she works harder.

"I bet my impostor syndrome was worse than yours," Adam pipes up.

"You? No way." Adam could face down anything without faltering. She didn't think he'd ever doubted himself, not for a single second in his life. His conviction had propped all of them up in moments of hardship.

Adam starts explaining to Sylvia, "I didn't know anything about coding, but Maggie was a genius at it. And she had this intuition—kind of like Charles's design intuition—about what people needed. That confidence I have? I developed it so people would look at me and not question why I was part of the team."

"You never told me that." She remembers the anxiety that battered her whenever she thought about Circle becoming realer and bigger and more impactful. Meanwhile, Adam had spoken grandly about Circle at interviews with reporters and sent eloquent emails to potential investors detailing all the future benefits. He'd played such an important role in driving the company forward, but if what he's saying is true, he'd still experienced some misgivings. He'd just done a way better job at hiding it. She has to respect him for that. He never let his emotions get in the way of Circle's future.

"I couldn't," Adam says, and she knows he's not putting on a show for Sylvia. "I had to be good enough for you."

Chapter Seventeen

DECEMBER 2005

To celebrate the end of finals and the official incorporation of Circle, LLC, they hiked up to the Big C, so named because of the giant yellow C graffitied into the slanted concrete. It was a popular place to watch the sun set, although Maggie had until then avoided making the ascent because she was challenged enough by the hills on campus.

On the way there, they picked up Hari's not-girlfriend. Priya Kumar was elegant and wore small gold hoops in her ears. She brought her camera, wearing its bulky case cross-body, telling Maggie about how she'd gone to India over the summer and realized how important it was to photograph where her family had emigrated from. Maybe it was because she was two years older and working a *real* job, but she seemed mature in a way Maggie was not. Maggie wondered if this was how she'd become after graduation, a world-weary adult who thought traveling the world would help her find herself.

The two of them ended up walking together, the three guys racing ahead of them up the hill. Maggie would've joined them, but Hari had made her promise to stick with Priya. Apparently, Priya had only come because Hari had told her there would be another girl.

The sun was beginning to turn everything a buttery yellow, and Maggie paused along the trail to take in the sprawl of Berkeley below them, and to catch her breath. Finals were behind her, and now she could pour all her energy into Circle. Adam's dad had lent them a lawyer, who'd been surprised to learn that they'd already figured out their equity split. Coming up with their roles had been a lot easier: Maggie would be CEO, Adam COO, Charles CTO, and Hari CFO. The paperwork was basically done, and a new year was ahead. She couldn't believe she'd only met Adam, Charles, and Hari a few months ago. It felt like she'd known them her entire life. Like all the friends she'd failed to make had guided her toward them.

"Where's your family from, Maggie?" Priya asked, interrupting her thoughts. Normally, Maggie wouldn't be opposed to conversation, but she kind of wanted to enjoy the view—and this milestone—in peace. "Are they immigrants, too?"

"Yeah, they came from China." The sky was clear, which meant they could see past campus and all the way to San Francisco. Staring across the bay, she thought she could glimpse the hopes of every person who'd passed through the city of gold on their way to grasp some piece of the American Dream for themselves. It was what had brought her dad to the US, and probably what had kept him here even when her mom stopped believing.

"Just your mom and dad?"

"Uh-huh," Maggie said without further clarification. She didn't want to explain how her mom wasn't there anymore. The guys had never asked her to, which was a relief. She didn't want them to treat her with pity.

Priya didn't take the hint. "Do you go back to visit your family in China? I remember the first time I went back to Mumbai, I was so shocked by how many uncles and aunts I had. I couldn't believe I was related to them all!"

"Cool," Maggie said. They'd reached the top, and she spotted

Adam at the crest of the yellow C, in the center of a small circle of other students. Steps curved around the side, and Charles was sitting farther down. Hari stood a few steps above him, searching for them. When he saw Priya, he waved enthusiastically, shouting, "You two look like best friends already!"

Maggie left Priya and Hari behind and made her way toward Charles. She stood above him, her hands on her hips. "Why do you look like such a loner? We're supposed to be celebrating."

Charles peered up at her. "This is me celebrating."

She grabbed him by the arms, tugging him up. The two of them started climbing the steps toward Adam while Hari lingered by Priya's side, holding her lens cap as she snapped photos.

"What did you two talk about?" Charles asked.

Maggie shrugged. "She was being nosy about my family."

"You don't talk about your family much." So Charles had noticed.

Everything related to her family seemed kind of depressing. Her lack of a mom. A dad who mostly left her alone beyond school pickups and taking her to doctor's appointments, which was why she'd found solace in computers. He'd never asked whether she was making friends or having fun in school. Not that he would have been able to help with that anyway.

She didn't like talking about her family because it didn't really feel like she had one.

"I guess . . . because it's not very normal." She found herself stumbling over the words. "My mom's not around."

Charles was quiet, then he said, "Once, when my older sister and I were fighting, she told me that I was a mistake. My parents denied it, but they gave her a huge grounding." He lifted a shoulder. "Everybody's families are fucked up in some way. Didn't Tolstoy write something like that?"

"Probably those exact words."

"Maggie!" Adam called, waving at her as she and Charles approached. "I was just telling everyone about the story of Circle, but you need to be here for the best part," Adam said, throwing an arm around her. "Here, give me your pinky." He smelled like grass and sunlight, and as she linked her pinky with his, someone said, "Oh shit, that's the logo!"

Adam grinned down at her, the sun cradling his face. Too soon, the moment was over. Adam released her, going to grab his backpack. She joined Charles, Hari, and Priya at their spot in the middle of the hill, facing the bay. The sun was now a blazing semicircle, disappearing behind the striking spire of the Campanile.

Adam returned with a six-pack of Miller High Life.

He winked at her before pulling one of the cans out of its plastic circle. "Ever shotgunned a beer before?"

She stared at him. "No . . ."

"I taught Charles freshman year. Charles, will you demonstrate?" Adam tossed a beer to Charles, who caught it one-handed.

Charles got down on one knee and unclipped the ring of keys from his belt loop. He ripped the key across the side of the beer can in one swift, sure motion, then pressed it to his mouth. He rapidly swallowed, crumpled the can, and stood back up, all in the matter of seconds.

"Charlie-*boy*! *That* is how you shotgun a beer," Adam said, fist-bumping him.

Priya scoffed. "Uncivilized." She looked to Maggie for agreement, but Maggie was busy grabbing a beer for herself.

Hari was already kneeling, asking Charles for advice on the best angle to puncture the can. "Wait, we should do this at the same time," he said. "Priya, can you take a picture of us?"

Priya clung to her DSLR like she wouldn't lower herself to capturing something so ridiculous. "Don't you guys want a nice picture with the sunset?"

"Maggie, come next to me." Adam reached for her hand. He

was kneeling too, and for a second, it was almost like he was proposing to her.

She flushed, crouching down beside him. Around them, people were staring. The ones above them were pointing at them, instead of looking at the sunset.

They formed a lopsided circle as they brought their beers to their mouths. "Wait, Charles, you're doing another one?" Hari asked as Priya walked higher up the hill to get a better angle with her camera.

"Beer is ninety percent water. I'm hydrating."

"Maggie, want to say something?" Adam asked. "You're the CEO, after all."

CEO. The title felt vast and powerful, like holding on to a jeweled scepter that towered far above her. She felt too short, too ordinary, for the role. She held the beer in her hand, the condensation slicking her palm. And yet, as everyone watched them, with Adam and the others beside her, she *did* feel powerful.

"To world domination," she said, raising her beer, the sunset and their spectators sending a surge of confidence through her. "To Circle."

"To Circle!" Adam roared.

"To Circle!" Hari and Charles echoed, and then they cut into their Millers.

Beer gushed over Maggie's fingers, and she hurriedly attached her mouth to the opening she'd created. Icy beer flowed through her lips, and all she could do was swallow as fast as she could.

Adam and Charles finished first, Hari and Maggie a few seconds behind. They stood, and a round of applause went up around the Big C. Someone screamed, "*Go Bears!*"

Everyone was clapping. Maggie was still clutching her empty can, shivering from ingesting so much cold liquid so quickly.

A warm arm came around her shoulders. Adam squeezed her

tight, grinning. "World domination," he said, repeating her words. "Sometimes, you really surprise me."

She returned his smile, exhilarated from the applause, the beer, Adam's glowing presence beside her. She felt immensely lucky, like today was one of those days where everything was destined to go right. Her secret fizzed and bubbled inside her, begging to be let out. Adam was still holding on to her, and she decided that she would tell him tonight. If there was even the slightest chance that he returned her feelings, it would all be worth it.

A high-pitched yelp tore their attention away from each other.

"Priya!" Hari yelled, and Maggie turned to see him rushing to where Priya was crouched, cradling her camera with one arm and holding her ankle with the other.

After some fussing, prodding, and examining, the conclusion was that Priya had rolled her ankle. Hari took control of the situation, eager to rescue his damsel. "Charles, we'll help her down."

"I told you, I can walk," Priya insisted, trying to get up on her own but obviously keeping her weight off her left leg.

Charles took her camera bag, hanging it around his own neck. "It would be better if Hari carried you." Was he trying to wingman?

Hari got the clue. "Come on, up you go." Charles helped Priya onto Hari's back, and he stood with a slight grunt.

"I'm too heavy," Priya said.

"You kidding me? I can barely feel you up there," Hari wheezed.

Charles looked like he was trying not to laugh. "I'll be right behind you."

At first, she and Adam followed closely, but then Maggie decided this was the opening she needed. She captured Adam's arm. He looked back at her, a question in his eyes. "We should take our time going down. I don't want either of us to get injured."

"You make a good point as always," Adam said, and she wasn't sure if that was mischief on his face, but he slowed.

The dark descended, and her head felt light from the beer. When she stumbled over a root, Adam caught her, grabbing her hand. Their fingers interlaced, and her heart went off to the races.

"It's a really nice night," she said, terrified that if she drew attention to them touching, Adam would let go.

"Mmm-hmm," Adam agreed. He rubbed his thumb over the skin between her thumb and forefinger. Her breathing went shallow. They had stopped walking. The twilight made everything soft and hazy as Adam took her other hand in his, facing her. If there was any time she should say something, it was now.

"I have something to tell you," she whispered.

She felt his hand move to the back of her neck, the slight pressure of him tilting her face up to his, bringing his lips to hers. The kiss lasted only for a second, so short that she thought she'd dreamed it. But then, Adam said, "Were you going to tell me you like me?"

He'd kind of stolen her thunder, but her mind was still caught up on the kiss, and all she could do was choke out a "yeah." She liked him so much that sometimes she went to his Circle profile and scrolled down to his friends section, just so she could see her name there. The digital equivalent of writing *Maggie Fink* in her diary and drawing hearts around it.

His hand slid down to her waist, and he kissed her again, deeply and thoroughly, like a boy who'd kissed lots of girls before but was still interested in kissing *her*. Then he pulled her off the trail, and she followed him, stumbling a little, dazed laughter on her lips. The grass tickled her ankles as he pinned her against a tree and kissed her again.

They made out until her mouth tingled and her hands had cautiously then fervently explored his skin.

When they returned to the hiking trail, holding hands, her

head was spinning so much she thought it'd fly off her neck. So this was what life could be. Sunsets with your best friends, making out with a boy who liked you back, working on ideas that might change lives.

"For the record," Adam said as they walked, "I like you, too."

She wanted to ask him to repeat it, but she didn't want to ruin the moment. So she did everything she could to capture the cadence of his voice, the feeling of his hand in hers, the sound of his sneakers on the dirt, so that she would be able to recall this memory perfectly later on.

Outside their apartment building, Adam released her hand as he reached for his keys. Before he unlocked the door, he turned to her. "We probably shouldn't let the others know. Just so we don't complicate things," he said.

She hadn't even thought about that, how this *thing* between them might exist in the light of the day, around the others. But she knew it was the right move. Circle had only just been born, and she would do almost anything to avoid jeopardizing what they'd built.

She nodded and followed him inside, his kisses still sweet on her lips.

Circle's Inner Circle: Part Two

"We had a perfect few months," Xu said as we stood at the viewpoint. It was a hike that he, Fink, and Acharya had done before, one that ended at the top of a mountain with picture-perfect views. I'd watched as the three of them convinced Tang, who looked pretty fed up, into completing the ascent. A few feet from us, Fink and Tang stood side by side, their backs to us as they appreciated the view.

Xu spoke with a wistfulness that made me think that their friendship really peaked at the very beginning of Circle. "Circle was just this weird little thing we were experimenting on together. Everything was low-stakes, so it felt like we could do whatever we wanted. It was astonishingly simple, when I think about it. I don't think anything has been that simple since."

Circle came with an irresistible story. "The App for Friends, Made by Friends," the *New York Times* article that first covered the company pronounced. The website was authentic and fresh. It was a departure from the clutter of MySpace, the anonymity of online message boards, the hyperspecificity of LiveJournal.

But was it that simple? I can't see how Fink and Tang, with their dueling visions for the company, could ever have coexisted in harmony. Back in 2007, I'd theorized that Tang was the bottleneck that prevented Fink from fully controlling the company's roadmap. Everyone knew that their disagreements had led to toxicity, internal divisions, and employee retention issues. After Tang left, Xu took over the product, but it was obvious that it was in service of Fink's vision. Despite his nontechnical background, Fink has since launched and popularized Public Profiles, leading to the rise of the "influencer" and a new era for Circle at the center of the information revolution.

But in the present, they seem to have made peace with all that. Fink doesn't shy away from showing his admiration for his ousted cofounder. Watching the two of them interact, I can see how they might have been when they were younger. Fink, the golden boy, and Tang, the girl genius. It's the irresistible pairing of rom-coms, reality TV shows, and Disney Channel Original Movies. I wonder if their particular relationship was special, and whether it affected Tang's role within their larger group. After all, she was the only woman, and that could have made her an outcast, the way that tech's bro-centric ecosystem always turns women into outsiders.

When I watch the three of them band together to convince her to complete the summit, like they will be incapable of finishing the hike without her, I am even more mystified by why they kicked her out of Circle. The prevailing narrative is that Tang's dismissal was a coup, a mutual agreement among Fink, Xu, and Acharya that she wasn't suited for the job. But I wonder if there was more brewing beneath the surface of this friendship.

Could it be that the ultimate failure of their partnership wasn't because the men didn't care enough for Tang, but because they cared a little too much?

Chapter Eighteen
JANUARY 2006

When Maggie let Adam into her room at midnight, she didn't think he was going to spend that time sitting at her desk, sending emails. Her roommate still wasn't back from winter break, and she'd kind of thought that they were going to do . . . other things. Now she felt like a pervert. But when Adam told her that he was sick of home and had pushed up his flight back to California, she quickly arranged for her dad to drop her off a week before classes started.

They'd had two weeks to sneak around before everyone went their separate ways for the holiday break. She and Adam had called each other, once on Christmas and once on New Year's. The knowledge that somebody liked her buzzed like a swarm of bees inside her chest, and she wished she could tell *someone*. But Hari and Charles couldn't know, and she knew her dad would disapprove. He disapproved of anything that threatened her studies. Plus, she didn't know if Adam was her boyfriend. They'd never gone on a real date. Usually, he snuck over late at night, when her roommate was already asleep, and they'd hide under her blankets, trying to be as quiet as possible.

"What are you doing?" she asked him now. He had come into her room, kissed her, then set up camp at her desk.

"This venture capitalist finally replied to me." Adam's voice was low and excited.

She lay back against the pillows again, trying to staunch her irritation. It wasn't like she didn't have things to do, too. There was code to debug, but she had put that off to spend time with him.

When Adam finally turned to her, it was to ask, "Can you get me the latest on the campuses we're on and how many users we have in each?"

Miffed, she turned on her side. It was 1:00 a.m., and she wanted to cuddle, not pull data.

Adam waited, then sighed. She heard him tap at his laptop a little longer before he shut it. Then, her bedsprings squeaked as he jumped onto the bed, nuzzling her neck. Maggie let out a shriek. He wrapped her in his arms, squeezing her tight. "I missed you," he said, lifting himself up to look down at her.

She lifted a hand and threaded it through his curls, the way she'd always wanted to. Then, she kissed him. His fingers pressed into her hips. His lips moved to her neck, a slice of pain accompanying the pleasure. They began moving against each other, and heat blossomed in her stomach—

There was knocking at her door. They wrenched apart, and Maggie dropped back against her pillows, panting.

"Your roommate?" Adam asked.

"She would never knock. Who is it?" she yelled.

"It's me," Charles called back.

She and Adam exchanged a panicked look. "Shit!" she said, pushing him out of the way and leaping off her bed. "Coming!"

She cracked the door open and slipped out. Charles was pacing in the hallway with his laptop half-open on his arm. "Charles? What are you doing back?"

He stopped, looking bewildered for a second. "You mentioned you were coming back today, and I know you don't sleep until three anyway."

Right, the two of them had been talking on the phone about the private chat feature they were building for Circle, and she'd told him she would work on it once she'd gotten back to her apartment.

Charles was still talking. "I figured I might as well come back, too. I was going to wait until tomorrow to come find you, but I had to show you this." He opened his laptop to reveal an impressive dashboard, with bar charts and graphs that were updating in real time. At the top was a number: eight hundred and fifty thousand. "I cleaned up our analytics tooling."

"First of all, that is way too beautiful for an internal tool. Second of all, is that number right? We're almost at . . ."

"A million," Charles finished for her. "And yes, it's correct. I triple-checked."

"A million," Maggie said softly. The number was impossibly vast. A million human beings using Circle. Logging on and seeing the home page she and Charles had built. Creating circles with their friends, posting about their lives. Pouring their thoughts, feelings, beliefs into this digital space.

She knew what Adam would say if he saw this. *We have to do more.* Circle was still limited to universities, but the requests were beginning to pour in from other demographics: older people, teenagers, even businesses. Maggie had found reasons to delay this growth. More people on Circle meant more things could go wrong. It meant leaving the safety of campuses, navigating the murky waters of providing for a far more diverse population.

The thing she would never admit to anyone was this: beneath the gratitude and thrill was deep fear. This wasn't a hobby anymore. It was real, to her and the guys and thousands of others. If they failed by launching a crappy feature or inadequately preparing for traffic spikes, she would be letting all of them down.

"We've done well," Charles said, like he could see the doubt naked on her face.

She ushered her doubt into a separate room. She couldn't live like this, numb to her accomplishments because she was so terrified of the future. She needed to be more like Adam, who spoke about Circle in grand terms without hesitation.

Adam! He was still in her room. "Thanks for showing me. We can talk more about it in the morning." She turned slightly, about to open her door again—

"Is that a hickey?"

Her hand flew up to her neck, covering the spot he was squinting at. She'd gotten a tiny thrill the first time Adam had given her one, like a mark of his possession. But she was going to have to politely ask him to stop if they wanted to keep this relationship to themselves.

"Probably eczema," she said. "I've been scratching at night again."

Charles's expression darkened. She waited for him to call her out on the lie. Was there a chance he knew? He'd asked her once if she knew why Adam kept leaving at night, and she'd nervously given him a half-truth: "Probably seeing some girl."

"You can talk to me," he said, shutting his laptop and holding it at his side. "You could say anything you wanted, and I'll listen."

The comment seemed out of nowhere, but it soothed some deep need inside of her. She hugged him. "Thanks for coming to find me."

For a moment, he froze, but then his arms wound around her. She felt the warmth of his laptop pressing against her back.

She pulled away. "Good night, Charles."

"Night, Tiny."

She went back inside her apartment. Adam was back at her desk, laptop open again. He twisted around. "What did Charles want?"

"We're almost at a million users," she said. A fresh wave of excitement swept through her.

Adam jumped out of his seat. "Seriously?"

She nodded.

He pumped his fist. "One million now, then five hundred million, then a billion. We're on our way. We should throw a party. I bet Hari will let us use his place. It's way bigger. This weekend? Or do you think we'll hit a million before that?"

Maggie shook her head, smiling, glad to be sharing this moment with him. Her thoughts drifted to Charles, alone in his room after coming to find her and deliver this news. A kernel of guilt formed, but when Adam sent off his email and cornered her back to bed, she forgot it entirely.

Chapter Nineteen

DAY 2: FRIDAY

By the time they arrive back at the lodge, it's late afternoon, and rain has started to fall. The sky is blotted out by thick clouds, waves slamming hard against the shore.

"Where's all the staff?" Hari asks when they enter. Everything's been cleaned and put away from breakfast, but there's no sign of the gray-clad waitstaff that Maggie saw hovering around this morning.

Adam clears his throat. "Here's the thing. I was going to cook. I told everyone they could have the rest of the day off."

"You?" Charles asks. "When's the last time you cooked something?"

"A while. But that's not the point. I wanted to make something for you guys. I was thinking we could use the grill."

Maggie looks outside to where the rain is now pounding against the windows.

"We can just use the kitchen," Adam says, gesturing toward the fully equipped kitchen next to the dining area. "I've got steak in the fridge and tofu for Hari."

"What are you marinating the tofu in?" Priya asks.

Adam stares at her like she's speaking in a foreign language. "Marinating?"

"You can't just grill a tofu without marinade," Charles says. "Otherwise it tastes like nothing."

"Interesting," Adam says.

Charles sighs. "I'll make a marinade."

"Mommy!" Jaya exclaims suddenly. "My tooth fell out!"

Everyone turns toward where she's poking her tongue in between the hole where one of her incisors should be. Jaya thrusts her small hand forward, and a tooth gleams there on her slightly bloody palm. "Daddy, look!"

Hari's head is dipped over his phone, but he looks up. "Oh, wow. Good job, sweetheart."

Priya shoots him an irate look that he misses. "Let's get you cleaned up, sweetie. There's blood on your shirt."

"Does that mean the tooth fairy is coming tonight?" Jaya asks eagerly. She gasps. "Will she leave me Norwegian money?"

"Of course," Hari says. "Every country has tooth fairies."

Priya ushers Jaya out, taking one of the umbrellas that are in the stand near the door. The moment they're gone, Hari asks, "So, anyone got any Norwegian money on them?"

"Why didn't you just tell her the tooth fairy is American?" Charles asks from where he's chopping onions. Beside him, Adam is unwrapping the steaks.

"It doesn't make sense for the tooth fairy industry to be only American. Their operating expenses would be out of control."

Adam places the steaks in the pan, concentrating. Smoke curls from the pan, spreading throughout the lodge.

Hari coughs, then coughs some more. He finally puts his phone away. "I need air. Maggie, want to come with?"

Charles has turned on the hood, but there's still enough smoke to make her eyes water, so she follows Hari outside to the patio. The sea is barely visible, everything shrouded in gray. Hari slides the doors closed, so that all they can hear is the rain falling around them, pattering on the eaves.

"Nice weather, huh?" Hari asks, holding a hand out to catch the drops.

"Feels appropriate."

Hari pulls his hand back and turns to her. "Sylvia was asking me about you and Adam on the way down. I didn't tell, though."

Alarm bells start ringing in her head. She plays dumb. "Tell what?"

Hari sighs. "We're still going to act like you guys weren't hooking up? Come on, Maggie. Nobody's that stupid."

She pretends to be entranced by the rain. The one thing she and Adam had always been in total agreement on was that Hari and Charles couldn't know about them. She'd thought they'd done a good job of hiding it from them, but evidently not. "He didn't tell you guys, did he?"

"Yeah, right." Hari is immediately dismissive. "Priya brought it up. I think it was after we had that million users party. Then I started paying more attention, and it was obvious."

"Why didn't either of you say anything?" She thought they would've confronted her or Adam about it. Unless they did, and Adam failed to mention it, but that wasn't his style. He wouldn't have kept something like that from her if it put Circle at risk.

"What were we supposed to do, barge in on you two and say 'gotcha'? Easier for everyone if we all just pretended it wasn't happening."

They'd started keeping secrets from one another so early. The cracks in the foundation forming before she really began paying attention. Even if Hari isn't mad about it anymore, he was definitely hurt about it back then. After all, this is the guy who got upset when Adam bought a pair of skinny jeans without consulting him.

This is why running OurSpot alone is better than bringing on any cofounders. There's nobody she needs to work hard to fool. "Don't worry, I'm keeping it clean this weekend," she assures him. "Nobody, especially me, wants to relive any of that mess."

Hari looks at her, his face uncharacteristically serious. He's grown up, Maggie thinks, with a jolt of sadness. "I know your heart's in the right place, but you're not the only one capable of disaster."

The doors slide open. Adam pokes his head out, a steak in his tongs that is on its way to resembling coal. "Let's eat!"

She and Hari put down place settings while Adam and Charles finish prepping the food. Priya and Jaya have returned from cleaning up her tooth, and Priya stacks pillows on a chair so Jaya has enough height to eat at the table with them. Jaya excitedly shows Charles and Adam the new hole in her mouth again.

"I've never been so glad to be vegetarian," Hari says, glancing at the blackened steak before reaching for the tofu.

"So," Sylvia says, "when did you guys all start turning on Margaret?"

Hari's hand freezes around his tongs. The tofu squishes between them.

Rain drums against the roof outside as Sylvia waits for their answer. Then, she supplements, "Because you all voted her out, but based on everything you've told me, things were going great. Where was the inflection point? Was it when you got funding?"

Maggie stares at Adam. This is his mess to get them out of.

Adam clears his throat. "Hard to pinpoint that. Here, eat. I don't cook for just anybody, you know." He thrusts the steak at Sylvia.

Sylvia's vestigial politeness kicks in, because she puts a piece of steak in her mouth. Chews and chews. Seems to realize she's made a gross miscalculation with the size she chose. She presses a napkin to her mouth.

"It's not that bad," Adam says. Then he eats a piece himself. "Oh, shit," he says, laughing, as he spits it into his napkin. "I don't remember the last time I tasted something this bad."

"I do," Charles says. "That offsite where you thought it was a good idea for us to catch and cook our own food, then the whole Marketing team got food poisoning."

The mood lightens considerably. The conversation veers away from Sylvia's show-stopping question and toward culinary disasters. It seems to bore Sylvia, who makes excuses ten minutes into the meal. Once she's gone, the guys stop chatting. The rain outside seems to lighten, too.

"I don't know if it was your plan to drive her off with your awful cooking, but it worked," Charles observes.

"Yeah, where's the real food?" Hari asks.

"This was supposed to be it," Adam replies, bemused.

"There's the basket you gave me," Maggie says, not wanting to sit through another misguided cooking attempt.

"What basket?" Hari asks, whipping his head around to Adam. "You've been holding out on us?"

"I got Maggie a welcome basket," Adam replies. "It's not a big deal."

Hari is outraged. "I've never gotten a *welcome basket*, and we've been friends for a decade!"

Charles is barely paying attention, his eyes on the surging waves outside. "It looks like a good day for a swim."

Adam and Hari settle down. "No way," Adam says sternly. "You're going to get fried."

"I don't hear thunder."

Adam folds his arms. "We'll all come, then. To keep an eye on you."

"Uh, not me," Hari says. "I'm going to go to my cozy cabin and doomscroll."

"No, you're not," Priya says. "Jaya needs to take a nap, and you're just going to keep her awake."

"It's settled then," Adam says. He goes into the kitchen and reappears with two bottles of wine. "We're going to watch Charlie-boy swim."

The water immediately soaks through Maggie's shoes when she steps onto the sand. There were only three umbrellas, so she's squeezed under one with Charles while Adam shares with Hari. Priya and Jaya already went back to their cabin with the third.

She knows Charles swims to clear his head and guesses that's why he wants to do it now, in this storm and after that grueling hike. She wonders what could be bothering him. Rain slides onto her right shoulder, soaking through her jacket, but she doesn't dare get closer to Charles under the umbrella. "Thanks for teaming up against Sylvia with me today." Today has shown her she's still terrible at interviews and that she needs to do better.

"Why didn't you say hi to Helen?" Charles asks out of nowhere. "At the Ranch 99," he clarifies, as if she doesn't know exactly what he's talking about.

She'd seen Charles's sister slapping melons a year ago, sporting a huge stomach. Her name had been on the tip of her tongue. She'd always liked Helen, who was a few years older and always knew exactly what to say to fluster Charles.

But Helen knew everything that had happened with the falling-out. She and Charles were close. Which meant Maggie was the enemy. Nobody wants baby felicitations from their enemy. "I thought she wouldn't want to talk to me."

"You hurt her feelings."

It takes her a moment; she's out of practice at reading Charles's expressions. The one on his face now is hurt. *He* is hurt that she did not say hello to his sister.

"How's her baby?" she asks.

"Healthy, but ruining her sleep. We share tips."

Maggie stops breathing. "You have a baby, too?"

He gives her an amused look. "Tips for *sleeping*."

"Really?" Charles could've gotten a PhD in sleeping. Not only could he fall asleep in any car, boat, or plane, but he also could sleep through alarms, loud parties, and once, a 6.2-magnitude earthquake.

He shrugs. "I guess I had a lot less going on in my head back then."

She wishes she could ask him what's on his mind, but they're all still trapped on this unbearably awkward hump of not knowing how to behave around each other. She decides for the both of them that they need to get over it. "Let's not be mad at each other this weekend. It's exhausting."

A soft laugh escapes Charles's lips, immediately unknotting the tension in her muscles. "I don't have a clue how to be mad at you, Tiny." They stop at the edge of the water, and Charles hands her the umbrella. At some point, he'd adjusted it so that it covered her instead, and half of his shirt is soaked. Maggie tries her best to cover them both while he shucks off his shoes. He looks up at her, amused. "I'm about to jump in the water. You don't need to shield me." He hands her his clothes. "Keep these dry for me?"

She takes them. They're still warm from the heat of his body. He turns toward the ocean, wading in. Doesn't make a peep even though she's certain it's freezing cold.

"Maggie, get over here!" Adam waves her to where he and Hari are huddled under their umbrella, handing the bottle of wine back and forth.

She clutches Charles's clothes to her stomach and joins them. Adam offers her the bottle. She brings it to her lips, taking a swig, then faces the water, searching for Charles. Spots his arms cutting through the waves, the quick flashes of his cheek as he breathes. It makes her feel better to keep watch over him, the same way she used to when he swam laps at the gym in college.

"You think he's still mad?" Hari asks Adam.

"He's *been* mad. You know he's not a fan of all the Circle Net stuff." A hint of frustration creeps into Adam's tone. Maggie pretends she's busy watching Charles swim, but their conversation pricks her ears.

It's only occurred to her now that when she left, she'd abandoned Charles. The two of them were responsible for the product side of the business. They'd functioned as a unit, together convincing Hari and Adam that certain investments or operations were necessary to help them effectively build, launch, and scale.

But Charles is fine without her. They all are. Aren't they?

She takes another big gulp of wine. There's a small itch starting behind her ears, a reaction to the alcohol. Turning to Hari and Adam, she asks, "Trouble in paradise?"

Adam shrugs, taking the bottle from her. "It's nothing new. Just Charles being his perfectionist self."

Charles's perfectionism was a precious thing. In the world of start-ups, where it was all about moving fast and breaking things, she'd admired his commitment to delivering something he 100 percent believed in. There was a purity to his design mindset, and she has a feeling that it's how Circle had managed to stay relevant, even now. Adam should be glad that Charles has held on to his values.

A flash of lightning suddenly streaks through the sky, followed by a *boom* seconds later. They all straighten, and Maggie immediately searches for Charles, out in the water.

"Charlie-boy!" Adam shouts, cupping his hands around his mouth. "Get out of there before you get crispy!"

Hari pats his stomach. "I'm still starving. Let's go to Maggie's cabin and eat the basket."

"You can't just invite yourself over," Maggie retorts.

"That's what you did all of junior year," Adam says.

"You said I was always welcome!"

Charles makes his way out of the water, hair sticking up from the salt. He holds his hands out to her, and it takes her a moment to realize he wants his clothes back. She thrusts them at him. This time, when they walk back, Maggie finds herself under an umbrella with Adam, while Charles and Hari share the other one. It's slow going. She has a buzz from the wine now, and it's making it hard to walk in a straight line.

In front of them, Charles drags Hari back before he goes plowing into a bush. "I think we're off-trail," he calls back to them.

Maggie looks down. At some point, they'd lost the dirt path, or maybe the storm had covered it with leaves. Mud clings to her sneakers and the hem of her pants.

"It does look that way," Adam says slowly.

"Isn't this *your* island?" Maggie asks. Her wet sleeves are cold against her arms. She has no idea how Charles doesn't have hypothermia, wearing his wet clothes after swimming in freezing water. Adam pulls her closer to him under the umbrella. He reaches an arm around, brushing rain off her shoulders.

"I have an idea." He hands her the umbrella to hold. "Tell me when to stop." Adam shuts his eyes, then spins in a circle with his finger pointing out. Maggie gapes at him, the rain landing in his hair and the mud coating his expensive shoes. With his eyes still closed, Adam says, "Hurry up, I'm getting dizzy."

She glances over at where Charles and Hari are under their umbrella, watching Adam with identical expressions of bafflement. "Stop."

Adam stops spinning, his finger still held up. "Okay. We're going that way."

"This is really not the time to be whimsical," Charles growls.

Adam smiles, and Maggie can't tell if he's drunk or just being himself. "Believe." He grabs Maggie's hand. His palm is warm, despite the weather. "Hold hands, everyone. So we don't lose anybody." He starts humming a Kelly Clarkson song as he waits.

Charles holds his hand out to Hari.

"*Charlie-boy*," Hari says in a seductive purr. "Are you trying to hold my hand?"

Charles makes like he's going to smack Hari in the face. Hari flinches, and Charles smirks, satisfied. He grabs Hari's hand and yanks him toward Adam and Maggie, before taking Maggie's hand, his skin a little damp from the rain. The four of them form a human chain, with Adam taking the lead. As the raindrops thud softly to the earth, Adam plots out what he claims is a straight path. At some point, he starts fully singing, and Maggie finds herself humming along. When the chorus comes, she hears Hari bawl, "Since u been gone!" in a horrendous off-key. Even Charles can't resist bobbing his head. When Adam flourishes a stick at her and demands she sing too, she does, the lyrics warped by her barely contained laughter.

At one point, Hari says, "Water break!" They all stop, and he passes around the wine bottle he's been clutching under his armpit. Everyone drinks, even Charles. The wine tastes sweet now, and Maggie finds that she's not so cold anymore.

They hold hands again, and against all odds, they make their way out of the forest, ending up on the beach. With the wine sloshing in her stomach and Kelly Clarkson lyrics ringing in her head, it feels like a miracle.

"See?" Adam says, smug. He squeezes her fingers. "When we're together, we can do anything."

When they finally reach the cabin, Maggie is so used to holding their hands that she almost forgets to let go.

Chapter Twenty

JANUARY 2006

Maggie and Priya stood in a corner of Hari's apartment, nursing the ass-flavored drinks Hari and Adam were mixing. Launching a company that was currently at nine hundred and seventy thousand users had not made Maggie any more comfortable in social environments.

She looked over at where Adam was pouring a guy a drink while keeping a conversation going with his other friends, laughing and smiling. She kept waiting for him to look in her direction. Give her an acknowledgment that even in a crowd, he would always find her.

"I don't know how they do it," Priya said. "Adam and Hari. You put them in any large gathering, and it's like attaching them to a circuit. We're just moths, trying to bathe in some of the glow."

Maggie didn't like the way Priya made it sound. She wasn't like her, hungering for morsels of a guy's attention. "I'm going to get another drink," she told her, then headed for Adam.

When he spotted her, his eyes lit up. He beckoned her close, smelling of liquor. "I need you, Maggie." His voice carried, and she saw some people glance their way.

Maybe this would be the moment they announced their relationship to everyone. She was caught between the desire to stop him and the urge to let the whole world know.

But Adam's thoughts were elsewhere. "We should project the countdown on that building." He pointed at the wall of a restaurant that was across the street, visible from Hari's large living room window. "Then everyone who walks by will see it. And I need *you* to use your big, beautiful brain to get us a projector."

"Where am I going to get a projector at this hour?"

Adam gave her an affectionate pat on the butt. "Take Charles. He looks like he's one chitchat away from combustion."

Charles was sitting on a corner of Hari's couch, bending over the coffee table, absorbed in some task. Someone roped Adam into another round of shots.

She contemplated sticking to Adam's side. But then she would have to talk to all these strangers that Adam and Hari had invited. If she had it her way, it would just be the four of them, a bottle of wine, and her laptop open on the floor, but Adam called the shots where social activities were concerned. She approached Charles. "Being a loner again?"

He fumbled with something in his hands and cursed as flecks spilled onto the coffee table. Her eyes snapped to the small container filled with something dry and green. The translucent paper held between his fingers. "Is that *weed*?"

"It's oregano," he said, deadpan, as he lifted a joint to his mouth, his tongue skimming along the edge of the paper.

Whatever she was going to say died in her throat as she watched him work his way down the joint, tucking it easily before using the drawstring of his hoodie to give it a good poke.

"How many times have you done this?" she asked, hearing the accusation in her voice.

"Not that many. I'm going outside. Want to come?"

"We have to get a projector. Adam's orders."

"Why do we need to follow them?"

Why *did* they? But then she thought about how disappointed Adam would be if they couldn't make his vision come true. He deserved this celebration. They all did. "Because. Will you help me or not?"

"Only if you smoke this with me. We can do it on the way to campus."

"Campus?" She caught on. "You want to steal a projector from one of the classrooms?"

"How else are we going to get a projector at this hour?" he repeated the question she'd just asked Adam.

"This seems like a bad idea. Especially if we're going to be . . . under the influence."

Charles lifted his eyebrows. "Tonight seems like a good night for bad ideas."

He was being playful, the Charles that he usually became late at night after too much caffeine. She'd seen less of this Charles, mainly because she'd been spending her nights with Adam.

Once they were outside, she let the cool night air wash over her. The moon was full overhead. She shivered, unused to the chilliness after the stuffy heat of the apartment. "Ugh, it was like the tropics in there."

Charles shrugged off his hoodie. "Here. It'll get cold soon." He dropped it around her shoulders, then put the joint in his mouth, cupping his hand around the tip as he lit it. Moonlight skimmed over his bare arms. He gave it a few puffs before handing it to her. "Breathe in and try to hold the smoke in your lungs before you breathe out." He demonstrated, and she nodded, following his movements closely.

"You're going to make sure nothing happens to me, right?" she asked, nervous. She had never smoked before.

Charles's lips up curved slightly, but he nodded solemnly. "I'll protect you."

She inhaled and smoke seared through her lungs. She burst into coughs.

Charles didn't laugh, just patted her on the back and handed her a bottle of water from his back pocket. "I coughed a lot my first time, too."

"When was that?"

"Summer break last year. My sister taught me." They started walking up Durant, toward Sather Gate. It was a Friday night, and they blended in with people on their way to house parties or headed home from the library.

"Isn't your sister a doctor?" she asked him.

"Yes, and I was a patient in need." Charles handed her back the joint, and this time, she managed to take a few puffs without coughing. "Actually, though, it helps calm me down."

"I've never seen you not calm. Wait," Maggie said. "Are you just high all the time?"

"I wish." The joint jutted out from his lips at an angle, making him look rakish.

They were behind the Valley Life Sciences Building now, the floodlights illuminating the base of its pillars. It had become cold, so Maggie shrugged his hoodie over her head. It smelled like the woods, with a hint of fresh fruit. Was this what Charles smelled like all the time? She hadn't noticed. She studied him as they walked, wondering what else about him she didn't know.

Charles spoke again. "I worry a lot, actually. Swimming helps. And smoking."

"What worries you?" She elbowed him gently. Her body felt looser, the inside of her mouth a little dry. "Not setting the curve for Data Structures?"

"Making the right choice," he said, passing her the joint again. His words came out slower, or maybe it was just her own brain's delayed processing. "I feel like, every time I've been given a choice, I always choose wrong."

She blinked slowly. Charles, who was so deliberate with design, who seemed so comfortable with who he was, had trouble making choices? "Give me an example."

"When I was ten, my parents let me choose our vacation destination. It was between Disneyland and the Grand Canyon."

"And you chose Disneyland?"

"No, I chose the Grand Canyon. My sister wanted Disneyland. We fought about it, and my parents sided with me." They were nearing Morgan Hall, and Charles brought her around the back of the building, away from the main entrance. "The weekend we went, a flash flood swept through the South Rim, and we had to evacuate. We were trapped in Tusayan for a week. Here." He'd found an open window about three feet above the ground and reached inside, jiggling it up farther. Inside, she could see the silhouette of chairs and a chalkboard. "Do you need a boost?"

She grabbed the ledge and tried to pull herself up, but she began sliding backwards, her arms too weak to get all the way.

Strong hands clamped around her waist, and she flew forward, her chest scraping against the ledge of the window. She scrabbled around and landed on the classroom floor. Charles followed, easily pulling himself up and through the window.

"Thanks," she muttered as she rose. She reached for the light switch, but Charles grabbed her elbow. A barely visible movement that she took for the shake of his head.

"I took a NutriSci lecture here," Charles says. "I remember it had a projector."

As they felt their way through the darkness, Maggie said, "I can't see shit. How are you doing this?"

"Here." A warm hand covered hers, navigating it until her fingers touched the cable connecting the projector to the power. The weed was heightening her sense of touch, and she turned her palm upward, relishing the roughness of his skin.

They unplugged the projector and Charles lifted it, carefully gathering the various cords on top so they wouldn't get tangled. Then he walked over to the window, tapping the joint, letting the ashes rain down to the dewy grass below, before passing it back to her. "We can probably leave through the door. We'll unlock it from inside."

Maggie pinched the joint and inhaled. There wasn't much left, and it was rougher against her lungs this time, sandpaper scraping against soft tissue.

"Can I tell you about my theory?" Charles asked as he took the stub from her, somehow managing to hit it without coughing. The weed seemed to have put him in a pensive mood. He paused by the window, studying the moon.

"Of course. You can tell me anything." She meant it. Gaining Charles's confidence felt like receiving something precious, especially when he wasn't as easy to talk to as Adam.

"Whatever I choose is cursed. I know it sounds irrational, but I can't help but think it's true."

"We're allowed our superstitions," Maggie said. "But, Charles, you *do* know how to choose. Look at all the choices you make, every day, for Circle. The font, the color theme, the interface, all the things that make users have a better experience. For any 'wrong' choice, you've made countless right ones."

Charles stubbed out the rest of the joint and stuck it back in a Ziploc. He faced Maggie and tucked it into the hoodie pocket. She blinked sleepily up at him. She didn't spend enough time looking at his face. When they were together, they were always focusing on a screen, never each other.

He looked at her for a long moment, then nodded and turned toward the door.

But she didn't want to leave yet, or for him to disappear into the darkness. She didn't want to go back to the party and try to talk to strangers. She wanted to be here, where it was comfortable.

"It's my turn to admit something," she said, drawing Charles's attention back to her. She thought she heard him take a breath.

"What?"

"I have no idea how we got to one million. Obviously, we made decisions to get here, right? You decided that Circle's color theme should be purple instead of blue. I wanted everyone to provide their real identities when they signed on. But most of these decisions weren't based on data. They were based on gut." Maggie chuckled, feeling like she was shedding a burden that she'd carried for a long time. "Isn't that scary? I don't even know how to unclog a toilet, yet here I am, making decisions that affect a million people."

Charles tipped his head toward her. The light from the moon sliced over his cheekbone, reflecting off his glasses. "Sounds like your gut knows what it's doing."

"And *you* should know that it's better to make wrong choices than sit around and let the world decide for you."

Her phone rang.

"Where are you?" Adam yelled over the noise of the party. "We're at nine hundred eighty! Get back here!"

"Coming, coming." She shoved her phone into her pocket. "Guess it's time to get out of here."

The two of them left the classroom, Maggie carefully holding the projector with two hands, Charles's hoodie lying on top. Like thieves, they tiptoed down the hall. She tensed as he pushed against the building's front door, but it opened, and no alarm went off.

Campus looked like a scene from a black-and-white movie as she and Charles walk-jogged toward Sather Gate. Weed aside, she felt lighter after talking to him. There was solidarity in knowing she wasn't the only one feeling around in the dark and hoping to land in the right place.

"You guys took forever," Adam said, when they got back to Hari's place. Charles began to set up the projector on the kitchen counter.

"It wasn't thaaat long," she said.

Adam pulled her in by the waist and looked straight into her eyes. She reached out and booped his nose.

"Dude, did you get her high?" She didn't hear Charles's response, but Adam laughed, burrowing his face in her hair as he hugged her. He smelled like liquor and cherry syrup, and she realized that he was very drunk. "My little stoner!"

The counter came to life against the neighboring building. They were already at nine hundred and ninety thousand. She could barely keep up with how fast the numbers were changing, but suddenly it was at nine hundred and ninety-five, and everyone was facing the wall, chanting the numbers. Someone outside screamed at them to shut up, but they were ignored.

One million came onto the screen and she heard popping noises. Sparkly paper rained down on them.

"Yes! Yes!" Adam was shouting at the top of his lungs, hugging everyone in proximity.

Hari was kissing Priya like it was New Year's Eve.

Adam grabbed Maggie and lifted her, spinning her in a circle before setting her down. "We did it!" he said, and then he dipped his head and kissed her, very quickly, on the cheek.

She searched the room and found Charles back on the couch. Their eyes met, but when she smiled at him, he didn't smile back.

Chapter Twenty-One

MARCH 2006

Maggie woke to the stickiness of oil and skin beneath her nails. The spot on her neck beneath her ear was burning. Her eczema had been worsening lately, with the all-nighters she was pulling to work on Circle and the fact that she hadn't washed her sheets in over a month. She glanced at the clock and then flew to her feet. She'd only intended to take a tiny nap. She and the guys had been up late, discussing Circle's expansion. Adam had finally convinced her to let nonstudents access the platform. They needed more headcount, more engineers to help them get work done. But for that to happen, they needed money.

Luckily enough, Adam's parents were visiting that weekend and wanted to take them all out to dinner. Maggie hoped that if they were sufficiently impressed, they would give Circle another much-needed cash infusion. She was also nervous because these were Adam's parents, and she was dating their son. She wanted them to like her, even if they couldn't know the true nature of their relationship. And now she was running late.

She cleaned herself up as best as she could, throwing on a sweater and jeans, before racing downstairs. There was a black town car idling at the curb, and as she walked out toward it, the passenger door opened and Adam got out, wearing a suit and tie. She stopped in her tracks, wanting to run back inside. But Adam smiled at her, pulling open the back door. "This way, m'lady."

She got into the car, squeezing in next to Charles, who was wearing a button-up, but no tie.

The man in the driver's seat turned around. He was handsome, with salt-and-pepper hair and the same smile as his son's. "So you're the girl genius!" he said. "It's an absolute honor to meet you."

They drove to Chez Panisse, a restaurant Maggie thought she'd never step foot in, where a meal cost the same as her rent. Adam's mom was already waiting there. She was blonde and dressed in all white, looking like she belonged at a country club.

As they sat around a table in the center of the wood-paneled restaurant, their wrists propped politely on the white tablecloth, Adam's father peppered her with questions. He had already done the same with Hari and Charles, asking about their upbringings and parents with genuine interest, marveling at how brave Hari was to come to school in the US while the rest of his family was in India, and complimenting Charles on his design portfolio, which he'd somehow managed to find online.

He had the same respect for Maggie. "Barely twenty, and you're already CEO of a company. See?" he said to Adam. "Margaret is the real meaning of self-made. She's an inspiration. I hope you're proud of yourself, young lady."

"Your parents raised you well," Mrs. Fink agreed in her soft voice.

The Finks were so nice. She wished Mr. Fink was her dad. Someone who could say *I'm proud of you* the same way you asked for a glass of water at a restaurant. Like it didn't cost him anything.

"Thanks, Mr. Fink. It's a team effort," she said, feeling a little warm from the wine. Adam had picked it with care, sampled it with concentration.

"How has it been, working with Adam?" Mr. Fink asked. "He never liked to share when he was little. I guess that comes with being an only child. You spoiled him, didn't you?" he asked Mrs. Fink. She lowered her eyes and sipped from her wine.

"I love working with Adam," Maggie replied honestly. Across the table, Adam stopped fiddling with his glass and looked at her. "He makes me feel like I can do anything."

Mr. Fink laughed, thumping the table. Her wine vibrated in her glass. "Just don't end up doing all the work for him!" Next to him, Mrs. Fink laid her hand on Adam's. Maggie noticed it was clenched into a fist. He slid it from her grasp.

After dinner, Adam's dad dropped them off at the apartment. Maggie went into her bathroom, where she peeled off her clothing and examined the red splotches on her neck. She was still hungry, but the night was a success. Adam's dad seemed to like her. Hopefully that translated into a check.

"Hey, your fuck-buddy's here again!" her roommate shouted, startling Maggie. The door slammed shut, probably her roommate going out for the night. Adam was supposed to have gone back with his parents to their hotel.

Maggie slicked Aquaphor over the redness, hoping it would be sufficient, then rushed out of the bathroom.

Adam sat on her bed, doing nothing. He was always doing *something*. Scrolling Circle, typing out an email, or texting someone. That was how Maggie knew something was wrong. Immediately, she wondered if she'd read tonight all wrong, and his dad had actually decided against giving them any more money. "Hey," she said gently, sitting next to him. "What's up?"

He clenched her blankets in his fists. "He pisses me off so much," he muttered.

"Who? Your dad?"

Adam slowly nodded. "All that shit he said during dinner. He was rubbing it in my face, the fact that I always run to him for help."

Maggie hadn't realized that was what Mr. Fink was doing. She'd thought he was simply being curious about their lives, but really, he'd been drawing comparisons between them and Adam.

"I couldn't do it, Maggie," he said, turning to her. It was the first time she had ever seen sorrow in his eyes. "I couldn't ask him for more money."

She took his hand. "Then don't. We'll figure something else out."

Adam squeezed her fingers. His mood seemed improved. "Have you thought about what you're doing this summer?"

She shook her head. She'd been taking everything day by day. There was so much to do. Classes to pass, expanding Circle at the pace Adam wanted, alone time with Adam when they could find it. Somewhere between it all, she knew she was supposed to obtain a summer internship. But if she thought too much about her future, she grew overwhelmed by how big it was. Everything that existed outside the constraints of this campus felt ambiguous and daunting. "Have you?"

"I'm going to stay here and work on Circle. I'll meet with investors and get us funding," Adam said, his expression tight. He didn't even seem to be in the room with her anymore, already dwelling somewhere in the future where the solutions for his current problems existed. "I don't need my dad's money. This company is going to succeed without him."

She could see then how seriously Adam was taking Circle. The sense of ownership he felt over the company that she seemed to be lacking. There were other competitors popping up, breathing down their necks, waiting for a misstep. It felt like they were at a pivotal moment, and if they screwed it up, that would be it for them. Circle would be forgotten, just like all the other social media companies that had flared bright before turning into ash. But Adam didn't just want Circle to survive. He wanted it to flourish. If she didn't want him to leave her behind, she would have to join him in this mission.

Chapter Twenty-Two

DAY 2: FRIDAY

Back in the cabin, Charles hops into the shower. Hari wobbles a bit on his feet before he finally collapses on the sofa in the living room. "Pretty waves," he says, before dozing off. In minutes, loud snoring rises from the couch.

Maggie can feel the wine too, as she stands in the hallway. But instead of drowsiness, her thoughts dart like fish. Holding hands with everyone earlier, making their way out of the forest, the sense of victory she'd gotten when they emerged unscathed—it's muddling her emotions. She is supposed to have her guard up around these guys. She tells herself that severely, then nearly falls over as she takes off her shoes.

"We still have a bit left," Adam says, shaking the bottle in front of her when she joins him in the living room. "Should we finish it?"

"I shouldn't," she says. But she finds herself sitting beside him on the carpet while Hari dozes above them.

Adam rolls the bottle between his palms contemplatively. "What if we turn it into a game? Loser finishes the rest of the bottle. Unless . . . you're afraid to lose."

He knows the exact flavor of taunt to make her participate. She sits down, cross-legged. "What game are we playing?"

Adam arranges himself across from her, putting the bottle in their midst. "How about . . . we take turns guessing whether the other person is telling a lie, or the truth. Whoever's wrong first drinks the rest of this bottle."

The bathroom door opens, steam puffing out.

"Charlie-boy!" Adam calls. "Maggie and I are playing for the last bit of wine. Join us?"

Charles stops by the kitchen first before returning with three tangerines held in his hand. He comes and sits, leaning against the couch Hari's on. For good measure, he pokes Hari in the side, but he doesn't stir. Shrugging, he turns back toward them. "Who's going first?"

"I'll go. We can go clockwise." Adam faces Maggie, his face composed. "There was one year that I woke up at five a.m. every day."

"Lie," Maggie immediately says.

Adam laughs. "What the hell, Maggie? Why did you respond so quickly?"

"You're dead to the world before eight a.m. But you wake up as the Energizer Bunny."

"He refused a meeting with the president once because it was before eight," Charles says casually. Maggie's jaw unhinges. The president should be worthy of an exception, but it seems that all of Adam's power has allowed him to bend the world to his schedule.

"It wouldn't have been productive otherwise. I was doing him a favor." Adam shakes his head ruefully. "Okay, you've escaped drinking this time. Your turn. Tell your truth—or lie—to Charles."

Maggie turns to Charles. He peels a tangerine, not looking at her. "I haven't smoked weed since college."

This makes him look up. Their gazes collide. He sticks a slice of tangerine in his mouth, eats it, then says, "Truth."

She gives a nod. Charles stares at her until Adam has to nudge him with a foot. "This wine isn't going to drink itself, Charlie-boy."

Charles pushes Adam's foot away. Then, he says, "I wasn't going to come."

The quiet is only punctuated by Hari's heavy breathing. Adam leans toward Charles, so close that they're almost nose-to-nose. Maggie watches them, breath suspended. His comment hints at some unspoken tension. He hadn't known that she was invited, so what reason was there for him not to show?

Adam pulls away and announces, "Lie!"

Charles's mouth is flat, but he nods. Adam gives him a friendly pat on the chest before stealing one of his tangerine slices. "I know you'd never pass up a chance to spend time with us, Charlie-boy." He rubs his hands together, facing Maggie. His competitiveness is beginning to show itself. He's eager for this game to have a loser. "I kept the Feels Chair."

He's made it too easy. "Lie," she says. There's no way that chair is still around. It was beyond saving.

Adam hops up, pointing at the bottle, gleeful. "You lose!"

The sudden movement makes Hari bolt up from the couch. "Huh? What'd I miss?" he asks. But Maggie is in a state of shock. Adam had really kept that old bacteria-ridden chair? She used to think Adam was careless with things and people. He would lose belongings into the mess of his room, and there were times he'd fail to show for things, even after she reminded him. And yet she thinks of how tightly he's held on to Circle for the past few years. How he never let her secret slip and orchestrated this trip so that they'd all be here. She's underestimated him.

Maggie reaches for the bottle, but Charles grabs it first. "You don't have to," he says.

She tugs it from his grip and drinks.

Chapter Twenty-Three

APRIL 2006

It took a few weeks to gather her courage and script out the talking points she would use with her dad. The day she planned to call him, she woke up at dawn, scratching at her neck. Her roommate was still sleeping, so she left the apartment to make the call. Her dad picked up on the first ring. He liked to get up early so he could brew fresh tea, pouring it into a thermos that he brought to work.

"Margaret, has something happened?"

"Hi, Dad." She focused on the script she'd memorized. "I wanted to talk to you about my summer plans."

A note of interest entered her dad's voice. "Did you get an internship?"

Her stomach turned over, and she pushed the words out before she could lose her confidence. "I'm going to work on my company."

"You have a company?" her dad asked slowly.

"Yes, it's called Circle, and we're now available in schools all over the world. You can check out the website if you don't believe me. Anyway, I won't be moving out of my off-campus housing. Do you think you could lend me some money for rent? We're planning on fundraising, so once we do that I'll pay you back."

There was such a long silence she thought he'd hung up. "Dad?"

"You are going to spend your final summer before graduation working on your hobby?" The way he said *hobby* made it sound like a dirty word.

"This is more than a hobby. There are over a million people using Circle." She emphasized *million*, as if that word would trigger something in his brain that would convince him she was doing something worthwhile, even if it wasn't paying her anything yet. She tried to channel Adam's certainty. "Soon the whole world will be on it."

"I didn't pay your tuition for you to waste your time like this."

"It's not a waste of time!" Bill Gates had dropped out of Harvard. Steve Jobs had only stayed in college one semester. She had sat in these courses that were supposed to make Berkeley one of the best universities in the world, and the reality was that they were taught by stuffy professors who knew more about scientific papers than real-life applications. She'd learned more from working side by side with Charles and brainstorming with Adam and Hari. School didn't make you smart—it was the people you chose to surround yourself with that mattered.

If she took one of these software engineering internships her dad cared so much about, she'd just be another computer monkey, someone whose job was to test whether blue buttons or red buttons made people click more. After creating something from nothing, she knew she would never be content with that.

"How can a child run a company?" her dad asked in disbelief.

Anger licked through her, and she scratched furiously at her wrist. "I'm *not* a child," she said. "I know what I'm doing."

"You have *no* idea what you're doing!" her dad exclaimed. "Let's say you try to run this company. You will go in front of people with Harvard MBAs, and all they will see is a little girl who doesn't know anything."

She moved the phone a few inches from her ear, keeping her mouth shut. This happened every time her dad yelled at her. She'd go numb, just waiting for the storm to pass. Later on, she would replay this conversation and think of the perfect comebacks.

"Do you know how much it costs me to be here?" her dad asked. "When your mother returned to China, I could have gone back with her. But I stayed because I knew you would have better opportunities here."

She hadn't known they'd stayed because of her. She assumed he'd chosen America because *his* life would be better here than in China. If he'd returned, would he have more friends, spend less time at home? Shame slammed through her. She'd deprived him of potential happiness.

"How do you expect anyone to respect you when you have so little experience?"

She leaned against the wall outside her apartment, tipping her head up and staring at the ceiling, heat building behind her eyes. Her resolve faltered. She was seconds from apologizing and saying that she would do as he said and look for an internship.

No. She had to forge ahead. Because on the other side of this conversation was Adam, Circle, and a future that they were going to build together. "I'm going to do this, even if you won't help me."

Her dad was silent. Then, he said, "I give you money because I want you to further your education. I will not pay for you to chase an irresponsible dream." With that, he hung up.

She went back inside. Her roommate was brushing her hair on top of her bed. She glanced over at her. "Were you breaking up with that guy down the hall?"

"No," Maggie mumbled, climbing back into her bed. Her head was throbbing now, and her wrist was an angry red. The conversation had somehow gone even worse than she'd imagined.

"Humph. Well, you always have his friend as a backup."

Maggie didn't have the energy to respond. She pulled the covers over her head and finally let tears loose. Was her dad right that this was all some ridiculous pipedream? Being around Adam warped her sense of reality—he made everything seem possible. But her dad's speech had reminded her that she was not qualified to run a company that millions of people used. There were other more experienced, more educated people out there, like the investors Adam was pitching, who would surely see that they were propping up their grand vision of Circle with sticks and duct tape.

She spent the rest of the day alternating between napping and crying. When she finally came out of the blankets to use the bathroom, the mirror showed that her eczema had gotten worse. There were red patches all over her face.

In the late afternoon, someone banged on her door. She jolted out of the blankets, suddenly remembering they were supposed to go to San Francisco today. There was a design fair Charles wanted to visit. Maybe if she pretended she wasn't home, they'd leave.

"Hey! Hey!" Hari's voice came from the other side of the door after a few minutes of pounding. "Your roommate said you've been, and I quote, 'crying like a freak' the whole day."

"Hari, don't announce it for the whole hall to hear," Adam scolded him.

There was a gentler tap on the door. "Maggie, please let us in," Charles said.

"Maggie!" Hari banged on the door again.

"There's nobody here!" she yelled back. Couldn't they take a hint?

"Oh, nobody can speak," Hari said. "Okay, guys, break down the door on the count of three?"

She threw off the covers. If they broke down the door, that would come out of *her* deposit. And now that her dad had abandoned her financially, she really couldn't afford any extra expenses.

"One!" Hari shouted. "Two!"

She sprinted for the door and yanked it open. Adam and Charles stood there holding the Feels Chair over their heads like they had planned to throw it at the door.

Hari stared at her, openmouthed. "Whoa, what happened?"

"Hari, learn how to filter," Charles said, starting forward before Maggie could shut the door on them.

Adam had a concerned look on his face. She'd told him about her plans to call her dad this morning, and promised to update him right after, optimistically assuming all would go according to plan and he would immediately transfer money into her account. She was a moron.

"Sheets, shower, Aquaphor," Charles announced, pushing her into the Feels Chair. She drew her knees up, putting her face behind her hands.

"I'm out of Aquaphor," she said.

"I'll get it," Adam said, jumping into action.

"I'll do the sheets," Hari volunteered.

"I'll get the water started," Charles said, leaving for the bathroom.

She sat on the chair, watching through the cracks in her fingers as Hari grunted and fought the sheets on her bed. From the bathroom, water started rushing.

"It doesn't look that bad, you know," Hari said. "Your eczema. I don't get the deal with girls. Priya complains to me every few days that she looks fat just because she ate some extra chocolate at dinner. Then I say she's always hot and she gets mad at me for not agreeing with her."

"Water's ready," Charles said, coming out of the bathroom. "I got you a fresh towel."

"Thanks," Maggie mumbled, darting past him. She took her time in there, letting the lukewarm water soothe her irritated skin. As she was toweling off, she heard Charles saying, "It's Aquaphor, not Aveeno."

"Isn't it the same?" Adam's voice came through.

"No, it's not the fucking same. Shouldn't you know this?" It was rare to hear Charles that annoyed. "I'll go buy it. I know what it looks like."

When she emerged from the bathroom, Hari had shuttled the sheets to the downstairs laundry room and Adam was sitting on their tiny love seat, looking chastened.

Hari pointed at the Feels Chair, placed opposite the love seat. "Talk." Priya's bossiness seemed to be rubbing off on him.

Slowly, Maggie made her way over to the chair. Felt the cushion give underneath her and gripped the armrests for comfort.

Adam's phone started ringing. He flipped it open, started rising. "It's my mom—"

"No distractions, Maggie's in the Feels Chair!" Hari slapped the phone out of Adam's hands.

"Dude!"

The door opened again, and Charles came through with a fresh bottle of Aquaphor, which he placed on the ground next to Maggie's feet before he shoved Adam down and took a seat beside him. She was aware that the three of them were here for her, and how troublesome she was for needing their care.

"Both of you shut up," Charles said to Adam and Hari. "I could hear your caterwauling from outside."

Adam picked up his fallen phone and returned it to his pocket before turning to Maggie. His blue eyes were knowing. "This isn't just about your eczema, is it?"

Maggie tried to sort through how much to share. Her dad's words weighed heavily on her, but she didn't want to infect the others with doubt.

"I told my dad I was going to work on the company full-time over the summer, and he didn't react well."

Adam sighed. He lifted his hand, and she wondered for a split second if he would touch her in front of Charles and Hari. But he rested it again on his knee. "It's okay, my dad was also not happy about it. He's been communicating with me through my mom."

"Wait, when did you agree on this?" Hari asked, looking between the two of them, brows furrowed. "The two of you are going full-time?"

Maggie froze. It was hard sometimes to remember what she and Adam had talked about in the privacy of her room, and what they'd discussed as a group. But it was out there now.

"This is a good time to talk about our summer plans," Adam said smoothly. "Maggie and I will be all-in on Circle. We don't want to lose out to competitors, so we need to expand as quickly as possible."

Maggie nodded, even though she wasn't sure she agreed that "as quickly as possible" was the right way to approach it.

Hari rubbed the back of his neck. "You know I have that internship with Goldman—"

"That's fine," Maggie said. She didn't want to mess with Hari's summer. He'd live with Priya, who was working at a venture capital fund in San Francisco, kill it at Goldman, then get a full-time offer that would help him stay in the country. And then maybe he could come to Circle once they figured out how to sponsor him.

"Charles?" Maggie asked, and she tried not to let on how nervous she was about his answer. Ever since they'd gotten high together, she'd felt a new camaraderie with him. Like their shared doubts had united them. She wished they weren't having this conversation now, so she could've had more time to come up with a convincing case for him to stay.

Charles rubbed a hand over the arm of her couch, his eyes on the floor. "I got an internship at Google," he said quietly. "I'm going to be in Mountain View this summer, with corporate housing. I'll still work on Circle, but I can't do it full-time."

"Congrats!" Adam was high-fiving him. "Why didn't you tell us sooner? That's huge."

Maggie scratched at her neck, before remembering her eczema. She lowered her hand, feeling the burning of her skin and her disappointment.

"Thanks," Charles murmured. He was looking at Maggie now, measuring her reaction.

She had known this was a possibility. Charles, who was smart and qualified and levelheaded, would have no shortage of opportunities. But a part of her had believed their partnership was special enough that he'd do anything for it.

At least she had Adam. They'd be able to focus solely on Circle and its growth. They'd do everything within their power to use their time wisely, and scale it into something even her dad would have no choice but to respect.

"I guess it's just us then," Adam said. He held out a fist for her to bump. "We've got this, Maggie. We'll make 'em proud."

Chapter Twenty-Four

DAY 2: FRIDAY

The knock sounds just as Maggie is laughing at Hari's attempt to deepthroat a banana. They have started unpacking the snack basket in the kitchen, and Hari insists on opening and tasting every single thing they take out. Maggie is lightheaded from that last pull of wine, and the lights whirl around her like stars. Adam's, Hari's, and Charles's faces are so dear to her, the sounds of their laughter an old track she keeps revisiting. She has all but forgotten their game, sinking instead into the cozy embrace of that last gulp of wine.

At the knock, they all freeze. Adam pads toward the door, peering through the peephole. He spins around, eyes wide. "Sylvia."

"What do you think she wants?" Maggie whispers, not very quietly.

"To talk to us, probably," Charles says dryly. He points at Hari, who's starting to choke on the banana. "You better eat that." Then he nudges Adam aside and pulls open the door.

Sylvia comes inside, wrapped in a thick robe, the strap of her swimsuit visible underneath. "I was going to pop into the sauna. Anybody want to come with?"

Hari is still working on his banana. Maggie waits for Adam to volunteer, but he actually looks a little ill, like he's regretting opening the second bottle of wine currently on the counter. Charles is probably the only one who's close to sober.

Sylvia's looking at her, though. "Margaret, how about it?"

This is a good opportunity to talk to Sylvia alone. If she doesn't let Sylvia boss her around with her questions, she might be able to talk about OurSpot. She feels extra bold from the wine. "Sure. Give me a second to change."

When she comes back out of the bedroom, a towel wrapped around her, Adam seems slightly more alert. There's a half-empty glass of water in front of him. Sylvia is leaning against the counter, vaping.

"Is that all you're bringing? You should wear the robe!" Adam pulls open one of the closets and extracts a fluffy white robe like Sylvia's, with *AF* embroidered onto the pocket. Maggie reaches for it, but he leans close to drape it over her. "Remember the plan," he whispers.

"Tiny." Charles holds a full glass of water toward her. "Drink this first."

She downs the glass and slams it on the counter. "Let's go," she tells Sylvia.

The sauna is the building that seemed to float in the middle of the ocean. As she approaches, she sees that the side walls are made of glass, but the wall directly facing the beach is pale wood. A series of small, rounded stepping stones lead to it from the shore.

Maggie considers the stepping stones with dread. They look slippery, and her balance isn't good even when her brain isn't so sluggish.

Sylvia gracefully dances across them. It looks easy, so Maggie tries to follow her movements. Immediately, she falls off the rock, her feet landing in the water.

She squeals at the cold. It feels like needles driving into her flesh, which helps clear up some of the fog in her brain. Sylvia has stopped five stones away, waiting for her. "Coming?" she calls.

"Coming!" she calls back through gritted teeth, as she curses Adam in her head for being fancy instead of building an actual path. She gets back on the stone and very carefully picks her way across the rest, keeping her eye on only the rock immediately ahead of her until she finds herself in front of the wooden dock.

She sighs in relief, stepping onto the smooth wood. Sylvia is already inside, and when Maggie opens the glass door, heat rushes over her. She drops her robe outside and climbs onto one of the benches. Nearby, a small furnace glows red. The rain has taken its gloomy gray shroud with it, and she can now see the mountains in the distance, disappearing into a thick coat of clouds.

"So," Sylvia says, and Maggie tenses, ready for the interrogation to begin. "Adam is a really bad cook, huh? I think pieces of that steak are still stuck in my throat."

"He hasn't changed in that respect," Maggie replies. It's nice to know there are some things Adam will always be bad at, no matter how hard he applies himself. In many ways, he's still the friend she had in college. Boyishly charming, spontaneous.

She glances over at where Sylvia is stretched out on her bench. It's hard to see her as a cutthroat journalist who makes tech bros perspire when she looks so relaxed. She finds herself curious about what Sylvia has observed so far. If she's caught onto the fact that they actually haven't spoken in years. "So, did you gather some good insights for your article?"

"You're not trying to probe me, are you?" Sylvia asks playfully. "I know what Adam's doing, by the way."

Her muscles tighten. "Do you?" She keeps her tone casual.

"He gave me this article because he thinks I'll throw him a bone. He thinks that I, along with all these other journalists he's 'partnered' with, will be so grateful for the opportunity to get access to Circle's billions of users, that we'll be nicer to him. Adam Fink might be one of the most powerful men in the world, but deep down, he still wants people to like him."

"Do you like him?" Everyone liked Adam in college. But maybe it's precisely because he's used to being liked that he doesn't know what to do when he's lost favor.

Sylvia gives her a close-lipped smile. "Not enough information to decide. I've got to say, following you today has been insightful. Usually, I'm observing the three of them in conference talks, news interviews, official stuff. Here, they seem looser. More . . . jokey. Maybe you bring out that side of them."

"What did you think they were like?" The way they were today is how she's always known them. She can barely imagine the three of them as Sylvia describes, though she thinks she caught a glimpse this morning. Professional, cool, weighing every word.

"Honestly? When we consider all the missteps Circle has made—their poor privacy policy, the predatory advertising, the insularity of the algorithm—the word that comes to mind is *soulless*."

"That can't be true," Maggie says. Their original desire was to connect people. By definition, that can't be soulless. "We created this company in the first place to help people."

Sylvia laughs. "Sometimes, Margaret, the things you say make me wonder if you even know these guys."

"You're the one who doesn't know them." She doesn't know why she's suddenly gotten defensive, but she finds herself extracting the memories she's hidden away all these years. The golden ones that had been some of the happiest of her life. "When Hari was super nervous for his driving test, we all skipped class so we could go with him to the DMV. Charles waited several hours in the rain outside GameStop the day the Wii came out because we wanted one for the apartment. One year, they got me three cakes for my birthday because I'd never had a birthday cake before. People like that are not *soulless*."

The wood creaks. Sylvia has sat up and is looking at her with impatience, and something like pity. "I get it, Margaret. You all looked out for each other, once. That's all in the past, though, isn't it?"

Is it? Have they all changed that much? Maggie curls her arms around her knees. Fine. If Sylvia doesn't want to hear about the past, she won't waste her precious memories on her.

Sylvia ladles water over the rocks. An angry hiss, then a wave of heat rises in the sauna. "I did want to ask you about Hank Wagner."

Hearing Hank Wagner's name is a bucket of ice water down her back. "What about him?" she asks carefully.

"Hank was involved in voting you out, wasn't he?" Sylvia waits for Maggie to give a single, stiff nod. "How have you dealt with how close he is with Adam now?"

Hank and Adam, still close? She shouldn't be surprised. She's not sure how much Sylvia knows about the relationship between her and Hank, but she doubts it's a good idea to insult him.

"Our philosophies might not align, but that's irrelevant. Adam can be friends with whoever he wants."

"*Friend* is putting it lightly. He's basically a father figure, especially after Adam's dad passed," Sylvia says.

"Mr. Fink passed?" Maggie asks, shocked. He'd been their first investor, technically. She thinks back to the awkwardness when she'd brought him up at breakfast, Adam's strange reaction when she'd asked about his dad.

Sylvia's looking at her oddly. "Did you not know?"

"Sorry, I, um, wasn't thinking. Sometimes it still feels like he's here." It's not a very convincing answer, but she's still stuck on the news that Adam's dad is gone. Adam must have been torn up, no matter how difficult their relationship was. She and Adam used to be the only two people who understood what it was like to hate someone yet desperately want their approval at the same time. Suddenly, she wants to call her own dad.

Sylvia's still studying her, as if she can see right through her.

"Even after today, I'm surprised you forgave them. That you let things go back to normal."

She doesn't like the how the question implies that she's weak. Almost wants to dispense with this whole scheme and admit that she has not remained friends with them, exactly because of everything they did.

But it's too late, now that Maggie is in on Adam's plan. Admitting their ruse to Sylvia now will only guarantee an implosion of her already raggedy reputation. Maggie wipes her hand against her forehead. "You have to move on at some point."

Sylvia arches an eyebrow. "Nothing wrong with a nice, strong grudge. It's fortifying, I find."

Now Maggie understands why Sylvia invited her to the sauna, isolating her from the flock. She wants to pry into her emotions around the ousting, unearth evidence of bitterness or vengeance. The Maggie of eight years ago would've gladly gotten into it with her, airing a laundry list of grievances. But she's tired of being characterized by who she was in college, and that goddamn GIF that experiences a resurgence every year. If she wants the world to see that she's grown up, she needs to acknowledge what happened and show that she's let it go.

She steers her thoughts toward their jaunt through the forest, Charles's and Adam's hands in hers. How opening her snack basket with them felt like pulling off the dust covers on antique furniture. Letting something old and precious finally breathe. "The best friends you had when were younger—aren't they still important to you, even if your lives have taken you in different directions?"

Sylvia seems intrigued by her question. She takes her time to answer. "I think you're allowed to outgrow the people who once might have been everything to you."

It's a complicated statement, one that Maggie can't fully figure out, with her mouth dry and her head beginning to throb. She gets up, descending the benches. "This heat's getting to me. I'm going to head back to the cabin."

"Margaret?"

One hand on the warm wood of the door, she turns to look at Sylvia.

"If you're going to report on our conversation to Adam, you can let him know that I'm going to write this article the way *I* want to. And he'll just have to wait and see." Sylvia sends her a sharp little smile.

Out in the chilly air, Maggie feels like her lungs are working again. She stands there for a while, gripping the sides of her robe. She has just begun to convince herself that some vestige of their friendship still remains, but Sylvia's comments have stirred up another cyclone of doubt.

She turns toward the cabin. Toward Charles, Hari, and Adam. Despite what Sylvia has said, being with them still feels safe. Time falls away and their old ways of speaking rise up like a forgotten second language.

Away from everyone, she lets herself admit it: she wants a circle to belong to again.

Chapter Twenty-Five

JUNE 2006

"Happy birthday!" Adam jumped onto the bed while Maggie was still waking up, nuzzling her neck. This was the problem with living with Adam. He woke up ready for the day while she needed at least an hour to stomp around like a zombie, which was why she'd decided it was better for them both if she just slept in Charles's room rather than sharing a bed with him. "You ready for that meeting with Hank?"

"Hold on," she said groggily, shoving him off her. "Let me wake up first."

"You're giving me sixty-year-old energy, not twenty-one," Adam complained as Maggie pulled Charles's covers over her head. She and Adam had been up late last night prepping their presentation for an investor meeting, so she hadn't dwelled on the fact that today was her birthday. Besides, birthdays in the Tang household were uneventful. Her dad would wish her happy birthday in the morning and give her a practical type of gift: a box of number 2 pencils even though she'd only ever used them on the SATs, an umbrella, a reading lamp.

As she and Adam rode the BART to San Francisco, she checked her texts. There were *happy birthdays* from Hari and Charles, even Priya. One from her dad. She didn't reply. He'd remained true to his word, not depositing any more money into her checking account. She knew tuition for fall semester was due soon but had no idea whether he planned to pay it or not, and she didn't want to be the first one to break the silence between them by asking.

Adam was nervous, alternating between flipping through his notes and glancing around the train. She put a hand on his knee, just so he'd stop jiggling it up and down. "What's gotten into you?"

"Just nervous. This is the first VC I've convinced to meet with us."

"There'll be others," she said. She could tell the rejections were beginning to wear on Adam. He coped by doubling down: sending cold emails, making calls, adding people to his precious spreadsheet. The summer had been even more intense than she'd expected. They were both so buried in Circle that even when they were together, it was all they talked about.

Hari had only visited once so far, with Priya. Charles had driven up the first two weekends, but then started having more weekend intern outings and stopped coming. They'd done a weird dance where Maggie tried to offer him his bed back, and he would refuse, either driving back the same day or taking the couch.

She and Adam got out at Montgomery station and walked down a narrow street with sagging fences. Trash littered the sidewalk.

"You sure this is the right address?" she asked Adam. She clutched her laptop tightly to her side as Adam matched the address to the building in front of them. There were silhouettes of women on the giant marquee, which also had the words *The Gold Club*.

A black car slid to the curb, and a balding man in a dark green quarter zip and tan pants emerged. He strode over. "You two must be from Circle."

"Hank," Adam said, and his voice sounded deeper. She was totally going to give him shit for this later.

"Adam, good to finally meet the man behind the emails." They shook hands, and Hank looked at her with a bit of confusion. "Who's this?"

"I'm Maggie," she said, stretching out her hand. "The CEO."

A beat passed. Then Hank let out a belly laugh. "That's funny."

Maggie glanced at Adam, hoping they could exchange a can-you-believe-this-guy look, but Adam was chuckling, too.

What is going on here? Maggie thought, but she kept her mouth shut. "Is this your office?"

Hank laughed. "Of course not. We can go somewhere else. I don't know if this place will be to your taste . . ."

No way was she letting him discount her that easily. "I'm game for anything."

As he led them in, Maggie poked Adam. "What is this place?" she asked.

Adam was peering around curiously. "My educated guess? This is a strip club. Not that I would know anything about one," he said hastily.

The bouncer nodded at Hank and checked Maggie's ID. "Happy birthday," he said.

Hank was tickled by this. "We'll have to get you a birthday lap dance!"

There were poles on the stage, tables surrounded by leather booths, servers who were women in lingerie. All the customers were male.

"I do *not* want a lap dance," Maggie hissed to Adam as Hank started talking to a scantily clad server. "I want to leave." There was no place on earth she would have stood out more than here, in her blouse and slacks, no makeup on her face.

Adam was drinking in their surroundings, a tourist in a foreign country. He was acting like a *boy*, Maggie thought with a flicker of distaste. She tugged his sleeve. "Adam, seriously." Repeating the request seemed to bring him back down to earth.

"We'll say our piece and get out as soon as possible. Promise,"

Adam said, and Maggie relaxed slightly, though she stayed close to his side.

Hank returned from his conversation with a man in a suit, who Maggie assumed was the manager or owner. "I requested Trinity. She'll take good care of you. Anyway, lunch. The fried chicken at the buffet is excellent." He led the way toward the buffet.

So that was how Maggie ended up sitting in front of a catwalk, fried chicken propped on top of her laptop, women shimmying onstage, trying unsuccessfully to get a word into Adam and Hank's conversation about pushing Circle public.

"Circle is going to be everywhere," Adam was telling Hank. "In some countries, it's going to be people's first brush with the internet. There are already people who go on our site first thing in the morning instead of the news. Not only do people use Circle, but it's *important* to them."

"But how do we turn that attention into money?" Hank hadn't looked at Maggie at all over the course of this conversation, besides when he asked if she needed space on the table to take notes. He sucked each of his fingers clean of chicken grease. Maggie eyed the stack of napkins next to his hand. This meeting needed to end.

"The money will come," she said, loudly enough that Hank couldn't just pretend it was the music. "Our priority this summer is making the site accessible to more users, not monetizing. Our investors should be on the same page."

Adam hastily said, "But obviously, we want to monetize. We wouldn't be a business if we didn't."

Hank glanced between them. "Here's the thing. We're being a bit more conservative with investments right now. But I like the two of you." This took Maggie off-guard. Was he just saying that, or did he actually like her despite how he'd blatantly ignored her? Hank continued, "We invest in people, not ideas. So before we decide on anything, I want to meet the rest of your cofounders.

I'll be hosting a get-together next week at my home in San Francisco. Bring them, and we'll talk."

At that moment, a woman in a sparkly bra walked up to them with a magnum of Grey Goose on her shoulder like it was a bazooka, a sparkler spitting off sparks from the tip. "Who's the birthday girl?" she sang.

Maggie shot Adam a panicked look. He got the clue. "Actually, Hank, we should probably get back to Berkeley. Thanks for meeting."

Hank held out his hand to shake, the same hand he'd been using to eat the chicken. Reluctantly, Maggie reached out to take it. Then, she grabbed her laptop to her chest and booked it out of there, rubbing her palm against her thigh as she went.

She heard Adam's footsteps behind her. "Maggie, slow down."

She waited until they were at an intersection before she spun around and faced him. "What *was* that?"

Adam frowned. "*That* was a successful meeting, if we don't count you sprinting off like Usain Bolt."

"Successful? He acted like I didn't exist, or at best, that I was your secretary!"

"He invited us to his party! I bet there are going to be all kinds of famous entrepreneurs there. You know Hank's BFFs with Peter Thiel?"

How was he not getting that she was upset? Who cared if Peter Thiel or George H.W. Bush or even Steve Jobs was at this stupid party? "That meeting did not make me feel like I was the CEO of this company."

"Maybe that's *your* problem!"

Her mouth dropped open. Adam's eyebrows were angry slants, his jaw hard. She waited for him to relax his posture, to apologize for what he'd said. But he didn't back down. "I worked really hard for that meeting." He was almost shouting now. "I know it didn't go *exactly* the way you wanted, but a *thank you* would be nice."

She'd never seen Adam this upset before. Whenever they disagreed, they usually found a way to come together again.

He fisted his hair. "I'm going to walk around for a bit. I'll meet you back at the apartment."

"Adam—" She could make him stop and come back to her. All it would take was *I'm sorry*, but the words refused to come out. She watched as he pivoted on his heel and walked away.

Chapter Twenty-Six

JUNE 2006

The hallway of their apartment was quiet when Maggie came back alone, but there were more shoes by the door than there had been when she'd left.

"Surprise!" The lights turned on as she opened the door, worrying over whether she'd messed everything up, and if Adam would be mad at her forever.

There was a sign across the living room that read HAPPY BIRTHDAY, though it'd been taped up crooked. There were also various photos of Maggie in unflattering poses: asleep at her desk with her mouth open, shoveling rice in her mouth, frowning down at one of her essays with her double chin on full display.

Charles came forward, holding a round, fruit-laden cake with HAPPY written in red frosting. He was singing, which she had never heard him do. His voice was mellow and sweet. "Happy birthday . . ."

"To you . . ." Hari and Priya came out next with a second cake, this one saying BIRTHDAY and covered in chocolate shavings.

Maggie pressed a hand to her mouth, genuinely shocked.

At the part where they were supposed to say her name, there

was an awkward pause. Then, Charles looked past her, to the door. "Where's Adam?"

She scrambled to come up with an excuse. "He had some stuff to do in the city."

"*What*?" Hari exclaimed. "This whole thing was his idea!"

Priya shushed him. "Let's finish the song." They finished the song, but with much less verve.

"How was the investor meeting?" Hari asked after, when they were sitting around the dining table and Priya was cutting the *HAPPY* cake. "Adam was really nervous about it."

"Fine," Maggie said, but it came out as more of a whisper. Here she was, eating this cake Adam had helped buy, while he stalked the streets of San Francisco furious with her. She should've seen how important that meeting was to him.

Charles glanced at her with concern, then said, "So how'd you manage to get away from work, Hari?"

"Told them it was a family emergency. Which is true. Maggie urgently needed the birthday song sung to her." Hari forked cake into his mouth, cream catching on his upper lip. "Honestly, I hate working there. I'd give anything to be working on Circle. Doing stuff that's actually exciting."

She heard the longing in his voice. Hari had spoken so confidently about getting a fancy corporate job, acquiring his H-1B, and spending the rest of his life in the US. She wished she could help him somehow, but that was in the government's hands.

"I wish you were working with us, too. Both of you." Her voice trembled. She missed them both.

The door opened again, and Hari, who was facing the entrance, straightened. "Adam, about time!"

Slowly, she turned. Adam held a box in his hands, a contrite expression on his face. He kicked off his shoes and walked slowly toward them, putting the box on the table.

"Open it," he told Maggie, smiling slightly, and she could tell that he wasn't angry anymore.

There was a third cake inside, covered in piles of soft white cream, and it said *MAGGIE*.

"Happy birthday Maggie," Maggie read, realizing why they'd been waiting for him. He'd had the last word of the sentence.

"You said you'd never gotten a birthday cake," Adam said. "So we got you several."

Her heart squeezed tight, and she knew in that moment that she'd forgiven him, too.

TWO CAKES AND several shots of Fireball later, Maggie had put the whole nightmare of meeting Hank Wagner behind her. When Hari asked again about the meeting, she let Adam answer.

"It went really well," Adam said. He'd had a few shots too, and his posture was more relaxed, his words beginning to slur together. At some point, he'd scooted his chair closer to hers. "He invited us to a party."

Priya's eyebrows lifted. "Some of the people at my fund have been to a Wagner party. Apparently, they're legendary. Usher was at the last one."

"Are we going?" Hari asked, excited.

"That depends on Maggie," Adam said, meeting her eyes.

A few hours ago, she would've answered this with a *hell, no*. But this was Adam's thing, and she didn't want to get in his way. She never wanted him to look at her again in the way he had in that alley. Not to mention, they *needed* that investment. "Yeah. We'll go."

"Really?" Adam asked, hopeful.

Hari suddenly climbed on top of his chair.

"Whoa!" Adam said at the same time Priya said, "Hari, get down from there."

Hari leveled a finger at her. "Maggie. Birthday girl. I have a question for you." He pointed a finger at himself, Adam, then Charles. "Fuck, marry, kill."

Maggie rolled her eyes, even as her skin tightened. "That's not a question." She was aware of Charles's and Adam's gazes upon her.

"Come on," Hari said. "Choose."

"I'd kill all of you."

"We're not asking you for state secrets. What's the problem?" Hari wheedled, before wobbling a little on the chair. Everyone moved, trying to put themselves in a position to help him.

"If I answer, will you get off the chair?"

Hari nodded. She deliberated, then pointed at him. "Kill, because you're making me answer such a dumb question."

Then she wiggled her finger from Adam to Charles. "Fuck. Marry." The two words tumbled off her tongue.

Hari got down from the chair, and Maggie heaved a sigh of relief. But then he began hip thrusting in Adam's direction. "Maggie wants to bang your brains out!"

"Oh, I know," Adam said, sending Maggie a wink.

Hari suddenly slumped onto the ground with a concerning thump. "So sleepy," he mumbled.

"Oh, jeez." Priya gave Adam a pleading look. "Help me get him to the car? He's got work tomorrow."

This made Hari stir. "No! I don't want to work tomorrow!" he wailed.

Priya and Adam dragged Hari out. Maggie wiped the table while Charles cleaned up the glasses. "I can finish up, if you need to drive home." He hadn't had any shots, only a glass of beer.

"I have one more gift." Charles withdrew a neatly wrapped box from his pants pocket and handed it to her. She opened it, revealing a translucent box with sparkling letters on the side that read *Juicy J.* "Happy birthday, Tiny."

Outside, she held the joint between her lips while Charles

flicked his lighter, leaning toward her. They looked at each other, their faces close. She sucked the joint before handing it back to him, cradling the smoke in her lungs before exhaling.

Charles watched her approvingly. "You're a pothead now," he said proudly.

"All thanks to you." They walked in silence toward campus. The air was still and warm, the light beginning to fade. Because it was summer, there were few students around. It was peaceful, and Maggie sank into the feeling.

"That's a nice gradient," Charles said, his face tipped toward the sky.

She stared at the intermingling of deep blues and pale orange. "What would you name that color?" she asked, pointing toward the center of the gradient, which was a pale pink.

Charles pondered this deeply. "'Tiny's Blush.'"

She shoved him. "That is so mean."

"It's the exact shade," Charles said, smirking.

They stopped in the eucalyptus grove behind the Valley Life Sciences Building, and she smelled the sharp tinge of the leaves. She came here more often now that there weren't so many couples making out with each other among the trees.

Maggie leaned against a tree while Charles puffed on the joint. When he handed it to her, he asked, "Why did you choose me as the one you'd marry?"

She groaned. "It was just a knee-jerk response to get Hari off my back."

"Your basic process of elimination, then."

She usually liked Charles's curiosity and his desire to understand her thinking. But right now she wished he'd find something else to interest him. She gave his question her best effort, hoping her answer would be enough for him to move on. "Because you're steady and reliable. Adam's perfect in small doses. Like, you're weed. And he's crack cocaine." She settled back, satisfied with this spur-of-the-moment response. It felt true. Charles would be a way better long-term partner than Adam. When she hung out with him, she got his full attention. With Adam, she always got the impression that he was thinking about five other things in addition to their conversation.

Charles took this in. "And what is Hari?"

"Alcohol. Because it's gross and makes me feel ill the next day."

This made him laugh, and she smiled in response. What was it about Charles's laugh that made it so rewarding?

"Maybe, now that you're twenty-one, you'll like drinking more," he said.

She tried forming a smoke ring and failed. Was she really twenty-one now? Sometimes she still forgot to brush her hair. She didn't understand health insurance and had never figured out what balancing a checkbook actually meant. It felt like twenty-one was the threshold to adulthood, one she wasn't ready to cross. "Do you ever get scared of growing up?"

"All the time." Charles blew out a perfect smoke ring. "I feel like, the older you get, the choices you have to make become more complicated, too. I like it when things are simple."

"Simple how?"

He shrugged. "Like, when you want to hang out with your friends, you go down the hall. When you think the visual hierarchy of your website isn't working, you shrink some navigation buttons. And when you like a girl, you ask her out."

She blinked at him. "Has that happened to you?"

"Poorly sized navigation buttons? All the time. I have a folder full of examples."

He was being deliberately obtuse. She felt like the two of them were circling around something, both not wanting to address it directly. "No, dummy. Did you like a girl and ask her out?"

He gave her a small smile. But instead of answering, he asked, "How are you feeling about Circle?"

She wanted to pretend she was happy with the way things were going, but Charles's question was an invitation to share what was on her mind. She didn't get many of those. There was a constant battle between her and Adam to showcase how well things were going. Because saying something was wrong would also mean admitting that one of them had made a misstep somewhere.

"It feels like priorities are shifting for the company. Like, now we've proven the product is good and people want to use it, perfecting it doesn't matter. All investors care about is how we're going to squeeze value out of it." She took a breath. "Part of me wants to go back to when it was just us and there were no expectations. When it was just fun. But I know that time is gone." It was her first time saying it aloud, and she realized that this was why, even with the knowledge that Circle was gaining traction, this summer hadn't fulfilled her the way she thought it would.

"Things are rarely going to go at the exact pace you want. But I think, as long as you like the general direction you're headed, you're good. If you ever feel doubt about that, you can come to me, and I'll tell you that the best is still to come."

Their eyes met. Something new bloomed in her chest. It made her notice the tenor of his voice and the way he held the joint between his fingers.

The two of them stayed out there for a long time, talking under the eucalyptus. When Charles dropped her off at the apartment, she got into his bed and tucked his blankets tightly under her chin.

Chapter Twenty-Seven

DAY 3: SATURDAY

The morning of her second day on Janteloven, Maggie wants to die. Her head hurts, her mouth is cottony, and she doesn't really remember what happened after she returned to the cabin last night and said yes to another bottle of wine.

She stares at the exposed wooden beams of the ceiling, trying to jog her befuddled brain. Adam had been eager to know how her conversation with Sylvia went, and when she confirmed that Sylvia was still committed to writing the article her way, Adam had commanded Hari to gather more intel on what Sylvia was writing.

"That's not very objective," Charles had remarked.

"Tyrant," Maggie had accused Adam gleefully.

"*Vigilant*," Adam had countered before he redirected the conversation. They bickered about irrelevant, senseless stuff, like how much they'd each pay to be part of a founding colony on Mars or which philosophers' brains they would want uploaded to the internet. Adam and Hari left at one, and Maggie and Charles fought over who would take the king bed until Charles sprinted to the fold-out bed and refused to budge.

It was the first time in a while that she'd fallen asleep without OurSpot as the last thing on her mind.

The doorbell rings, a deep peal that makes her head throb. It keeps ringing.

The bathroom door is closed, which means Charles is inside, so Maggie reluctantly gets up. On the doorstep, Hari stands dressed from head to tie in purple, a purple tote with a giant C dangling from his fingers.

Hari eyes her. "You look as bad as I feel. Ready for the photo shoot?"

"What photo shoot?" she croaks, rubbing what might be dried saliva from the corner of her mouth.

Hari's gaze goes behind her. "Charles, put on your Circle Purple. We're meeting at the main lodge at nine for the photo shoot."

She turns. Charles stands a little behind her, wearing a thin gray T-shirt and pajama pants. His hair is rumpled, his eyes sleepy. "Sylvia requested a photographer," Charles says. "To take photos for the article."

"Which is why we have to coordinate outfits." Hari opens the bag wider, and Maggie sees purple cloth inside. "Imagine how good it'll look on camera."

"I'm not going to wear Circle swag," Maggie says. In the sober light of a new day, she realizes it's up to her to establish boundaries. They might've bonded last night, but she doesn't work at Circle anymore.

"You're not going to look like a team player."

"We're not on the same team." With Adam's help, they've made it clear to Sylvia that Maggie was an important part of Circle. Now she has to show that she will be able to take the best parts of what she did at Circle and do it again. There's a difference between a reunion and reassimilation.

"Charles, a little help here?" Hari asks.

She feels his shrug. "It's up to her."

"Whatever. Fine. You can explain yourself to Adam when he

goes disappointed-teacher on you later. I'll leave these here, in case." Hari plunks the tote bag on the doorstep. "Don't be late!"

"WHERE'S YOUR CIRCLE purple?" Adam asks the moment Maggie arrives at the main lodge. She spotted the purple blob of people outside from far away. Even Jaya's wearing a purple beanie with a C.

"I didn't want to look like another member of One Direction." She's wearing all black and has tried to comb her hair, but there are still baby flyaways that refuse to stay down. There's nothing she can do about the dark circles beneath her eyes or the sour taste in her mouth. Drinking in her thirties is just as bad as it was in her twenties, but now it seems to take her twice as long to recover. "I feel like shit."

"I do, too," Adam says, even though he looks like he got a full eight hours of uninterrupted sleep, calm and put-together in his purple Patagonia vest. Must be that smart mattress. "I've got a doctor on the mainland. Should I fly him out to give us IV drips when we get back?"

Maggie waits for him to say he's joking, but it appears to be an earnest offer.

Sylvia swaggers down the path toward them in a white puffer vest whose hood is lined with fur. Following her is a mousy-looking man weighed down with camera equipment.

"Everyone, this is Manny. He'll be taking photos today, but don't pay any attention to him. Act like you normally would." Sylvia turns to Maggie. "Why is everyone else a grape while you look like a black hole?"

"I'm an iconoclast that way."

"I'm going to show you the best parts of the island today," Adam informs them, though he doesn't provide more detail beyond that. They pile into a van driven by the same tall, silent Norwegian man who picked her and Sylvia up at the airport the other day. Maggie realizes she hasn't heard a word of Norwegian since they left the Oslo airport. They could be anywhere in the world, really.

She ends up in the back row, grabbing the window seat so that she can focus on the view.

But then Sylvia sits right next to her. "Adam, come here," she says, gesturing to their row.

Adam takes a seat across the aisle, looking slightly apprehensive. Maggie can *feel* the energy rolling off Sylvia, like a predator set loose. In the sauna yesterday, things had been casual and off the record, but this is Sylvia the journalist, ready to dig up her story. "Maggie and I talked about Hank Wagner last night. I forgot how much of a role he played in Circle while you were raising your Series A. And now, he's basically the only person you listen to."

Maggie compacts herself farther into her corner, resting her pounding head against the cool wall of the van. So Hank Wagner is the thread that Sylvia wants to tug on. She definitely doesn't want to get pulled into this.

"I listen to him, but my opinions are my own." Adam sounds slightly defensive. Two rows up, she sees Hari's head swivel backwards, like he senses trouble.

"But you hold so many of the same perspectives. You usually donate to the same political campaigns."

Maggie stares hard outside the window, watching the blur of meadows and ocean. Talking about Hank Wagner always makes her feel nauseous, and the hangover's not helping.

"Part of the reason Hank and I are friends is that we care about these topics. We're constantly debating them and refining our beliefs."

Sylvia nudges Maggie. "What do *you* think of Hank Wagner?"

Maggie glances at Adam, who has one hand on the headrest in front of him, a frown on his face. "I already told you."

"You said your philosophies didn't align, which checks out. Hank tends to impose his values on the businesses he invests in. What was it like, having him around?"

Maggie stays silent. *Connect everyone.* That was the original mission. But after Hank, that message got reinterpreted and twisted.

The van comes to a stop. "We're here!" Hari calls from the front.

Adam quickly gets up and makes his way off. But Maggie is fenced in. Even after everyone gets off, Sylvia doesn't move. "Margaret," she purrs. "Why do I feel like you're holding back with me?"

"Why don't you go ask Hari or Charles some questions for a change?" Maggie asks. "Do you not care about them?"

Sylvia's eyebrows arch, and Maggie knows she's made some fatal error. Exposed her belly somehow. It's only the two of them and the driver now, but they're far enough in the back that he can't hear. "Because you're the interesting one. One girl, working with three passionate guys. There must have been . . . *tension.*"

Maggie wishes a meteor would impale the van right this instant. Instead, there is just silence while Sylvia waits for her to answer. "I don't see how my gender has anything to do with it."

"Oh, Margaret." Sylvia's voice is sympathetic. "I think we both know how much gender works against us in a field like this. You've worked with Hank Wagner, after all."

A chill rustles through her bones. Her eyes meet Sylvia's, but the journalist's face is impassive. *What do you know?* she wonders.

Someone steps onto the van. Charles is at the end of the walkway. "Are you two getting off?"

Maggie rises, and Sylvia stands too, making space so that Maggie can go around her. She prays that Sylvia does not pursue this line of questioning and is relieved when the reporter does not follow.

Chapter Twenty-Eight

JULY 2006

Maggie needed a break. Funds were running dry, and she was doing the job of five engineers. She'd taken on some of the front-end work so Charles could focus on his internship, along with her existing back-end responsibilities. Maintaining a site with as many users as Circle was like caring for a misbehaving puppy. It required oversight at all times, else it would shit on your living room carpet. From the moment she opened her eyes in the morning to when she closed them at night, she was sitting in front of her laptop. It was Adam who reminded her to eat lunch and go outside once a day.

Adam was always out and about. He'd trespass on industry conferences to collect business cards and names, Caltrain down to Palo Alto where he'd pitch VC execs in the cafés they frequented. He'd come back reenergized by the conversations he'd had, and Maggie would pretend she felt just as invigorated from languishing in her codebase.

In her mind, Hank's investment became the only answer. With the money, she and Adam could hire experienced engineers. They could get an office and a lawyer. Because the legal issues were beginning to crop up, and unlike buggy code, Maggie wasn't sure how to solve them. They had to develop a privacy policy, rules around harassment and discrimination, and respond to harmful content. Apparently, if they didn't want to be "sued up the ass," which Adam had quoted verbatim from the Fink family lawyer, they needed to get this right.

And maybe, with a bigger team, Maggie could actually get some sleep.

The day of Hank's party, she was tired and itchy, but she managed to summon her enthusiasm over hanging out all four of them again. They hadn't all been in the same place at once since her birthday.

They met up at Adam and Maggie's apartment, with Priya planning to drive. Adam had told them to bring their swimsuits, since there was a hot tub. Maggie owned exactly one, a ratty red one-piece that she'd used for PE swimming classes that most definitely was not VC-party-caliber. She put it on and stood in front of the mirror, pressing down her stomach, observing the stretch of spandex around her butt.

Looking at herself like this, she felt a burst of self-consciousness. Her stringy hair, her scrawny legs, the paleness of her skin. Sometimes, she wasn't sure what Adam saw in her. If not for Circle, maybe she would've been just another girl he'd flirted with and forgotten.

She cracked open the bathroom door, sticking only her head out. Adam was in the kitchen, preparing pregame drinks. Charles was at his desk, putting in an order for Circle swag. Hari had wanted T-shirts, but Charles took over the job when he discovered Hari had no idea how to turn their logo into a PNG.

Priya was hanging out on the couch next to Hari, wearing a dark blue cover-up with a white-diamond pattern, the halter of her swimsuit visible around her neck. To Maggie's surprise, her absence this summer had been a bit jarring, too. Maggie missed the times she'd drop by with groceries or mercilessly tell Hari that his nose hairs were getting too long.

"Priya?" she asked now. "I need your help with something."

Priya moved her legs off Hari's lap. He'd been massaging her calves. "What's up?"

Part of her wanted to shrink back into the bathroom, but she pushed on. "Um, can you come in?"

"Hey, Charles." Hari scooted to the end of the couch closer to Charles. "Would you rather have no balls or no brains?"

Priya rolled her eyes, getting up and walking to the bathroom. Maggie closed the door behind them and turned toward her. "I need help with my makeup."

Surprise wound its way through Priya's features, quickly replaced by purpose. "Okay. Do you want to use your stuff or mine?"

"Yours." Maggie had no *stuff*, unless they were counting the free lip balm she'd gotten from her dentist. She plucked at her one-piece and watched the spandex send her thighs jiggling. "And, um, you wouldn't happen to have an extra swimsuit, would you?"

Priya left to get her things and returned with a bright patterned bag overflowing with what Maggie could only assume were torture devices, along with a chair from the kitchen, which she set in front of the stained mirror.

Priya pushed Maggie into the chair. "You can choose from here," she said, dropping a large tote into Maggie's lap. "There are cover-ups, too. Do you have a brush?"

Maggie handed her one, and she pulled it through Maggie's hair. Almost immediately, the bristles snagged, and Maggie yelped.

"I changed my mind. I don't want this." She half rose out of the chair.

"Stop being dramatic." Priya forced Maggie back down.

"Are you okay in there?" Hari yelled through the door.

"Fine," Priya called out. She extricated the brush carefully. "I shouldn't have been so hasty. This will take time." She turned on the faucet and ran her hand underneath the water before combing it through Maggie's hair. The pressure of the strands pulling against her scalp and the graze of Priya's fingers felt oddly comforting. For some reason, it had never occurred to her to wet her brush before combing her hair. Another thing her mom might've told her, if she were still here. There was so much knowledge her mother had taken from her. How to brush her hair, what to do when your period came, when it was time to start wearing a bra, things that might've spared her from the disdain of other girls.

Priya ran her fingers through Maggie's hair, and Maggie found herself leaning into her touch. "Have you ever watched *The Princess Diaries* or *Pretty Woman*? There's always a makeover scene," Priya said happily. "The ugly duckling transformed into a beautiful swan. I've always wanted to participate in someone's makeover."

"Are you calling me ugly?" Maggie asked, offended that she would come right out and say it.

"No! Just . . . ungroomed. Your appearance is your armor. And you don't want to head to a party like this without protection of some sort. The guys don't have to worry about this stuff, but things are different for us girls."

Maggie frowned as Priya set aside the brush. It *was* pretty unfair that she was in here while the guys were chilling outside. Why wasn't Adam freaking out about how his swim trunks made his legs look?

Priya put her hands on Maggie's shoulders and studied Maggie's face in the mirror. "We don't have enough time to curl your hair. Eyelash curler and eyeliner," she decided before proceeding to bring them far too close to Maggie's eyes. She ducked, and Priya said irritably, "You need to trust me, unless you want to lose an eye."

She felt the cool gloss of eyeliner, then dabs of eye shadow as Priya colored in her lids. She seemed to know exactly what to do, despite their differing complexions. "How did you get good at this?" Maggie asked, in awe. She used to browse the makeup tutorials in *Seventeen* magazines at the library, but knew her dad would never give her money to buy things like mascara or brushes. She'd convinced herself she didn't need them, even as she admired the cheerleaders in her classes, their shimmery smiles and highlighted cheekbones.

"I wanted to impress boys," Priya replied. "Not a very feminist reason, but oh well."

"You're already pretty, though." Hari was smitten with Priya, and it wasn't because she put on lipstick.

"Thank you." Priya finished her work and clapped her makeup palette shut. "Want to take a look?"

Maggie turned to face the mirror. Her eyes were lined with something dark and smoky, and her lips, courtesy of something shiny and pink Priya had smeared onto them, seemed fuller.

She turned back to Priya, speechless.

Priya smiled, as if she knew everything going through her head. "Wait until the boys see you. Have you decided which swimsuit?"

Maggie went through the bag, arriving on a lavender bikini that clasped at the back, small golden tassels dangling from the sides of the bottoms. Regular Maggie would never dare to wear such a thing, but Priya had made her look like someone who could pull it off.

"You'll look gorgeous in that," Priya said, and Maggie understood on a deeper level why Hari was drawn to her. Priya had this capable steadiness, like she could tell the future and knew everything would be alright. "Pair it with the white cover-up."

Gorgeous. Adam sometimes called her cute, never gorgeous. She tucked the word away carefully. "Thank you," she told Priya sincerely. Maybe when the school year started up again, they would hang out more like this. She might ask Priya to teach her some of her skills.

Priya affectionately tucked a strand of Maggie's hair behind her ear, then pulled the door open. "Guys, come look!"

"Wait—" But it was too late. Adam, Hari, and Charles had obeyed Priya's summons. They hovered in the doorway, gawking at her.

A big grin broke out over Adam's face, his blue eyes blazing with admiration. "I don't know exactly what you did, but she looks amazing. Good job, Priya." Priya beamed.

Maggie had a feeling Adam would've said that even if Priya had turned her into a clown. Then, she looked at Charles. The expression on his face . . . she'd seen it before, when he looked at art. *Slow looking*, he'd called it. He'd described it to her on a trip to the MoMA, when the two of them wanted inspiration for Circle's brand identity. She'd wanted to race through every exhibit. He'd gotten her to slow down and really look, explained how a great piece of art made him feel something he couldn't yet name.

"I like the way you usually look," Charles said finally. "But this is nice, too."

Priya gave an offended scoff, but Maggie smiled.

"I don't get it," Hari said, confused. "What am I supposed to be seeing?"

Chapter Twenty-Nine

DAY 3: SATURDAY

The air is so crisp it sears her lungs as she gets out of the van. She realizes they are very high up, almost eye level with the peaks of the neighboring mountains. There are glass stairs leading up to a glass deck that stretches precariously over the valley beneath.

Maggie trots behind Charles, eager to get away from Sylvia. The woman is on the hunt for scandal, and Maggie knows she absolutely reeks of it.

Adam leads them toward the stairs, walking backwards like a tour guide. "Before this island came into my possession, there were a few structures scattered across the acreage. I didn't want to tear them down, so I fixed them up a bit. If you're brave enough, you should walk out onto the deck. No more than two people out there at once. I didn't get it load tested." He punctuates this with a chuckle.

Maggie climbs the stairs, remembering to snap photos for her dad. The glass is stable, but there's only a low railing around the deck, and seeing the entire valley spread out beneath her is a little terrifying, especially given how clean the glass is. Far below is the blue snake of a river, framed by sharp gray granite.

"I have cleaners come out here every week to Windex. Nothing like smudged glass to ruin the near-death feeling," Adam says, and she realizes he's followed her out. He comes to stand beside her.

Sylvia has remained near the van, speaking to Charles, but Manny has positioned himself near the stairs, his camera pointed toward them. She realizes how this looks, her and Adam on the deck, that dramatic view behind them, his head dipped toward hers. There is something she wants to say to him, though.

"Sylvia told me about your dad." She watches his expression twist, grief momentarily shadowing his features. "I'm sorry, Adam."

He shrugs. "He was old, and sick. It was bound to happen."

"Still. I know you loved him." She almost reaches out to touch him, but she's conscious of Manny's camera lens. The last thing she wants is for Sylvia to start speculating about romances. If what happened between her and Adam made it into the article, it would completely destroy her credibility. "I wish I could've been there for you."

"You're here now." The sadness is gone from his face, and he steps closer. "Us, being together. Haven't you missed it?" His eyes are the same blue as the river beneath them. She feels like he's been testing her since the drinking game last night. Prodding her with these shards of their past to see what will make her bleed.

Maggie spots Priya climbing the stairs. Relieved, she sidesteps Adam and calls, "Hey, how come you're not the one taking photos? Didn't you used to be into photography?" There's a momentary blankness on Priya's face. "That DSLR you always toted around," Maggie clarifies. "You brought it everywhere."

"Oh, that. I don't take photos anymore. Everyone's got a camera on their phones now, anyway."

"Hari abuses his," Adam says. His hands are in his pockets, and he seems to respect Maggie's need for distance, because he stays by the railing. "He takes photos of everything. I think he's just building up a blackmail catalog."

"Priya's probably still better at photography than he is," Maggie says.

"Everyone's better than him. He always cuts off my feet when I ask him to take photos." Priya opens her purse. "Here," she says, tucking something into Maggie's hand. Eyedrops for her definitely bloodshot eyes.

Maggie closes her fingers around it. "Thanks." She looks through the glass floor and shudders slightly. The height is beginning to make her dizzy. She goes down the stairs, leaving Priya and Adam on the deck, to where Jaya is plucking wildflowers and Hari is scrolling through his phone.

"There's service here?" she asks.

"Nah."

"Margaret!" Sylvia is striding toward her, a smirk on her face that spells trouble. Charles is hot on her heels, and she can tell that something is wrong by the pinch of his mouth.

"Did you and Adam disagree over whether to accept Hank's offer?" Sylvia asks her.

She glances at Charles. His arms are folded, the corners of his eyes tight.

Hari lowers his phone, his eyebrows coming together. "Maggie's the one who accepted Hank's offer."

Sylvia raises a hand, eyes still on Maggie. "I want to hear it from her."

Aware that Manny is lurking on the sidelines with his camera, Maggie remains calm. She can tell Sylvia is excited over sniffing out something provocative. Everyone is staring at her.

She hears Adam's footsteps on the stairs behind her. Adam, who considers Hank a stand-in for his dad. Adam, whose dad is dead.

Her fingernails bite into her wrist as she lies through her teeth. "Of course not. We were in total agreement."

Chapter Thirty

JULY 2006

They made their way to Hank's party in Priya's cramped Prius, Maggie squished into the back between Adam and Charles while Hari got the passenger seat.

"You should ask Priya if you can keep her swimsuit," Adam whispered in Maggie's ear, his breath sweet, like the margaritas he'd mixed back at the apartment. His thigh rested against hers, his fingers sneakily playing with the bikini's golden tassel.

Maggie darted a look toward Charles on the other side of her, but he was staring out the window, a muscle playing in his jaw, probably nervous about the party.

"Hey, why don't you share with the class?" Hari asked, squinting at them in the rearview mirror.

Maggie's breath caught. Was this it, then? Had they been found out?

Instead, Adam said, "There's a rumor that if Hank invites you into the hot tub, it's a test. He wants to see if you can outlast him."

"Can you stop worshipping this guy when you barely know him?" Charles asked, irritation threading through his voice. He'd been on a short fuse since they'd squeezed into the car, leaning toward his side so that his legs only touched hers when Priya took a sharp turn.

Adam reached across Maggie to punch him in the shoulder. "Why are you so moody? Are you mad that you're not playing Ping-Pong and riding your rainbow bike around Mountain View with your Google friends?"

"Do your lips hurt?" Charles threw back.

"What?"

"From making out with Hank Wagner's asshole."

"Guys, stop," Maggie said. She yanked the strings of her bikini out from under Adam's fingers. She was nervous, too. Today would be pivotal in convincing Hank he could trust her to make the most of his investment. She wanted to use this opportunity to show Hank there was a reason *she* was the CEO.

They arrived at Hank's house, on top of a hill with an unobstructed view of the Golden Gate Bridge, its red columns soaring out of the fog. Priya spent twenty minutes trying to parallel park on a sixty-degree hill between two designer convertibles.

Hank owned the corner lot, and the house had huge windows facing the bridge. As they approached, she could hear the noise of the party, see men moving within, holding glasses and tiny plates.

Hank greeted them at the door in a Hawaiian shirt and Bermuda shorts. Maggie saw Adam make a move to shake his hand, but she stepped in front of him, taking it upon herself to introduce the group. "I'm looking forward to getting to know you," she told him, making sure to maintain strong eye contact and give his hand a solid shake.

Hank boomed out a laugh, taking his other hand and cupping it around their fingers. "Let's get you all drinks."

He was a welcoming host, introducing Hari to a friend who was a managing director at the Goldman San Francisco office. From what Maggie had learned about banking internships, mere grunts like Hari rarely got to be in the same room as senior people. Hank said jovially, "What are you guys doing, making this kid do analyst stuff when he's over here running an entire company's P&L?"

The MD laughed. "We'll have to do something about that."

Hari gave Maggie an *OMG* look before peeling off to talk to him.

Hank led her, Adam, and Charles up the stairs, where there was an astounding art collection. "I thought this Lichtenstein vanished," Charles said, leaning against the banister and examining a modestly sized painting nestled in a shadowy section of wall. He'd been withdrawn during the tour, but now he was interested. "Is it real?"

"Who knows?" Hank said, but he winked at Maggie. She smiled back, liking being on the inside of a joke. "Let me introduce you to my art adviser. I think the two of you would have a lot to talk about."

Maggie felt herself warming up to Hank. They'd both started off on the wrong foot at the strip club, but that had been a mistake of setting and her lack of preparedness. This time, their conversation flowed easily. It helped that she kept asking herself, *What would Adam say?* Adam would keep the conversation casual and act interested in everything Hank said, while slipping in information about Circle and the good work they were doing. All with a big smile on his face.

Hank was responding to it, too. Even as other people tried to draw him into conversation, he kept coming back to her, ostensibly to continue their tour of his massive home. Adam, who had stuck with them, tried to ask a few questions in the beginning but gave up. She only felt slightly bad about it. Adam had already gotten his quality time at the Gold Club.

The tour ended in front of a closed door. A burly man dressed in all black stood in front of it like some kind of bouncer. "Steven, why don't you let these two check out the refreshments?" Hank said. He gave Maggie a lightly chiding look. "You're bad, distracting me from my other guests."

"Way to cut me out of the conversation," Adam muttered to her as they watched Hank descend the stairs, shouting something to one of the Larrys.

The glow faded with Adam's accusation. "You could've jumped in whenever," Maggie replied, defensive.

"You going inside?" Steven asked. "No loitering here."

They went through the door into a dark room, Steven shutting it behind them. There were curtains pulled over the windows, the main source of light coming from candles placed around the circumference. Maggie realized the room was full of people, lying on the floor or sprawled across beanbags. A table against the wall had a neon sign that said *Refreshments*. Instead of bowls of punch or platters of food, though, there were small bottles, each of them made of colored plastic. Maggie approached them, stepping over a couple that was spooning each other. Two men were making out on the couch next to the table, their movements languid. She tried not to stare.

The bottles held pills of different shapes and colors. Many of them were stamped to look like tech logos.

"This is weird," she said to Adam.

Adam picked one up. "I think that's molly." Instead of backing away, he scanned the bottles. "Hey, look. There's a Circle pill." He popped open one of the bottles, and small pellets spilled into his palm, circular and stamped with their cursive C. "Should we try it?"

She'd never taken Ecstasy, and she wasn't about to start here in this room of cuddling strangers. She needed to be alert while they were trying to close this deal with Hank. "No!" It came out louder than she intended, and some of the bodies stirred, like she was the most disturbing thing here.

"Maggie, chill," Adam said. She was already pivoting toward the door, but not before catching a glimpse of someone who looked a lot like the married billionaire CEO of a network company, groping a woman who was not his wife. Outside, she let the light streaming in from the windows clear her mind. What the hell was that? Why had Hank told them to go in that room? Had he thought he was doing them a favor?

She realized Adam hadn't followed her out.

Steven cleared his throat, and she jumped. "Right. No loitering." She went back downstairs, hoping Adam would be able to emerge on his own.

"There you are. You all just disappeared." Maggie almost fell over herself with relief at the sight of a familiar face. Priya stood in front of her holding a small plate of miniature food items.

"I just saw the weirdest shit of my life," she said to Priya.

"Weirder than watching one of the PayPal founders use a TI-84 with his feet?"

"Um. I'm not sure, actually. Let's go outside, and I'll tell you." She needed someone to tell her she wasn't freaking out over nothing. Had Adam really stayed behind to take the Circle molly? Should she have stuck by him in case anything happened? A shudder went through her. She was glad to be free of that strange room, but if she didn't see Adam in the next ten minutes, she would have to go back in.

She and Priya went to the roof where a DJ played bouncy, tropical music on one side while another guy in a chef's hat manned a pizza oven on the other. Overlooking the view of San Francisco was a wooden deck with a hot tub built in. The people up here were milling about in swimsuits, holding beers and looking relaxed. Maggie felt like she'd entered a new room in some kind of twisted funhouse.

"So?" Priya asked. "What were you going to tell me?"

Just as Maggie was about to spill, she heard her name being called. Hank had come up the steps, and he'd managed to round up Hari, Charles, and—thankfully—Adam.

"Hot tub!" Hank said, indicating the tub. He was shirtless now, the hair on his chest thick and curling.

"Oh my god," Maggie said quietly. "He's inviting us into the hot tub." Adam had mentioned this. If a founder was invited in, it meant Hank was seriously considering funding you.

This was her chance. If she stayed in longer than he did *and* impressed him while doing it, they would get his money. They were so close.

Priya wrinkled her nose. "Looks a bit cramped for six. I'll sit this out."

"Maggie, come on!" Adam called, and she could tell he was delighted by the invitation. He peeled off his shirt, tossing it aside without a second thought. Hari followed behind him, letting out a whoop as he slid into the hot water.

The people on the roof were watching now. They knew the symbolism of the hot tub. This was history in the making.

She tugged at the hem of her cover-up as she neared the tub. What if she screwed this up?

Charles hadn't gotten in yet, either. His shirt was still on, and he was sipping a Coke on the edge of the tub, his legs dangling in the water. Maggie walked over to him.

"Not getting in?" she asked, stalling for time.

He looked up at her. "If you want to stay out here, I'll keep you company."

In the hot tub, she watched Adam clink beers with Hank and Hari. If Hank didn't offer them funding because she failed to get in the hot tub, she wouldn't be able to forgive herself. Adam had already done the work, first asking his dad for money, then securing that first meeting with Hank. It was her job to close.

She stepped around Charles and toward Adam and Hank.

"Did you save me a jet?" she asked Adam, wondering if he'd taken any of the drugs in that room. But he seemed clear-eyed.

"Right here," Hank said, sliding over so she could get in between them.

Quickly, she shed the cover-up and slid in before too many people could get a glimpse of her body. The water was blisteringly hot, and she knew her skin was going to be unbearably dry tonight. She'd probably have to apply several layers of moisturizer when she got home. At the other end, Charles took off his shirt before getting in, too.

"So, I'm trying to understand each of your roles," Hank said as the water bubbled around them. "Charles here is the reason the site is so addictive. Hari is the finance guy. Maggie is the brains of the whole operation. That leaves you, Adam." He leaned his head slightly to look past Maggie at Adam. "What's your job?"

Adam's face was red, though that might have been because of the heat. "I make sure we go after the right opportunities. We offer a lot to our users, Hank, but there's a lot we can learn from them, too. Imagine if we found new ways to leverage the information our users give us."

Maggie gaped at him. This had not been part of their pitch. Adam had previously mentioned possible use cases of aggregating data and packaging it for buyers, but she'd had her hands full, and they'd tabled it. Or so she'd thought.

Hank was waiting for Adam to elaborate. But she would not let him promise things that weren't part of their product roadmap. She turned toward Hank slightly, blocking Adam from view. "We're committed to delivering a seamless experience for our core users. That always comes first. I want Circle to inspire as much loyalty as Apple products, or Nike shoes. We can do it without your money, but we want to work with you because of what you can offer us."

There was a glint in Hank's eyes, and she feared she'd overstepped, her overblown confidence off-putting somehow. Her ears filled with the bubbling of the water, her nerves buzzing.

Then, Hank said, "You'll get a lot more than funding. We're

focused on getting our teams the support they need, and our network is vast in the Valley and beyond."

A hand cupped her knee. Adam, calming her down. She realized she'd risen slightly from the water, and the cool air had made goose bumps rise along her skin. She gave Adam a grateful glance, but his attention was on Hank.

"I think we could have a very productive partnership." Adam rested his arms along the edge of the hot tub, and that was when Maggie realized there was still a hand on her knee.

Despite the heat of the water, her entire body iced over. Slowly, she turned to look at Hank. When they made eye contact, the hand on her leg gave a squeeze.

She yanked her knee from his grasp, rising out of the water, splashing Adam and Hari in the process.

"Argh!" Hari shouted as he wiped water off his face. Hank was calling someone over for towels.

Adam was looking at her, his eyes wide. This time, he did touch her. His fingers wrapped around her arm, and he tugged her back down toward the water. "We don't get out before him," he murmured.

Numbly, she sank back in. Across the hot tub, Charles was watching her, a small furrow of concern between his brows. *Okay?* he mouthed at her.

"Everything good?" Hank asked. His arms were resting on the edge of the tub now, and he had a pleasant smile on his face. A female attendant was standing there in a sequined bikini, holding a stack of towels, and she flashed back to the Gold Club. She'd thought she was in control, but with Hank Wagner, that was never the case. "Do you need to get out?"

Her teeth chattered. If she rationalized enough, that touch could've just been errant bubbles from one of the jets. That room she'd seen, with those people draped over one another—

that was harder to explain away, but she would find a way to forget about it.

"No," she said, her voice firm. "Nobody's getting out." She stayed there until her skin pruned and her face hurt from the smile she was forcing. Until Hank finally got out, promising to get in touch soon.

Chapter Thirty-One

DAY 3: SATURDAY

Their second stop is on the bank of a lake, at a white structure with curving walls that resembles a deflating marshmallow. It's a perfect day to explore the island. The sky is wonderfully clear, its blue hues reflected in the crystalline water, but Maggie is too busy thinking about Hank. She will never forget the feeling of his palm on her flesh, the confusion, and most of all, the doubt. Doubt that it had happened at all.

Adam is bouncing on his heels, excited to show them this next building. Maggie makes sure there are at least two people standing between her and Sylvia as they follow him through a giant concrete door that he has to push open with both hands.

Inside, there are pictures on the walls, each spaced several feet apart for a gallery effect. Circular skylights dot the ceiling, creating natural spotlights on the walls.

"This is the museum," Adam says with a little flourish, like *ta-da!*

"A museum for what?" Sylvia asks, but a closer look answers her question.

On the nearest wall, Maggie identifies a framed copy of their lease, accompanied by a picture of the apartment the four of them had moved into together senior year. The next wall features a printout of their first landing page, back when the site was still called Clubb.

"When we moved to our larger headquarters, we had to empty the old office," Adam says. "I kept everything in storage, until I bought this place, and I realized we could showcase everything here. Circle history. *Our* history."

Her eyes go to the chair sitting in one of the circles of light. That greenish leather, the smooth walnut arms. She searches it for the stab wound, but the Feels Chair seems untouched. As if she had never gotten angry, never stormed out.

"Is that . . ." Hari begins.

"The Feels Chair," Maggie breathes. *I kept it*, Adam said last night. Part of her had refused to believe it was true until this moment. She looks at him now, a little awed. Adam's smiling widely, as if he's been anticipating this for a while.

"What's that?" Sylvia asks.

"It's this old chair I picked off the street," Hari tells her. "I thought we tossed it after . . ." he trails off, realizing where he was about to bring the conversation.

Maggie hears the sound of Manny's camera, greedily snapping pictures.

"Hold on." Sylvia's eyes are wide. There's a glimmer of realization there that Maggie doesn't like. "That GIF of you stabbing a chair before you left . . . Was that the Feels Chair?"

Even though she'd been furious and destructive when she was ousted from Circle, Maggie should have taken it out on some other object with fewer memories attached. Sometimes, she still dreams about the Feels Chair. The cracked green leather surface and its smooth walnut arms. The way the cushion was always warm because one of them was constantly sitting on it.

Every time she thinks about it, she cringes. She could have held her head high and exited with a little bit of dignity the day she quit. But she'd decided to blast it all to hell and got caught on camera going apeshit on a piece of furniture.

"I shouldn't have done it," she admits. She never got to apologize, and she has always felt terrible about how badly she messed up that chair.

"Why did you?" Sylvia asks.

Because she'd been young, and reckless, and eager to get back at everyone for how badly they'd wronged her. Now, seeing that Adam has refurbished the chair and the damage she'd done wasn't permanent, she feels like she can own up to it.

"I was angry. The chair represented our friendship, and at that moment, I thought our friendship was over." She pauses, then forces the next sentence out. The lie. "I was wrong, obviously. Because we stayed friends."

"Right," Adam says, catching on. "You forgave us pretty quickly after that. Because you realized that our friendship is separate from the company, and that we still cared about you."

She can't bear it, all of a sudden. How Adam kept all these things, restored the Feels Chair so it's like the ousting never happened. It should be her holding on to these artifacts, being the steward of their past. Yet she was cut out of this timeline years ago.

"I need to use the bathroom," she blurts, rushing out of that gallery, away from the memories.

There is an all-gender bathroom outside the gallery, and she goes inside, locking the door behind her. She takes the eyedrops that Priya gave her and squeezes them onto her dry eyeballs, then plants her hands on the sink and stares at herself in the asymmetric mirror. The skin at her wrists itches, and when she blinks, the eyedrops leave shiny tracks on her cheeks. She doesn't know how long she can keep up this pretense anymore. Like she's made peace with all the fuckups she committed, when this is the first time in years that she's revisiting them.

There's a knock on the door.

"Yo!" It's Hari. "Let me in."

"I'm peeing!" Maggie replies.

"No, you're having a meltdown. If you don't let me in, I'll tell everyone."

Maggie opens the door, and Hari nearly falls inside. She shuts it again.

He goes to the sink and turns on the faucet, splashing water on his face. "That woman is going to kill me," he says. "And I'm not talking about Priya."

"Same," Maggie mutters, digging the heels of her palms into her eyes.

Hari turns around, water dripping through the foliage of his beard. "You're not part of Circle anymore, though," Hari points out. "Even if you slip up and call Adam a shit, it's not going to affect your ability to do your job."

"It definitely would. I'm not the one who has eight years of friendship backing me up."

"Is that really what you think?"

Maggie peers closely at him, noting the deep furrows in his brow. "Yes. Am I wrong?"

Hari sighs. "The last time the three of us did something like this together was five years ago, when we hiked Kilimanjaro after the IPO. It just didn't feel right, getting to the top of that mountain without you there to celebrate with us. For someone who's been absent, your presence has *always* been felt."

She rubs at her wrist. There's no way she's haunted them the way they've haunted her. They're the reason she hasn't stepped foot in Berkeley since she dropped out. She studies Hari, his elbows against the sink, his face wearier than she's ever seen it. "But you're all here now. Isn't that good?"

The drip of the faucet echoes against the stone walls of the bathroom. "Adam and Charles hung out while I was out on pat leave, but by the time I got back, they'd stopped. Neither of them has told me why, but I know they must've had some kind of disagreement. And now I have Priya, Jaya, my podcast . . . I don't have the energy to figure out what went wrong."

Sadness seeps in. Charles and Adam used to be tight. Before she showed up, they did everything together. She'd thought that her absence would've brought them back together again.

The doorknob rattles, startling them both.

"Hari, I *know* you don't have explosive diarrhea." It's Adam's voice. "Is Maggie in there with you?"

Hari glances at Maggie. She nods.

Hari opens the door. Adam comes inside, followed closely by Charles. "I knew it. You were hiding. You always complain you're not quoted enough in the press, and now look at you."

"Sylvia started asking about that happy hour where one of the engineers got too drunk and dove into the bay," Hari replies. "You know I'm not equipped to answer that without Legal."

Maggie pays closer attention to the distance between Adam and Charles. She thinks of Adam's comment about how Charles doesn't reply to texts, how irritated Charles was with Adam for putting them in a cabin, the lie Charles offered during the drinking game. *I didn't want to come.*

They're all crowded into the bathroom. A beat passes, then Hari asks, "If you're both here, who's with Sylvia?" The answer dawns on him, and he leaps into action. "I need to save Priya!"

The door clicks shut after him. Adam asks Maggie, "Are you feeling sick? Should I ask our driver to take us back?"

"I'm fine." She gets up off the toilet. "Is Sylvia still asking about Hank?"

"She'll stop if Charles tells her there's nothing to share." Adam's voice is sharp.

Charles folds his arms. "I don't give a shit about Sylvia's article, but I want the truth. I know—and I've had plenty of time to think about it—that something changed when Hank invested in us."

He's right. Everything began falling apart after that summer.

Adam runs a hand through his hair, frustrated. Maggie wonders how often Charles has done this, pulling Adam's plans off-track because there's something he disagrees with. That used to be her role, but it seems like Charles has taken it up since she's been gone. "If you want to know what happened, Maggie is the only one who can tell you. I need to get back out there." Then, he leaves.

They look at each other. The stubbornness slips from Charles's face. "Will you tell me?" he asks quietly. "Hasn't it been long enough?"

Her body tenses. It's hard to refuse his request when it's so direct. "It'll change the way you see me," she whispers. It should be easier now to tell him. They aren't friends anymore. But damn it, she still cares what he thinks.

"No," Charles says firmly. "You're always going to be the same person to me."

Their gazes hold. She could get up and leave this bathroom, and he would probably let her go. But she does not want to lose this connection between them again. She chooses to believe him.

Chapter Thirty-Two

AUGUST 2006

They didn't hear from Hank for a few days following the party, and Maggie grappled with the fact that it had to do with her. Her inability to be whoever Hank Wagner wanted her to be.

She'd tried to erase the party from her mind. But Adam wouldn't stop talking about it, reveling in the famous people he'd met and the information he'd gleaned about technology that wasn't even on the marketplace yet. Maggie wished he would stop. She'd avoided his bedroom, going straight into Charles's room each night, lying awake even though she was tired. She couldn't stomach the thought of anyone touching her, not even Adam.

She'd thought of telling him. But she didn't even know how to describe what had happened. Did this count as sexual harassment? The phrase sent a frisson of terror through her. It seemed so extreme for what had transpired. After all, it could've been a slip of his hand, or the pressure from the jets. The more she thought about it, the less sure she was.

On a Monday, she was deep in writing code, her headphones over her ears, when she felt Adam tapping her shoulder.

"You've got a call," he said, holding her phone out.

She picked up. "Hello?"

"Maggie? This is Hank."

Goose bumps sprouted along her spine. Adam was watching her. *Who is it?* he mouthed.

"Hank, hi." The moment she said his name, Adam's eyes lit up.

"Put him on speaker!" Adam said, crouching in front of her.

She didn't know why Hank had called her instead of Adam, who'd been handling all their communication. "I'm putting you on speaker. Adam's here, too," she said.

"Good, glad you're both here. I wanted to give you a call to talk about the offer." Adam rooted through Charles's desk to find a pen and paper while Hank began talking about pre-money and post-money. Maggie didn't need to be a finance nerd to know that he was offering them a ton of money. It barely registered. All she knew was that there was no way they could ever turn this down.

She hadn't realized Adam had taken over the conversation until he was saying, "Looking forward to discussing more" and ending the call. He held his arms out for a hug. "We got it!" When she didn't hug him, he lowered them slowly. "Maggie? You in there?"

She slapped on the biggest, widest grin she could muster. "We got it!" she said, trying to inject the appropriate amount of enthusiasm.

Adam frowned at her. "You sound like your pet iguana just died." He put his hand on her knee, in the exact spot Hank had touched. She flinched away from him and stood up. Adam stepped closer, concerned confusion still on his face. "Tell me what's wrong. Is it because you want to break up?"

She stared at him. "What?"

"You've just been avoiding me, so I thought . . ." Adam glanced away, uncertainty making its way onto his face. "If you do, I get it. I'm not exactly the world's best boyfriend."

Any other day, she would've been delighted to hear him utter the word *boyfriend*. She drew breath through her nose, then looked at him. There were a lot of feelings swirling through her at the moment, and she didn't know how to sort through them on her own. "He *touched* me, Adam."

"Touched you? Like how?"

She could feel the tears welling behind her eyes, even as anger swelled in her heart. She should be feeling the thrill of success, not hands where they didn't belong. "When we were in the hot tub, Hank grabbed my leg in the water."

"Like he bumped into you? It was probably an accident. It was pretty crowded in there."

This, embarrassingly, was what made the tears start to fall. She'd expected him to accept her experience, not rationalize his way out of it. She had plenty of her own excuses she could offer him, the ones she'd come up with trying to convince herself that it wasn't real, wasn't a big deal.

But this was Adam. She'd lost her virginity to him. Of all of them, he was supposed to get it.

Through gritted teeth, Maggie said, "I *know* it wasn't an accident."

Adam rubbed his neck, looking bewildered. "Okay. If you're sure, I believe you." Through the blurry veil of tears, she saw him retreat into the bathroom before reappearing with a roll of toilet paper. He offered it to her. She dried her eyes as he began pacing. She felt useless and miserable, the cause of their current predicament. But Adam was a problem-solver. He'd find them a way forward.

Adam walked from one end of the room to the other, then punched the wall in a sudden motion that made her jump. "Fuck!"

Maggie dropped her toilet paper roll, shaken by the outburst. "A-are you okay?" she asked.

"Everything was perfect," Adam said, drawing his fist to his side, wrath threaded through every single word. "But you're right. We can't take that asshole's money."

She knew how many meetings he'd had with Hank, the emails he'd pored over, all the research he'd done. It sucked to know that work had gone to waste.

"I'm sorry." She didn't want to work with Hank, but the thought of turning down the offer also made her stomach tighten. They'd been operating under the assumption they'd secure an investment this summer—Adam had started looking at office spaces, and Maggie had begun interviewing potential employees—but school resumed in a few weeks. They were going to miss their deadline and have little to show for it. Secretly, she had hoped the money would be enough to justify her dropping out of Cal, so she wouldn't need to ask her dad for tuition for senior year. She could already imagine his disapproval, the *I told you so* that would echo through her ears for eternity.

Even if they refused Hank, then what? She couldn't tell anyone the truth about what happened, how she'd been alarmed by a leg touch. If this got out, people in Silicon Valley wouldn't know her as Margaret Tang, founder of Circle. They would know her as the girl who made a big deal out of nothing.

Adam had come to her. He took her hand in his, and she noticed that his knuckles were bruised. "I'll call him tomorrow and turn it down." The dismay was clear in his tone. He dropped her hand and went into his room, shutting the door behind him.

Maggie sat back down at the desk, but all she could do was stare blankly at the wall, as if the stucco held answers. As if she wasn't the only one standing between Circle and its success.

She heard a key in the lock. Turning, she saw Charles coming in, his Google backpack hanging from a shoulder. He immediately zeroed in on the dent in the wall and Adam's closed door. "What's wrong?"

"Nothing." She could've told him then about Hank. The explanation perched on the tip of her tongue, but she didn't want him to react the way Adam had. To ask if she was sure, like she didn't know herself. Because she wasn't, and she didn't. "What are you doing here?"

Charles took the toilet paper roll she'd abandoned and tore a piece off, before folding it into a smaller square. He came over, hesitated for a second, then reached out and dabbed at her right eye. She hadn't realized she was still crying. "Adam texted me and Hari, said there was good news."

She grabbed Charles's hand and stilled it. His hair had gone a while without a cut, and it curled a bit at the edges. The way Charles was looking at her . . . she had to look away. It was too pure, too honest, a poor match to her own shame and disgust. "If you had to make a decision that would make someone you cared about a lot happy, would you?" she asked. "Even if it wasn't great for you?"

A flicker of surprise in his expression. "If you're asking for you, I would say, fuck everyone else."

"I'm asking what *you* would do."

"Someone I cared about . . ." Charles was still studying her, trying to parse out the meaning behind her question. "If it was someone who mattered a lot to me, I would do anything."

She was never going to be as selfless as Charles, but she wanted to be even a fraction as good. It wasn't just Adam who mattered here, but Circle's future. Charles's and Hari's, too. She got up. "I'm going to talk to Adam for a sec."

Charles tossed the tissue in the trash. Hurt clouded his expression, but she was too busy contending with what she was about to do. "Okay. I'll be out here."

Adam lay on his bed. The room was dark, and he wasn't moving, but she knew he was awake. She took three steps inside and shut the door.

"We're taking it," she said to him. She knew how much he wanted this, and it was wholly in her power to give it to him. If she cared about him, wasn't this the right thing to do? Besides, she trusted Adam. He would look out for her, especially now that he knew about Hank.

Adam sat up. Shook his head. "Maggie, no."

"I'm the CEO, and I've made my decision."

The company was *all* of theirs, and if her only reason for rejecting this deal was personal, that was unacceptable.

She had no way of knowing that soon, Circle would not be hers at all.

Circle's Inner Circle: Part Three

Spending the weekend with Circle's founders has been an adventure. We've hiked mountains, eaten overcooked steak prepared by Adam Fink himself, and even visited a museum dedicated to the company. All of this reminds me that Circle is merely topsoil on the deep-reaching roots of the friendship that existed beforehand. There's a comfort that these four have around one another, the kind you can only really have with very old friends. People who knew you when you were still in the process of becoming. Tang speaks of their past with a clarity that makes me think she revisits these moments often. She mentions their early mistakes at Circle with humor, like when they had to get in a room and define "nudity."

"You would not believe the amount of work it took to get there. I've never had to think so hard about what constitutes a nipple in my whole life," she recalled, shaking her head with a trace of amusement. But back then, it was easy for them to reach agreements. They challenged one another frequently, but "everyone was willing to come to the table," Acharya said. That can perhaps be best reflected through their decision to split the equity evenly, with nobody coming out ahead.

"There are so few moments in life when you really feel like you belong. But it always felt like there was a place for me in that group," Acharya told me as the two of us walked through the gleaming shrine that Fink has erected toward their memory. Within it are various tchotchkes, including the chair that stars in the infamous GIF we all know. They call it the "Feels Chair," a funny little premonition for how significant this chair came to be.

Fink is adamant that the friendship existed separately from the company. It appears that the four were able to repair their differences shortly after Tang was voted out, judging by her willingness to show up to this reunion. It seems to me, though, that this friendship has only survived by being fed through a filter. Conversations stay on the past, and anytime I bring up the present, the responses become more evasive, as if there's a balance they don't want to upset. There are taboo topics, too: the state of Circle now, any possibility of sexual tension, and Hank Wagner, one of the Valley's most notorious VCs.

Once we're outside the museum, I pull Fink aside and ask when he knew she had to go, and whether he sees her new company as a threat. "I don't remember exactly when," he tells me, squinting against the sunlight. "All I know is that it's the hardest thing I've ever had to do. And no, I don't see OurSpot as a threat. I'm happy that she found something else to care about."

It sounds too diplomatic, even if the two of them are friends. Fink has his sights set on positioning Circle as a major player in politics and world news. There are rumors around the relationships he's exploring with authoritarians and his eagerness to meet with world leaders to discuss how Circle can power information distribution in their countries, especially with the launch of Circle Net. If Circle wants to please its shareholders, it will need to keep finding ways to demonstrate growth and hold its competitors at bay. And despite Fink's assurances that he and Tang are on good terms, someone as shrewd as him definitely knows she can also be a threat.

"Have you thought of bringing her back?" I ask him. It's not such a ridiculous question. After years of exile, Steve Jobs returned and made Apple the most valuable company in the world. Howard Schultz reimagined Starbucks and ensured its survival after the financial crisis. It wouldn't be so odd for Circle to look to its past for solutions to its future woes.

"Of course," Fink says with a laugh. "I also think about immortality and self-sustaining extraplanetary civilizations." At the moment at least, he seems to consider it impossible.

Chapter Thirty-Three

DAY 3: SATURDAY

Charles seems to be at a loss for words. Maggie tries to read his face, search for disgust or recrimination. She finds neither. Instead, there's a rawness to his expression, and his voice is rough as he says, "That *fucker*."

He stands, and she catches his hand. "Charles. Please don't make this into a big deal. Adam—"

At the sound of Adam's name, Charles's jaw clenches. "Don't tell me you want to protect him. Not when he didn't do the same for you."

"It was my decision to take Hank's offer. Don't punish him for that."

"I'm sorry, Tiny. That's not something I can promise you." Before she can stop him, Charles is leaving the bathroom. Maggie chases after him, hoping he's not about to start a brawl in Adam's very white museum, in front of Sylvia. She should've anticipated this. Charles is a terrible actor. Asking him to pretend not to be mad is like asking a slasher-film extra to star in a Broadway musical.

Everyone else is in the museum. Adam turns toward Charles when he enters, and Maggie sees his expression tighten, an alertness come into his eyes.

"Where were you two?" Sylvia asks curiously.

"I wasn't feeling well," Maggie says quickly. "What did we miss?"

"Manny got a bunch of photos of the museum, but we should do some group photos outside," Sylvia says, ushering them out of the museum and onto the grass. It's approaching late afternoon now, though the sun is still high in the sky. Manny maneuvers them, putting Adam in the center and directing Hari and Charles to stand on either side of him. Charles won't move from where he stands a few feet away, even as Hari follows Manny's instructions.

"Charles," Adam says with good humor, even though Maggie is pretty sure he's gritting his teeth, "we need you in this photo."

Charles walks over to Maggie, who's on the sidelines beside Priya. Jaya is at their feet, braiding grass. He puts his hands on Maggie's shoulders and steers her toward the group. "Then Maggie should be in it, too. We're not complete without her."

Maggie feels like a rotten grape in her all-black ensemble. "You guys should take a few photos without me."

"No, Charles is right," Adam says, his smile forced. "Get in here!"

She ends up squished between Charles and Adam, Hari on Adam's other side.

"Let me guess," Adam says, his voice low, as Manny bends behind his camera. "You're pissed at me again?"

"You are correct," Charles says, matching Adam's tone. "Because you chose a deal over your friend. Like some kind of raging asshole."

"*Whoa*," Hari says from Adam's side. "What's with the name-calling?"

Manny lifts his head from behind his camera. "Do we want to try a smile?" he asks hopefully.

Maggie attempts to lift the corner of her lips.

"Never mind," Manny says. "I'm going to take a few more. How about something candid? You guys should face each other, like you're having a chat."

Adam's turns fully toward Charles, Maggie still between them, as Manny snaps away. "Maggie said yes. *She* picked up the phone and called him back. Not me. I didn't want her to. You don't know how shitty I've felt about it." Real distress bleeds through his voice.

"He did," Maggie says, trying to nip this in the bud. Part of her had blamed Adam afterward for forcing her hand. But that would be a denial of her own agency. It was her need to prove herself that had eventually made her call Hank back. "Really, it's behind us now—"

"Is this about Hank Wagner again?" Hari asks. "Look, I lowkey think he's a bit creepy, but he's on our board, like it or not—"

"Great!" Manny calls approvingly. "You guys look like you're having a real conversation."

"You probably made her feel like she had no choice," Charles says to Adam, ignoring Hari entirely.

Adam looks at her, his gaze searching. "Is that true, Maggie?"

She'd always given outsized weight to Adam's opinion of her. From the very beginning, she'd wanted to impress him, to be worthy of his friendship. Even when they were together, she had always felt like she didn't quite match up to him. "I didn't want you to have to start over again."

Adam says, almost pleadingly, "It wasn't my fault."

It happens in a blink. A thudding noise, then suddenly, Adam is on the ground, clutching his face.

She snaps her head around to look at Charles, whose hand is clenched, a storm in his eyes.

"What the fuck?" Hari exclaims.

"Whoa!" Manny shouts, but this is accompanied by the sound of the camera shutter.

Adam runs the heel of his palm against his chin. The corner of his mouth is bleeding. In a somewhat dazed voice, he says, "The fuck?"

"I asked you," Charles says, standing over him, his voice no louder than it was before but brimming with anger. "After we signed the documents, I asked you multiple times if there was something you weren't telling me because Maggie refused to go to any of our meetings with him. And you just said they didn't *vibe*." He looks disgusted, like he hates himself for even repeating the word. "Do you ever give a shit about anyone? Or are people just tools to you?"

"Maybe you should think about why she told me and not you." Even with his bloodied mouth, Adam smiles, but it's not one of his sunny, deal-making smiles. It's all thunder and wind. He's pissed now, too. "You might not talk about your feelings ever, but you don't have to when they're written so fucking clearly all over your face."

Charles moves forward, like he's about to even out the damage he's done to Adam's face.

Hari's the one who steps between the two of them, roughly shoving them apart. "Break this up, right the fuck now! Have you two forgotten where we are?"

Maggie had been too stunned to move, but now she goes to Charles, blocking his view of Adam. "This isn't worth fighting over," she says to him, her voice hard.

Charles tilts his head up at the sky. When he looks at her again, the rage has cleared from his brown eyes, leaving remorse in its place. Slowly, his fist unclenches. "Adam was right. It wasn't his fault. Not all of it, anyway." He releases an unsteady breath.

Sylvia jogs over, and she looks like she's barely holding back a delighted smile. "What was *that* about?"

Adam slowly gets up. His mouth is still bleeding. Priya, who's been shielding Jaya's view of the whole situation, tosses him a wad of napkins from her bag. He presses it to his face. "The staff should be setting up lunch for us soon," he says through the napkins. "Why don't we explore the area and then reconvene in an hour or two?"

Charles pivots on his heel and walks toward the lake. Sylvia glances after him, then back at Adam, as if deciding which source can be squeezed for the most juice. She decides to stay put.

"Sylvia," Priya says in an authoritative voice, "Can you look for the first aid kit? And Manny, maybe you can go take some landscape photos. Look how nice the lake is!"

Manny doesn't need any further encouragement. He wanders off, probably questioning what he's gotten himself into.

Sylvia stands there for a moment, as if debating whether to argue.

"I'll be back," she promises before she heads back into the museum.

Adam massages his jaw and winces. He looks pitiful, sprawled on the ground.

"Let me see." Maggie pushes his hand away and studies the wound. The bleeding has slowed, and his teeth are intact. "I'm no doctor, but it doesn't look too bad."

Hari is having his own moment of panic. "If Manny actually got a picture of Charles clocking you, we're screwed, Adam. This is *not* what we need right now. God, sometimes I want to strangle the both of you."

Maggie pats Hari's shoulder. "I know how you feel. Breathe."

Adam grabs Maggie's arm, forcing her to look at him. "Go after him. You're the only one he'll listen to now."

Her hand is still against his cheek. She lets it stay there for a second longer, reassuring herself that he is really fine. Then, once Sylvia returns with the first aid kit, her mouth already half-open around a question, Maggie grabs it from her and goes after Charles.

Chapter Thirty-Four

SEPTEMBER 2006

The desk Hari had been screwing into place suddenly collapsed, and he let out a guttural scream-cry. "Why are you *doing* this to me?"

"Because you're not worthy," Charles said as he put the finishing touches on another Loberget swivel chair. They were panic-assembling IKEA furniture at midnight on a Saturday because the new office was opening Monday, and the semester had started, so they were back to juggling classes, projects, and a company that now had a valuation to live up to. Her dad had come through on her tuition. Maggie meant to call him and say thanks, maybe even apologize. She felt bad for how they'd left things, even had the alarming thought that if she never spoke to him again, she would be no better than her mom, someone who disappeared without a thought toward the people she was abandoning. But every day brought a million other things to do, and she never got around to it.

Hari threw his hex key at Charles, who ducked. It disappeared into a pile of Styrofoam.

Thanks to Hank's investment, they'd signed the lease on the office last month, and Maggie had already hired several new engineers. They now had an obscene amount of money, enough for them to hire the best people and pay Maggie a small salary that she put toward a new laptop and subletting a tiny, one-person space in Berkeley.

She should've been ecstatic. All their wildest dreams were in the middle of coming true.

Yet every time they hit a new milestone, all Maggie could think was that this was Hank Wagner's success, too. If Circle hit it big, he'd be able to tell people that *he* was the one who'd made it so. Now that he'd invested in them, he basically owned them.

"Maggie," Adam said, "will you help me with the boxes?"

The two of them took the folded cardboard boxes to the back for recycling. When they'd finished violently compressing them into the already packed dumpster, Adam turned to her. He took her hands in his. They'd had so little time for each other in the last month that the action felt foreign. "You can't keep avoiding meetings with Hank, Maggie. He's on our board now, which means he's going to be crucial to Circle's future."

She hadn't realized how obvious she'd been about avoiding Hank. They'd had a board meeting with him last week, which she'd ducked last-minute by saying she had an interview. "You don't need me there," she said. Her voice quavered.

Adam looked pained. "You're the CEO. Of course we need you."

She knew she was the CEO, but this was the first time that she realized she was *missed*. They were collectively governing Circle, sure, but she was the one in charge of their vision. As they hired more people, she'd be expected to behave professionally, not like a college kid who could skip a class if she overslept. She wondered if Adam was speaking for Charles and Hari, too. If they all thought that she was behaving incompetently.

"I know it's hard," Adam continued, his voice soft. "But we're in this together. Anytime you're in a room with him, just remember I'm right behind you, backing you up."

Together. That was what she needed to hold on to. Sometimes, she felt utterly alone, but Adam was still here. So were Charles and Hari. They were counting on her. "Okay. Forward me all the materials for the next board meeting. I'll lead it." She pulled her hands out of his.

"Wait. Maggie." Adam blocked her from the door. "*We're* okay, right?"

She looked at him, trying to summon the passion that had driven her toward him that day on the Big C. Yet all she felt was resignation. Whatever flame had burned between them had snuffed out. When she thought of another semester sneaking around, lying to Charles and Hari, she felt a deep fatigue. It didn't feel worth it anymore, not when she had to get serious about running a company.

"Yeah, of course. But what we were doing . . ." She gestured loosely in the air, not finding any better way to convey what that was. "I think it's better if we stop."

She saw Adam's expression dip, grow bewildered. "Fine," he said, resignation in his voice, before pulling open the door. The two of them silently went back inside, Adam lagging behind, where Hari and Charles were arranging the desks.

They'd eschewed cubicles because Charles said they prevented collaboration, and the result was something that resembled a mess hall. Knowing Charles was the most artistic out of all of them, Maggie had let him handle the design of the space. Along the walls were whiteboards and a vibrant purple rug that Charles insisted they splurge on, creating a walkway toward the conference rooms.

"Tiny, do the honors. Name our first conference room," Charles said, pointing at one of the glass-walled boxes.

Maggie shook off her conversation with Adam. A good CEO didn't let her personal feelings prevent her from doing her work. "We could name it after places we really want to go." Soon, this place would be filled with people working for them, sharing the belief that Circle was doing something important and worthwhile. She wanted to remind people that there was always a destination, a place their good work would carry them. "I'll call mine Norway." The vision came to her suddenly: toy boats, posters of fjords, maybe a life-size cardboard cutout of a hot Viking and some real-looking swords . . .

"Why Norway?" Hari asked.

"When I was younger, I took a pop quiz that asked which country was the farthest from the United States. And I wrote Norway. I was wrong, obviously, but it's always seemed remote. And it's supposed to be one of the happiest places in the world. Doesn't that make you want to go?" She wasn't sure what Norway had besides Thor and fjords, but it felt like the rugged last frontier of her younger self's imagination.

There was a hard knock that made her jump. Priya waved at them through the windows, pointing furiously at the Feels Chair next to her. Maggie had suggested inviting her to check out the office, though she'd let Hari take credit for the idea.

Hari ran to open the door. "You brought it! Guys, where should we put it?"

"Over there," Charles said, indicating an empty corner by the wall of whiteboards.

"By the way, while you and Adam were gone, Charles and I decided something," Hari said as he and Adam set the Feels Chair down.

"*You* decided," Charles said. "I tried to talk you out of it."

Hari ignored him. "We should break our leases and all move in together!" He then went on to list all the reasons for cohabitation: Charles, Adam, and Maggie essentially had already lived together; Maggie was subletting in the boonies; Charles needed a place with parking because he was bringing his car to campus . . . "And I'm the only one who hasn't gotten to live with you guys. So we should do it. That is, if it wouldn't be awkward."

Maggie laughed, valiantly keeping her eyes from going to Adam. "Why would it be awkward? That's a great idea."

"Yeah," Adam said, piling on. "I *love* this idea. Hari, you're brilliant."

She glared at him, and he smirked back at her, the humor not reaching his eyes.

Charles stepped toward the whiteboard, giving it a decisive smack. "Before we go, I was thinking we could christen this place." He held up a stack of Post-its. "Maybe we can each write a piece of advice that we'd give to our future employees."

Charles distributed Sharpies. Adam immediately wrote something down, sticking it to the whiteboard. His handwriting was too messy for her to read from where she stood.

Maggie tapped the Sharpie against her chin, applying herself diligently to the prompt. Should she say something about not giving up on your dreams? That was cheesy. Be uncompromising about what you believe in? That rang false. Being part of a team meant being open to compromise.

"Let's do a family photo," Priya said. She'd pulled out a Polaroid camera and motioned at the Feels Chair.

"Family photo!" Hari crowed.

Before she knew what was happening, Adam had picked Maggie up, princess-style. He deposited her in the Feels Chair. Their eyes met, and she smiled tentatively at him. *Are we good?*

Adam nodded once. *We're good.*

Charles sat by her feet, arms looped under his knees, while Hari and Adam crouched on either side of the chair.

The flash went off. Hari taped the Polaroid in the place of honor, right at the center of the whiteboard. By then, Maggie had finally come up with her answer. She approached the board, sticking her Post-it right next to Adam's. Then she surveyed the room, imagining the unoccupied desks full of people. Monday, they would welcome their new employees into the office on Cedar Street, twenty minutes from where it all started.

Adam read her Post-it. "That's a good one." He reached out and smoothed the corners down so it wouldn't fall off.

As the others prepared to leave, Maggie lingered, admiring how the Feels Chair fit in perfectly, the whiteboard populated with their Post-its. She stepped closer to read what the others had written.

Adam—*Leave a legacy.*

Hari—*Make it a good time.*

Charles—*Simple is beautiful.*

And hers—*Never forget who your friends are.*

Chapter Thirty-Five

OCTOBER 2006

Living together was a good idea. In theory.

There hadn't been many options when they started searching so late in the semester, so the four of them had ended up in a two-bedroom house close to the Shattuck BART with a ceiling that leaked when it rained and a noisy in-unit washer/dryer that sounded like a UFO trying to take off. They affectionately called it the Shithole. Adam was paying more for the single bedroom, Hari and Charles were sharing the second one, and they'd created a janky fake bedroom in the living room for Maggie with curtains and a Chinese folding screen of peacocks. Priya had gifted it to them on the first and what would become the last day she stepped foot in the house.

They had fun that first month in the Shithole. While working on Circle, they scavenged for furniture, played DDR, and watched YouTube videos on Charles's giant monitor. Then, change came. Charles decided to do a double major. Priya got mad at Hari for not spending enough time with her, so he started spending weekends with her in San Francisco. In between classes, Maggie was constantly in code reviews at the office, making sure her new engineers didn't crash the whole site with their deployments. Adam was always in meetings, talking to some new investor Hank had introduced him to or getting to know a new hire. Their interactions narrowed to hallway run-ins, or urgently hollering through a bathroom door when one of them needed to pee.

They would all be in the same place only once a week—in the office, during their weekly check-in. Maggie always looked forward to these because it was just the four of them, and it was never very serious. They would catch up on what they needed to do, but they'd also talk about mundane things, like whether Hari should get the wart on his butt cheek looked at or the odds that the Microsoft Zune was going to flop spectacularly.

This time, though, as she barreled into the office, once again late because of a bus that had failed to show up, she saw through the conference windows that they had an unwelcome guest.

Hank Wagner sat at the long conference table in Norway, looking far too old and serious next to the cutout of a hairy Viking with mouth open in a soundless war scream. Adam sat beside him, Charles and Hari opposite them.

She noticed how subdued the rest of the office was too, everyone at their desks diligently working. There was nobody perusing snacks in the microkitchen, or playing at their newly acquired Ping-Pong table.

"Long time no see," Hank said pleasantly as she opened the door. Was it just her, or did he do a full-body scan? It was a reminder that he was still an old perv, except now he was an old perv *and* a stakeholder. Fuming, she grabbed the seat at the head of the table, which happened to be the farthest from him.

"Hank was in town, so I invited him to observe," Adam said. "We can get started now that you're here."

"To observe, or to chaperone?" she asked. She'd agreed to be in the same room as Hank, but that didn't mean she needed to play nice. She heard Hari make a small choking noise. The good-humored atmosphere was gone, now that there was an adult in the room. "Who wants to give an update first?"

Hari spoke up. "Spoke to our general counsel, and we should be clear to go live." They'd been preparing to let teens onto the platform, which Maggie had not taken lightly. She remembered how impressionable she'd been as a kid, how easily influenced by her peers, the mark that sites like MySpace had left on her psyche. If they were going to do this, they needed every single guardrail in place.

"Did you run the announcement by her, too?" Maggie asked.

"Not the exact wording—"

"Do that first. We don't launch until every single piece of messaging has gone through PR and Legal."

Hari rubbed his forehead. "That's going to take another week at least."

"Then we'll wait another week. We don't rush; we do it right." That was her motto.

Charles gave an update on the new developer platform that they were creating, which would allow software developers to create applications using Circle data. As expected from Charles, they were ahead of schedule.

"So you'll let people build applications around Circle data for free," Hank said, "but you won't give user data to advertisers?"

Maggie clenched her hand into a fist beneath the table. Advertising was the last frontier she wanted to cross. She didn't want Circle to turn into a swamp of pop-up ads, no matter how much advertisers were clamoring to get on. "Only one of those things makes the user experience better."

Hank put his arms on the table, regarding her with the coiled deliberation of a snake. "Have you asked the rest of your cofounders if they agree with you?"

"They do," Maggie replied, staring him down. She heard Hari shift in his chair, but the guys stayed quiet. "And you're awfully talkative for someone who's here to observe."

Hank shrugged, leaning back again. The chair squeaked beneath him, and she uncharitably hoped that it would break and bring him crashing to the ground. Unfortunately, it held.

Adam, sensing the darkening mood, said loudly, "Looks like I'm last. We've been invited to speak at a few conferences, and there's a journalist at *TechCrunch* who wants to interview you, Maggie. Are you up for it?"

Maggie had turned down all interviews so far. She just didn't think she had the skill set for representing Circle well, and Adam was so much better at it. But Hank was watching, and it wasn't a good excuse if she rejected an interview due to stage fright. Besides, she read *TechCrunch*. It would be kind of cool to have her name on there. "Sure. Send them my way."

She was about to end the meeting when Hank said, "Things aren't moving fast enough. I want you to have a plan for who's going to be in charge, all the time. Someone who isn't going to show up late to meetings because they had to go to class."

"*I'm* in charge," Maggie said, staring Hank down. She had developed her own way for staying on top of everything happening at Circle. Every day, she sent an email with a question mark to an employee. The recipient was expected to respond within twenty-four hours with a status report of what they were working on, their next milestone, and what they had most recently achieved. It terrified people, but it gave her the context she needed. "Ask me any question about the company, and I'll answer it."

Hank shrugged, unconvinced. "What about your plans to start generating profit?"

"We've got a plan for that," Adam said. Maggie's eyes shot to him. They did? So far, she'd been focused on keeping the company running smoothly. She was embarrassed to admit that she hadn't spared much thought toward long-term strategy. It felt like enough of an accomplishment to keep the whole, unwieldy beast online.

Adam ended up walking Hank out.

"What plan was he talking about?" Maggie asked, when they were both gone.

Charles and Hari exchanged a look.

"What?" she demanded, suddenly getting that familiar feeling of being on the edge of a playground, watching the other kids playing.

"It's called Public Profiles," Hari explained. "Adam thinks Circle is too insular. People talk to friends in their circles, but then what? He thinks there's this untapped opportunity in letting public figures on the platform and having them pay for the chance to talk to Circle's users."

"That's not our mission," Maggie said immediately. "We connect people with each other. We facilitate communication. It's not our business to sell our users' attention. And why am I hearing about this from the two of you?"

"I thought he already talked to you about it," Charles said, looking troubled. "He mentioned that he was going to walk you through the proposal. I already lent him the engineers for the work."

Her hands clenched tightly in her lap. Charles and Hari were both peering at her, concerned. She couldn't believe that Adam hadn't consulted her first about this. This had eroded her credibility in Hari and Charles's eyes, too. Now, they saw how little Adam valued her input.

This wouldn't do. "Oh, right! Adam did mention this." Her voice sounded too high and false. She was pretty sure she was fooling nobody. But she forged on. "Hari, do you mind forwarding me whatever materials he shared with you? I remember him sending them to me, but they've gotten buried under other emails."

Hari nodded slowly.

Hank didn't think she was doing enough. Adam was furthering his own agenda. She felt like the company was turning on her, threatening to eat her whole.

In that moment, she felt young, tired, and completely inexperienced.

"Being CEO sucks." The words escaped before she could stop them.

Hari and Charles looked at her with twin expressions of sympathy. It wasn't as if they didn't have their share of problems, running their respective parts of the company, but in that moment she seemed to be the only one buckling under the pressure.

Chapter Thirty-Six

DAY 3: SATURDAY

Charles is sitting by the lake, his back to her. The sunlight picks up the brown strands in his hair. Maggie feels a bit guilty that she left Adam and Hari to deal with Sylvia, but she also just doesn't have the energy. Not right now.

"You're not thinking of going for another swim, are you?" she asks to warn him of her presence.

"I was considering whether it's worth getting a possible bacterial infection." Charles straightens his hand out in front of him, wincing slightly.

Maggie sits next to him. "Let me see?" He lets her take his right hand. It's heavy and warm in her palm. She lays out the Q-tips and disinfectant from the first aid kit.

"He's okay," she tells Charles, because he'll want to know but won't ask. "You won't be getting a hospital bill."

He doesn't reply, and she shakes his hand a little. "Hari said the two of you haven't been on great terms."

"Hari should mind his own business."

"*Charles.*" She isn't going to force him to talk to her, but she's given him one truth. She feels like she should get one in return.

In one sudden movement, Charles pulls her toward him with his left arm, and she falls into his chest. The Q-tips go flying. He buries his face in her hair and says, "After you left, it felt like I was the only one who remembered what Circle used to be. Hari, Adam, Hank—they've always wanted it to be something else."

There's an ache in her chest as she lifts her hands to his back, clutching the fabric of his jacket between her palms. To her and Charles, Circle was perfect from the moment of conception. She'd been so happy just handwriting Post-its and building cheap furniture, dreaming of a future that hadn't arrived yet with all its dark realities.

Charles murmurs, "Staying at Circle to work for Hank Wagner is probably the worst choice I've made in my life."

It sends despair spearing through her to hear him say that. Maggie pulls away and clasps his face in her hands. "I don't blame you for it. So don't blame yourself. Okay?"

He swallows. Closes his eyes briefly. "I didn't fight for you."

"How would you have known?" Adam's earlier words ring between them. Something kept her from telling Charles back then, and she doesn't know how to tell him that it was because she was terrified of losing him.

Charles gently takes her hands and lowers them. "We should check on Adam."

They walk back to the museum, their steps not quite in sync. Maggie has done her best at wrapping Charles's hand with the small roll of bandages from the kit, but there's a reason she's an engineer and not a nurse. She can already see the end she didn't manage to fix in place flapping about.

Charles pushes open the door to the museum. Inside, Adam is sitting alone at a table with a medley of sandwich-making ingredients, like a PTA mom managing a bake sale that nobody's showed up for, an ice pack pressed to his face. He looks up when they enter. "Hey. I called another car to take everyone else back. Thought it was for the best if we ended things for today."

"How did you, er, explain things to Sylvia?" Maggie asks.

Adam shrugs. "Told her it was a bit of roughhousing gone wrong."

There's no way Sylvia bought this explanation. Maggie suspects the only reason she agreed to go back early is so she can strategize how best to leverage it during the group interview tomorrow.

Charles is looking around at the walls of the museum. "The art in the main lodge and our cabin," he says slowly. "They're all by my favorite artists."

"That's because I don't know shit about art, Charlie-boy."

Charles finally returns his gaze to Adam, who has grown tired of holding his ice and switched arms. When he moves the bag, Maggie lets out a sharp breath. The skin there is blotchy, a web of broken capillaries. He'll be sporting a massive shiner tomorrow.

"Does it hurt?" she asks.

"What do you think?" It's the first time Adam has sassed her, and she's glad that he's done acting nice.

Charles holds out his shoddily bandaged hand like a peace offering. "I feel your pain."

Adam smacks it aside, but the movement lacks real force. "Get that out of my face, asshole. The two of you should make sandwiches for the trip back. Car's coming in fifteen."

"What about you?" Maggie asks.

"I'm still full from Charles's knuckle sandwich." Adam's voice is wry, and Charles snorts.

"If it'll make you feel better, you can punch me, too," Charles offers.

"Nah," Adam replies. "Your self-flagellation will probably be far more effective." He gets up to change out his ice pack, and Maggie and Charles make sandwiches out of rye bread, mayonnaise, brown cheese, and ham.

When the van arrives, Charles takes the seat next to Adam. Things aren't quite back to normal, but Charles clearly regrets getting physical. He even offers Adam half of his sandwich.

As they bump over the gravel road back to the cabins, Adam gets up on his seat and twists around to face Maggie. "I want to ask you more about OurSpot."

Maggie has been waiting for this. She would've been curious too, about an old friend who went off to start something of their own. She's cautious about what she shares. There's no telling what he might use against her. So she focuses on the positive. The user response, the app downloads, their low churn.

Adam whistles when he hears her engagement numbers. "Those are some good numbers, aren't they, Charles? I wish Hari was around to hear this."

Charles hasn't turned around, but he says through a mouthful of sandwich, "It's got a lot of potential."

"Maybe," Maggie says. Adam bends her head toward her.

"What?" she asks, ducking a little from his scrutiny.

"You don't have to make it sound good just for us, you know." Adam puts his arms around the headrest, hugging it as he speaks. "It's very shitty running a company. I get woken up at three a.m. because some terrorist thinks it's a good idea to threaten people on Circle. And I have to look alive and decide what to do, because nobody else will. I think people might have died because of decisions I've made. In fact, I might be responsible for a massacre or two."

"Don't give yourself too much credit," Charles says. "You've got hundreds of people helping you."

Adam shrugs. "But it's still on me, in the end."

"I get it," Maggie says. And she does, even if on a smaller scale.

Adam rests his chin on the headrest, a question in his eyes. "What keeps you up at night?"

Maggie reflexively wants to say that everything is great. She complains to her dad about work all the time, but there's little he can offer besides his sympathy. Adam and Charles have both been in the trenches beside her. They've developed a shared understanding that doesn't exist anywhere else. "Sometimes, I think I've just built a pale Circle imitation, and everyone knows it." Maybe Circle was the only good idea she has ever had, and all she's doing is iterating on the same, tired idea. The possibility has bothered her for a long time, but there's been nobody she could talk to who would understand.

"It's not," Charles says, crumpling his sandwich wrapper and turning around, too. "You build around the same themes—connection, belonging, memory—but that doesn't mean what you're making is a carbon copy. Anyway, the use case for OurSpot is completely different from Circle. People join because they want an intimate place to connect with their friends. Circle is a discovery tool."

Maggie looks at Adam and Charles, both of them peering down at her. They share the same posture, their arms hugging the headrests. All this time, she'd viewed Circle as some kind of paragon of success for a social media company. But OurSpot does serve a separate audience. Adam had pivoted Circle toward discovery by turning it into a platform where people shared their views for the world to see. But OurSpot is for groups. Friends join because they want to deepen their connections. If the two are different, then she needs to think about success differently, too. "You sure know a lot about OurSpot," she says.

"So does Adam," Charles says, and there's something strange in his voice. "He's done a lot of research."

There's a wistful note to Adam's voice when he says, "I always think about the four of us, working in the Shithole together. Those were good days. But look at you now. I guess you never needed us."

By the time they'd all moved into the Shithole, Maggie had been struggling to stay afloat. Her "good days" were way before that, when it was just her, Adam, Charles, and Hari, lounging in Charles and Adam's room, sharing snacks, and brainstorming company names that didn't have inappropriate double meanings. The good days were gone before they'd even known it.

The van drops them off at the main lodge. By now, it's late afternoon, and even though she wasn't the one who got punched in the face, Maggie still feels drained. Priya and Hari are waiting on the curb, Jaya between them.

"Where's Sylvia?" Adam asks when they get off.

Hari folds his arms. "She said she was going to get some writing done in her cabin. Which gives us time to talk about how we're going to save this article when there is now a photo of our CTO punching our CEO! Our shareholders are going to piss themselves if this gets out."

Adam is calm. "The photographer is a freelancer. We'll buy the photo off him. In fact, I'm surprised you haven't already tried that."

Hari looks grouchy. "I did. He agreed to sell it. But that doesn't change what Sylvia saw. If we're going to get through this group interview unscathed, we need to agree on our story."

"Actually, I need to talk to the two of you about something," Charles says. "Privately."

Maggie straightens, wondering what this could be about. Why she's being left out.

"That sounds ominous," Adam says with a laugh.

"Jaya needs to take her nap," Priya says. "Maggie, should we let the guys speak?"

Maggie lingers a second before reluctantly following Priya, glancing over her shoulder at the men's backs as they head into the main lodge. They've been so open with their lives this weekend that she forgot there are still things she isn't privy to.

"Mommy, when's Daddy going to come back?" Jaya asks.

"In a bit," Priya assures her. "He's just busy."

Jaya kicks a pebble. "Daddy's always busy."

Their cabin is located in the forest, halfway between Maggie's cabin and the main lodge. Maggie is about to head toward her own cabin when Priya says, "Would you like to come inside?"

In Maggie's mind, Priya was always Hari's girlfriend first. After everything happened, she wanted to reach out, but it had felt like something that wasn't allowed.

Priya is looking at her expectantly, and it occurs to Maggie that she's probably felt like the outsider on this trip, too. That she has felt like one for far longer than Maggie has.

"Sure," she says.

There are picture books and toys strewn all over the cabin. Jaya refuses Priya's attempts to get her to nap. "I want to play games!" she shouts, jumping up and down on the bed. Maggie marvels at how Priya could possibly put up with this sort of energy every day. It seems way harder than being a CEO. At least her employees know how to cook for and clothe themselves.

"Here," Maggie says, unlocking her phone and giving it to Jaya. "Five minutes, then will you get in bed?"

Jaya snatches the phone from her hand, nodding eagerly. She swipes through the screens like a little tech savant. "You have the same games as Uncle Charles!" she declares.

"I do?" Maggie asks, smiling a little. Looks like Charles's taste is still the same as hers.

"They're all in his tiny folder," Jaya says as she starts playing *Cut the Rope*. She giggles. "Why does Uncle Charles have a tiny folder?"

"Maybe he only keeps bits in it," Maggie says, amused by Jaya's fixation on this. "Although, the typical app is at least a few megabytes."

Jaya does not register her explanation of data storage units. "It's so tiny he named it Tiny."

The smile slips off Maggie's face. It can't be a coincidence, that she's been getting these games all these years. She'd only stopped receiving new ones in 2013. The same year she'd started OurSpot.

The epiphany hits her then. Not a mysterious benefactor, after all.

"Jaya!" Priya eventually takes the phone from Jaya's hands, her voice stern. "It's been more than five minutes. You promised Aunt Maggie, and what do we do in this family?"

"We keep our promises," Jaya says in a monotone, pouting. She squirms beneath the blankets and within a few minutes, her small chest is rising and falling.

Maggie feels Priya's hand on her shoulder. "Let's go to the living room."

They sneak out of the bedroom, into the much larger living room. Maggie notes the art on the walls. More funky interpretations of everyday items. It does seem like something Charles would like.

Priya offers Maggie a glass of water before she sits down next to her on the couch. She has a pile of clothes beside her that she's folding into neat little squares. "I feel like the two of us haven't really gotten to catch up. How has everything been?"

Watching her carry out her responsibilities with graceful assertiveness, Maggie is reminded of Priya's thumb gently pressing against her brow as she drew on eyeliner before Hank's party. She used to think Priya was fierce and a little scary, but there's always been a gentleness to the way she's treated Maggie.

For the moment, she shoves aside her revelation about the games. "I think it was a bad idea for me to come here."

"Why?"

"Because it makes it seem like our story didn't end."

"Things didn't end when you left, you know," Priya says, creating a neat tower of folded shirts. "The guys had to figure out how to run Circle without you."

"They kind of brought that problem on themselves." As she watches Priya color-code her stacks, Maggie falters. This is the story she's told herself. The guys kicked her out, and she'd had no idea it was coming. But she was also wrapped up in her own insecurities, fixated on one-upping Adam and protecting Circle from Hank.

Normally, she would not so openly welcome constructive criticism. But what's been missing has been an outsider's perspective on this whole thing, and she's not about to ask Sylvia for her take. "Actually, what do you think?"

Priya stops folding. "Do you really want to know?"

Maggie braces herself. "Yeah."

"I think you all cared about Circle, and you were all trying your best. But you and Adam both wanted to control the company in your own way, without compromise. I've seen a lot of start-ups go through the same thing, and it almost always ends with one person leaving. That doesn't mean the person who stays is the winner. In a situation like that, everyone loses something."

"I don't think Adam lost anything."

"He did." Priya doesn't clarify. She selects a green puffer and holds it out to Maggie. "We're supposed to go somewhere cold tomorrow. Try this on."

Maggie marvels at Priya's supernatural ability to sense that she's underpacked. She zips the puffer up. It's warm, and smells like cinnamon. She thinks about the criticism she received when she was barely twenty-one and struggling to run Circle, from investors, employees, her peers. She used to hate the girl she was. One with an open heart, who let those comments get under her skin. "People were always harder on me." She hears how petulant she sounds, but she doesn't think Priya will judge her for it.

"I think you know that's not true."

She stuffs her hands into the pockets of the puffer as she mulls over Priya's comment. She thinks of Adam, saying he wanted to be good enough for her. Perhaps she's guilty of the same thing that she's blamed others for. She'd wanted him to fulfill so many roles: object of her admiration, friend, crush, cofounder. It's no wonder that she'd been constantly disappointed.

Losing their friendship was like watching her house burn down. She had fled the flames, run as far away from them as she could to start over again. Maybe Adam had felt that way too, except he had actually bothered to salvage some things from the wreckage. Unlike her, he had realized that there might be value beyond the exterior.

Priya zips up a suitcase, after somehow managing to shove a mountain of clothes inside. Maggie watches her move around the cabin, tidying up, her hands constantly moving.

"Will you tell me why you don't take photos anymore?" Priya's old DSLR used to be attached to her. Maggie knows what passion looks like, and Priya used to be passionate about photography. Something must have happened for her to give it up completely.

"I told you. Jaya and part-time VC work keeps me busy."

It's Maggie's turn to give Priya that faintly censorious look. "That kid can entertain herself with a square foot of dirt and her own spit. Also, you and Hari are rich, so it's not like you have to lift a finger if you don't want to. What's the deal, really?"

Priya presses her lips together, and Maggie thinks she has pushed too hard. But then she says, "The work he's doing, it's important." There's a fierce pride in her voice, but Maggie also hears the implication. *More important than what I want.* "Those first few months after you left were tough. Hari came home past midnight every day and was out of the house by six in the morning. He and Adam were trying to fill the gap you left behind, and morale was pretty low. They got their feet under them, eventually, but Hari needed me. So I did whatever I could to help, whether that was picking him up from the office when he was too tired to drive or scheduling Jaya's birth before the IPO."

"You didn't mention Charles."

Priya shrugs. "He wasn't super cooperative in the beginning."

Hearing Priya talk about Circle and Hari's struggles resurfaces her anxiety over returning to OurSpot after this weekend. The crushing weight of responsibility that she can't share with anyone else, not if she wants people to see her as capable.

But she pulls herself back to this conversation. OurSpot can wait. "Things are better now, aren't they? You deserve to pursue what you're interested in, too."

"I guess. But Hari's changing the world, and he inspires so many people. That's why he has to be online all the time." Priya's voice grows smaller, unsure. "Whatever he does will always dwarf anything I do."

It's such a departure from the Priya Maggie remembers, who ordered people around and once got a root canal without localized anesthesia. That Priya would never have been content staying in Hari's shadow. Maggie puts a hand on Priya's arm, hoping that what she says next gets through to her. Hari would hate that Priya has limited herself because of him. "The things you want are not any less meaningful. Don't make yourself small because of him. Besides, he shouldn't be on social media so much anyway. I've cofounded *two* social media companies, so I would know."

Priya is quiet for a long moment. Then, she touches Maggie's hand. "You have always looked really lovely in colors," she says.

Chapter Thirty-Seven

NOVEMBER 2006

The *TechCrunch* interview turned out worse than she had feared. Maggie entered the Shithole, hoping nobody would be home so she could sulk in her living room–bedroom while eating peanut butter out of the jar and scrolling through her friends' Circle posts. Charles had read about something called an *infinite scroll* on a blog, and they'd rolled out the feature last week. Average time spent on their home page had skyrocketed. Even Maggie found herself scrolling for hours before retiring, bleary-eyed and melty-brained, to her actual work. It was brilliant, as long as she didn't get sucked into it, too.

They'd managed to assemble their mega-desk by the front door, and as she stepped inside, Charles immediately looked up from his monitor, pushing his headphones down. "Hey, want to take a break and play this game with me? It's like *Invaders* but you destroy the aliens with hex color codes."

Maggie sighed, walking past him and pushing aside her divider so she could put her backpack down. "Charles, what do you do if the world hates you?"

He spun his chair around to face her. "Surely the world has better things to do."

"Oh yeah? Look at the home page of *TechCrunch*." She flopped onto her bed, staring at the ceiling as she listened to Charles type the web address into his computer. She should've accepted that giving interviews was her weakness and sent Adam in her place, like she always did. But she needed to stop depending on Adam. He was all in on Public Profiles, despite her lingering skepticism over pivoting away from their core users. Adam had been sheepish when Maggie confronted him about it.

"I totally thought I talked to you about it," he'd said apologetically. "It's pretty far along, but if you want to get involved, I'll make sure someone from the team catches you up." It had been simultaneously nice and dismissive, and it had irked Maggie. She didn't want to glom onto Adam's idea, and besides, she didn't think it was a good one. And now, to add to the headache, there was this *TechCrunch* article.

Charles read silently. "It's not that bad."

She stood up and peered over his shoulder at the screen. Saw her face splashed on *TechCrunch*'s website with the header: "The CEO of Circle Might Be the Least Important Person There." Someone had lifted a crappy headshot she'd had taken back in community college. The article went on to make an argument for her utter lack of experience, starting with her age and ending with a quote from someone at the Engineering Honor Society saying that she'd started Circle as a site to gossip about classmates, and had merely gotten lucky with its popularity. The article quoted a Circle post made by some random chick named Sylvia Kim that had somehow risen to the top of Circle's home feed: *Congrats Circle on raising. Hank Wagner's specialty: removing testy CEOs. Bets that it's Margaret Tang?* followed by a giant photo of Hank's smarmy face. The pièce de résistance was a quote she herself had given: "I'm only one of the many people who make Circle successful." She'd been trying to share the credit, but the reporter had positioned it as evidence that she was an amateur.

Every word of the article was tattooed onto her brain. It was extra awful because of how it nailed her own insecurities. She *did* lack experience. She *had* gotten lucky. They weren't wrong about any of that.

"I bet everyone at Circle has read it." She was supposed to be at the office right now, reviewing the launch plan for Circle in Eastern Europe. But she'd rescheduled the meeting. She didn't think she could order a roomful of people around when her self-confidence was so low.

"It's just an article. Reporters make money off controversy. You really don't want to play *Hex Invaders* with me? It'll make you feel better."

She lay back down. "Maybe my dad was right," she muttered. People looked at her and saw a kid. She wished she possessed an iota of Adam's confidence, or even Charles's cool composure. Instead, she was awkwardness anthropomorphized. It wasn't like she'd learned social skills from her dad, whose most frequent interactions were with the duck butcher at Ranch 99 and his car insurance agent every time he wanted lower monthly premiums.

"If you want, I'll make a bunch of fake websites about how great you are and SEO them until they bury that *TechCrunch* article."

"Very gallant, but no."

As she got up to make herself a snack, she glanced at Charles's screen. It was of Circle, but it looked like he was testing something in staging.

"What is that?" she asked, pointing.

"The algorithm for the new home page."

Maggie blinked. Had they discussed this previously? She was starting to lose track. Her instinct was to pretend that she knew what he was talking about, but she didn't like lying to Charles, who was always honest with her. "Why do we need a new one again?"

"Adam wanted to replace the current feed." Charles looked perturbed. "For Public Profiles."

She stepped closer, leaning over his shoulder to read the code. There was nothing wrong with their current home page, which was sorted based on how recently people posted. "I knew he was working on Public Profiles, but I didn't know he was making us change the home page algorithm. And you of all people shouldn't be involved."

"What's that supposed to mean?" Charles pushed away from his desk, folding his arms.

Maggie grew still. She didn't know what she meant, except that something dark and possessive uncoiled at the thought of Adam taking Charles away from her. "It's just . . . we're a team." It was a weak line. She knew it, and Charles knew it too, judging by the way his eyes narrowed. He was still in his chair, and she was leaning over his shoulder, her face close to his. Quickly, she pulled back.

"We're all on the same team," Charles said, his voice growing gentle. "Unless this is about something else?"

She suddenly found it hard to swallow with him looking at her, his eyes probing. "I just don't think this is the right move. And I don't know how to tell Adam." Adam recruiting Charles to make updates without her knowledge—this felt like a new betrayal.

Charles rolled his chair back to his desk. "You two need to sort your stuff out." He said it bluntly. His patience was running thin, too.

He was right. She needed to put Adam back in his place. Or else that *TechCrunch* article would come true.

SHE PLANNED CIRCLE'S anniversary celebration for the Sunday after Thanksgiving.

Maggie arrived at Ocean Beach, strangely nervous. She'd arranged the whole thing in secret, and she wasn't sure how the guys would react. There was a group calendar invite, so they knew where and when to show up. Charles had been home for the holiday, Adam had been nowhere to be seen, and Hari was convalescing with Priya in San Francisco after his harrowing Friendsgiving injury—a Ping-Pong ball to the eye during their office party.

She popped the trunk of her Zipcar, taking out a box of firewood, and headed down to the beach. Her feet sank into the cool sand, and the ocean breeze wound around her bare ankles as she made her way toward the fire pits. She had to make several trips because it was just her, and the logs were heavy.

The sun was beginning to set when she finally had everything on the beach. She got busy starting a fire. While it wasn't difficult with lighter fluid, she'd still come here a few times the past week to practice.

As the fire ignited, she noticed a couple approaching her.

"Are you Margaret Tang?" the woman asked. She looked around Maggie's age.

Maggie straightened, wiping her dirty hands against her pants. Nervousness spread through her limbs. "Yes. Are you here for the Circle Community Gathering? Grab a drink and a shirt." She nodded toward the bins she'd carried onto the beach.

More people started arriving, and the group became easier to spot, as everyone donned shirts and milled around the fire. Maggie wished one of the guys would show up, so she wouldn't be on her own, forced to make small talk. Charles's voice whispered in her ear that there was no user experience if she didn't talk to users, so she pushed down her discomfort and joined the crowd.

It wasn't too bad, actually. People told her how Circle had been the reason they'd found their best friend, their spouse, and in one guy's case, his long-lost cousin who had moved to Mongolia. A couple shared their love story. They'd broken up during college because long-distance had been too difficult, and then reconnected on Circle. Gradually, everyone started mingling, and Maggie backed away from the group, wanting a break from talking.

A mix of emotions churned in her chest. She'd given something of value to all the people on this beach, somehow grown from loner outcast to an entrepreneur with purpose. She was proud of herself, she realized. And yet . . . here she was, still standing away from the crowd. It was a hard habit to shake, not when she'd grown up in mostly solitude.

She let out a soft sigh. No matter what she did, she would always be someone who didn't quite belong.

"The party is over there, you know."

She turned and found Charles standing there, outlined by the firelight. He'd put on one of the shirts, a purple tee with Circle's logo on the chest pocket. They rarely used the full logo now, preferring a cursive C to represent the company on the webpage and internal documents. But this was Maggie's party, so she'd used the logo in its entirety: *Circle* written in cursive, Charles's sketch of hers and Adam's fingers in their pinky promise framing the word. She wondered if Adam even remembered their promise.

"I'd rather be the planner than the participant. What do you think?" She'd come up with the idea two weeks ago and hustled to pull it all together—blasting out an invitation to Circle's first-ever community gathering in San Francisco, monitoring sign-ups, fretting over how many shirts to print.

"I can't believe you didn't let any details slip while you were planning this."

"I'm full of surprises."

Charles smiled affectionately, like this was something he already knew. "I've got a surprise for you, too. It's why I'm late. I had to pick it up."

He pulled something out of his pocket. It was rectangular and flat, the glass screen gleaming. A device of some sort.

Maggie plucked it out of his hand. Examined it closely, like it was a newly discovered specimen in a lab. If she wasn't mistaken, this was a full touchscreen.

"It's an iPhone," Charles said. "And it's not supposed to be announced until next year, so you're going to have to keep this a secret until then."

"How did you get your hands on this?" She handled it gingerly, almost regretful that she was smudging its pristine surface. When she flipped it over, she saw something engraved on the metallic back, reflecting the firelight. *For Tiny.*

"I'm not going to tell you so you don't get implicated." He turned it on, and the Apple logo blinked at them before transitioning to a screen of jewel-toned icons.

She marveled at how cleanly the graphics flowed across the screen, the camera, the pleasure of pressing the home button and seeing the windows shrink back into the home page. The innovation took her breath away. "This is going to change everything, Charles." She was already thinking of the implications. A phone that could be used for more than texts and calls. A pocket-sized browser from which you could access Circle.

"Just like Circle is," he said. "I think we've barely scratched the surface of what technology can do. You're taking us into a new era."

A new era. The semester was coming to a close, and then there would be only one more left before they were officially catapulted into the real world. She'd mostly been dreading it, but Charles was reminding her of how much there was to look forward to. New gadgets, groundbreaking ideas, and moments like this, with the foam from the crashing waves sparkling in the air, the chatter of people in purple shirts, Charles looking at her like her face held the sun.

"Sorry I'm late!" They both looked up, Maggie slipping the iPhone into her pocket, to see Hari sprinting over the dunes, still wearing his eyepatch from the Ping-Pong incident. "Whoa, Maggie, who are all these people?"

She grinned at him. "Why don't you talk to them and find out?"

Accompanied by Hari and Charles, Maggie joined the group again. Their presence sandpapered away the edges of her awkwardness, and conversation flowed more easily than when it had just been her.

It was beautiful to meet the people whose lives Circle had touched. Maggie wanted to stay in this night forever. She would distill it into the purest elixir so she could take small sips of its vitality whenever she needed it.

But as the night wore on, there was still no sign of Adam. Where r u? she texted him. She kept flipping her phone open, thinking she'd missed his response. Until, finally, when almost everyone had left and Hari and Charles were dousing the fire, she received his reply.

Can't make it. Sorry

Chapter Thirty-Eight

DAY 3: SATURDAY

After she says goodbye to Priya and walks back to their cabin, the olive puffer providing another layer of warmth, she finds herself unable to sit down. It's been at least two hours, and Charles is still not back. She wants answers. To confirm that she's not delusional for jumping to conclusions based on what a five-year-old blurted out before naptime—and to begin to understand what it all means.

She feels like she has just downed an energy drink, her nerves buzzing. This many years should have dimmed those feelings, but she feels twenty-one again, her stomach overrun by butterflies. He'd voted against her, hadn't he? These games he'd sent her—were they his way of apologizing?

From her window, she finally spots Charles on the path leading to their cabin, then picking his way over the rocks. He stands there, regarding the water for a minute. Then, he tears his shirt over his head and jumps straight in.

Maggie runs to the window, nearly pressing her face to the glass. "Again?" she mutters to herself. Something must have happened. He swims outside of her view, and she paces the room for several minutes before racing outside, just in time to see him swimming toward the floating sauna. He's not going to run—or swim—away from her. Not until she's gotten answers.

She runs along the shore until she can see the curved lines of the sauna. Has war flashbacks of hopping over those minuscule skipping stones. She shucks off her clothes, leaving herself in only her bra and Kohl's undies, before sprinting into the water.

She howls, her entire body going electric. How does Charles *do* this? She's a block of ice being shaved down. But she fights through it, powering her arms through the water until she hits the dock where the sauna is located. Planting her palms on the wood, she pulls herself up, gooseflesh frighteningly prominent all over her arms.

Hot hair blasts her as she opens the door to the sauna. Charles is in the corner, wearing only his boxers. His head snaps up at her approach. Moisture glistens at his throat, though she's not sure if it's sweat or seawater. He is, for some reason, holding an orange. They stay like that, drinking each other in.

She realizes how she must look. Soaking wet, pressed to the sauna door, wearing only her bra and underwear. Her teeth are clacking too violently for her to say anything. Instead, she walks to the benches and climbs up to where Charles is. Sits right next to him. Water drips from her hair, pattering onto the planks below. Slowly, warmth enters her body, and the pleasure of it is so immense that her entire body feels weightless.

Charles resumes peeling his orange. Then, he stretches out his arm. A familiar ritual, the splitting and sharing of fruit, one that Chinese kids everywhere understand. After she'd moved home, her dad had peeled an apple for her every day. It sat there, on their dining table, a symbol of all the things he didn't know how to say.

She reaches for the orange slice, the tips of her fingers brushing against his palm. The fruit has warmed in the heat of the sauna, and it coats the cavern of her mouth with sweet, hot juice. The membrane clings stickily to her lips. She finally can feel her toes, and she stares down at them as she speaks, suddenly shy. No words seem sufficient. "My favorite game was *Florence*. Because I felt like

I was actually part of a story. My least favorite? *Candy Crush*. Do you know how many times I told myself, 'Just one more level,' and then five hours would pass? I actually had to delete it, or else I would've ended up spending real money just to destroy fake candy. So, sorry about that. But that was the only one I deleted."

Charles's voice is low. "Why are you telling me this?"

She turns to look at him. "You spent five years sending me hundreds of dollars' worth of games, and you're not going to own up to it? Were you ever going to tell me?"

They stare at each other. Juice glistens on his lip. Then, he clears his throat. His eyes flick away. "It was my way of being there for you."

"*You* voted me out. *You* took Adam's side." The words come out furious. The emotions war inside her—anger over what he did, tenderness because he'd been thinking of her this entire time, and a deep yearning to talk to him the way she used to. "Why do all of this?"

Shock ripples over his face, closely followed by comprehension. "Maggie, I didn't vote against you. Is that what you thought this whole time?"

It knocks the air out of her lungs.

"Adam called the meeting. I didn't realize until I saw Hank that it was about removing you."

They would've been able to get a majority, even without Charles. Still, she almost doesn't want to believe it. To accept that she had been wrong this entire time. She watches the sweat beading on her knees. "But you didn't say anything. You let security cart me out." The shame of being escorted out of there, everyone in the company watching while none of the guys lifted a finger, burns through her.

"When you burst in, I was trying to negotiate with them. So that they'd agree to bring you back eventually." Charles is clenching his fist, the skin around his bruised knuckles stretching. "How was I supposed to know that you'd just disappear without a trace?"

Seeing him in that conference room, she had believed that Charles and Adam had banded against her. After all, they had been friends and roommates first. She'd been so furious that Charles had been part of the conversations that it had never occurred to her that he'd been trying to help. "I'm sorry, Charles." She well and truly means it.

"I thought of reaching out when you started OurSpot." It comes out of him in a rush.

"Why didn't you?"

"I thought you'd moved on. And . . . I was stuck." Charles cradles the peel between his hands, examining it. "I used to want to build stuff with my hands. I thought I would design things that people could hold and delight in. Instead, my greatest accomplishment is making people addicted to a website. Circle doesn't make people happy, Tiny. It makes them feel anxious and inadequate, but they stay on it because they can't bear to delete it, either."

He sounds so miserable that she lurches forward onto her knees and put her arms around his neck, hugging him hard. Her fingers dig into the hard muscle of his back, as if she can force the pain out of his body. She hears his disappointment with himself, and it makes her heart hurt. Charles has always wanted to create beautiful things, but it sounds like that dream was put aside in service of Circle.

Charles's arms wrap around her tightly. They hold on to each other, breathing in the scents of cedar and citrus. Her dad is not a hugger, and she has forgotten how nice it is to be held like this. Like she is providing comfort in addition to receiving it.

Charles's breath is warm against her neck. "I'm glad that you're here, Tiny."

She squeezes her eyes shut. Lets the truth of the words ring through her as she says, "Me, too." He releases her, and she sits back on the bench, even though she wants to touch him again. Questions swarm inside her. She wants to know more about his life now.

"Remember that night we got high and stole the projector?" Charles asks. "We talked about what choices we get to make. I thought about it a lot after you were gone. And I told myself that if I ever was in the position to choose again, I'd choose you."

I'd choose you. He says it with the steadiness of someone who has considered every angle and arrived at the same answer, again and again. Moisture gathers in the small of her back and along the back of her knees. Here, in this sauna, she feels cocooned in so many possibilities, but she is only certain of one: that she chooses him, too.

She leans forward and kisses him. His mouth tastes sweet from the ripe orange.

For a second, she thinks he's kissing her back. Hears his hand land hard on the bench beside her hip, feels the pressure of his mouth against hers.

In the next moment, he is pulling away from her. His body is rigid, and she realizes that he's gripping the bench with his injured hand.

"Maggie," he says, his voice sounding like it's been scraped over rocks. "We can't do this."

He can't look at her, and she remembers—the girlfriend. He'd sent her those games because he felt sorry for her, and she's jumped to conclusions yet again.

She is a puddle of embarrassment. She can't believe she just tried to make a move on him like a horny teenager.

She stands up abruptly. "I'm going to head back," she says. She needs to find a cool, dark corner to scratch her wrist and contemplate how badly she's just messed things up.

Charles gives a rough shake of his head. "Hold on, let me explain—"

She doesn't wait for him to finish. She rushes out of the sauna, shivering and cursing under her breath as she hops over those damned stepping stones toward the rest of her clothing. She runs back to the cabin, showers and quickly retreats to the bed, sliding under the covers. When she hears Charles come in, she pretends to be asleep.

Chapter Thirty-Nine

DECEMBER 2006

"You're going to have to take another semester of classes if you want to graduate," the pitiless academic adviser said, referring to Maggie's three failed classes and five unfulfilled requirements, which she hadn't discovered until she signed into the university portal for the first time since the semester started.

"I can't afford that." The thought of telling her dad, who she hadn't called in months, made her feel faint. She would rather take on a zombie army than admit to him that she'd failed. "I've been working on this company—Circle, maybe you've heard of it? That's why I couldn't study—"

The woman rolled her eyes. "Next you'll tell me you've been auditioning for *Star Trek*. Go talk to the financial aid office. Maybe they'll help."

Maggie descended the steps of Sproul Hall, fuming. What was the point of school, anyway? So she could get a paper degree and drive around with a license plate frame that said *Cal Alum*?

"Maggie!" She lifted her head and saw Adam jogging toward her. "Were you just in for academic advising, too?"

It figured that Adam would appear while she was not in the mood to talk to anyone, when she had been unsuccessful at hunting him down for the past month. At first, she'd been angry about how he'd hijacked the home page and tried to get him alone so she could yell at him for it. But his calendar was full, and an entourage followed him everywhere he went in the office, providing a very effective meat shield. Then, the anger had bled away, replaced by defeat. There was no pinning Adam down, unless he wanted to talk to her, too. After their breakup, it was too visible how his priorities had shifted. They might still be friends, but her importance to him had diminished. "Where have you been?" she asked.

"Working, obviously! Where have *you* been?"

She bristled at the insinuation that she hadn't been working, too. "I've been keeping my head down since that *TechCrunch* article."

"That article was such bullshit," Adam said. "I hope you didn't let it bother you too much."

"Of course not." Good thing Adam hadn't been around to see her print it out and shred it into confetti while Charles cheered her on. "Are you done with finals?"

"That's why I was here, actually. I'm officially a college dropout." Adam said it like he was announcing he was going to the Olympics. "I stopped turning stuff in, like, a month ago."

Her stomach bottomed out. Another thing added to the list of stuff he hadn't mentioned to her. "I've been trying to talk to you one-on-one. You know that, right?"

Adam stuffed his hands in his pockets. "Things have been busy." She thought she detected a glimmer of regret in his tone. Maybe he'd also noticed how they barely spoke anymore. Charles was right. They needed to sort this out.

"We need to talk about Public Profiles," she said. "I get that you want something you can own, but you have to keep me in the loop. Especially if it's going to affect the assets we already have."

That made Adam look at her. She was surprised by the flicker of defiance in his eyes. "If I'd gone to you first, it never would have happened."

She faltered, taken aback by the combativeness of his response. She almost backed down, until she remembered that she needed to advocate for herself. It was becoming clear that she couldn't rely on Adam to steer the company in the right direction. Steeling herself, she said, "Keep me in the loop. Or else we're going to have bigger problems." She hated how much it sounded like a threat, but she didn't trust him anymore.

They stared each other down, and she half expected Adam to blow up, the way he had when their first meeting with Hank had gone poorly. She wanted him to get mad at her, so they could yell at each other, get it out, then forgive each other again. But instead, he shrugged and said, "Sure."

AFTER MAGGIE READ through everything on Public Profiles and perused what their engineers had done, she concluded it was completely wrong for Circle. Adam's theory was that Circle had become a hub for information. After making it publicly available, they'd seen famous people joining: celebrities, politicians, public figures. These people wanted to leverage Circle as a place to share their views in an authentic way, things they couldn't get through the filter of normal media. Adam wanted to capitalize on this, charging these people for access to audiences that they normally didn't have.

Maggie hated the idea. She didn't want people like the president or actors to encroach on the space that she shared with her circle.

On Christmas Eve, she stayed late at the office, putting together a counter to this strategy. There had to be other ways to make money. If Adam had been at her bonfire and spoken to their users, he would know how sacred the Circle feed was and that they shouldn't mess with it. She knew Adam wouldn't like what she was doing, but if he wasn't going to change his plans to appease her, she'd have to take action.

Charles was sitting next to her at Norway's conference table, headphones around his neck, messing with a Circle-branded Rubik's Cube. Hari had been buying a lot of custom swag lately, from coasters to beanies. It was his retail therapy as he waited to hear back from Goldman.

"You can go home, you know," Maggie told Charles. "You don't have to stick around if you're done."

Charles didn't lift his eyes from the cube. "I'd rather hang out with you." Charles was working on reducing their technical debt, a thorny problem that conveniently absolved him from taking a side. She wished he would just take her side, but she also understood his reservations over offending Adam. They were bros, after all.

Her phone rang, and she saw that her dad was calling. She'd finally called and invited him to the Circle office, hoping it would be an effective prop to her announcement that she was dropping out. It was not financially responsible nor logical to stay in college another semester. It would just cost her on all fronts. And what would it look like, if her COO was willing to go all in with the company, but she was still over here, trying to turn in English papers on time? It would just be more proof that she hadn't grown up.

She rushed to the front of the office and saw her dad waiting outside the glass doors. She was excited for him to tour the office, to show him that this was what happened when she had the freedom to pursue the things she loved. She pushed the door open, stepping outside. "Hey, Dad. Come in—"

"A coworker showed me an article about you," he said.

The door shut behind them. She looked at her dad, the grave expression on his face, and knew he was referring to the *TechCrunch* article.

"The writer made some good points," he said. "You shouldn't be running a company, in addition to being a student. You'll just end up being bad at both. Best to focus on school first, graduate with a good GPA."

She could tell that the article had embarrassed her dad. His coworker had probably been nice about it—*look, your daughter's in the news!*—but he'd taken it as an insult.

He hadn't asked if she was okay, or bought up all the magazines in town and set them on fire. Instead, he'd agreed with every criticism leveled at her. "Actually, I *am* going to focus on one thing. Circle. I'm dropping out of school."

Her dad spoke calmly, but she saw the flicker of outrage in his eyes. "You have one more semester left, Margaret."

She didn't bother explaining that it would definitely take her more than one semester to graduate. "I don't care. This company is the one thing that makes me feel alive." Her dad didn't understand the importance of doing this *now*. Everything could be different in six months. She needed to be *here*. Already, she was seeing the consequences of her split attention. An entire company strategy advancing without her, doubt from reporters over her competence, Adam's vision beginning to overrule hers. "I'll pay off the loans. You don't need to worry about that."

"I don't want you to make a mistake and regret it forever. A degree, an education—nobody can take that away from you."

"You keep telling me I'm making mistakes, but what about *your* mistakes?" she asked harshly. Her dad's injured expression confirmed that she'd hit true. "If I don't do this now, I *know* I'll regret it for the rest of my life. Unlike you, I'm actually going to do something about it." She looked him in the eyes, making sure he understood that she was absolutely serious. After a minute, her dad turned his back on her. Began walking away in his unhurried way. She watched him go. She wouldn't follow. She wouldn't return to their quiet house where he would give her the cold shoulder, and she would have to take it because she had nowhere else to go.

"Maggie? How long have you been out here? Where's your dad?" Charles was beside her all of a sudden, ushering her back into the warmth of the lobby. He brushed her cheek with a thumb, and she realized she was crying.

She rubbed her eyes. "It's late. You should go."

"What about you?"

"I'll call a taxi to take me back to our apartment."

"I'll drop you off."

"No, you should be with your family. Not dealing with—" She motioned frantically at her face. "All of this bullshit."

He was taking off his hoodie and wrapping it around her shoulders. It smelled like his blankets when she'd slept in them that summer. "I want to be with you right now. I'd rather be here, with you, than anywhere else."

The way he said it had her looking up, her vision blurry from her tears. Charles was standing close, his hands still on her shoulders. His voice was low and sincere. Suddenly all the moments they'd spent together—spooning Golden Curry in their mouths over the pot, arguing about whether Neopets actually died, sharing all those joints—flooded back to her, creating a tapestry whose full design she only now could see.

Sturdy, sensitive Charles. Brilliant designer, fellow weeb, the best listener in the world. All this time, she had only seen Adam.

She reached up and framed his face with her hands. He leaned in, and she met him halfway. Their kiss was warm, earnest, and tender.

He pulled back, pressed his forehead to hers. And then he smiled, his eyes bright, and fireworks went off in her chest. "What if you came to my house for Christmas?"

Chapter Forty

JANUARY 2007

"I have something to ask you," Maggie said to Charles, stopping in the middle of the Glade and tugging him to face her. The two of them were walking around campus, stoned, thanks to a medicinal weed cookie. It was almost like old times, except now they were holding hands. She'd gone to his house for Christmas, eaten dinner with his raucous family. It had been noisy, fun, and cozy, but her enjoyment had been tempered by the thought of her dad at home by himself. She'd shrugged off the thought. He should be glad she wouldn't be asking him for money anymore, relieved he wouldn't have to support her.

"Sure. Anything." It still warmed her whenever he said that. It felt like she could ask for the world, and he would give it to her. Charles sat on the grass, pulling her down beside him. She rested her head on his shoulder, taking in the smell of grass and citrus from the Cuties he was always peeling.

"Do you think Circle is headed in the right direction?" She could feel Charles tensing, as he always did when she mentioned Circle. But she had to talk about this with someone. Adam used to be that person, but he was too absorbed by his own aims to listen.

Sometimes, she felt like she was the only one who thought things were off. Yes, Circle's users were from all over the world, and people spent an average of three hours a day on it. They'd recently onboarded the Canadian prime minister. But Maggie felt like they were straying further from why they'd created Circle. "I've been thinking a lot about our original mission, and I have a new idea. Code name: Spot. Cute, right?" She'd been playing with the idea of launching a separate, decentralized platform that allowed users to choose what content they saw. Already, she'd assembled a contingent of loyal engineers and started sandboxing.

Charles's shoulder shifted under her head, and he faced her, frowning with faint disapproval. "Maggie, you can't recruit me into this feud you and Adam have going."

"I'm just asking your opinion," she said a little defensively. She'd thought he would've agreed with her, simply out of affection. Even with the marijuana high, she felt a prickle of warning at the thought, for how presumptuous and manipulative it was.

Charles shook his head. "Sometimes, it's impossible to separate you from Circle."

"Why's that bad?" Circle was part of her. Without it, she was another average, awkward kid, part of the nameless masses passively moving through life. Circle had given her purpose. A reason to wake up every morning.

"No, Maggie. You exist apart from this company." Charles put his hands on her cheeks, his palms warm, looked straight into her eyes like he was telling her something extremely important. "Even if it's no longer a part of you anymore, you'll keep going."

She laid her hands over his, even as her thoughts drifted. He was wrong. Charles would never get her desire to build her life around Circle. The way that Circle's failures were her own failures.

This would always be something that divided them, in the same way it had brought her and Adam together. But she didn't want to think about that now. She planted a kiss on his lips, then jumped up, liking the flash of heat in his eyes. "Race you back home!" She took off, certain he wouldn't be far behind.

When they got back, baked and laughing, Adam and Hari were sitting at the kitchen table, drinking beers.

"The whole crew's together!" Hari cried. He lifted a bottle, letting loose a belch. "Beer?"

Maggie, with her sluggish thoughts, glanced from him to Adam, who seemed to be a few bottles in by the glazed look in his eyes. He was staring at her and Charles's joined hands. She resisted the urge to drop his hand and lifted her chin. "Fancy seeing you here. I thought you were living at the office now." Their employees talked about how Adam kept a sleeping bag under his desk. They tittered about how some of them had stumbled on him brushing his teeth in the bathroom. For some reason, this only enhanced his status. Maggie had once fallen asleep at her desk at work, and someone had taken a photo and posted it to 4chan, where it had instantly garnered comments like "my woman when I tell her to use critical thinking."

Adam's eyes narrowed. "It definitely feels a lot more like home."

Hari swiveled his head between the two of them, a frown on his face. "Is something wrong?"

"Nope." Adam finished his beer, got up, and went into his room.

Chapter Forty-One
DAY 4: SUNDAY

On Sunday, Maggie wakes up far too early again and dresses before hurrying out of the cabin. When she arrives at the lodge for breakfast, she sees Adam pacing outside on the deck, alternating between staring out at the scenery and speaking into the phone. The corner of his mouth is dark and puffy.

The coffee machine whirs and grinds diligently as she waits. The morning is crisp and clear, the waves the smallest she's seen them so far, shimmering underneath the sun. There's not a cloud in the sky. It's at odds with how she feels, like the earth has cracked open beneath her. Just when she's accepted that she's still in love with Charles, she's lost him again.

This time, she has nobody to blame except herself. If she had stuck around all those years ago and actually given him a chance to explain—she doesn't even dare to imagine how everything would be different. This weekend has revealed how much her loneliness has been by her own design. She has always held herself in a state of preparation for people to follow her mom's footsteps and leave her. She'd driven Lisa away, maintained a chilly distance from her employees, rebuffed the Wongs' well-meaning advances. She'd left first. Just like her mom.

The machine beeps, signaling her drink is done. She glances out the windows at where Adam's pacing and decides that today, at least, she can choose not to be lonely. Making a second cup, she heads outside.

"We need to move fast," Adam's saying. "Especially now, with Charles—" He looks up and notices her. "Send me those documents today," he orders, then he hangs up and smiles at her. She hands the cup of coffee to him. "Thanks. You're up early."

"Haven't gotten used to the jet lag. What's your excuse?"

"Trying to knock out some work." Adam rubs his forehead, takes a sip of the coffee. "Mm. I feel more alive now."

"What happened?" she asks.

He faces her fully. She tries not to stare at his bruised cheek. "He didn't tell you?"

"Who?"

"Charles is quitting Circle. He told us last night."

So that was why he'd jumped into the ocean. She'd been so consumed with forcing a confession out of him that she hadn't given him the chance to speak in the sauna. Now she feels even worse for mauling him instead of listening.

Adam sighs, going to the railing. He leans his elbows against it as he sips his coffee. The wind jostles his curls. "I wonder if I did this to myself by sticking the two of you together."

Charles's rejection from last night stings anew. For all of Adam's meddling, none of it has worked out. She walks to the railing, leaning on it next to him. "The forced cohabiting was a stroke of genius. Not."

Adam smirks, glancing over at her. "Don't tell me you didn't appreciate it."

She rolls her eyes. "Your support is coming a little late." She flashes back to Charles's reaction in the sauna again and shudders slightly. How could she have forgotten the girlfriend? She's an idiot.

"I wouldn't be so sure." Adam has finished his coffee, and he bends down to put it beside his foot. "I think he liked you from the moment he saw you. I was the dick who kept you two apart." His eyes go to her thumb, which is rubbing against her wrist again. She immediately stops. "And I think you *definitely* still like him."

She can tell that playing matchmaker is how Adam has been trying to redeem himself, regardless of how Charles feels. Charles and Adam may be best friends, but she'd bet her old iPhone that they never talk about feelings. Adam would have no idea how wrong he is this time. She brings the topic back to the resignation. "I hope you're not going to try to force him to stay at Circle. He was probably already thinking about leaving before he even showed up here. Charles isn't the type to make spontaneous decisions."

"You're right," Adam concedes. "Actually, while Hari was on pat leave, he brought it up. I didn't react well, and he didn't bring it up again. It's just . . . the timing couldn't be worse. I need him."

"It's never the right time. You'll forgive him," she says. It hits her then. She's not sure when it happened. Somewhere between that cursed hike and now, her anger toward the guys has dissipated like mist under the sun. She sends Adam a smile that she hopes is comforting. "You forgave me, right?"

Adam is incredulous. "*I* forgave *you*?"

She taps her fingers against the rail. Blows the steam off her coffee. Buys herself a bit more time before she explains. "I've blamed you for everything that happened without acknowledging what I did wrong. It was easier that way, but I know I messed up, too. I wanted to run Circle my way, and I forgot how to be a good friend in the process. So . . . I'm sorry."

Adam shakes his head slightly. "There's nothing to be sorry about," he mumbles.

The feeling that has been building up in her this weekend finally thrashes its way to the surface. She'd resisted its pull in the beginning, but it seems that the yearning is still alive. "I'm always going to miss what it was like when you were in my life."

Adam smiles softly. "I've missed you too, Maggie. There were a lot of times when I wished you were still there. When I could've used your voice in my ear. You know, I always thought to myself that if we saw each other again, we would pick up right where things left off. Talk like no time had passed. I think that's true, don't you?"

If he had asked her on Friday, she would have said *hell, no*. After all, if friendship is a plant that needs to be watered regularly, theirs should have withered to nothingness long ago. But maybe real friendship is not a plant. Maybe it's a mountain. Sometimes difficult to ascend. But there, always, through the storms and the seasons.

Chapter Forty-Two

MARCH 2007

Maggie was the one who planned the trip to Norway. It was their last spring break, even if she and Adam weren't enrolled anymore. Mostly, she wanted to return to normalcy. After that night she and Charles came back together, hers and Adam's relationship had tipped completely into chaos. He'd gotten pissed at her for taking engineers from Public Profiles and putting them on Project Spot. She'd gotten pissed at him for putting spies on her. He still wouldn't admit it, but she was sure that hot Chinese intern from Stanford didn't do anything besides eavesdrop on people in the microkitchen. She stopped trying to hide that the two of them were completely at odds. If someone was working for her, they were sure as hell not working for him, too.

Hari had gotten his full-time offer from Goldman. At the end, he'd accepted the offer. Maggie could tell he was dreading it, but they all knew that Goldman was the lower-risk path to getting his green card. All of this made him sullen, withdrawn. Once he was working full-time, Maggie had the sinking feeling that they would lose him.

Charles was the only one who seemed relatively unbothered by Circle burning to the ground. He wanted to use spring break to catch up on sleep and swim every day at the gym. He'd told Maggie how much he wanted to go fully offline.

The difference between them was that Circle's problems were her only problems. To Charles, Circle held the same level of importance as his homework, his swimming, and . . . her. "We should do something non-work-related. Just me and you," he'd said, his sincerity disarming her like it always did. Being with Charles took some getting used to. He was so direct about what he wanted. She didn't know how to meet him halfway. With Adam, she had never wanted to be so transparent with her affections. The more obvious she was, the further he'd push her away.

Charles had eventually agreed to Norway, like he usually did when she begged hard enough.

Adam, shockingly, had also agreed. It gave her some hope that he missed the way things were, too. Perhaps Norway would be where they figured out a better way to run Circle together.

The original plan was for them to head to SFO from the Shithole. But the night before, Adam said, "Hari and I are heading there from the office. Need to finish a few things, so don't wait for us."

Sometimes, she thought Adam just liked the feeling of appearing important.

"Maggie, you and I can head there together," Charles said, sensing her displeasure.

Yet when she woke up the morning of their flight, the Shithole was still as a tomb, all the guys gone. She checked their rooms, feeling abandoned, especially by Charles.

It was only when she picked up her phone to call him that she saw five missed calls from Priya.

Priya didn't even say *hello* when Maggie returned her call. "They're discussing removing you. You need to get to the office," Priya said in one quick breath. "Now."

She stood there, frozen, in the living room. Charles had left his half-empty mug of coffee on his desk, and she picked it up, frowning at the water ring it left behind. Charles always cleaned up after himself. "What are you talking about?"

Priya spoke fast, like they were on a long-distance call and she was being charged by the minute. "They've been planning this for a while. Hari's going to kill me for telling you, but I had to. Hank's with them."

Maggie dropped the cup of coffee. It fell onto the carpet, brown darkening the beige.

Her heart pounded so hard in her chest that she thought she might faint, but she heard herself say, "You're a good friend." All this time, maybe Priya had been her *only* friend. She leaped into action, grabbing her backpack and calling a taxi. For a second, she looked at her packed suitcase. Then, she grabbed it, like there was a chance she'd still be able to make her flight after this.

The ride to the office was excruciatingly long. She shoved a fifty into the driver's hand and told him to floor it. Surely, Priya was incorrect. There had to be a good reason they were all at the office without her.

They've been planning this for a while.

At the office, she launched herself out of the car, not realizing until she burst through the doors that she'd left her suitcase in the trunk. She stopped short when she saw the four of them in the Norway conference room: Hank, Adam, Hari, even Charles, standing with his back to the glass.

Her mind went blank. All the excuses she'd come up with in the car vanished. There was no good reason for them to be meeting without her right now, just as they were supposed to go on vacation.

She stepped to the door. Adam saw her first. His face paled, which told her enough: Priya was right.

Slowly, she pushed open the door and walked in, dropping her backpack on one of the chairs.

Silence stretched through the room. She turned in a slow circle, taking in the scene. Hank, with his hands behind his head, a stack of papers in front of him. Hank liked all his presentations to be printed out, which Maggie thought was further confirmation that he was scourge of the earth. Adam, beside him, watched her like she was a dangerous animal that had escaped its enclosure. Hari sat across from them and refused to meet her eyes. Finally, Charles, the only one standing. He stared at her and gave the slightest shake of his head. *Calm down*, that shake said. *Don't overreact*.

For a second, she considered being polite. There was a misunderstanding somewhere here, and if she was *really* patient, maybe they would have time to feed her some kind of bullshit.

But then she saw how Charles's eyes flicked to where Adam was sitting. The two of them communicating in a secret language. Her anger surged.

She chose to face Adam as she said, "Anyone want to explain why I was not invited to this *very cozy* gathering?"

Hank rose to his feet. "I'll hand it off to our new CEO to give you the news." He pulled his fleece on, tugging it over his belly. "Make it quick. Lots to do today."

The moment he was gone, Maggie snapped, "New CEO? What the fuck is he talking about?"

"You're being replaced," Adam said. His voice was calm. "Hank approached me about it a few months ago. I told him that if he was going to do this, we couldn't put a stranger in your role. He was worried about my limited product knowledge, but the success of Public Profiles has convinced him otherwise."

"Oh, so you did me a *favor*." Her voice dripped with derision, even as her heart clenched. Adam had kept this from her, not even bothered to discuss it from the start. Once, they might've laughed at Hank's use of the word *mature*, like that was any indication of someone's competence. Instead, he'd completely left her out in the cold.

Adam was watching her from across the table, expressionless. "Hank says that this company needs a CEO with vision."

Vision. That was always what she'd lacked. She did not have Adam's hunger or ambition. She did not try to leave her flag on every piece of land she touched. She should have seen this coming. And Adam was just going along with it? Had he always seen her as replaceable, or was it this particular prize that made her dismissal worth it?

Adam continued. "If you still want to work here, we could change your title. Charles suggested 'Chief Innovation Officer.'"

She spun to stare at Charles. He'd been in on it, too. "You asshole," she said. Shouted, actually.

Charles shook his head. "That's not—"

But Maggie was already turning back to Adam, feeling her lips twist into a sneer. "You're delusional if you think I'll work for you."

Adam clenched his jaw. He looked angry, and she felt a surge of satisfaction. She found herself itching for a fight, so that everyone could see perfect Adam Fink lose his temper, too. "That's what it's about, isn't it? You don't respect me. You think it's an insult to work for me, when everyone else at this company would rather work for me than you."

A punch in the gut would've been less vicious. Had he always felt this way, and she'd just been naive, thinking a boy as popular as him would actually like her?

"We *all* agreed that you need to take a break," Hari said, and his voice carried a note of warning.

Suddenly, she felt like a fool for ever sharing anything with any of them. They should never have seen her struggling to solve a problem, or frustrated over Hank. She'd directly fed them evidence that she wasn't suited for this job.

Sympathy worked its way onto Adam's face, but she thought it looked forced. A mask over his triumph at dethroning her. "I know how hard this is to hear. But the truth is things have been unraveling for months now. Something's got to change."

"I'm not the only one to blame for that." Why wasn't *he* the one leaving?

"Public perception of you hasn't been great since the *TechCrunch* article," Adam said. "You want to know why it's me, and not you? It's because I'm actually likable."

Maggie was thrust back to that summer camp. Watching Adam at the bonfire, surrounded by friends, caught in a quagmire of jealousy and desire. How she'd thought about approaching him and introducing herself, before dismissing the notion. She was weird, nerdy, not worthy of his friendship.

Perhaps they never should've been friends. It was only Circle that had kept them in each other's orbits for so long.

She hated him. She wanted to hurt him. To show him that even if they weren't friends, she still understood who he was at his core. She leaned over the table so that she and Adam were almost nose-to-nose. "Yes, you're likable. Do you ever wonder why? It's because you give people exactly what they want. People like you don't leave legacies. They get forgotten." She saw Adam twitch and knew she'd hit her mark.

"*Okay*," Hari said, sounding a little panicked. "This conversation isn't productive anymore. Let's—"

She could barely remember how to breathe. In the absence of oxygen, fury came billowing through, blurring her thoughts and blanketing all common sense. She relished it, letting her feelings do the talking instead of picking through her words carefully. "Why *the fuck* would I keep working here?" she asked, her voice raising into a shout. "To work with some assholes who think I'm a shitty plug-in they can delete when they feel like it?"

"Maybe you should lower your voice," Hari said meekly. "The soundproof walls aren't that good."

"Oh yeah? Is there something you don't want everyone to hear?" She grabbed the heavy collectible sword leaning against their cardboard Viking and marched outside.

"Maggie, stop!" She wasn't sure who shouted it. Charles? All of them? All she knew was that she needed to let out this smoldering anger before it burned her up on the inside. She spotted the whiteboard with the Post-its from when the office first opened. Utter bullshit. She looked for the photo of the four of them, but it was missing, an obvious patch of blank wall where it should've been.

She zeroed in on the Feels Chair, sitting there innocently with its green leather and walnut arms. Even after she was gone, this goddamn chair would still be here, outlasting her.

She walked to it, lifted the sword, and stabbed it right through the center of the chair cushion. And because that didn't feel satisfying enough, she yanked it out and stabbed it again. And again.

It was only once her arm muscles were straining from the weight that she dropped it. It clanged against the floor. Her brain cleared. Slowly, she turned around. Everyone in the company was staring at her. One guy was pointing his Razr at her, taking a photo. In their blasted open-office layout, everyone had a front-row seat to her meltdown.

The guys were inches away, regarding her like she was a stranger. Like they were afraid of her. Hari was putting his phone away, and she knew he'd called security.

She had burned through all her anger. In its ashes, grief arrived, torrential and overwhelming. She had to get out of here before everyone saw her cry. So she ran for the exit.

Outside, the wind cooled her tears, even though she was still breathing hard. The taxi that had brought her was still idling at the curb.

The cabbie popped his head out. "Miss! You forgot your suitcase. And you didn't tip me!"

"Maggie!" Charles sprinted out after her, and for a moment,

she wanted him to pull her into his arms. "I'll go back with you. You shouldn't be alone."

She thought of him in the room with everyone else. How she'd woken up this morning, and he hadn't been there. Charles was supposed to be on her side, and yet, when it came to it, he had chosen Adam.

"I'd rather be alone than with you," she said.

She could see how the words hurt him. But he didn't give up, seizing her hand. "We exist separately from Circle," he said, and it almost sounded like he was pleading.

She shook him off. "No. We don't."

Then she got into the taxi.

THE FIRST THING she did at the apartment was get on her laptop and log into Circle, tears stinging her eyes. At the very top of her messaging bar, she saw Hari, Adam, and Charles's icons. They were all online.

How mistaken she'd been to think she needed friends. It was better to be alone than have this raw, throbbing pain in her chest. She had shown these people her true self, and they'd deemed her not good enough. They had taken Circle from her. She would never forgive them.

Charles's bubble popped up with a red 1, indicating that he had sent her a message. She ignored it and clicked on her settings, scrolling to the very bottom, where *Delete Your Account* resided in warning red letters. She and Charles had purposely made it difficult to find. "Who would ever want to delete their Circle anyway?" she'd joked. "It's the best thing that's ever happened to everyone."

She selected it. A pop-up asked, *Are you sure?*

She hesitated for a moment, then pressed the button down and watched her account disappear.

Chapter Forty-Three

DAY 4: SUNDAY

Maggie would have stayed outside and spoken to Adam longer, but the serenity of the morning is interrupted when Sylvia pulled open the doors and sticks her head through. Today, she's in a pink vest and a pom-pom beanie. "You're still here!" she observes when she sees Adam. "I thought you and Charles might've killed each other in the night."

Adam clears his throat. "We got it out of our systems."

They follow her back inside, and the others file in shortly after. Finally, Adam tells them what the surprise is: "We're boating through one of the strongest tidal currents in the world."

They take two helicopters to a town on the mainland called Bodø, where they then get in a van that drops them off by the strait. Adam leads them onto the bridge that overlooks the river, and Maggie follows behind him. She peers over the railing at the churning water below. A slim channel of deep blue runs underneath the bridge, the water there looking smooth and soft, like stretched taffy.

"Tiny," Charles says suddenly. He's right beside her. "About last night—"

She holds up her hand, already flushing. "That was my bad, Charles. I got carried away. I'm sorry I forgot about your girlfriend."

Charles frowns. "She and I broke up." So Charles rejected her purely because he didn't want to be with her. That's even worse.

"You don't need to explain," she says. She starts heading back down the bridge, where Sylvia is gesturing for them all to join her. Priya takes Jaya to the bank of the river so that Jaya can touch the water. Sylvia doesn't seem too bothered by how noisy the river is. She claps her hands together, expression bright, tucking her vape into her fanny pack. "I think this is a great place to do our group interview. Let's start. I want you all to tell me your secret."

Maggie tries not to glance at Adam in a panic. Has Sylvia finally caught on? But Adam isn't looking at her. Instead, he is staring out at the water, an oddly strained expression on his face. As if he's wrestling with himself over something.

"What secret?" Hari asks, and Maggie detects the nervousness in his voice. He's worried, too.

Sylvia gives him an exasperated look. "The secret to your friendship! I've got to say, I had my doubts in the beginning. But you all convinced me. And I'm sure that the public wants to know—how have you managed to stay close, even after everything that has happened?"

Nobody moves to answer. Even Adam, who can always be depended on to jump in, stays mute. "Um," Maggie begins, then feels the pressure of everyone's eyes on her. "Communication is important." She rewinds through the events of this weekend. Learning of Adam's dad's death, telling Charles about Hank, bonding with Hari in the bathroom. Gains a bit more confidence as she continues. "I made a lot of mistakes in college. Did a lot of embarrassing stuff. So did they," she says, indicating Hari, Charles, and Adam. Charles is staring at her now, pained. "I think that taught us to give each other grace. And when you manage to forgive one another, that makes your friendship much stronger."

She ends it there, letting the current punctuate her statement. This time, it was not hard to find the answers to Sylvia's questions.

Hidden in her own answer is a genuine hope that they've somehow made it to the other side.

Then, Adam speaks. "That was really well-put." But he doesn't seem pleased. "Actually, Sylvia, I don't think you've had enough time to talk to Charles and Hari. Why don't you—"

"No," Charles interjects. "You're not still going through with this."

Maggie glances between them, confused. Are they talking about the interview?

Jaya runs up to them, pulling Priya by the hand. "Daddy, can I play on your phone?" she asks.

"Jaya, not now," Hari says.

"Of course I am," Adam replies to Charles, irritation in his voice. Maggie sees Sylvia noting this with her sharp eye. Adam is usually so measured whenever she is present. "*Especially* now, after your decision."

"Why not?" Jaya complains to Hari.

"People are allowed to move on, Adam," Charles says, his hands spread out in a gesture of peace. "I gave you a heads-up as a courtesy, not because I needed your permission."

"Wait," Sylvia says, quick on the uptake as always. "You're leaving Circle?"

Jaya starts yelling. "I want to play on your phone!"

"Jaya, quiet!" Hari snaps.

"Don't speak to her that way," Priya says suddenly. "All she wants is your attention."

Jaya starts crying. Hari is arguing with Priya now. "I give her plenty of attention!"

"You're always on your phone. Even when you're supposed to be watching her, you're on your phone. Do you know how that affects a child, when they have to fight a *device* for their parent's time?"

Priya pulls Jaya away, throwing Hari a poisonous look, then

walks off, whispering comforting things to her daughter. Jaya's sobs fade, leaving the five of them standing there uncertainly.

Hari seems to debate following them, but then he turns back to their group. "I agree with Charles. We've made good progress this weekend, but let's pick it up when we're back."

Adam scoffs. "You two spend a weekend with Maggie, and suddenly you're both pussyfooting around what we came here to do. In the end, it always has to be me who does the hard thing."

Sylvia has her arms folded and is watching them silently. Maggie's eyes dart from Charles, to Hari, to Adam.

"What is it?" she asks quietly.

Adam rubs his face, then seems to remember part of it is swollen and quickly drops his hand. "We didn't invite you here because of the article, Maggie."

A cold wind brushes her cheeks. She's on the edge of learning something she's not sure she wants to know.

"We invited you because we want to buy your company."

Chapter Forty-Four

DAY 4: SUNDAY

There is something familiar about this situation. She might be standing in an oversaturated Windows XP background instead of a gray conference room, but it all comes back to her. Standing on the outskirts of a conversation that happened without her. The way the guys are looking at her with this terrible knowledge in their eyes. Once again, she has been outplayed. She let her guard down, allowed these men back into her heart so that they could let her down again. The five of them stand on the bank of the river, in a deformed pentagon with her at the tip.

Her entire body is numb. Adam edges closer. "Maggie?"

"Are you serious?" she asks. The words come cracking out of her. "You brought me to this island so you could buy me out? And both of you went along with it?" This she directs at Hari and Charles. Hari suddenly can't meet her eyes, but Charles holds her gaze. Her mind starts to pick apart all their interactions this weekend. Everything they'd said had been said with purpose. A motive.

"We were testing it out. Seeing if you might be amenable to it," Adam says.

"There was no *we*," Charles says. "I told you not to do it."

"You still came, didn't you?" Adam snaps. "I gave you the push you needed. There was no way you weren't showing up after I mentioned Maggie might come. You could've reached out to her years ago. Instead, you distracted yourself with your string of girlfriends rather than admitting that you didn't have the balls to go after the person you're actually in love with."

Maggie's mouth dries. She waits for Charles to jump out and deny it, but he doesn't. Sylvia is still standing there, hitting her vape and observing them with wide eyes. A bird twitters overhead.

Hari rubs his temples. "For fuck's sake. Both of you, stop being dicks to each other."

Adam turns to Maggie. "This weekend could be every single day, Maggie. Us working together, except this time, we have infinitely more money and resources. You could build *anything*. Don't you want that?"

She does. Operating a tiny start-up is like sprinting with a weighted vest while juggling a dozen eggs. Every day is a fight, both to keep giving users what they want and to reassure herself that what she's doing is worthwhile. The fatigue is such an ingrained part of her. If she had limitless resources, she wouldn't have to worry about getting the most out of every dollar. She wouldn't have to mark the date they run out of runway in her calendar and feel her anxiety mount with each tick of the clock. Most importantly, she wouldn't be doing it all on her own.

Adam's plan was to convince her that there's still a friendship to come back to. It had worked. She'd basically told him so, an hour ago. She wants them back in her life, like some kind of damn fool.

"Don't do it," Hari bursts out. "Circle is nothing like what you remember, Maggie. You'd hate it—"

"*Hari*," Adam says sharply. "We discussed this before we came here. You were onboard."

"You'd already decided. All you wanted was for me to nod and agree." Hari runs a hand through his hair, looking as if he's debating if he should give voice to his thoughts. "Eight years ago, I took your side because I owed you one. You got me the immigration lawyer, which I'm still grateful for, but I haven't been allowed to disagree with you since."

"Wait, what immigration lawyer?" Maggie asks, at the same time that Adam says, "You don't *owe* me for that, Hari. I wanted to help."

"Back when I wanted to quit Goldman so I could work at Circle," Hari explains to her. "Adam got me a lawyer who helped me stay. He paid for all of it, too. And yeah, Adam, you can say you did it out of the goodness of your heart, but how do you expect me to say no to you after a favor that big?"

Maggie gapes at him. She'd felt Hari's frustration over his immigration troubles, but it was yet another thing she'd been powerless to change. She can't summon any anger at Adam for how he'd one-upped her there; if she'd had his connections, she would have done the same thing.

"You've still got free will," Charles says, coming to Adam's defense. "Don't pretend you don't love the status that being Adam's right-hand man has given you."

Hari gives Charles a betrayed look. "Is this because you're upset I asked him to be my best man?"

Charles exhales. "*No*, dude. You spent half the time we were in Kilimanjaro checking notifications. You wonder why we haven't hung out? Because even when you're with us, you're never a hundred percent there. Priya and Jaya are suffering because of it, too."

His last comment turns Hari defensive. "I've always made time for my family. Everyone knows that."

"I don't think Priya's idea of a good time is to tag along on a business trip," Maggie says, her conversation with Priya fresh in her mind. She shouldn't get involved, but she feels compelled to speak up for her. "She and Jaya should get time with you, irrespective of everything else."

"Are you saying I'm a shitty dad?" Hari demands.

"No," Maggie says, but Hari is already raising his voice.

"You know how hard it is to balance everything? Especially when I'm also trying to be a good friend and preventing the two of *you*—" he points accusatory fingers at Charles and Adam "—from disgracing us during shareholder calls?"

"I think it's time we were honest with ourselves," Charles cuts in. "We haven't been friends in a long time."

That is what makes them all go quiet. An orange RIB zooms by, its roar filling the silence. When the thrum of its engine fades away, Sylvia speaks. Maggie had forgotten the reporter was there, hanging on to every word they exchanged. They all had. A sense of doom descends over their group.

"It seems that you guys have some things to talk out," Sylvia says, very belatedly. "I'm going to give you some privacy."

With Sylvia gone, it's like they have run out of words. Maggie glances from one guy to the other. There are identical looks of frustration on their faces, as if they have all found themselves in the same labyrinth, none of them with any idea of how to find each other or get out.

Chapter Forty-Five
DAY 4: SUNDAY

Hari is the one who breaks the silence. It seems that his panic over Circle's impending PR disaster has superseded his anger at each of them. "We are *so* fucked. Might as well let Manny release that photo too, so the whole world can see what a mess this company is."

"It will be fine," Adam says, a curious flatness to his voice. "People will be talking about the acquisition, not this."

Maggie stares at him. "I didn't say yes." Everything has tilted into an alternate dimension. She cannot believe she was going on earlier about forgiveness and wanting Adam back in her life. "You lied to me. Again."

"Technically, I didn't lie," Adam says. "I obscured some details, but that's because I wasn't even sure if the acquisition play was the right move. I wanted to make sure we could still get along. We could've kicked off the conversation after we returned. But Charles leaving changes things. There's an immediate hole we'll have to fill."

Her first instinct is anger at how rationally he's laying everything out, as if her feelings are another chess piece he's maneuvering around a board. But the root of his statement isn't false. She had felt compelled to come here. She'd wanted to see them again, regardless of whatever ulterior plans they had.

"Why don't you think about it?" Adam asks more gently. His eyes are pinned on her, hopeful, despite her reaction. "I know you didn't find out in the best way, but I really want you back, Maggie. Whatever it takes."

"What if I asked you to kick Hank Wagner off the board?" She shouldn't even be entertaining this. But if there's the tiniest chance that she does go . . . no way is she working at a company that has anything to do with Hank Wagner.

Adam doesn't even blink. "I was going to do that anyway. What he did to you is inexcusable, and I should have recognized that a long time ago."

"Wait, why are we talking about Hank Wagner again?" Hari asks, his anger melting into confusion. "Goddammit, what else are you guys not telling me?"

Maggie takes a deep breath. Tries to settle the emotions roiling inside her. Her eyes go to Charles. He's examining her, worry settled between his brows. Unlike Adam or Hari, he has no stake in her decision, not when he's quitting. His concern is for her, not the company. "I'm going for a walk. Charles, will you come with me?"

His face displays surprise. "Yeah."

"I'm going to find Priya," Hari grumbles. "At least she gives a shit about me."

"Hari, no," Adam says, putting a hand on his shoulder. "I give a shit about all of you. That's why we're here."

Hari shakes him off. "You've made it clear that you only give a shit when it's convenient for you. Go talk to Sylvia and see if you can get her to not eviscerate us in her article. I'm done cleaning up your messes."

Maggie doubts that even Adam's charisma can stand between Sylvia and her juicy scoop. But if anyone has a shot, it's him. They split up.

She and Charles walk along the strait, the path surrounded by small wildflowers, little splashes of purple, blue, and creamy yellow that poke out from the grassy carpet. The path isn't very wide, and they walk close together. There are so many thoughts scrambling her brain right now, but they scatter as her shoulder brushes his. If any one of them hadn't come, her understanding of the past would have been incomplete. She feels like she almost has the full story. Like she can see each of these guys for who they are and what they became.

"What happened last night?" she finally asks. She was still drawing her own assumptions, cutting Charles off because she feared what he had to say. But if the truth is that he's moved on, then she needs to let him say those words. She needs to hear them, and accept them.

"I wanted to make sure you knew everything before anything could happen between us. So that you know I'll be here, no matter what you decide."

She finally understands why he'd pushed her away last night and been so chilly at the beginning of this weekend. He hadn't wanted to complicate things for when Adam told her the real reason she was here. All of this had been Charles's way of protecting her.

They stop on the bank of the river. The current here is weaker, the water collecting in mini pools of seagrass and polished stone. Further downstream, she sees another orange RIB packed with tourists making its way up the river. Keeping her tone placid, she asks, "Should I take Adam's offer?"

"That's your decision. But if you do take it, and you want me there . . . I don't have to leave right away."

She shakes her head immediately. "No, Charles. Don't trade your happiness like that."

She takes her phone out of her pocket. Pops off the case, so he can see the metal backing. The engraving is still there. *For Tiny.*

"You kept it," Charles says, and his voice is a fuzzy scarf she wants to wrap around herself.

"I've used it every single day for the past eight years. Even learned how to change the battery myself, once Apple stopped supporting it." The phone had become a reminder that once someone had cared enough about her to carve her name into something, and in a world barren of anybody who really loved her besides her dad, it was infinitely precious.

She puts the phone away and looks up at him. Sees that his walls have come down, too. Hesitantly, she brushes her fingers against his cheek. "If you hadn't sent me those games, I wouldn't have known what to play. I didn't know what to watch, what music to listen to." Losing them had meant losing everything they'd loved together. A compendium of songs, movies, and jokes, cast away.

"I miss you," she breathes. The confession feels like smashing through the concrete poured around her heart. She still misses him, even though he stands right in front of her, because there is so much about him she doesn't know anymore. She has spent longer missing him than being with him.

"Me, too," Charles murmurs.

She lifts her head toward him, a question on her lips. He clasps her face with both hands and kisses her. It's a kiss brimming with sadness, forgiveness, and hope. There's so much they need to catch up on, so much time gone that it feels a little futile. But maybe that doesn't matter. Because they're here, now, and there's a lot of life left to live.

When they separate, Charles's eyes are glittering, sunlit pools. "When I saw you for the first time in eight years on Friday, it put me right back in that hallway junior year. Seeing you looking completely lost."

She shoves him. "Thanks a lot."

"Even then, all I wanted was to get you to where you needed to be. I'm happy wherever you are. Whether that's at Circle, or somewhere else. You and I are a place all of our own."

She has never given Charles a real chance. Not in college, when she was consumed by herself and all the ways she fell short.

But she gives that girl some grace. She was growing, and mistakes are part of learning. Now she feels better prepared for a love like this. To do it right. She pulls him closer and kisses him again.

"Woo!" someone shouts, and she pulls away to see another RIB floating by. "Get it, girl!"

"Oh, God," she mutters. Charles laughs, then wraps his arms around her.

She hides her face in his chest. She wants to go back to their cabin, lie in bed next to him and stay up all night talking. But that will have to wait. She still has to face Sylvia and give Adam an answer.

They return to the dock. A long inflatable RIB waits for them. Adam and Sylvia are already seated. She tries to read their faces but can't tell if Adam was successful in convincing Sylvia to leave the fight out of the article.

Their guide is a stoic Norwegian man who hands them neon windbreakers and tells them to keep their arms and legs inside the boat. He directs Maggie to sit beside Adam, and Charles takes the seat by Sylvia.

"You two are good now?" Adam asks, glancing over at her.

She nods.

"I'm glad," Adam says, and it sounds like really means it. "Are you still mad at me?"

Maggie nods again.

He sighs. "I'm sorry I wasn't up-front. But would you have come if I'd told you the truth?"

They both know the answer to that.

"Why, though?" she asks. She refuses to believe that all Adam wants is another jewel in his crown. OurSpot isn't worth that much presently, though the potential is there; she can admit that.

Adam seems to have a moment of indecision, like he is struggling with something. A truth that he isn't ready yet to admit. "Because I'm lonely, and you are, too."

His words sink in, and she can feel herself bending to his will again. Reminds herself to stay strong. "I agreed to all of this because I wanted to tell Sylvia my version of our story. Will you still let me do that?"

Adam considers her, and she knows he's weighing the pros and cons. There's a lot she could say that could damn him. "Yeah," he says. "If you really think about what I'm offering."

"I will."

Hari, Priya, and Jaya come down the dock, interrupting their conversation. Hari is piggybacking Jaya, but there's a sour look on his face. Priya follows behind, fuming. Whatever has been going on between them has not been resolved.

They get into the boat, taking the last row. Their guide starts the engine, and they glide out onto the river. As he speaks about the origin of the strait, the age of the land that surrounds them, Maggie sneaks a look at Adam. His head is tipped up, his curls rippling in the gust, and his eyes are closed, as if he is fully lost in the moment.

The boat slows, its engine groaning, water swirling past them in aquamarine eddies tipped with white. "Feel that?" their guide shouts excitedly, stoicism transforming into childlike wonder. "That's four hundred cubic meters of water trying to force us back! But we won't let it, not today!"

With the wind blowing her hair into her mouth and eyes, she decides to focus on the people around her and their surroundings. The business stuff can wait for when she's not on a boat going through nature's largest washing machine.

Adam nudges her. "Amazing, isn't it?" he yells over the water and the engine. "This river is going to be flowing long after we're gone. We're so insignificant to the world, we might as well try to make our mark while we can!"

It's such an Adam thing to say. There were so many times Adam challenged her, supported her, gave her confidence. Circle would never have existed without him. He has always been able to separate out his emotions, see what needs to be done and do it. It's something she admires deeply and can't imitate, no matter how she tries. It's why he's Circle's CEO.

The boat is nearing the tall concrete bridge that overlooks the maelstrom. The sound of the engine escalates. Around them, puffins float on the waves, chubby and unbothered. A flock of seagulls lands, lazily surfing the spirals, their bodies silvery white.

"Sir!" Their guide sounds frantic all of a sudden. "You shouldn't be standing!"

Maggie turns around and sees Hari wobbling, arm extended, fingers clutched around his phone, trying to get some precious shot that only he can see. Priya, who's sitting in front of him, is twisted around, yelling something she can't make out, but which is probably a version of *sit your ass down*.

Then, as if in slow-motion, they bump over a rapid and Hari's phone goes shooting out of his hand, right into the river.

"Noooo!" Hari howls, except there's no audio, just the horrified O of his mouth. He looks like he's going to dive into the water after it, but Charles grabs a handful of his jacket and yanks him back into his seat.

Priya smacks Hari once, lightly, in the face. His mouth snaps shut, and he stares at her with his hand pressed to his cheek in shock. But something has been unleashed in Priya, and it makes her louder than Maggie has ever heard her, loud enough for her words to be audible over the engine and the waves. "Do you hear yourself right now? The only thing you've cared about on this entire trip is your phone and whether you have service. Why don't you focus on what's around you instead of constantly thinking about how good it will look to other people?"

Hari goes slack-jawed, and Maggie grins at Priya, momentarily lifted out of her own agonized deliberation. How satisfying it is to watch another woman go feral.

Then, Hari reaches out and grabs Priya. And kisses her in front of them.

She pushes him away, a look of embarrassment on her face, but he just hugs her tight. Charles starts clapping, then she and Adam join in.

"There it is!" their guide calls, a note of relief in his voice. "Eyes ahead!" Priya hauls Hari back into his seat.

Maggie turns back around. The water beneath the bridge looks deceptively calm, dark and smooth like the surface of a stone. But the boat veers right, and Maggie suddenly sees hundreds of whirlpools, water churning and thrashing below. She finds herself entranced by the way water under pressure has the ability to turn into this beautiful dance. Their guide reduces their speed, and she enters a strange, reflective state as they glide over the whorls. Life has exerted its own pressure on her, molding her into who she is now. She has learned to ride the current alone, but just because she is capable of bearing loneliness, doesn't mean she is better this way.

She's lucky to have been part of this circle, even if it wasn't forever. As hard as she is on her past self, she envies her, too. For approaching life with an open heart, innocent to the consequences.

Adam is nudging her again. She meets his eyes, and she hears him, in her head, saying, *I'm lonely, and you are, too.* Even though their lives went in different directions, loneliness has come for them both.

The craving for connection has not deserted her. Being around everyone this weekend has shown her just how much she needs it. And now, here she is, being given another chance to redo what all of them had messed up all those years ago.

"Look," Adam says, pointing overhead, and she hears him

telling the others to look, too. She tips her head back and sees the eagle circling. Its wings are flung wide against the blue sky, and it rides the wind effortlessly. In that moment, she and everyone else in this boat are the same: heads tipped up, admiring the eagle as she soars on the wind.

Chapter Forty-Six

DAY 4: SUNDAY

There is a picnic waiting for them, a neat little spread of pickled fish, rye crackers, cheese, standard Norwegian fare, spread over a gingham blanket. It looks straight out of a food magazine shoot, especially with the sun shining overhead, turning the colors around them searingly bright. In an hour, the van will return, and they will make their way back to Janteloven.

Hari is arguing with their tour guide at the boat, pointing wildly at what appears to be a scuba diving class taking place on the opposite bank, probably asking if one of them can retrieve his phone from the grasp of the river.

Despite the brief distraction of the cruise and the reminder that nature doesn't give a shit about whether she should sell her tiny start-up to a Fortune 500 behemoth, the moment Maggie's feet touch the ground, she starts thinking again. This new possibility is almost too easy to imagine. Adam's offer comes with a huge payout. She'd get to work with him and Hari again. Charles won't be there, but he'll still be around. It will no longer be solely on her to find a path forward. Suddenly, all the worries that had been heaped on her shoulders before she arrived on this trip seem like they could be wiped away with this single deal.

Hari trudges back, looking more despondent than he has this whole trip. "It's gone," he moans. "It had everything on it. My transcripts for the podcast. Notes from Circle meetings. Photos of the four of us." This is what makes his shoulders sag.

"It'll be okay," Charles reassures him. "We have a lot of shared stuff together. Adam and I can send it to you."

Hari looks at him doubtfully. "I don't know. Seems like I've missed out on a lot."

"We'll catch you up," Adam says. "Promise."

Then Priya cuts in, her voice no-nonsense. "I backed everything up to our family iCloud."

Hari's love for Priya blazes so brightly from his face that Maggie almost feels like she has to look away. He squats next to Jaya, pressing a hard kiss to her head. "Daddy loves you," he tells her.

Jaya looks up at him, then points at one of the fish. "Nobody eat Billy!"

"Let's all sit." In all the excitement, Maggie had forgotten that Sylvia was here, witnessing the dissolution. Now she looks like she means business.

One by one, they sit down. None of them touch the herring out of respect for Jaya's wishes. Maggie is about to eat a cracker just for something to do, when Sylvia says, "I believe all of you owe me an explanation." The congeniality is gone, but Maggie catches the unhappy twist of her lips.

She feels a throb of sympathy. Sylvia had no idea what she was getting into, but she doesn't deserve to be lied to. She was just another woman trying to do her job well.

She'd lied to Sylvia because she wanted to protect herself, but it's time that she admitted to her own mistakes. "I'm sorry. If you'd be open to hearing the truth, I'll tell it to you."

Sylvia eyes her. Then, she reaches for her vape. Takes a hit, before opening the recording app on her phone. "I'm listening."

Maggie takes a deep breath. Starts from the very first lie they told. "I haven't seen most of the people here for eight years."

"Why?"

"Because I ran away." It sounds so cowardly to admit it. But she has to live with that choice, the way it has reverberated through her life, made her distrustful and afraid. "There wasn't much of a friendship left at that point." She isn't even sure if they can classify what they had as friendship, not after the first few months. It was messy, complicated by Circle and her ill-conceived romances with Adam and Charles. She was the reason so much of it went wrong.

"I wasn't convinced in the beginning," Sylvia says. Some of the flintiness has disappeared from her eyes. "There were some comments that seemed off. But the more time I spent with all of you, hearing you reminisce, and seeing the way you behaved around one another . . ." She trails off, contemplative. "There was a comfort and a rhythm to it. And you remembered the past so clearly. Like these were stories you'd retold over and over again."

Adam lets out a soft laugh. "You weren't the only one convinced."

Sylvia leans back. "And Hank Wagner. I know he played a big part in all of this."

"He just isn't very likable," Charles says. Still protecting her.

Maggie fingers a blade of grass, gathering strength from the people around her. Across the circle, Priya gives her an encouraging smile. "Off the record?"

Sylvia nods, pressing pause on her phone.

So Maggie tells Sylvia what happened in the hot tub. Sylvia doesn't react, only listens, and by the end, she doesn't look surprised. Instead, she says, "A colleague of mine is doing a story on Hank Wagner. You're not the first woman to have issues with him. Your story would be very valuable to her."

Maggie doesn't make any promises. She's not sure if she's ready for this story to reach a wider audience.

Hari's shaking his head, the only one who is having trouble accepting this. "Hank? Really?" He's looking at Adam with newly distraught eyes, like a kid finding out he's adopted. "You knew this the whole time?"

Adam's head dips, but Maggie still glimpses the regret on his face. "Yeah."

Now, Hari looks at Maggie. "I wish you'd told me," he says.

"Or me," Priya says, fire in her eyes. "I would've helped you put that bastard down."

"I know. I messed up." She has to own up to the part she played in this. "I didn't know what was worth fighting for, and when I had to let go. I forgot that Circle was all of ours."

When Maggie's finished talking, she takes a huge gulp of water. Sylvia helps herself to a cracker with cheese before asking Adam, Charles, Hari, "And the three of you stand behind everything she's shared? No adjustments?"

"She told it perfectly," Adam says. Their eyes meet, and it feels like the end of a late night debating a new Circle feature, the two of them in full agreement. At that moment, she knows that whatever Sylvia ends up publishing, they will all accept it.

"Just one last question," Sylvia says, and Maggie feels the group collectively grow tense. Wondering what she could possibly still ask them, after everything's she's laid out. "When you look into the future, what do you see?"

There's a hesitation that resembles the beginning of every icebreaker when nobody wants to be the one to go first.

Charles volunteers. "Like you heard earlier, I'm leaving Circle. Not immediately. I'll be around, to help with the transition."

Sylvia tilts her head. "And how do you feel about this?" she asks Adam.

Adam purses his lips, forehead wrinkling. "It's a big loss. After Maggie, Charles is the best engineer in the world." Then, his eyes crinkle, and he smiles. "I guess it's about time I let him do some real good."

"What are we going to do without you?" Hari asks plaintively.

"You'll be fine," Charles says. His posture is looser now, and Maggie can tell that Adam's words have assuaged his guilt over leaving. "Also, you have a key to my house."

This improves Hari's mood.

"What about you, Hari?" Sylvia asks. "You've got your podcast, your Public Profile on Circle, and you're leading the charge on partnerships with media companies for Circle Net. The only thing missing is a TV appearance."

"TV does sound nice," Hari says. Priya purses her lips. "But I'm going to try to spend more time with my family." Jaya has finally sat down in his lap, and he runs an affectionate hand over her braids, looking over at Priya. The wind blows Priya's hair across her face, but Maggie glimpses a smile. "I *am* a family man, after all."

Adam, who's sitting next to Hari, squeezes his shoulder. "You're a good guy, Hari. I'm glad you're my friend." There's a tremor in his voice. He releases Hari and says to Sylvia, "Circle remains my priority. It's the one thing I have to get right. That's about all I'm certain about."

There's a swoop of disappointment in Maggie's stomach. She wanted Adam to say something definitive about their friendship. To send her a message that even if she walks away from his offer, there will be something of them after all this. It seems that beyond this weekend, nothing is certain.

Chapter Forty-Seven

DAY 4: SUNDAY

The interview ends shortly after that. Maggie didn't expect to feel better afterward, but there's a hard, heavy feeling in the pit of her stomach. The future is up to her now. If she chooses to join Circle, she could have it all. Her past, her friends, her loneliness vanquished. There's a lot for them to rebuild, but she's seen the glint of treasure in the wreckage.

"That went as well as it could've," Adam says, once Sylvia leaves to go for a walk along the river. He rubs his neck. "Actually, who am I kidding? She's going to skewer us. Even if I stop her from posting on Circle Net, this article is going to make its way into the world."

Hari doesn't look as bothered. "It might not make us look great, but it'll get views. You said it yourself, Adam—our cultural relevance is decreasing. If we get to announce an acquisition of OurSpot through Circle Net, we'll be back on the map again." His hand brushes his pants pocket, and he sighs again. "I forgot I don't have a phone anymore. I can't even give the team a heads-up."

Maggie stiffens at Hari's language. Priya elbows him. "She hasn't said yes."

"Right," Hari says, unconvinced. "Take the time you need,

Maggie. Just letting you know that as the CFO, I can find a way to make the numbers work for you." At Priya's glare, he adds, "But no pressure."

Jaya climbs to her feet, bored by the adults talking. She starts wandering over to the river. Priya and Hari get up to make sure she doesn't fall in.

That leaves Maggie, sitting between Adam and Charles. She stares at the red checked pattern of the picnic blanket, the cheese sweating on its wooden cutting board.

Adam reaches for plates. Hands one to Charles. "We should talk about your transition plan," he says.

Charles accepts the plate. "We can do that when we're back. Let's just . . . enjoy the scenery."

Adam mulls this over. "Yeah," he says finally.

Maggie nibbles on a slice of cheese, eyeing the two of them as they awkwardly attempt reconciliation. It's so obvious that they're both tired of being at odds, but they're incapable of letting *I'm sorry* pass their lips. She can sympathize. "Adam, what do you think Charles can do with all his new free time?" she asks.

Adam's eyes light up, the way they always do when he's given the freedom to brainstorm. "There are so many options. Color consultant. Interior designer. Art adviser. Actually, the children's wing I just funded at Stanford Hospital could use a designer—"

Charles stops him there. "You're not going to sneakily have me work for you again. But we *will* still hang out after I leave. If you want."

Adam's mouth opens in dramatic protest.

Maggie stands, taking her phone out. There is service here, which means she can make an international call. "I'll be right back."

She walks away from them, toward the bridge. Her dad picks up after the first ring. "Is everything okay?" he asks. The same thing she asked him when he appeared a few days ago at the Wongs' to check in on her.

"We need to stop greeting each other this way," she says, and then, absurdly, she's crying. She doesn't know what's wrong with her and why the waterworks keep going. Maybe it's because they've been locked up for the past eight years, and the pressure is beginning to create cracks. "Dad, I don't know what to do."

Her dad's voice is calm, a beacon lighting the way through a storm. She pictures him sitting in one of their old Windsor chairs, pulling a cup of hot tea toward him as he says, "Slow down. Start from the beginning."

"It's a long story, and this is an international call." She sniffs, realizing she hadn't bothered to check what time it is over there. "Do you have time?"

"I always have time for you. Tell me everything."

At first, it's hard to get the words out. She keeps thinking that she's wasting her dad's time. But he doesn't tell her to hurry up and finish. He just listens.

So she explains it all. How things are different, and yet the same. Bonding with Hari. Being with Charles, who still knows his way around her heart. Remembering how alike she and Adam are, in their ambitions and their loneliness.

Her dad isn't quick to speak, but when he does, it's slowly, as if the thoughts are coalescing in real time. "This reminds me of when your mom left."

Maggie's breath catches in her throat. Although things have improved with her dad, the subject of her mom is one she never dares to broach. It feels like the one thing that could risk sending them plummeting back to the stony silence that consumed most of her childhood.

"Your mom was unhappy with life in America. When she told me she wanted to return to China, I felt so betrayed. I'd worked so hard to find a way here for us, yet she had decided both you and I were not good enough to make her stay. You were only two. In those first few years, I kept regretting staying. All our family back home thought I should have returned with her. Maybe we would be happier if we'd returned to China. Maybe your mother and I would still be together."

Maggie feels a sudden, fierce respect for her dad. How hard he must have clung to his American Dream and the future he'd imagined for them. The future she is living right now. The future she could live tomorrow.

Her dad says, "The hardest was when I got laid off. I felt like I was all by myself in this world."

"Me, too," Maggie whispers, clutching the phone tightly.

"But then you came into my room one day, and you made me get out of bed. And I realized I wasn't by myself. I had you. I had spent so many years missing your mom and not seeing that you were still here." He clears his throat, the only indication that emotion has crept in. "My point is this: losing people can teach you how strong you can be on your own. But it doesn't mean you should close your heart to the relationships that matter."

"I want to take this offer," she admits, the first time she allows herself to say it. To be paid well, to stop having to work herself to the bone, to be back in the embrace of a friendship that used to make everything seem possible. "If Mom had asked you if she could come back, what would you have said?"

Her dad doesn't answer for a long time, and Maggie is worried she's crossed the line. But then he says, "I probably would have said yes, when you were little and I had no idea how to raise you. Now, though? I have a good life. Good friends and a good daughter, people who have never wanted anything from me but stayed anyway. But all of that is easy for me to say without your mother standing right in front of me."

Good daughter. She loves him for trying. "When I get home, will you tell me more about Mom? Can we have . . ." Her throat gets tight, and she has to clear it. "Can we have more talks like this?"

"Yes." They chat a little longer, but when Maggie goes to hang up, her dad says, "Whatever you decide, I'm proud of you."

Chapter Forty-Eight

DAY 4: SUNDAY

The return to Janteloven is quiet. During the helicopter ride, Maggie soaks in the view of Norway's landscape from above. The green, the blue, the white edges around the coast like foam left on lips after the first sip of a cappuccino. When they get off at the helipad, it sinks in that this is their last day. They'll go back to their lives after this, and if she doesn't take Adam's offer, she has no idea when they'll all be in the same place again.

They gather a final time on the helipad, the helicopter blades still beating above them. It's afternoon now. Everyone waits for Adam to tell them the next step in the itinerary.

But Adam says, "I don't have anything else planned. I figured we could all use this time to pack and get ready to leave." He seems surprised too, at how quickly time has flown. They head toward their respective cabins.

On the walk back, Charles tugs her to him. "Can I take you on a date when we're back?" he murmurs, his fingers dancing along her hips, and she feels suddenly shy at the formality.

"I'll give you my number."

In the cabin, Charles showers while Maggie sits on one of the armchairs and picks up the iPad that came with each of the rooms. She hovers her finger over the Circle app, the sans-serif

C on a purple background. It had been a very special kind of torture, after she deleted her account, not to immediately log into the site that had been the subject of her every waking hour for two years. Even a month after her ousting, she sometimes found herself typing the URL right after opening a new browser, through habit alone.

But if she's going to take Adam's offer and return, she needs to face what Circle became. She taps the icon.

The thing that opens on the iPad is a far cry from the Circle she knew. The home page is *loud*. There are all kinds of ads, posts from random people from the furthest reaches of the internet. Low-quality content. She sees now why Adam is betting on Circle Net. The original home page doesn't work anymore.

She looks up Adam's profile. It's got a star that marks it as a Public Profile. There's a picture of him grinning on the new Circle campus, which looks like a gleaming futuristic city. Most of his posts are about the company. Celebrating various achievements, interviews he's given. Some other announcements about nonprofits he's supporting, pictures of him and various politicians. She gets that strange sensation that she is not even looking at a real person, followed by the unctuous twist of disappointment. Adam has truly shaped Circle around his own vision. There's little she can do to pull him off the path he's chosen.

Hari's profile is similar. Even his headshot is polished, a crisp image of his face on top of a blurred background. He has dutifully posted on every one of Priya's birthdays and their anniversaries, thanking his wife for everything she does.

Charles is the only one who hasn't adopted a Public Profile, so she's locked out of most of his activity. All she can see is a photo of him in front of a familiar-looking, demure yellow house, smiling a bit shyly. She recognizes the house from the Christmas she spent there.

"That was the day we paid off their mortgage."

She'd been so absorbed that she hadn't heard Charles sneak up behind her. He smells of forest-scented body wash.

She's a little embarrassed to be caught cyber stalking, but Charles doesn't seem weirded out by it. She sets the iPad aside. "You all became such important people. I guess I'm lucky you guys all came on this trip." How many chances like this come along now? Adam had done her a favor, she realizes. He'd helped her revisit her past and tie off the loose threads, the ones she hadn't had the courage to touch before.

Charles curls his fingers around her cheek, his gaze soft. "No matter who we become, we're nothing without our friends."

ADAM IS LYING in the grassy field next to the stairs that lead up to his cabin. Maggie observes him for a while from a short distance away. He doesn't move, doesn't even raise his arms to shield his face from the blinding sun. Eventually, she walks over, casting her shadow over his squinting eyes.

He lifts his head slightly. "Oh. Hey." He lies back down. "Sometimes, my whole body hurts. My back screams at me until I lie down. I have to do it at the office, too. Had to get frosted windows."

In the tall grass, he looks small. She recalls how he'd struggled on the hike, the fleeting pain she'd glimpsed when he lifted her duffel. "How long?"

Adam sighs. "A few months before my dad died. Chronic pain is an appropriate punishment for the bad guy, huh?"

She lies down beside him. The grass tickles her neck, and she can already guess that her skin is not going to be happy about this. Unlike Adam, she has to shut her eyes against the sun. She has the odd feeling of being on a movie set, a place where the ending is something she can erase and rewrite. "You're not the bad guy."

"I am. I grew Circle, but at what cost? Our users have stopped trusting us. I feel like I've checkmated myself." There it is again, that tremor in his voice that tells her he's being honest against his own instincts. "You were always the one who cared about giving people places online to feel safe."

"Adam, I can't take your offer." She says it to the sky. Being here, with them, has reminded her that there is beauty in opening her heart. But opening her heart is not the same as surrendering it. If she lets Circle acquire OurSpot, that would be surrender. It will never get the chance to thrive on its own. One day, OurSpot might even be bigger than Circle. But she will never know if she says yes today. Even if it could put their friendship back together again and give Sylvia's article a happy ending.

The grass tickles her ears as she turns her head slightly to look at Adam. His eyes are trained on the clouds. Then Adam says, "I need you, Maggie. I'm not sure I can do this by myself anymore. It could be just like old times."

"Just like old times," she repeats to herself. One more chance to give a different answer, and she's tempted. There's an irresistibility to being *needed*, the certainty of her importance in someone else's life. But there's a tug in her gut that tells her she didn't come on this trip to rewind time. It's time for her to leave Circle behind for good and run full-speed at what's ahead. "I'm sorry, Adam. I know you can do this without me."

He lays his hands on his stomach. "You realize that if we can't be collaborators, then we will have to be competitors?"

It could be a threat. She has no doubt that Adam will protect what's his. But this time, alongside the current of fear is a thrill. Nobody has ever challenged her the way he has, and she is a little excited for what the future may bring. The hard problems still left to solve, the limitless opportunities left for her to learn and grow.

She props herself up with an elbow, turning to him. He tilts his head toward her, his blue eyes the same shade as the sky. He's not smiling, and she knows she's disappointed him, maybe even devastated him a little. "Then bring it on." She understands him far better than the rest of the world, though that understanding will never be complete. Whatever he throws at her, she'll be ready.

This coaxes a smirk onto Adam's face. He finally gets up, facing the horizon. "We've got one more night," he says. "What should we do with it?"

Maggie has gotten used to the eternity of the sun here. The way that this whole weekend has felt like one very long day. At first, it felt relentless. Now she doesn't want it to end. "I don't know, but I think we should spend it together."

"ANOTHER HIKE?" SYLVIA ASKS, panting slightly as she follows Maggie up the incline. "You're trying to kill me. I'm not made for the mountains, Margaret."

"You won't want to miss this," Maggie assures her. Adam showed Maggie how to find this viewpoint, the small sandy trail that follows the sea to a cliff overlooking the water.

But doubts trickle into her mind as she leads Sylvia to the viewpoint. She'd told Adam to round everyone up, but she's not sure if he was successful.

Then, she hears a bullet of laughter. Adam's and Hari's. And when she enters the clearing, she sees them fencing with sticks while Charles tallies their wins in the dirt. Behind them is the ocean, vast and blue, the sun a white orb still hanging high in the sky. Priya is sitting on a log, and Jaya is picking dandelions beside her.

Adam and Hari drop their sticks. "We were waiting for you," Adam says, not the least bit self-conscious about their antics.

Maggie raises her eyebrows, but she can't help a smile from escaping. "Looks like you were keeping busy."

Charles rubs his shoe through the dirt, smudging the tally he'd drawn. Then, he bends down and opens his backpack, extracting cans of beer. The first one he tosses to Adam, who catches it with one hand. Charles distributes the rest, although Sylvia and Priya politely refuse.

"What's the beer for?" Sylvia asks.

"A milestone," Maggie says, as she gets down on one knee. One by one, the guys join her, until Adam's the only one standing. Then, slowly, he kneels. It seemed fitting to resume the tradition, probably for the last time. "We made it through the weekend."

"To Circle?" Adam asks.

"No," Maggie says. "To friends."

"To friends!" Their voices combine into a victorious chorus. Maggie rips open the side of her can, pressing it to her lips. Her knee feels creakier, and the beer surges out of the opening so quickly she nearly chokes, but then she starts chugging and it feels like she's back at the Big C, full of bubbles and gratitude for the people around her.

She's done before she knows it, and as she rises a little unsteadily, she sees the others doing the same. Sylvia is shaking her head, a smiling slipping out. "Thanks for inviting me. The rest of the night is yours. Enjoy it."

Circle's Inner Circle: Part Four

It's in the final stretch that I discover everything I'd observed that weekend has been a lie, elaborately fabricated, put together using the residual ashes of their long-dissolved friendship. In reality, Tang and the guys hadn't spoken in eight years. I am shocked when they confess to this, because I'd been sucked into the illusion, too.

It appears the same qualities that made their partnership work were the ones that damned them in the end. Their selfishness, their individualism, their obsessions. It comes to a head that weekend in many ways, through fistfights and drowned phones, culminating in an acquisition offer for OurSpot. I'm certain Tang will take it—an acquisition offer from a company as big as Circle is, after all, the exit that so many start-ups dream of. But she surprises me and turns it down. After, I come to understand why. She is done tethering her identity to Circle. If there is a friendship here to be had, it must be strong enough to stand on its own.

I let them have their last evening together. Later that night, from my cabin, I see what might be four heads bobbing in the arctic water. They're too far away, but as I slide open my windows, I think I hear loose, open laughter, as if this weekend has unlocked something they've each been hiding within themselves. No matter how many words I use, how each of these people feels about one another is far too complex to be contained inside this article.

On Monday, there is barely a goodbye as everyone departs, hurrying back to their lives.

Xu leaves Circle shortly after. Acharya stays, but his podcast goes on hiatus. Hank Wagner resigns from Circle's board, or maybe is asked to leave. OurSpot eschews investor funding, instead crowdfunding from users so that it can continue creating products to service them. It raises a million dollars within the first hour. Circle continues its digital domination with Adam Fink at its helm, despite failing to add Our-Spot as a shiny new feather in its cap. The capitalistic tech engine rumbles on.

As journalists, we must remain sufficiently detached from the subjects we observe, so that we can report objectively and truthfully. Perhaps I have failed in that respect, because there is one thing I hope holds true: that the story of these four is not over yet.

Chapter Forty-Nine

DAY 4: SUNDAY

During the two-ish years that they knew each other, plenty of things went wrong. Like the time they got tickets to a Nickelback concert but pregamed with so much Fireball that they never made it out of the apartment. Or when Charles borrowed an extra *Dance Dance Revolution* mat from a friend and Adam organized an entire tournament, but Maggie and Hari went way too hard on "Sandstorm" in the first round and both ended up twisting their ankles.

Maggie supposes this is just what happens when you throw four chaotic, individually weird people together.

But their last night in Norway goes perfectly.

They decide to watch the *Lord of the Rings* director's cut together because Adam apparently hasn't watched a movie in five years and it's still unchecked on Maggie's bucket list.

Charles brings edibles, and they all partake. Adam and Priya boil water on the same stove where Adam so disastrously tried to cook steak two days ago. Adam has the enlightened idea to melt brown cheese on top of instant noodles, which looks disgusting but tastes delicious, but Maggie's also not sure if it's because she's high and *everything* tastes delicious.

Adam reveals that the main lodge has a speakeasy movie room, which infuriates Hari.

"You mean I could've been marathoning *Breaking Bad* instead of going on emotionally fraught hikes?"

They make a fort with pillows and blankets that Jaya delights in crawling through, though Maggie insists Adam take one of the leather recliners, for his back.

Maggie leans against the base of Adam's recliner and spends more time watching the movie's light play over Charles's jaw than the movie itself. Hari leans over and whispers "whipped" in her ear while Frodo and Sam are rowing toward the eastern shore, and Maggie tries to suffocate him with a pillow, which leads to the movie being paused until they broker a peace.

Halfway through *The Two Towers*, Adam gets a phone call. He tiptoes out of the room and returns looking troubled. Maggie can see the specter of tomorrow hanging over him. He will have to go back to work at Circle, knowing he's failed to acquire OurSpot, Charles is leaving, and without any certainty over how Sylvia's article will turn out. It's a reminder that she has her own mess waiting when she gets back. The movie fades into the background as she begins to assemble a to-do list in her head. The first thing for her to do when she returns is to give Lisa a call. If she has to grovel, then so be it.

As the credits roll, Hari says, "I think we should make a Spot."

That yanks Maggie out of her thoughts. "We don't have to do that."

"I like that idea," Adam says.

"You can join mine," Charles says. It turns out he's had his own Spot this whole time, but has been using it to organize his photos, notes, and links. Maggie tries not to bemoan the fact that he was using her friendship app as a productivity tool.

It's them against her, so she gives in. She opens the app on her phone, a little ashamed of how bare her account is. OurSpot users can only add up to five friends a week, and Spots are kept active through regular posting and interaction. It doesn't matter if the user is a celebrity or someone's mom; the rules are the same for everyone.

Charles sends around an invitation link.

"Wow, this site is slick," Hari says, peering over Priya's shoulder as she opens the app.

"You don't need to pretend," Maggie says, eyeing him. "I know you guys probably ran a whole competitive analysis on us."

Adam clears his throat. "We need to add photos, right? Should I open up my Circle and download some from there?"

Maggie's forgotten how many photos they have, how committed they once were to capturing memories during a time when it was so much more inconvenient to do so.

"Do you guys remember this?" Adam shows them a photo of the four of them, Maggie holding a half-eaten cake with her name on it, looking a little bashful.

"The three-cake birthday," Maggie says, a lump rising in her throat. Her twenty-first has always been connected to that disastrous meeting at the Gold Club, and she's disappointed in herself for giving a negative moment so much power. There are probably other moments of joy she's overwritten, all for the sake of a narrative that was easier to accept.

"I bet you've never had that many cakes for a single birthday again," Hari says.

"I also have stuff to add," Priya says. "Hold on, they're loading. Adam, you really do need to improve the service on this island. It's embarrassing for a tech CEO."

Photos *of* photos. Them shotgunning beers on the Big C. And a Polaroid. The one of the four of them, on their first day in the office.

"I took it off the wall when I was visiting during one of your office happy hours. I felt like, with how heated things were, someone was going to try to do something to it. Rip it up, or draw a mustache in Sharpie," Priya explains. "It's in my nightstand drawer, if you want it back. Sorry," she tells Hari.

Hari looks dumbstruck. "You're the only one who would've been able to keep that photo without losing it."

They fill the Spot with photos. The prompt appears to write their first post. So Maggie writes down what they had each written on those Post-its. OurSpot is intended to be a place for friends to capture their most important memories throughout their friendships, yet Maggie knows that what is being recorded on this Spot could be all there is left after the weekend.

"No more phones. You're making me feel left out," Hari says. "Let's go outside."

Priya takes Jaya to bed while the four of them head outside. It's cold now, the sky overhead a deeper blue, though not fully dark.

Maggie turns to Charles. Shoots him a smile. "Race you." She plucks off her clothes and dives into the water. Behind her, she hears a splash, then a howl. Hari's.

"Fuck, it's cold. You two are maniacs!"

Charles swims by her. "You're falling behind," he calls, and she speeds up, chasing him to the sauna. To her surprise, she sees Adam swimming toward them, too. He stops, looking like he might drown, and she meets him halfway, concerned. Sees Charles doing the same.

But then Adam recovers. "Eat my dust, losers!" he shouts before he submerges his head. When he comes up again, he lets out a loud, exhilarated laugh. The race resumes.

The combination of her mounting tiredness and the fullness of the day seems to transport her through some warped timeline, until she's not sure where and when they are anymore. It's 2006, and this is just another day of hanging out with nothing that important to do, the buoyancy of youth drawing them along. When she looks at these people, she sees them as they were. Full of hope, in love with life and one another.

THE NEXT DAY, Maggie wakes up by herself, blinking in the brightness of the sunlight. Panic streaks through her, and she leaps out of bed, just as Charles exits the bathroom, a towel around his neck. She sags in relief.

"You're still here."

But Charles's expression changes, and she senses it, too. The island feels emptier. As if some important presence has left.

It turns out Adam was called about an urgent meeting last night. He took the helicopter when everyone else went to bed, and Hari, Priya, and Jaya flew out earlier that morning.

There isn't a real goodbye. Just life, continuing.

Maggie and Charles catch the same flight back. They split up at the airport, but not before Charles drags her to him and kisses her, hard. "I want to see you tomorrow," he says.

She laughs and kisses him. "Me, too. Tomorrow, and all the days after that."

She returns home, accompanied by a large dose of determination over what she needs to do next. Back at the Wongs', she ducks into her garage-bedroom and calls Lisa. The flight home gave her time to reflect on how she's been running OurSpot. She thinks of how Adam has come to rule Circle, the way Hari and Charles have mostly let him have his power unchecked. She doesn't want to become like that. She needs people who will ground her.

Lisa picks up, which is a positive sign.

Maggie says, right off the bat, "I made a huge mistake, and I want you back."

Lisa isn't convinced, and Maggie can't fault her for it. But she agrees to meet in person, and Maggie hangs up, undeterred. She still has a shot.

On Monday, she takes some of her engineers to lunch. They're quiet and nervous around her, but she doesn't shy away. The first time she jokes about how she and Adam Fink are rivals for life, everyone stiffens. But then someone asks, "What was it like to work with him?" So she tells them about Circle. About how special it is to create something with your best friends, even if at some point you might have to let it go.

She and Charles spend almost every evening together. She makes sure that she carves out the time. If he senses her attention drifting to OurSpot, he asks if it's a right-now problem or a next-day problem. It's almost always a next-day problem. He and her dad get on a first-name basis, and now she has another person to help explain memes to him. The Wongs are disappointed on behalf of their still single son, but they understand once they meet Charles.

"What a catch!" Mrs. Wong whispers to Maggie, squeezing her elbow like Maggie's a daughter she can finally give away. Sometimes, they will have fruit and tea together: Maggie, Charles, her dad, the Wongs, and her Circle mug. Until one day, when Charles says, "If you just moved in with me, we could have everyone over and not have to squeeze into a shoebox." By July, she is living with him, and they celebrate the Fourth with both of their families and the Wongs. Maggie apologizes to Helen for running away from her at Ranch 99 ("I *knew* that was you!").

One day while at work, Maggie gets a text from an unknown number. A photo taken from the top of the Big C, the Campanile proud against the sunset. *No sprained ankles today*, it says.

She grins down at her phone. Priya's taking photos again.

That's how they start talking. It's a nice break from work for Maggie to check her texts and see a photo of the Golden Gate Bridge in the fog, or Jaya, hands pressed against the glass of an aquarium. A reminder that there's a whole world beyond work, like Charles says.

She learns from Charles that Hari and Adam are busy with Circle, searching for his replacement and preparing for the Circle Net launch. Charles is slowly transitioning out of the company, and Maggie worries that once he leaves, she will lose her last tie to Adam and Hari.

She debates calling up Adam to ask if he's doing okay, but she's not sure if he wants concern from her, so she never follows through. After all, they're competitors.

Sometimes she opens OurSpot and goes to the Spot they created their last night in Norway. Scrolls through the memories just to remind herself that the weekend was real. With each passing week, the possibility of reaching out to Adam and Hari fades a little more.

Six months later, while she and Charles are driving back from her dad's, a notification pops up on her screen. *An update has been made to your Spot.*

She sees Charles checking his phone. "Who posted?"

"You should see for yourself."

"Can you give me a hint?"

"It'll ruin the surprise if I say." He lets loose an alarmed "ahh" when she attempts to pick up her phone and swerves the car. "It's Adam. Keep your hands on the wheel."

This makes her accelerate the car accidentally. "Tell me what he said!"

"It's a photo."

"Describe it to me! Every single detail!"

"Please exit the highway first. I fear for my safety."

She exits early and screeches into a gas station. Charles sighs. "Maybe we should switch."

"You're the one who made me drive because you wanted to work." Charles has been consulting with various companies on designs for objects ranging from spice organizers to cordless blow dryers. This is on top of the little things he's built in his apartment to make her life easier, like the mini shelf he installed for her to charge her phone by their bed, or the cord organizer he made for her out of redwood. Maggie, far less impressively, shows her affection by planning dates to Berkeley, Monterey, San Francisco, and whupping his butt in *Mario Kart*. When she finally tells him she loves him, he laughs and says, "I knew that already."

Now she holds her breath as she swipes over her OurSpot notification. It expands into a photo of Maggie, Hari, and Charles in that slate-blue sea, their faces turned rose gold by the midnight sun. Adam must have taken this right before he got in.

Maggie's fingers tremble. How does she respond? *Should* she respond? Suddenly, she feels fifteen again, struggling to draft a text, the whole of the English language not feeling sufficient.

"He probably went through his photo album from the weekend and realized he never shared that photo," Charles observes.

Maggie settles against the seat. "Oh." This is a very rational explanation.

Then, a message appears from Hari, along with the selfie they took at the top of their first hike: *Just tell them u miss them, u sissy*

Adam replies. *I miss*

The sentence dangles there, and he goes offline.

Her stomach flips over. Was that it? Was this her chance to say something to him, but now it's too late?

But then his icon turns green again, and he types.

A moment later, *brown cheese* appears in the chat box.

"Asshole," Charles says, but he sounds amused. He clicks Send on something, and in their Spot, a photo of Maggie asleep after a day of meetings appears, her head tipped back against her chair, all chins showing.

She's just leaped on top of him and is sentencing him to death by tickling when Adam replies: *same*

She rolls off Charles, picking her phone up again. Her thumbs hover over the keyboard. She deliberates over what she could say that is confident but not cavalier, that shows she's open to friendship but not desperate for it. She stares down at her screen, the last message from Adam hovering there. An outstretched hand, waiting for her to grab it.

"Whatever you want to say, say it." Charles is gazing at her, that expression of exasperated affection on his face, even as he rubs at where she jabbed him too hard under the armpits.

Right. It doesn't matter how she says it, only that she says it.

She types quickly and presses Send before she can reread her message.

Her question hovers there, forlorn, as her heart races. It contains all the hopeful idealism of her young self. The one who'd pressed the button launching Circle into the world, excited for whatever happened next because her friends were right beside her.

Then, she sees, along the top bar of the chat:

Multiple people are typing . . .

★ ★ ★ ★ ★

Acknowledgments

Writing this book may have been one of the hardest things I've ever done. At one point, I didn't think I would ever reach the end, but now here it is. As I write these acknowledgments, I can't believe I've made it. I feel so grateful for the people who have been here for it all:

Mike—you have always stood by my side. Through everything publishing has thrown at us, you have remained a steady, trustworthy partner. You are truly my rock!

Melanie—you played a big part in what this book became. Thank you for always challenging me and pushing me to find the heart of the story.

Meredith—thank you for adopting *The Social Circle*, getting us that beautiful cover and everything you did to push it over the finish line.

To the marketing, sales and publicity teams who were so instrumental to *Women of Good Fortune*'s release, and the librarians and booksellers who recommended the book to potential readers—I feel so lucky to have your support.

I read a lot of books in order to write this one, but among them, *Brotopia: Breaking Up the Boys' Club of Silicon Valley* by Emily Chang is a bracing, shocking look at the inequality that runs rampant in Silicon Valley. I highly recommend it.

There are many friends who read an early version of this book and talked me through my doubts so I could find the real story within. Thank you for being interested enough to read the whole thing, for pointing out the facts I got wrong and for encouraging me to remember that my writing is only a part of who I am. The best parts of the friendships in this book are inspired by all of you.